CREATED BY
**ROBERT KIRKMAN &
LORENZO DE FELICI**

ROBERT KIRKMAN
WRITER/CREATOR

LORENZO DE FELICI
ARTIST/CREATOR

ANNALISA LEONI
COLORIST

RUS WOOTON
LETTERER

SEAN MACKIEWICZ
EDITOR

LORENZO DE FELICI
COVER

ANDRES JUAREZ
LOGO & PRODUCTION DESIGN

FOR SKYBOUND ENTERTAINMENT

ROBERT KIRKMAN *Chairman* • DAVID ALPERT *CEO* • SEAN MACKIEWICZ *SVP, Publisher* • SHAWN KIRKHAM *SVP, Business Development* • BRIAN HUNTINGTON *VP of Online Content* • ANDRES JUAREZ *Art Director* • ARUNE SINGH *Director of Brand, Editorial* • SHANNON MEEHAN *Public Relations Manager* • ALEX ANTONE *Senior Editor* • JON MOISAN *Editor* • AMANDA LAFRANCO *Editor* • JILLIAN CRAB *Graphic Designer* • MORGAN PERRY *Brand Manager, Editorial* • DAN PETERSEN *Sr. Director of Operations & Events*

Foreign Rights & Licensing Inquiries: contact@skybound.com

WWW.SKYBOUND.COM

IMAGE COMICS, INC.

TODD MCFARLANE *President* • JIM VALENTINO *Vice President* • MARC SILVESTRI *Chief Executive Officer* • ERIK LARSEN *Chief Financial Officer* • ROBERT KIRKMAN *Chief Operating Officer* • ERIC STEPHENSON *Publisher / Chief Creative Officer* • SHANNA MATUSZAK *Editorial Coordinator* • NICOLE LAPALME *Controller* • LEANNA CAUNTER *Accounting Analyst* • SUE KORPELA *Accounting & HR Manager* • MARLA EIZIK *Talent Liaison* • DIRK WOOD *Director of International Sales & Licensing* • ALEX COX *Director of Direct Market Sales* • CHLOE RAMOS *Book Market & Library Sales Manager* • EMILIO BAUTISTA *Digital Sales Coordinator* • KAT SALAZAR *Director of PR & Marketing* • DREW FITZGERALD *Marketing Content Associate* • HEATHER DOORNINK *Production Director* • DREW GILL *Art Director* • HILARY DILORETO *Print Manager* • TRICIA RAMOS *Traffic Manager* • MELISSA GIFFORD *Content Manager* • ERIKA SCHNATZ *Senior Production Artist* • RYAN BREWER *Production Artist* • DEANNA PHELPS *Production Artist*

WWW.IMAGECOMICS.COM

CHAPTER SIX

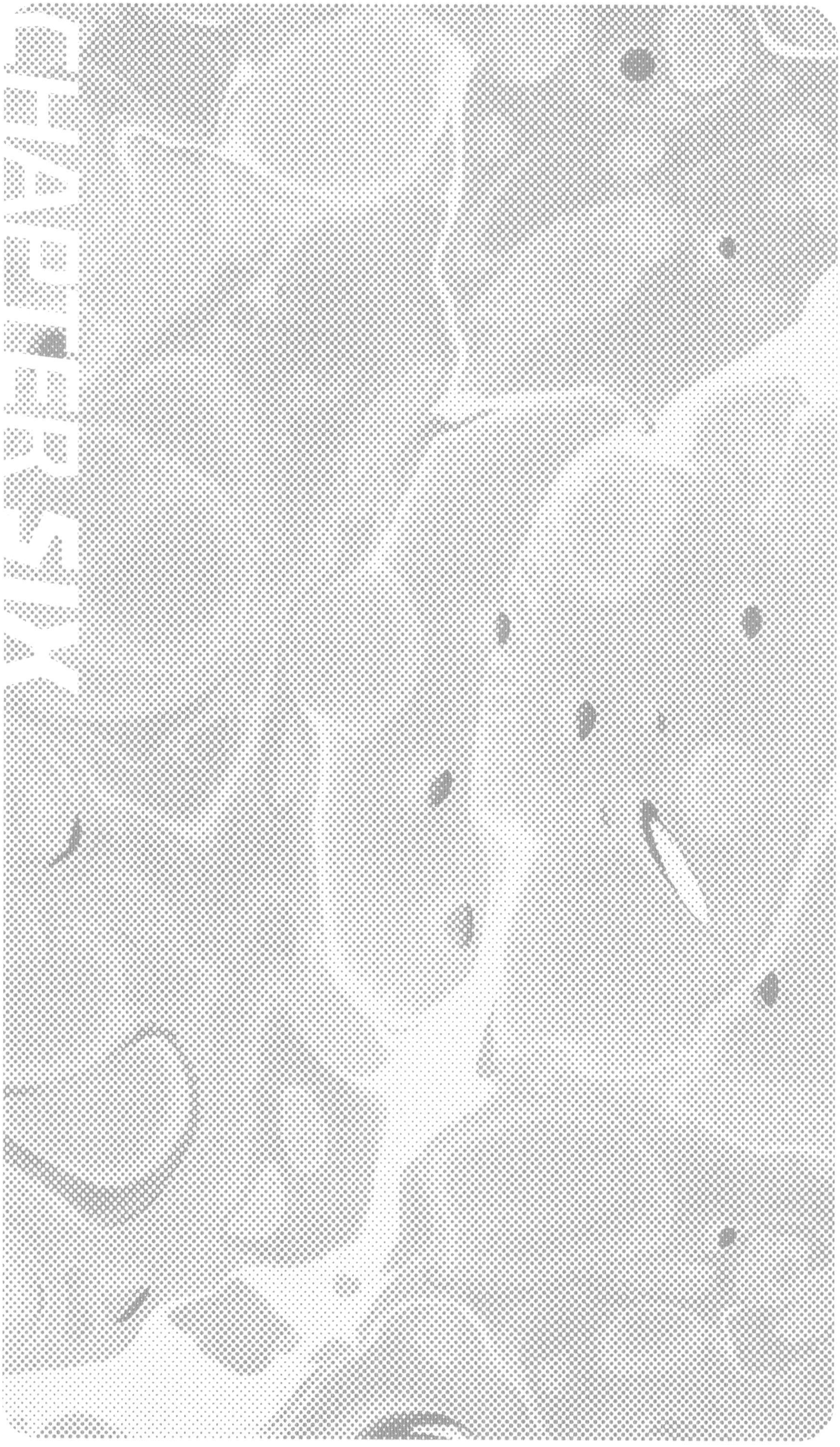

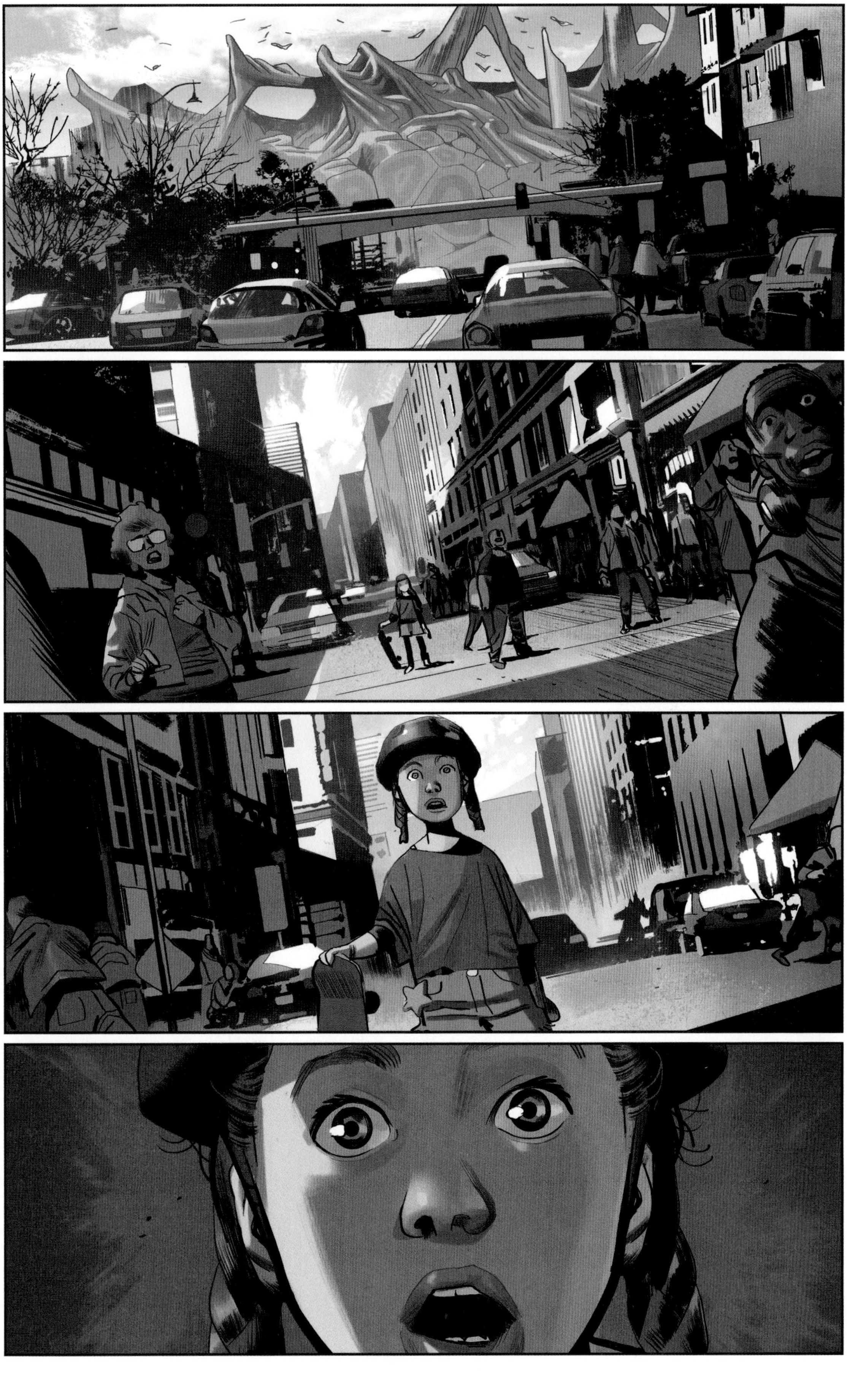

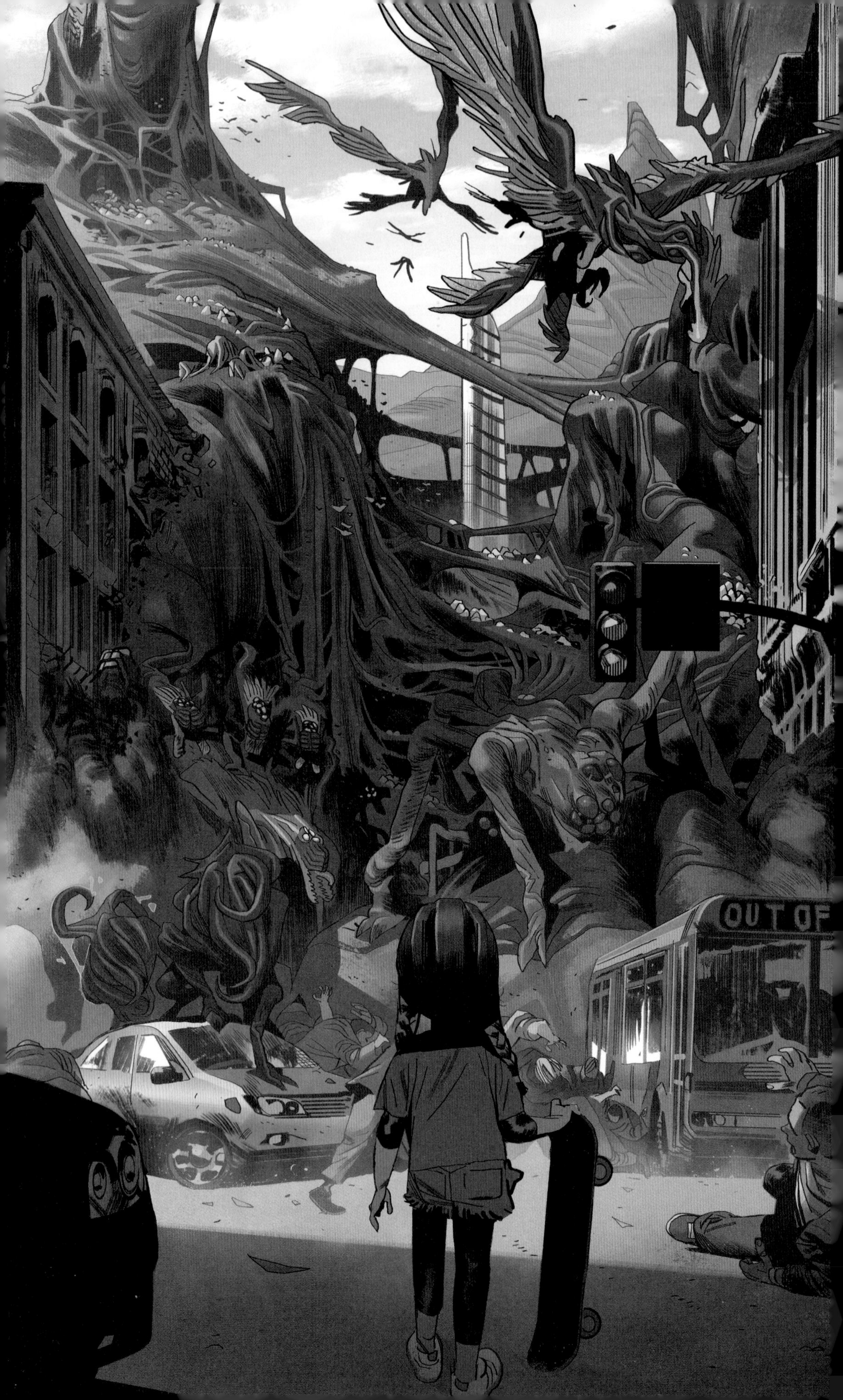
OUT OF

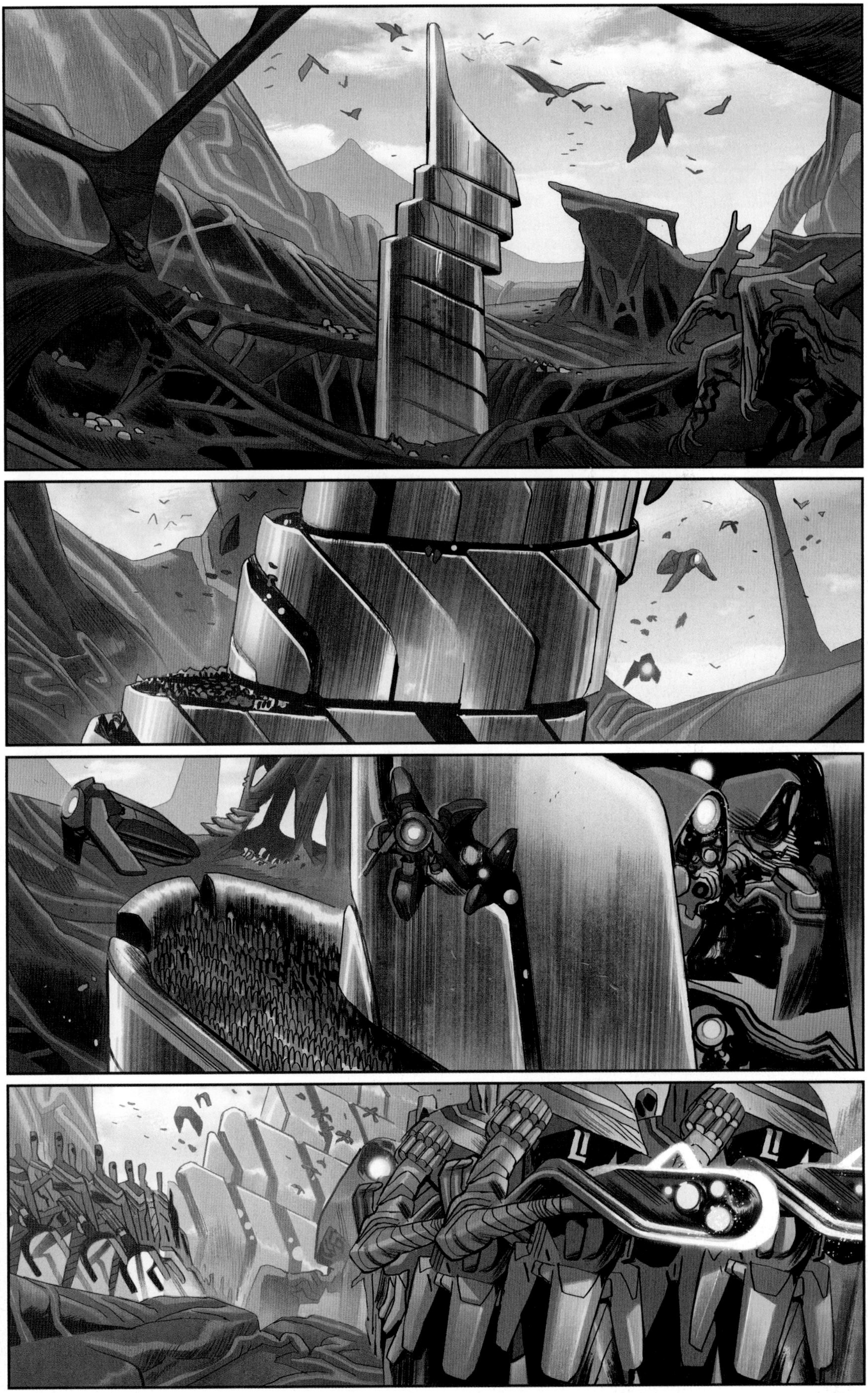

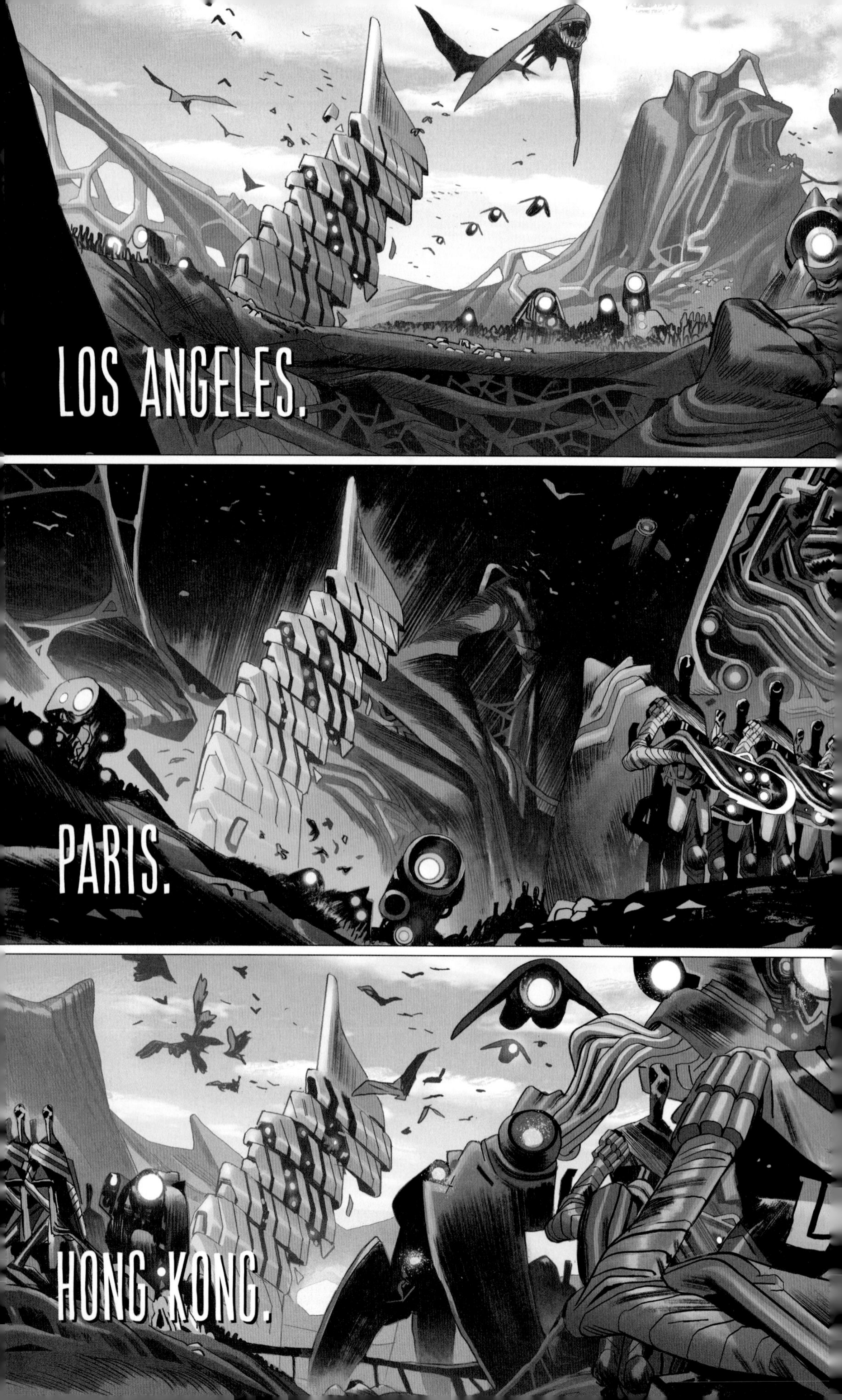
LOS ANGELES.
PARIS.
HONG KONG.

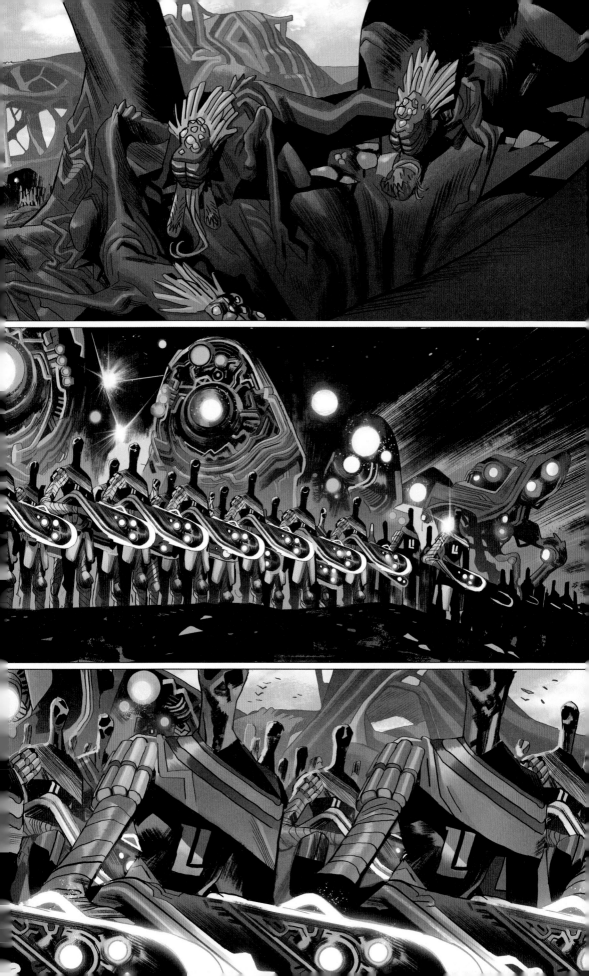

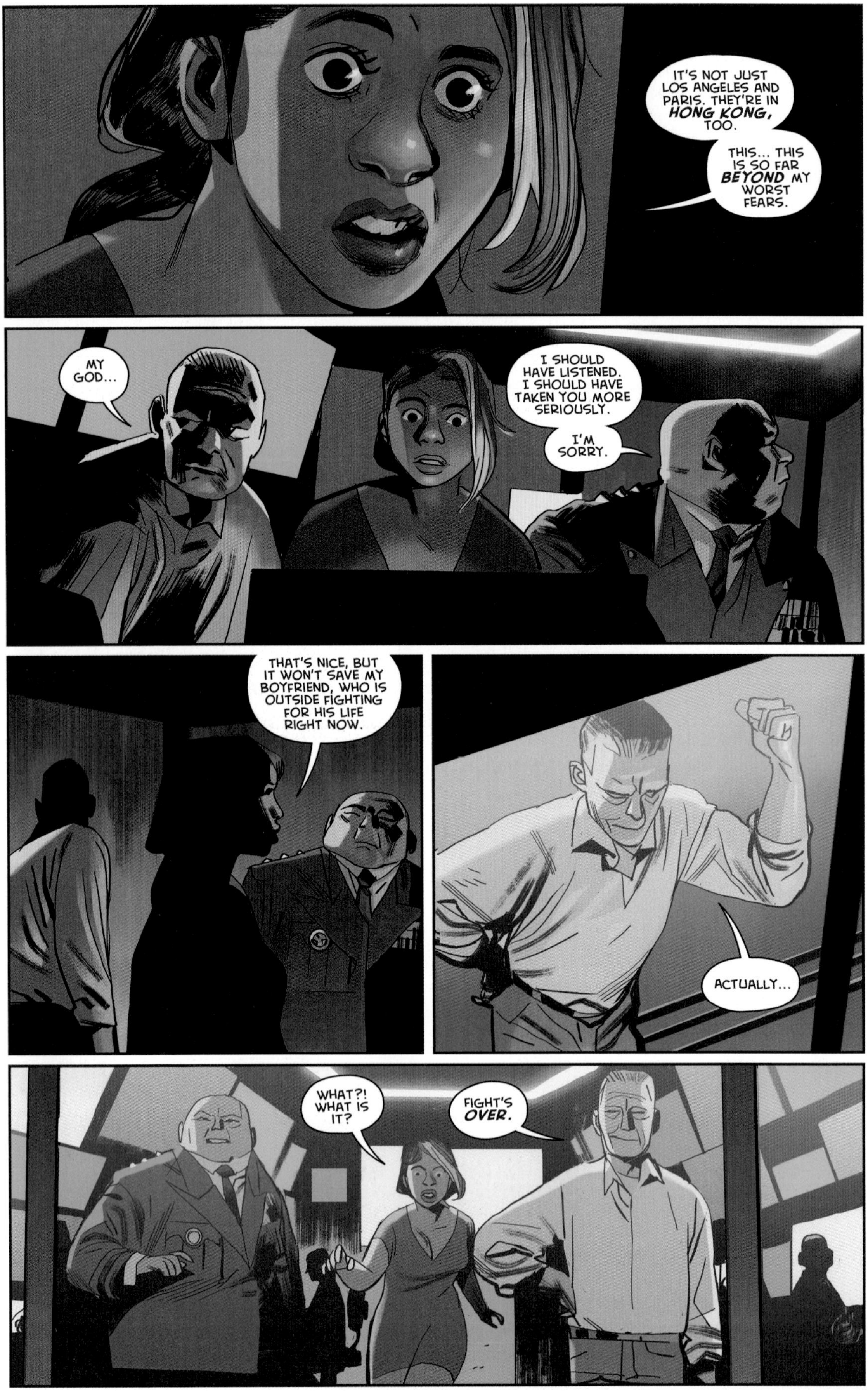
IT'S NOT JUST LOS ANGELES AND PARIS. THEY'RE IN HONG KONG, TOO.
THIS... THIS IS SO FAR BEYOND MY WORST FEARS.
MY GOD...
I SHOULD HAVE LISTENED. I SHOULD HAVE TAKEN YOU MORE SERIOUSLY.
I'M SORRY.
THAT'S NICE, BUT IT WON'T SAVE MY BOYFRIEND, WHO IS OUTSIDE FIGHTING FOR HIS LIFE RIGHT NOW.
ACTUALLY...
WHAT?! WHAT IS IT?
FIGHT'S OVER.

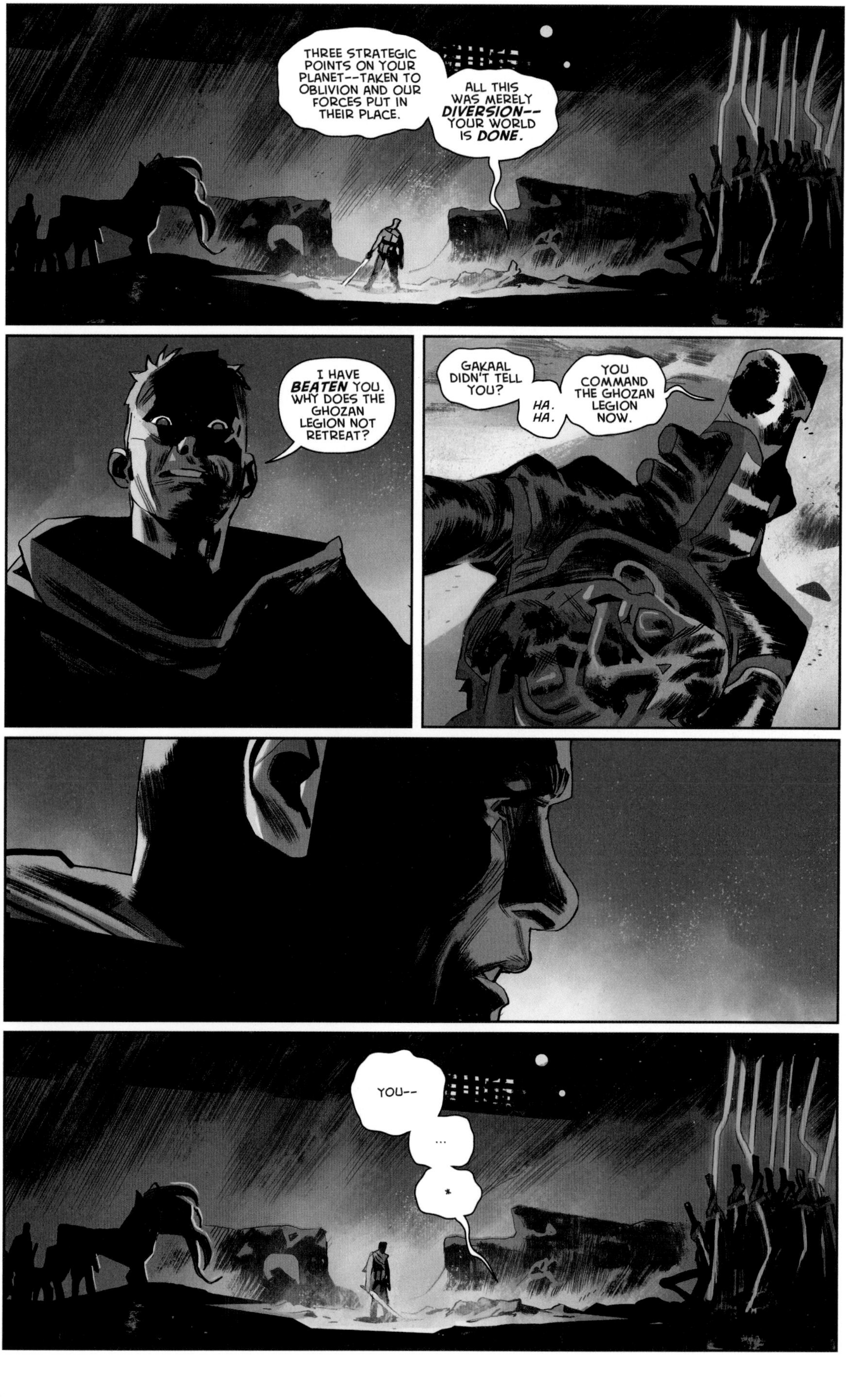
THREE STRATEGIC POINTS ON YOUR PLANET--TAKEN TO OBLIVION AND OUR FORCES PUT IN THEIR PLACE.
ALL THIS WAS MERELY **DIVERSION**-- YOUR WORLD IS **DONE.**
I HAVE **BEATEN** YOU. WHY DOES THE GHOZAN LEGION NOT RETREAT?
GAKAAL DIDN'T TELL YOU?
HA. HA.
YOU COMMAND THE GHOZAN LEGION NOW.
YOU--
...
*

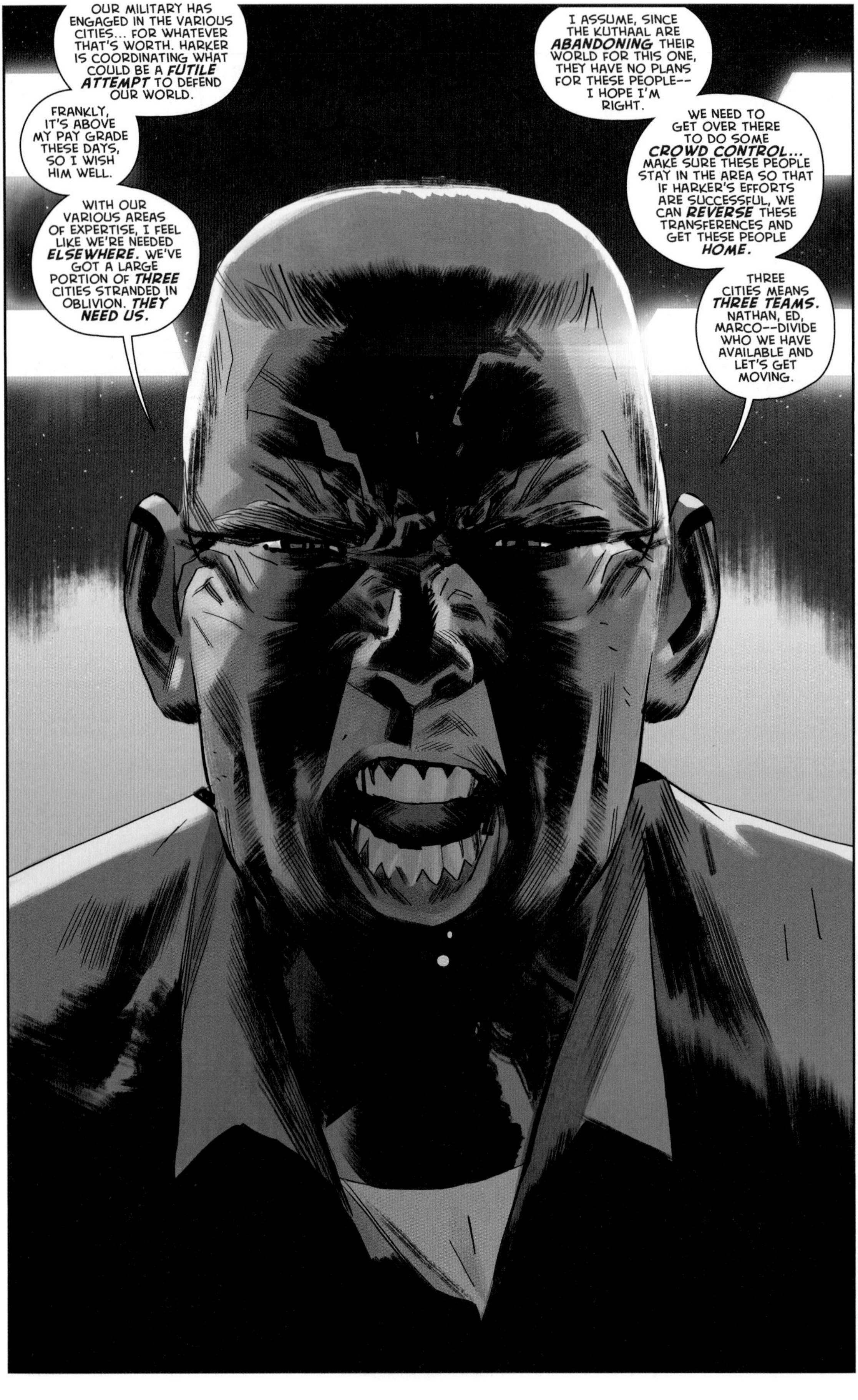

OUR MILITARY HAS ENGAGED IN THE VARIOUS CITIES... FOR WHATEVER THAT'S WORTH. HARKER IS COORDINATING WHAT COULD BE A ***FUTILE ATTEMPT*** TO DEFEND OUR WORLD.
FRANKLY, IT'S ABOVE MY PAY GRADE THESE DAYS, SO I WISH HIM WELL.
WITH OUR VARIOUS AREAS OF EXPERTISE, I FEEL LIKE WE'RE NEEDED ***ELSEWHERE.*** WE'VE GOT A LARGE PORTION OF ***THREE*** CITIES STRANDED IN OBLIVION. ***THEY NEED US.***
I ASSUME, SINCE THE KUTHAAL ARE ***ABANDONING*** THEIR WORLD FOR THIS ONE, THEY HAVE NO PLANS FOR THESE PEOPLE-- I HOPE I'M RIGHT.
WE NEED TO GET OVER THERE TO DO SOME ***CROWD CONTROL...*** MAKE SURE THESE PEOPLE STAY IN THE AREA SO THAT IF HARKER'S EFFORTS ARE SUCCESSFUL, WE CAN ***REVERSE*** THESE TRANSFERENCES AND GET THESE PEOPLE ***HOME.***
THREE CITIES MEANS ***THREE TEAMS.*** NATHAN, ED, MARCO--DIVIDE WHO WE HAVE AVAILABLE AND LET'S GET MOVING.

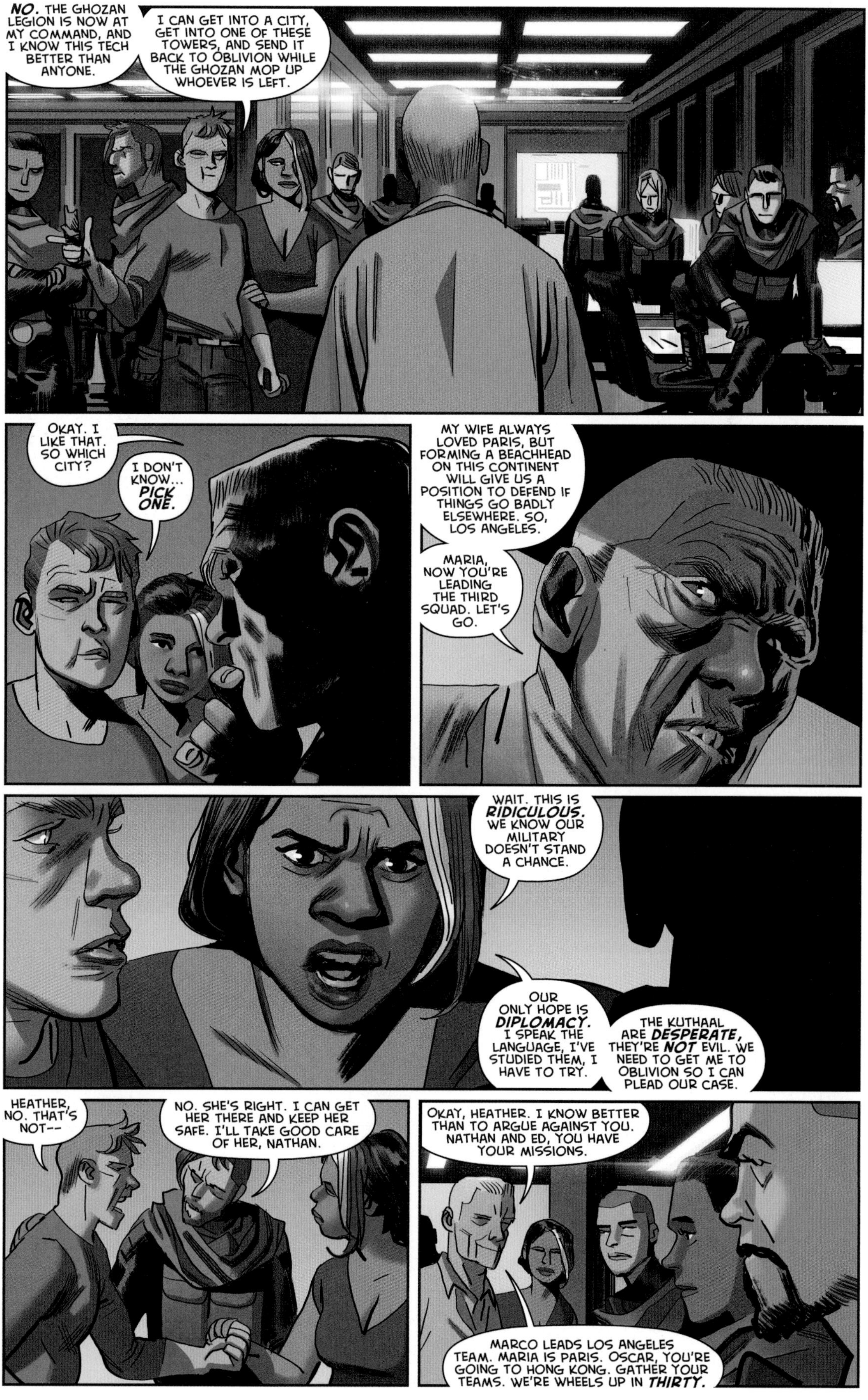

NO. THE GHOZAN LEGION IS NOW AT MY COMMAND, AND I KNOW THIS TECH BETTER THAN ANYONE.
I CAN GET INTO A CITY, GET INTO ONE OF THESE TOWERS, AND SEND IT BACK TO OBLIVION WHILE THE GHOZAN MOP UP WHOEVER IS LEFT.
OKAY. I LIKE THAT. SO WHICH CITY?
I DON'T KNOW... PICK ONE.
MY WIFE ALWAYS LOVED PARIS, BUT FORMING A BEACHHEAD ON THIS CONTINENT WILL GIVE US A POSITION TO DEFEND IF THINGS GO BADLY ELSEWHERE. SO, LOS ANGELES.
MARIA, NOW YOU'RE LEADING THE THIRD SQUAD. LET'S GO.
WAIT. THIS IS RIDICULOUS. WE KNOW OUR MILITARY DOESN'T STAND A CHANCE.
OUR ONLY HOPE IS DIPLOMACY. I SPEAK THE LANGUAGE, I'VE STUDIED THEM, I HAVE TO TRY.
THE KUTHAAL ARE DESPERATE, THEY'RE NOT EVIL. WE NEED TO GET ME TO OBLIVION SO I CAN PLEAD OUR CASE.
HEATHER, NO. THAT'S NOT--
NO. SHE'S RIGHT. I CAN GET HER THERE AND KEEP HER SAFE. I'LL TAKE GOOD CARE OF HER, NATHAN.
OKAY, HEATHER. I KNOW BETTER THAN TO ARGUE AGAINST YOU. NATHAN AND ED, YOU HAVE YOUR MISSIONS.
MARCO LEADS LOS ANGELES TEAM. MARIA IS PARIS. OSCAR, YOU'RE GOING TO HONG KONG. GATHER YOUR TEAMS. WE'RE WHEELS UP IN THIRTY.

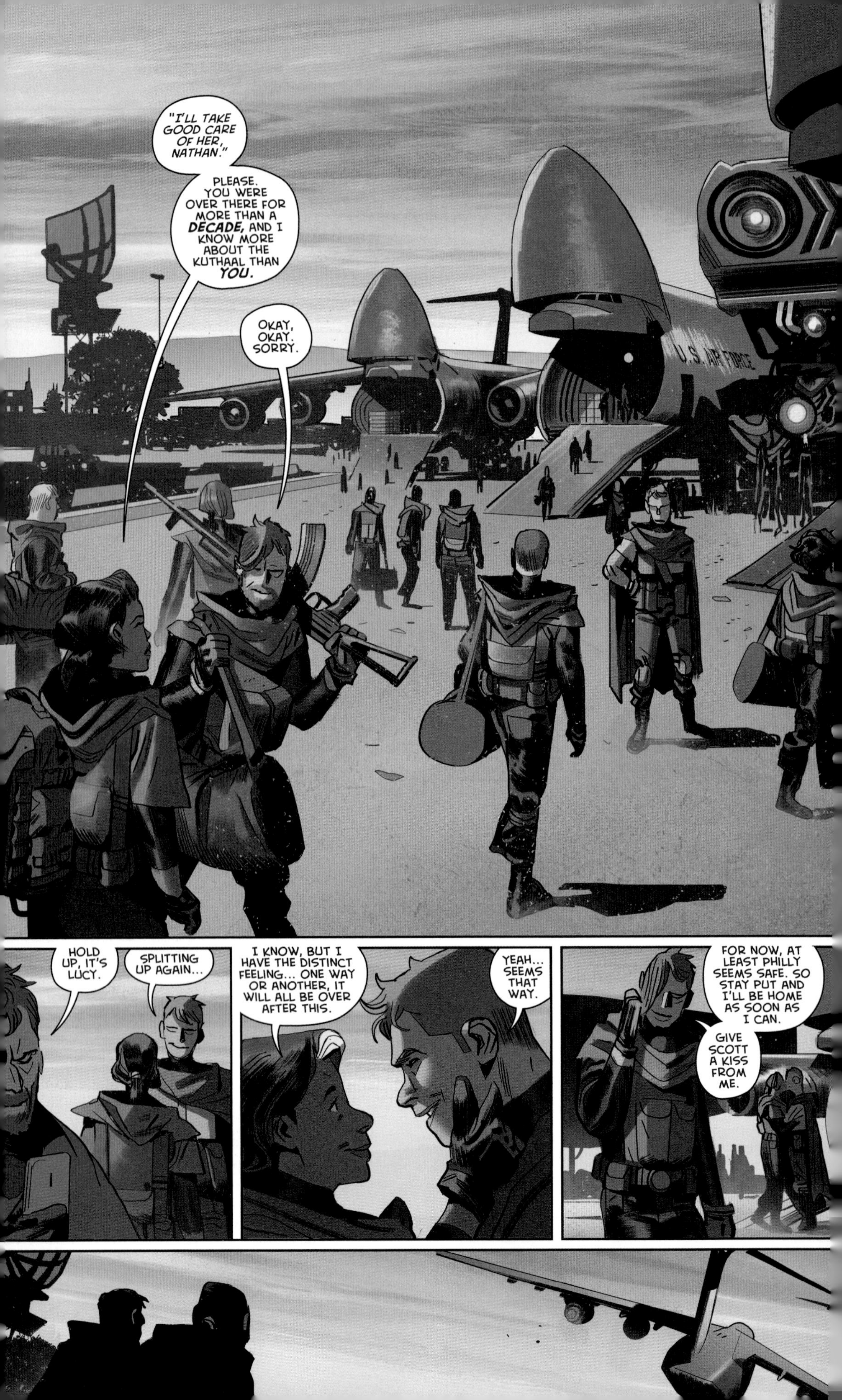
"I'LL TAKE GOOD CARE OF HER, NATHAN."
PLEASE. YOU WERE OVER THERE FOR MORE THAN A DECADE, AND I KNOW MORE ABOUT THE KUTHAAL THAN YOU.
OKAY, OKAY. SORRY.
U.S. AIR FORCE
HOLD UP, IT'S LUCY.
SPLITTING UP AGAIN...
I KNOW, BUT I HAVE THE DISTINCT FEELING... ONE WAY OR ANOTHER, IT WILL ALL BE OVER AFTER THIS.
YEAH... SEEMS THAT WAY.
FOR NOW, AT LEAST PHILLY SEEMS SAFE. SO STAY PUT AND I'LL BE HOME AS SOON AS I CAN.
GIVE SCOTT A KISS FROM ME.

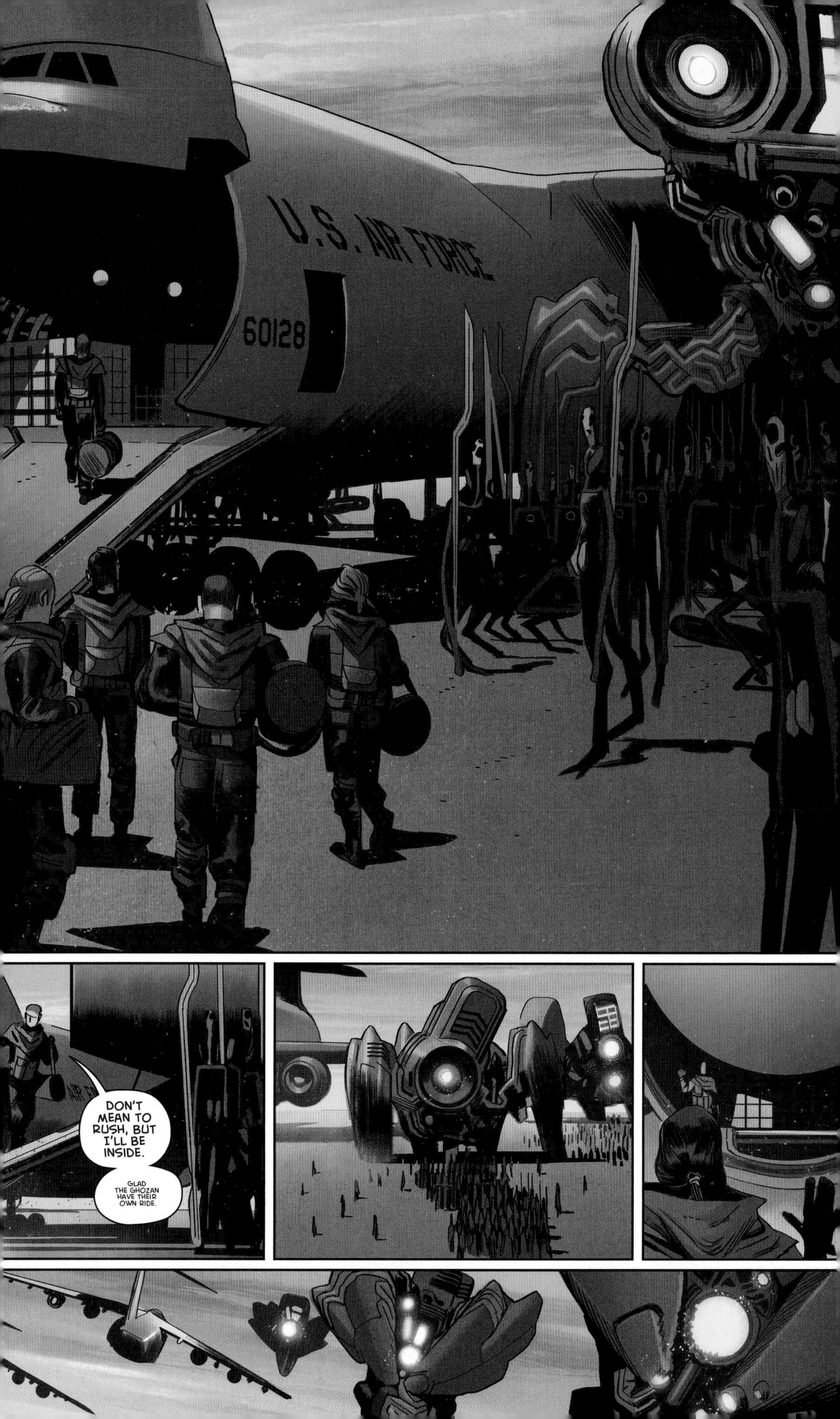
U.S. AIR FORCE
60128
DON'T MEAN TO RUSH, BUT I'LL BE INSIDE.
GLAD THE GHOZAN HAVE THEIR OWN RIDE.

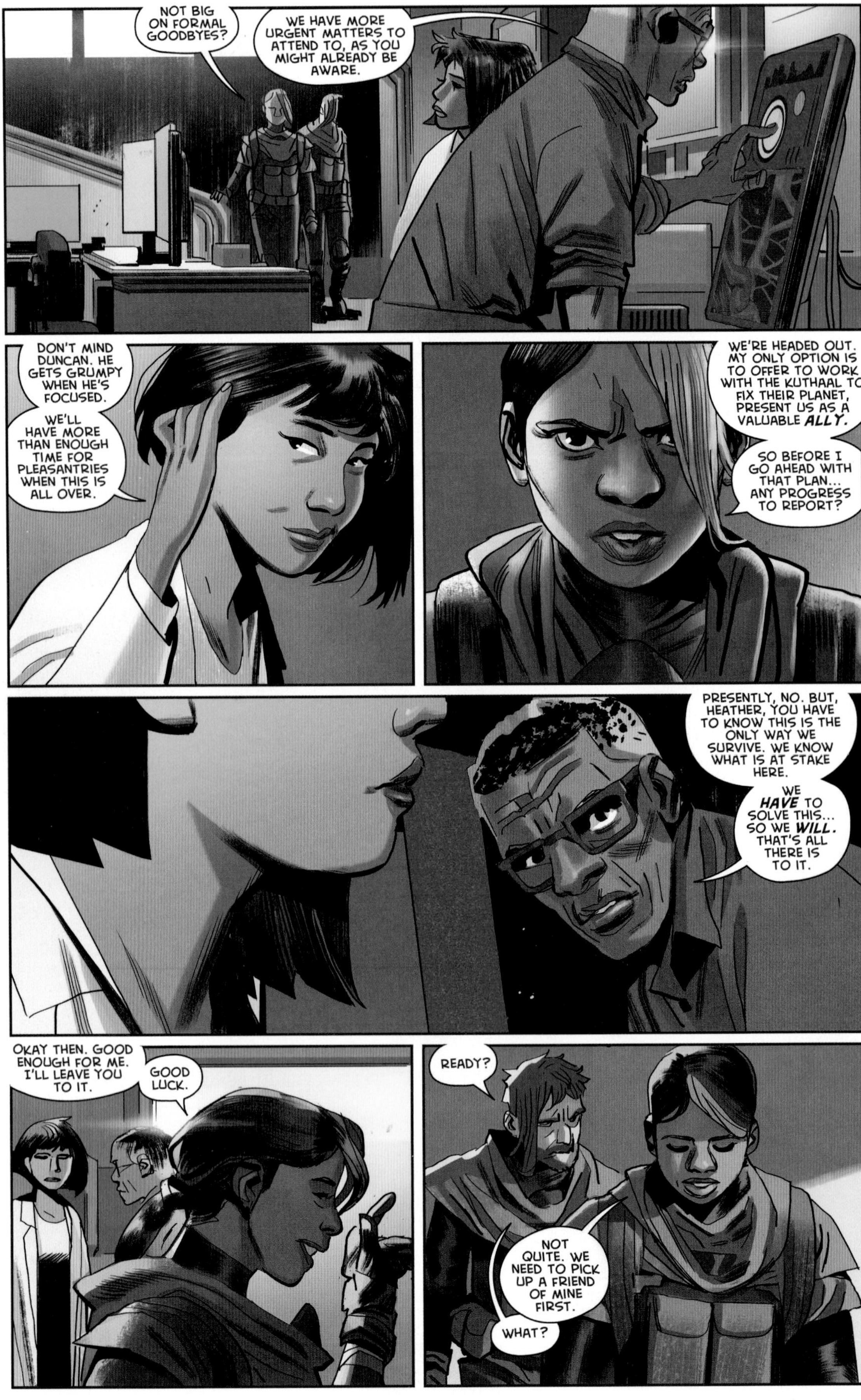
NOT BIG ON FORMAL GOODBYES?
WE HAVE MORE URGENT MATTERS TO ATTEND TO, AS YOU MIGHT ALREADY BE AWARE.
DON'T MIND DUNCAN. HE GETS GRUMPY WHEN HE'S FOCUSED.
WE'LL HAVE MORE THAN ENOUGH TIME FOR PLEASANTRIES WHEN THIS IS ALL OVER.
WE'RE HEADED OUT. MY ONLY OPTION IS TO OFFER TO WORK WITH THE KUTHAAL TO FIX THEIR PLANET, PRESENT US AS A VALUABLE ALLY.
SO BEFORE I GO AHEAD WITH THAT PLAN... ANY PROGRESS TO REPORT?
PRESENTLY, NO. BUT, HEATHER, YOU HAVE TO KNOW THIS IS THE ONLY WAY WE SURVIVE. WE KNOW WHAT IS AT STAKE HERE.
WE HAVE TO SOLVE THIS... SO WE WILL. THAT'S ALL THERE IS TO IT.
OKAY THEN. GOOD ENOUGH FOR ME. I'LL LEAVE YOU TO IT.
GOOD LUCK.
READY?
NOT QUITE. WE NEED TO PICK UP A FRIEND OF MINE FIRST.
WHAT?

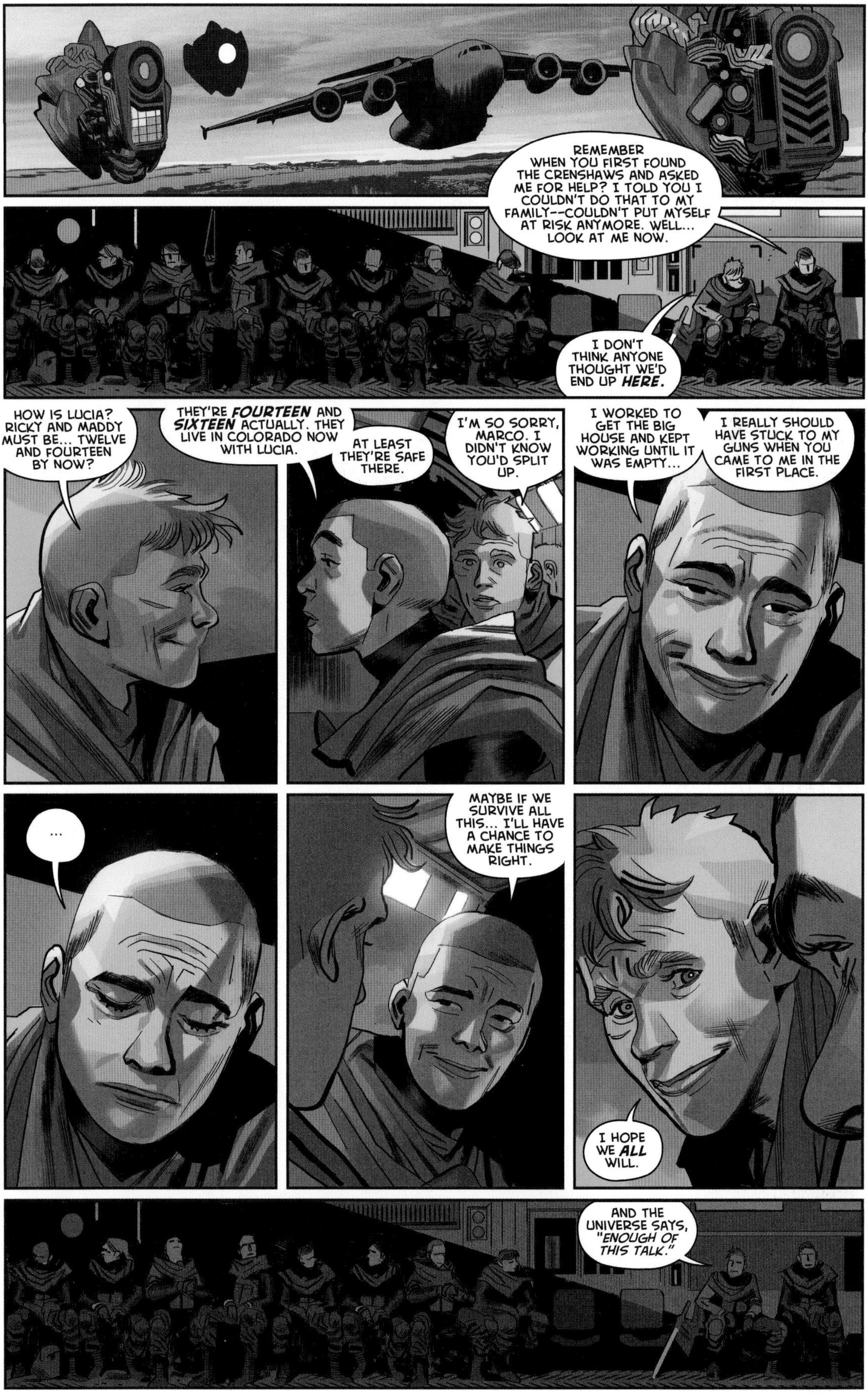
REMEMBER WHEN YOU FIRST FOUND THE CRENSHAWS AND ASKED ME FOR HELP? I TOLD YOU I COULDN'T DO THAT TO MY FAMILY--COULDN'T PUT MYSELF AT RISK ANYMORE. WELL... LOOK AT ME NOW.
I DON'T THINK ANYONE THOUGHT WE'D END UP *HERE.*
HOW IS LUCIA? RICKY AND MADDY MUST BE... TWELVE AND FOURTEEN BY NOW?
THEY'RE ***FOURTEEN*** AND ***SIXTEEN*** ACTUALLY. THEY LIVE IN COLORADO NOW WITH LUCIA.
AT LEAST THEY'RE SAFE THERE.
I'M SO SORRY, MARCO. I DIDN'T KNOW YOU'D SPLIT UP.
I WORKED TO GET THE BIG HOUSE AND KEPT WORKING UNTIL IT WAS EMPTY...
I REALLY SHOULD HAVE STUCK TO MY GUNS WHEN YOU CAME TO ME IN THE FIRST PLACE.
...
MAYBE IF WE SURVIVE ALL THIS... I'LL HAVE A CHANCE TO MAKE THINGS RIGHT.
I HOPE WE *ALL* WILL.
AND THE UNIVERSE SAYS, *"ENOUGH OF THIS TALK."*

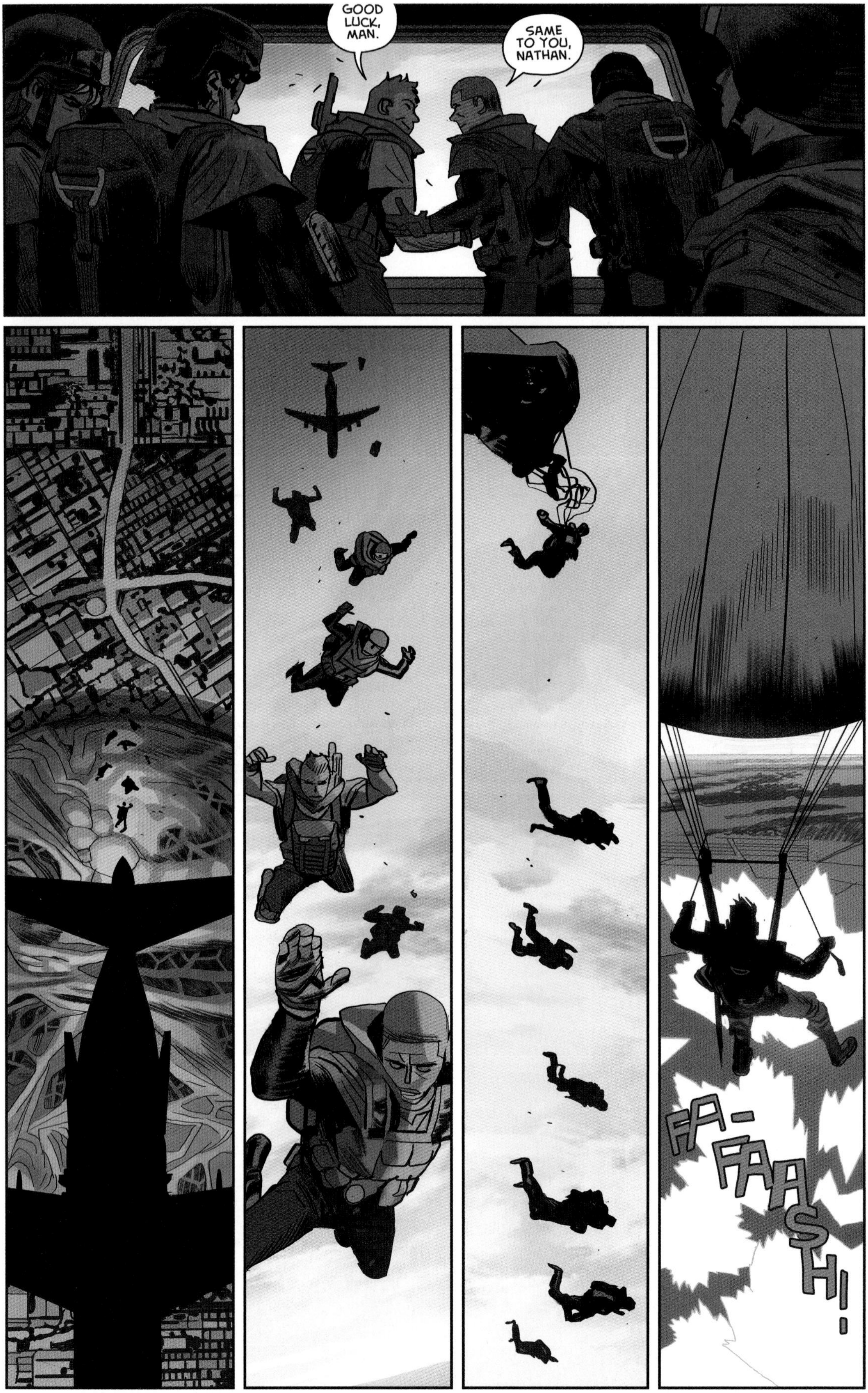
GOOD LUCK, MAN.
SAME TO YOU, NATHAN.
FA-FAAASH!!

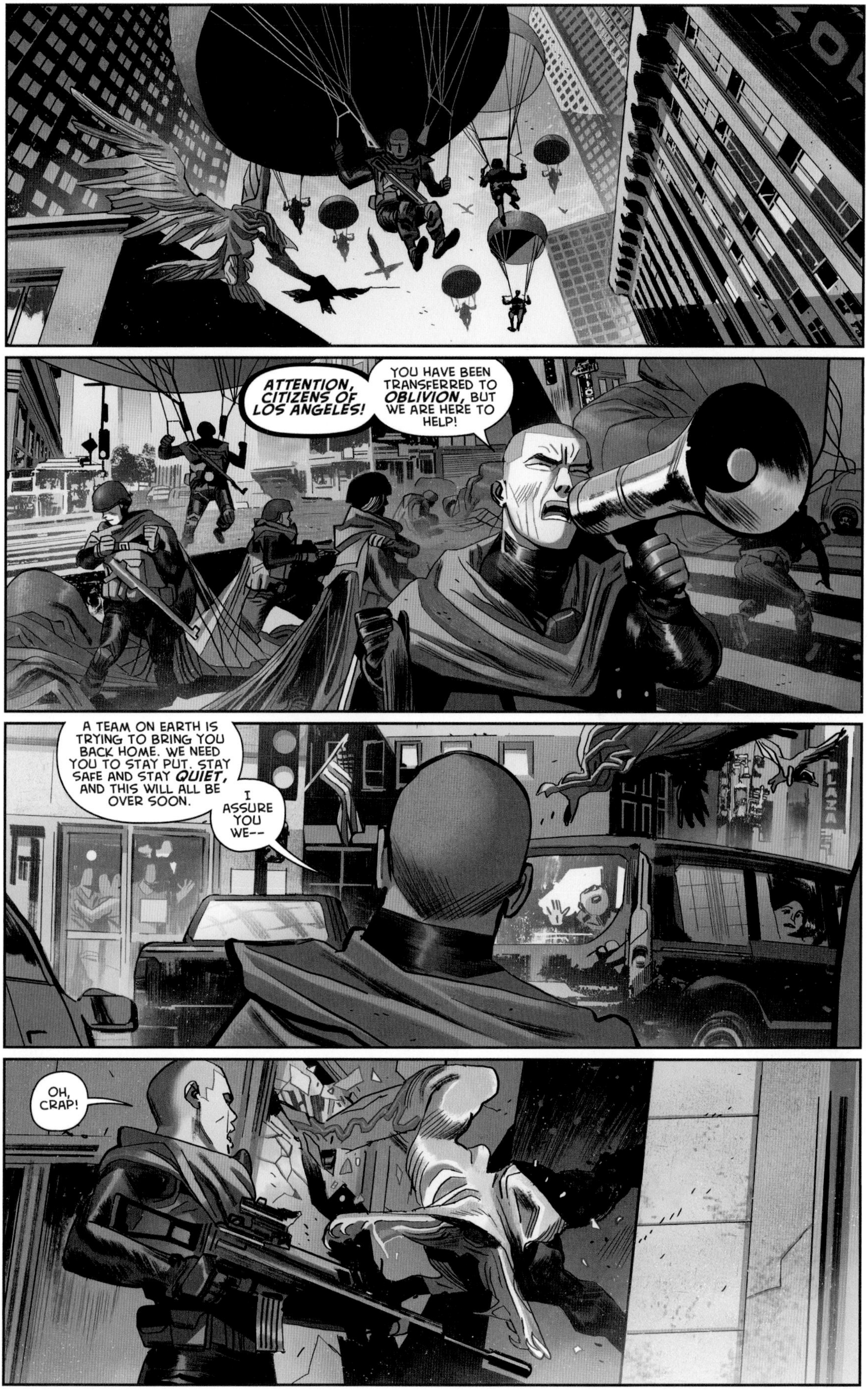
ATTENTION, CITIZENS OF LOS ANGELES!
YOU HAVE BEEN TRANSFERRED TO OBLIVION, BUT WE ARE HERE TO HELP!
A TEAM ON EARTH IS TRYING TO BRING YOU BACK HOME. WE NEED YOU TO STAY PUT. STAY SAFE AND STAY QUIET, AND THIS WILL ALL BE OVER SOON.
I ASSURE YOU WE--
OH, CRAP!

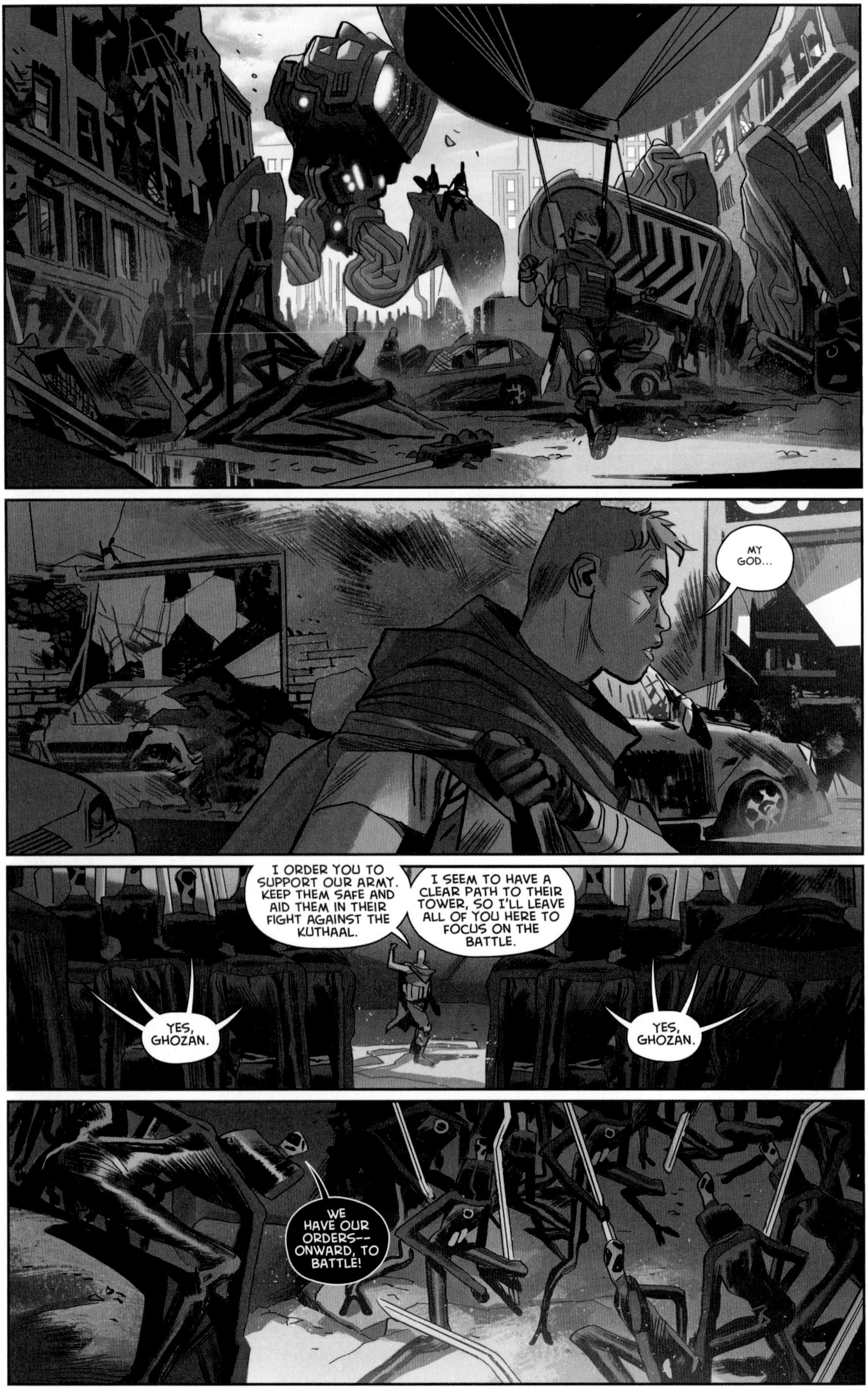
MY GOD...
I ORDER YOU TO SUPPORT OUR ARMY. KEEP THEM SAFE AND AID THEM IN THEIR FIGHT AGAINST THE KUTHAAL.
I SEEM TO HAVE A CLEAR PATH TO THEIR TOWER, SO I'LL LEAVE ALL OF YOU HERE TO FOCUS ON THE BATTLE.
YES, GHOZAN.
YES, GHOZAN.
WE HAVE OUR ORDERS-- ONWARD, TO BATTLE!

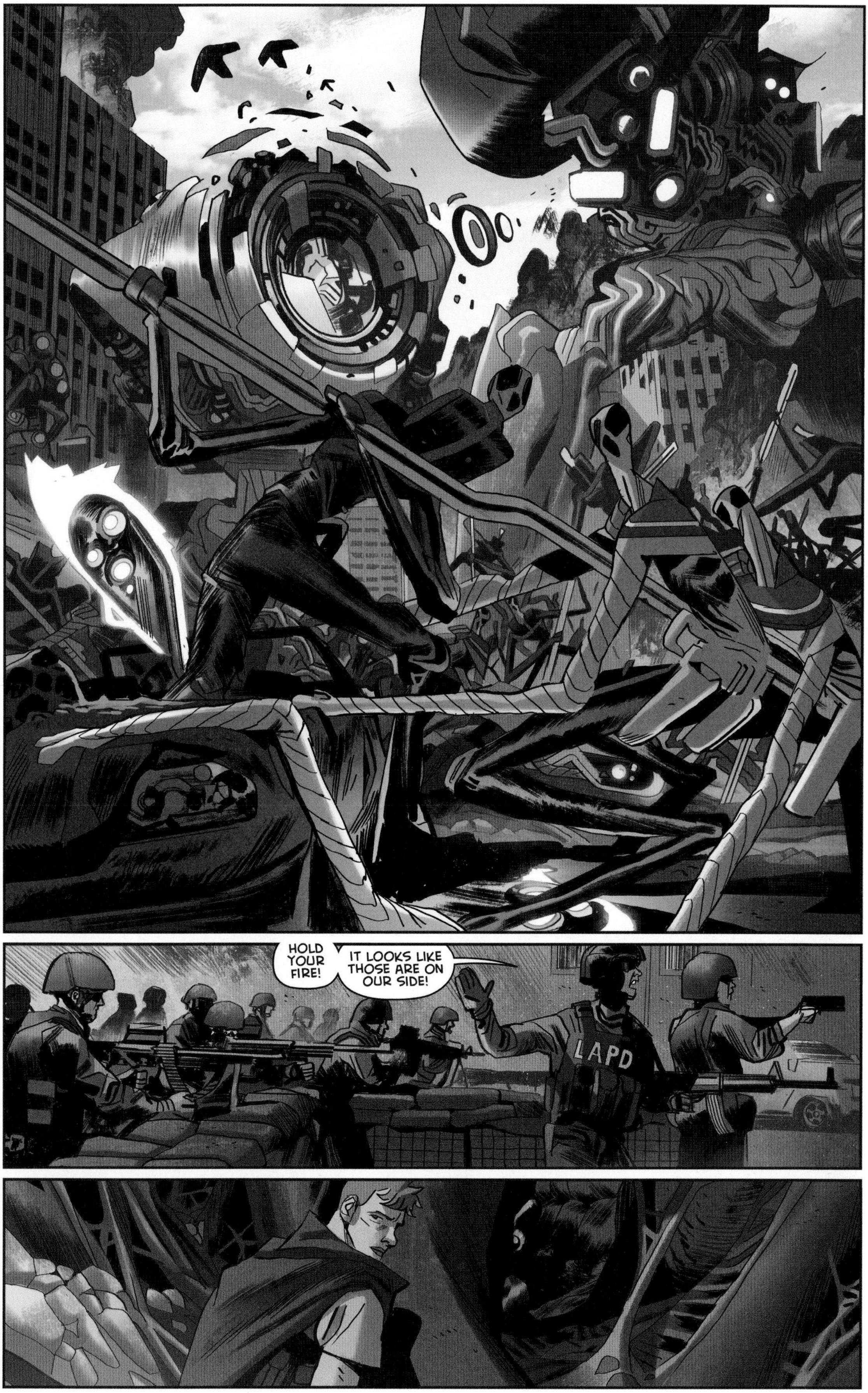
HOLD YOUR FIRE!
IT LOOKS LIKE THOSE ARE ON OUR SIDE!
LAPD

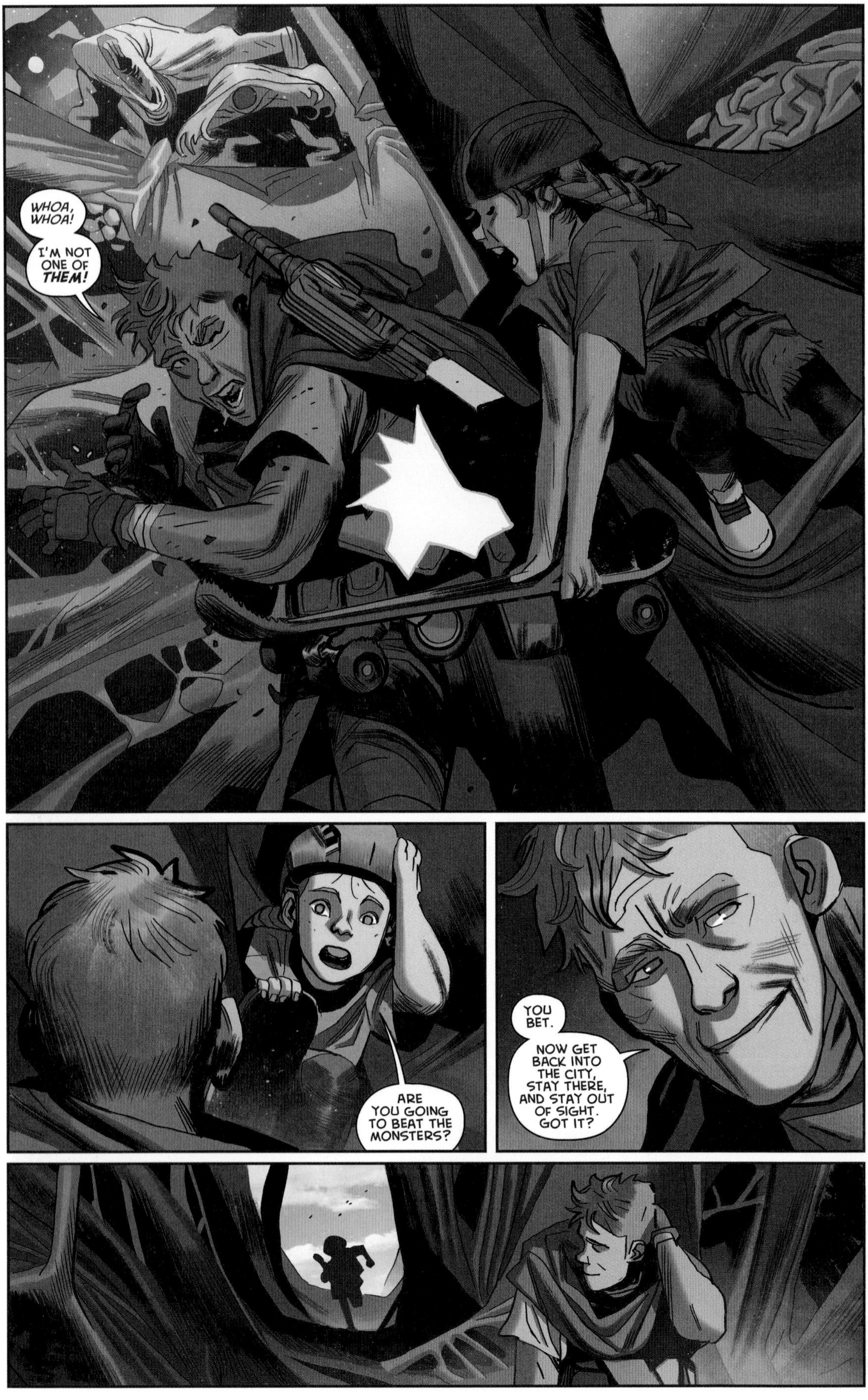
WHOA, WHOA!
I'M NOT ONE OF **THEM!**
ARE YOU GOING TO BEAT THE MONSTERS?
YOU BET.
NOW GET BACK INTO THE CITY, STAY THERE, AND STAY OUT OF SIGHT. GOT IT?

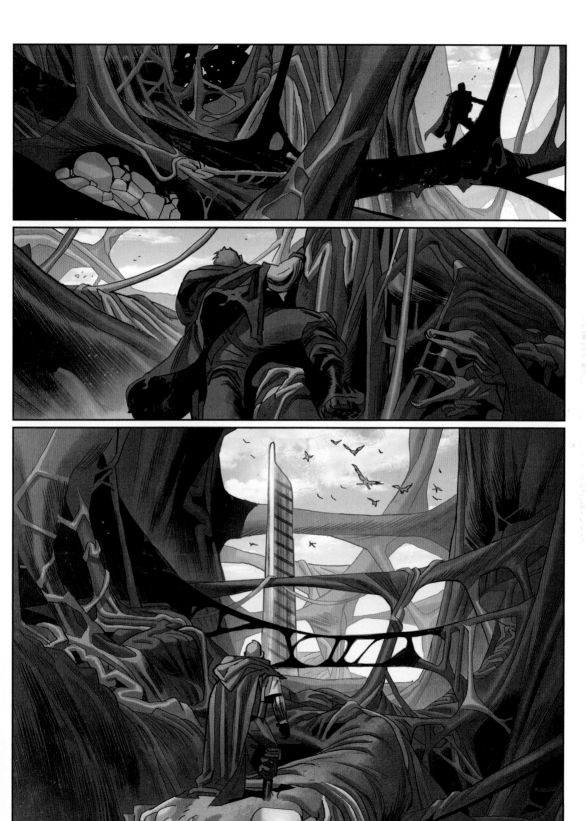

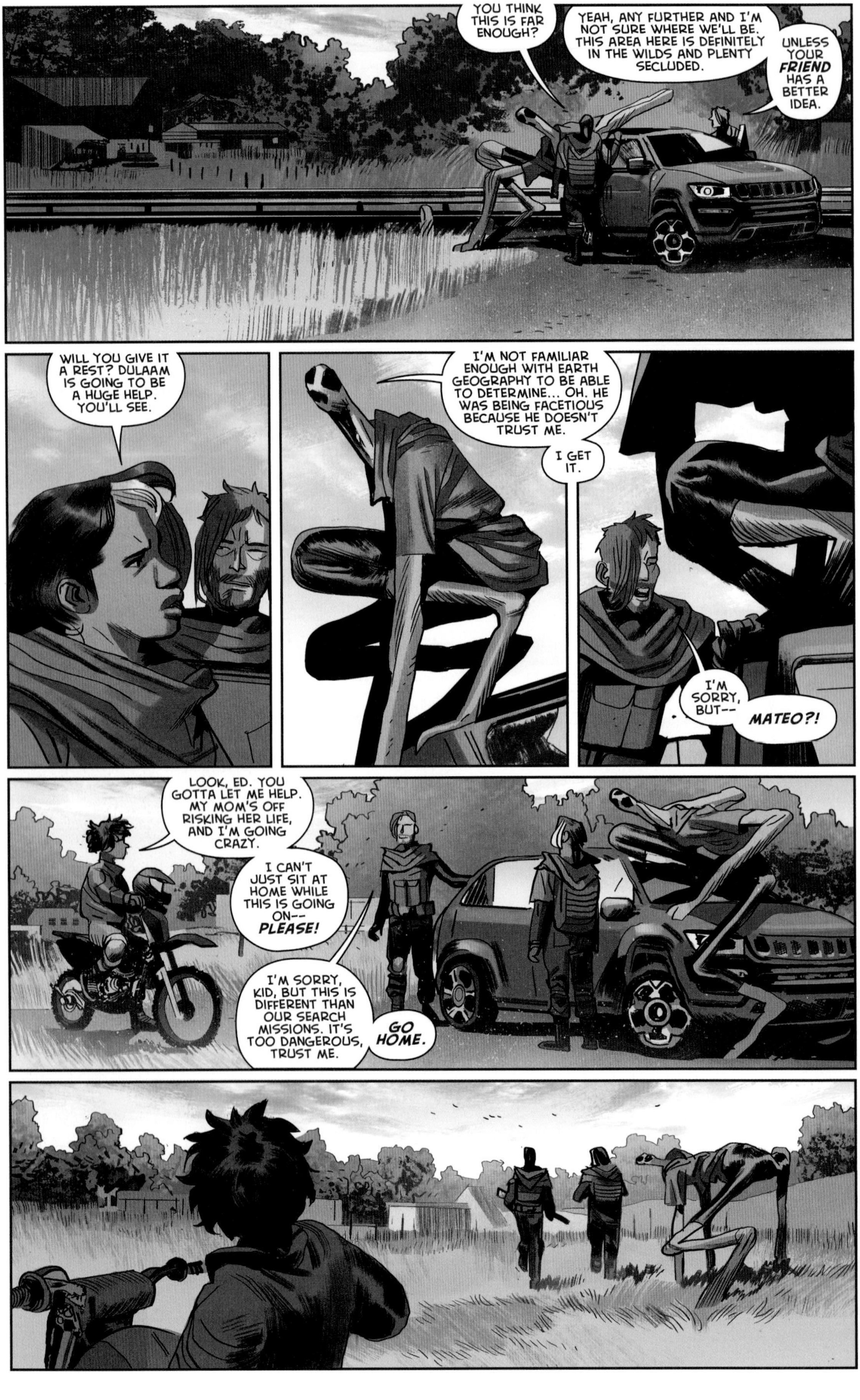
YOU THINK THIS IS FAR ENOUGH?
YEAH, ANY FURTHER AND I'M NOT SURE WHERE WE'LL BE. THIS AREA HERE IS DEFINITELY IN THE WILDS AND PLENTY SECLUDED.
UNLESS YOUR FRIEND HAS A BETTER IDEA.
WILL YOU GIVE IT A REST? DULAAM IS GOING TO BE A HUGE HELP. YOU'LL SEE.
I'M NOT FAMILIAR ENOUGH WITH EARTH GEOGRAPHY TO BE ABLE TO DETERMINE... OH. HE WAS BEING FACETIOUS BECAUSE HE DOESN'T TRUST ME.
I GET IT.
I'M SORRY, BUT--
MATEO?!
LOOK, ED. YOU GOTTA LET ME HELP. MY MOM'S OFF RISKING HER LIFE, AND I'M GOING CRAZY.
I CAN'T JUST SIT AT HOME WHILE THIS IS GOING ON-- PLEASE!
I'M SORRY, KID, BUT THIS IS DIFFERENT THAN OUR SEARCH MISSIONS. IT'S TOO DANGEROUS. TRUST ME.
GO HOME.

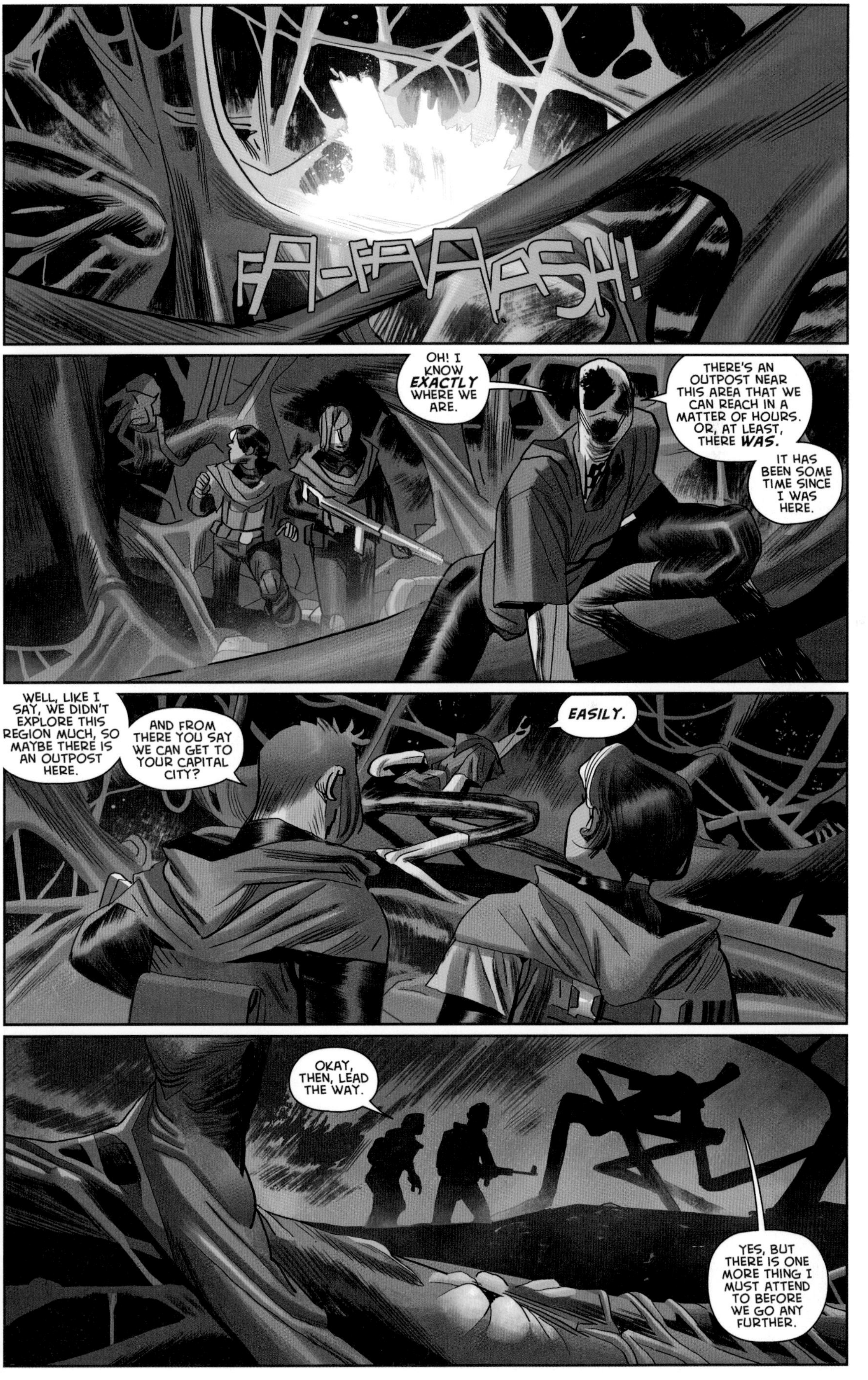
FA-FAAASH!
OH! I KNOW EXACTLY WHERE WE ARE.
THERE'S AN OUTPOST NEAR THIS AREA THAT WE CAN REACH IN A MATTER OF HOURS. OR, AT LEAST, THERE WAS.
IT HAS BEEN SOME TIME SINCE I WAS HERE.
WELL, LIKE I SAY, WE DIDN'T EXPLORE THIS REGION MUCH, SO MAYBE THERE IS AN OUTPOST HERE.
AND FROM THERE YOU SAY WE CAN GET TO YOUR CAPITAL CITY?
EASILY.
OKAY, THEN, LEAD THE WAY.
YES, BUT THERE IS ONE MORE THING I MUST ATTEND TO BEFORE WE GO ANY FURTHER.

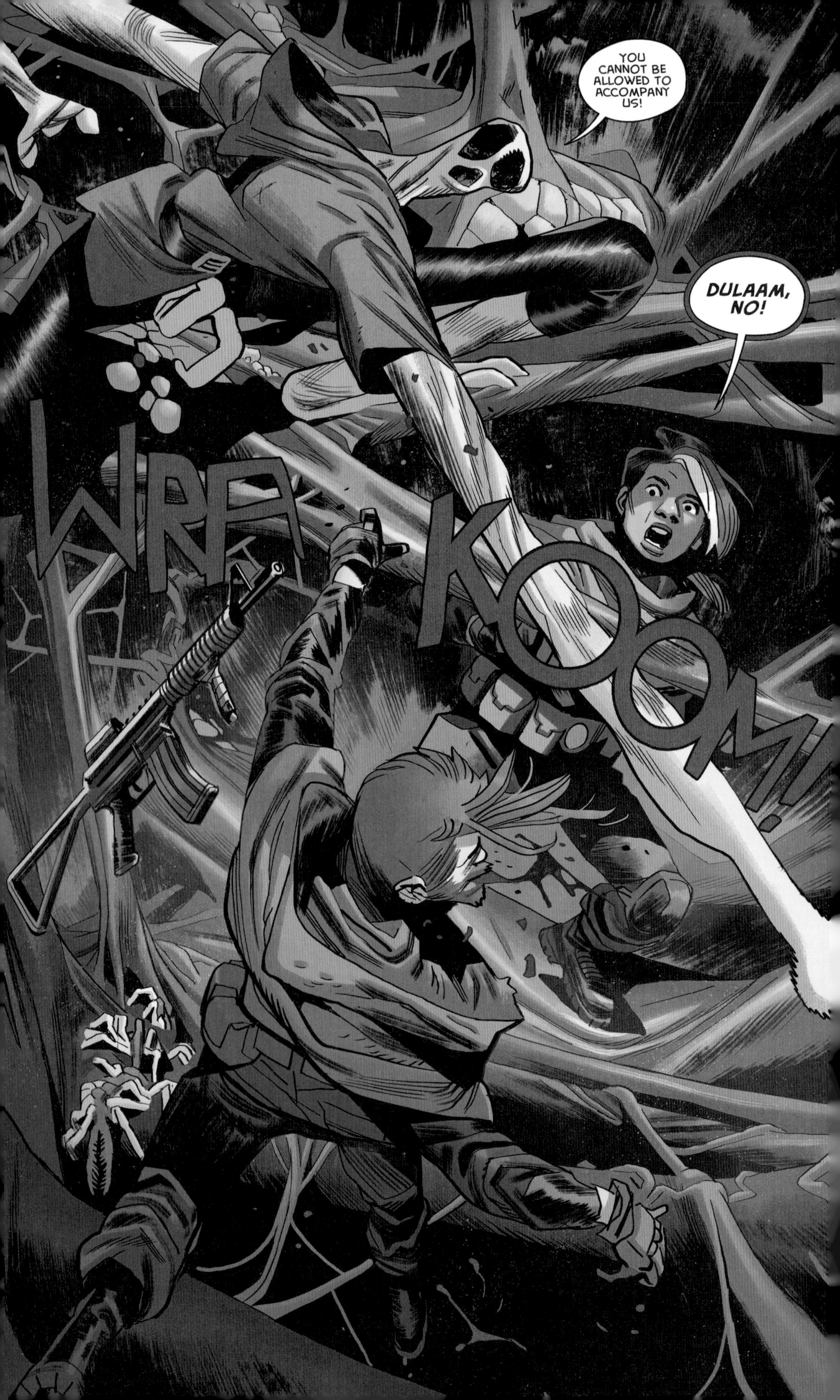

YOU CANNOT BE ALLOWED TO ACCOMPANY US!
DULAAM, NO!
WRRAKOOOM!!

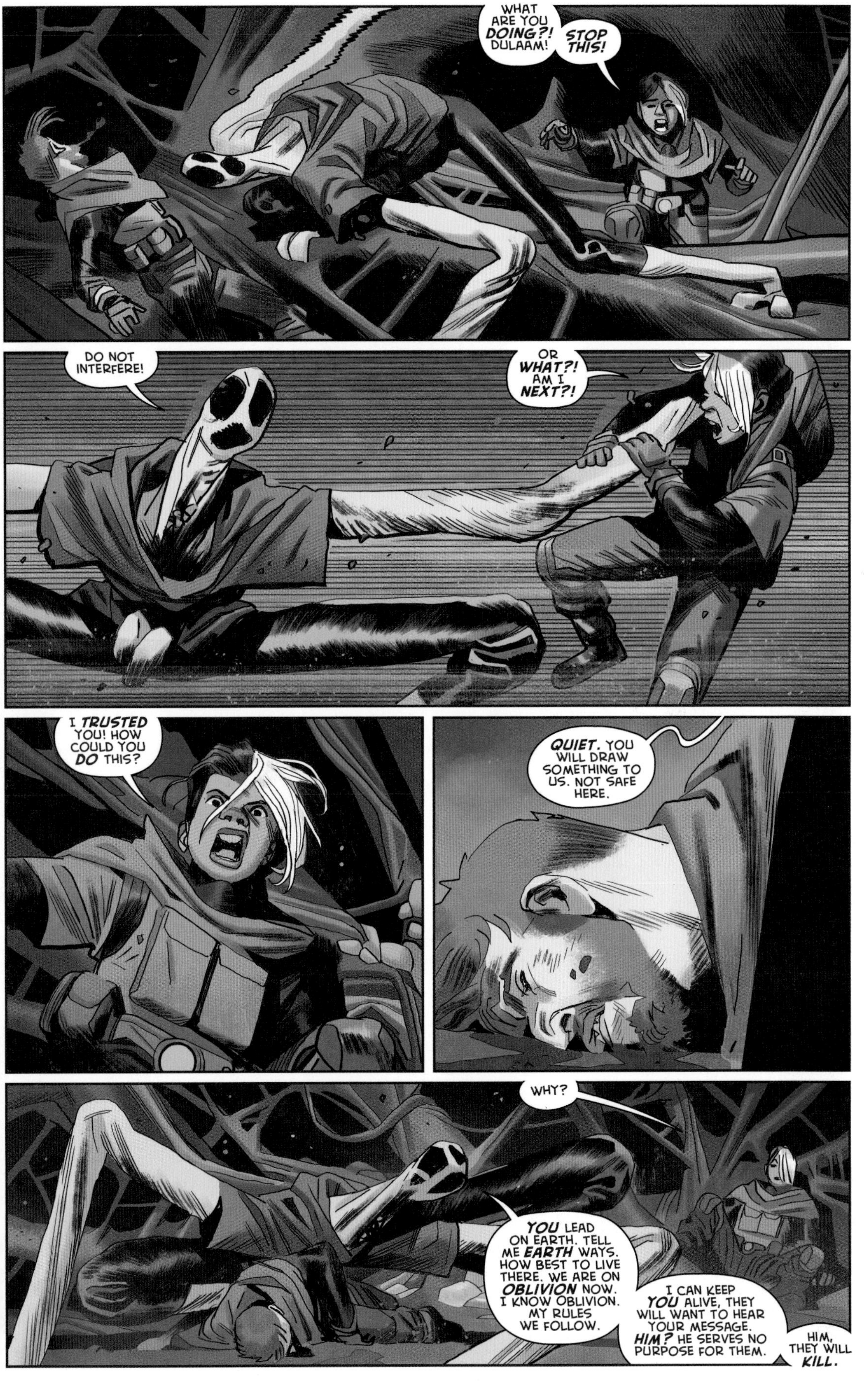
WHAT ARE YOU DOING?! DULAAM!
STOP THIS!
DO NOT INTERFERE!
OR WHAT?! AM I NEXT?!
I TRUSTED YOU! HOW COULD YOU DO THIS?
QUIET. YOU WILL DRAW SOMETHING TO US. NOT SAFE HERE.
WHY?
YOU LEAD ON EARTH. TELL ME EARTH WAYS. HOW BEST TO LIVE THERE. WE ARE ON OBLIVION NOW. I KNOW OBLIVION. MY RULES WE FOLLOW.
I CAN KEEP YOU ALIVE, THEY WILL WANT TO HEAR YOUR MESSAGE. HIM? HE SERVES NO PURPOSE FOR THEM.
HIM, THEY WILL KILL.

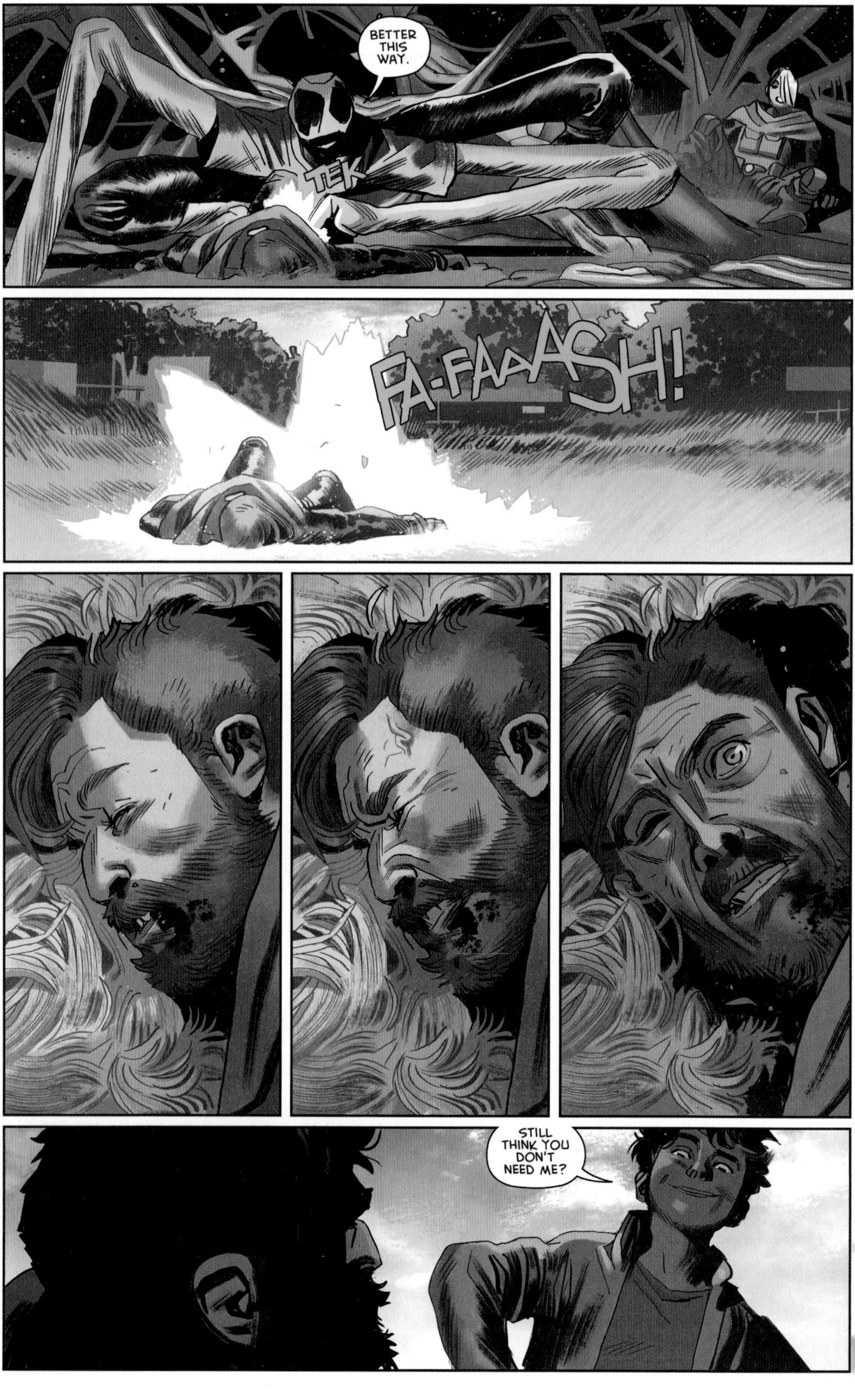
BETTER THIS WAY.
TEK
FA-FAAASH!
STILL THINK YOU DON'T NEED ME?

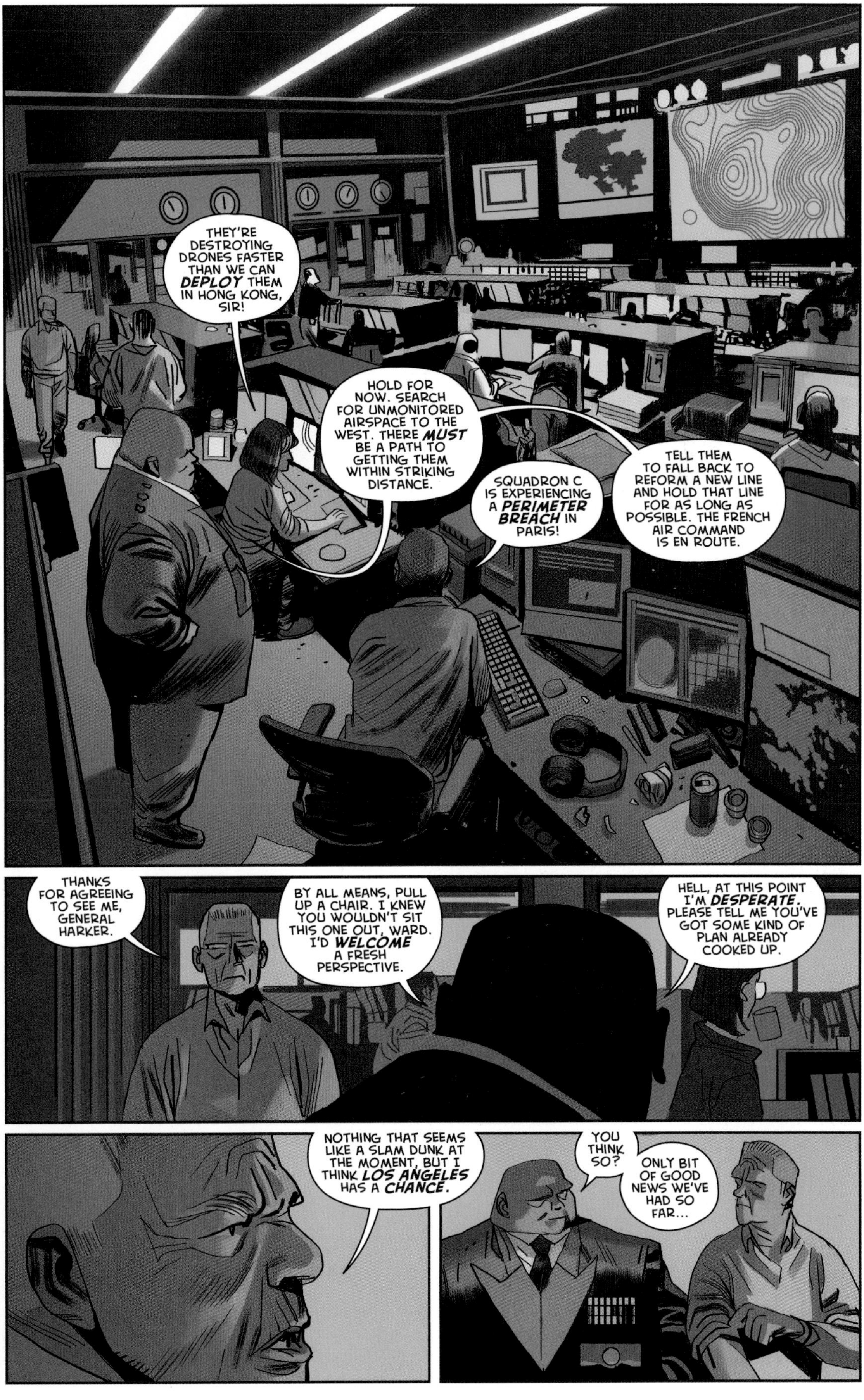
THEY'RE DESTROYING DRONES FASTER THAN WE CAN DEPLOY THEM IN HONG KONG, SIR!
HOLD FOR NOW. SEARCH FOR UNMONITORED AIRSPACE TO THE WEST. THERE MUST BE A PATH TO GETTING THEM WITHIN STRIKING DISTANCE.
SQUADRON C IS EXPERIENCING A PERIMETER BREACH IN PARIS!
TELL THEM TO FALL BACK TO REFORM A NEW LINE AND HOLD THAT LINE FOR AS LONG AS POSSIBLE. THE FRENCH AIR COMMAND IS EN ROUTE.
THANKS FOR AGREEING TO SEE ME, GENERAL HARKER.
BY ALL MEANS, PULL UP A CHAIR. I KNEW YOU WOULDN'T SIT THIS ONE OUT, WARD. I'D WELCOME A FRESH PERSPECTIVE.
HELL, AT THIS POINT I'M DESPERATE. PLEASE TELL ME YOU'VE GOT SOME KIND OF PLAN ALREADY COOKED UP.
NOTHING THAT SEEMS LIKE A SLAM DUNK AT THE MOMENT, BUT I THINK LOS ANGELES HAS A CHANCE.
YOU THINK SO?
ONLY BIT OF GOOD NEWS WE'VE HAD SO FAR...

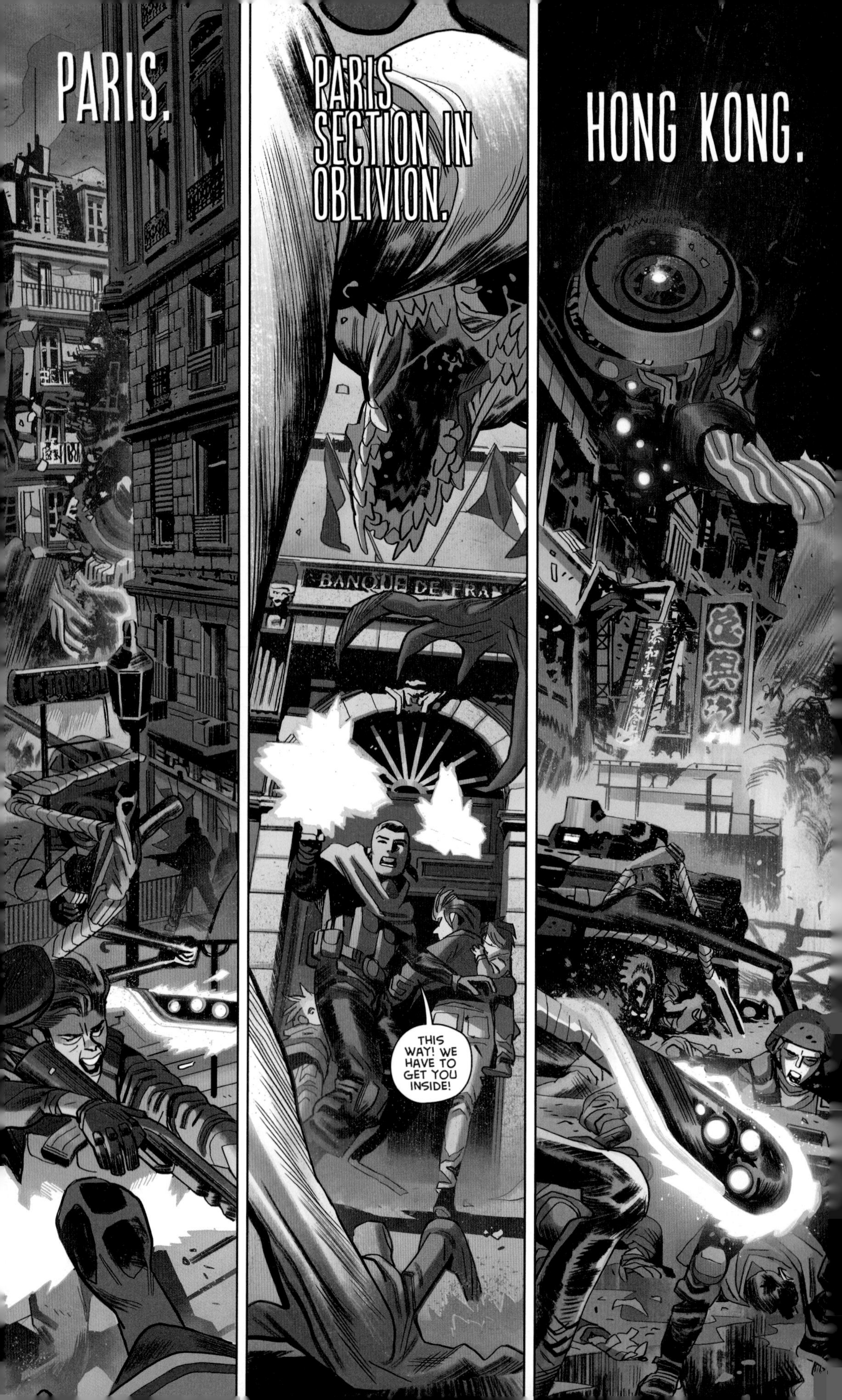
PARIS.
PARIS SECTION IN OBLIVION.
BANQUE DE FRA
THIS WAY! WE HAVE TO GET YOU INSIDE!
HONG KONG.

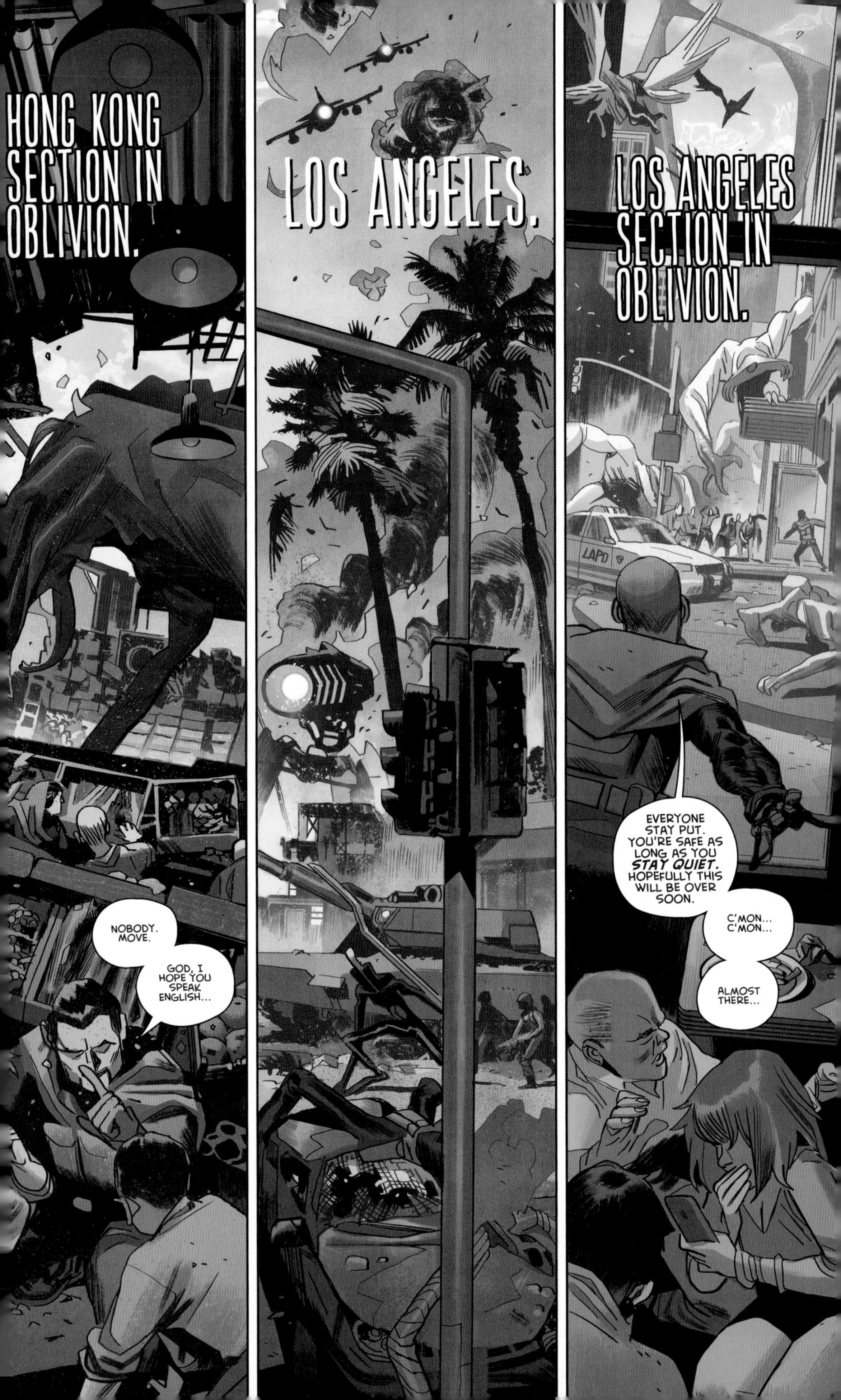
HONG KONG SECTION IN OBLIVION.
NOBODY. MOVE.
GOD, I HOPE YOU SPEAK ENGLISH...
LOS ANGELES.
LOS ANGELES SECTION IN OBLIVION.
LAPD
EVERYONE STAY PUT. YOU'RE SAFE AS LONG AS YOU STAY QUIET. HOPEFULLY THIS WILL BE OVER SOON.
C'MON... C'MON...
ALMOST THERE...

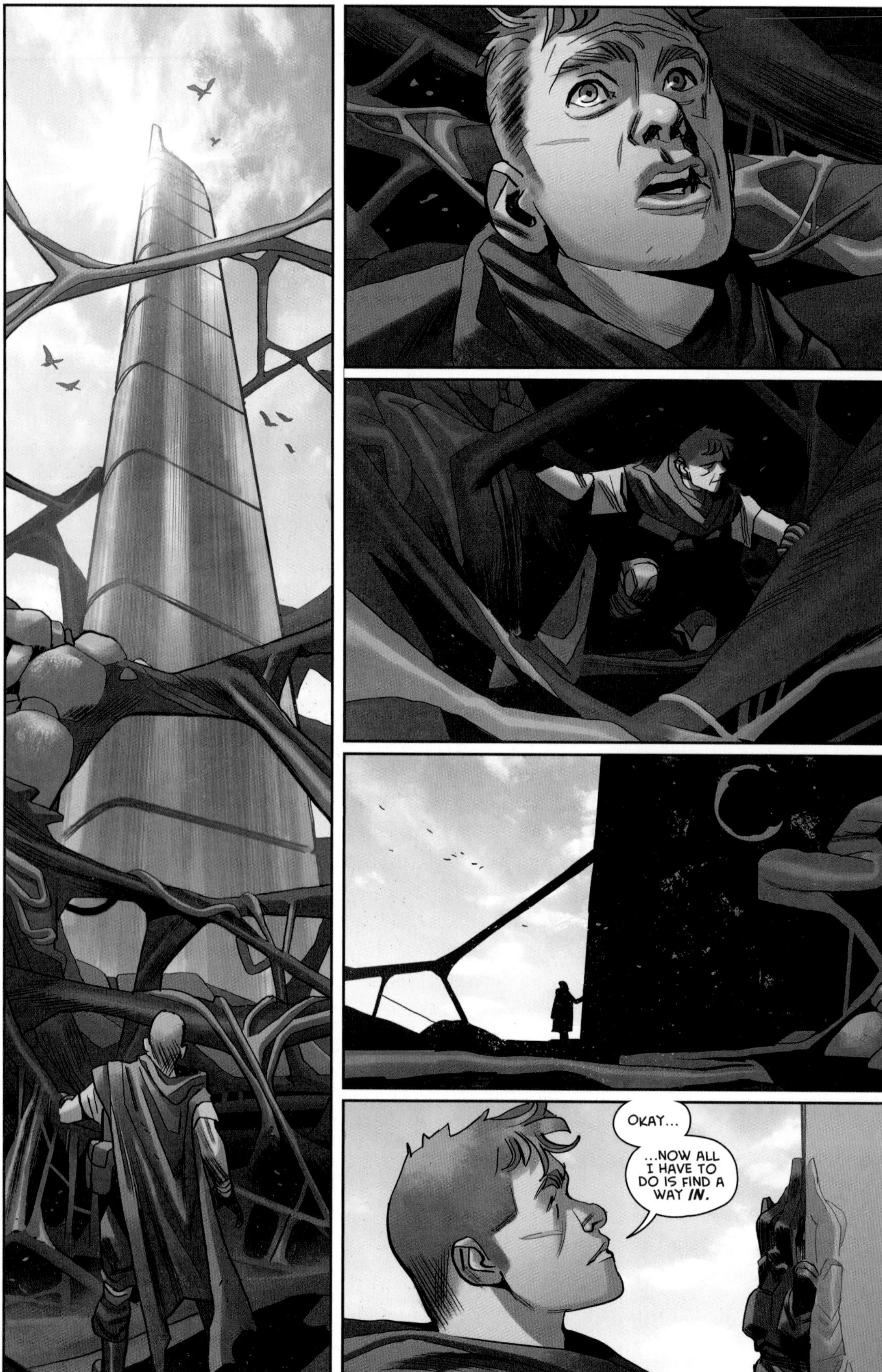
OKAY...
...NOW ALL I HAVE TO DO IS FIND A WAY IN.

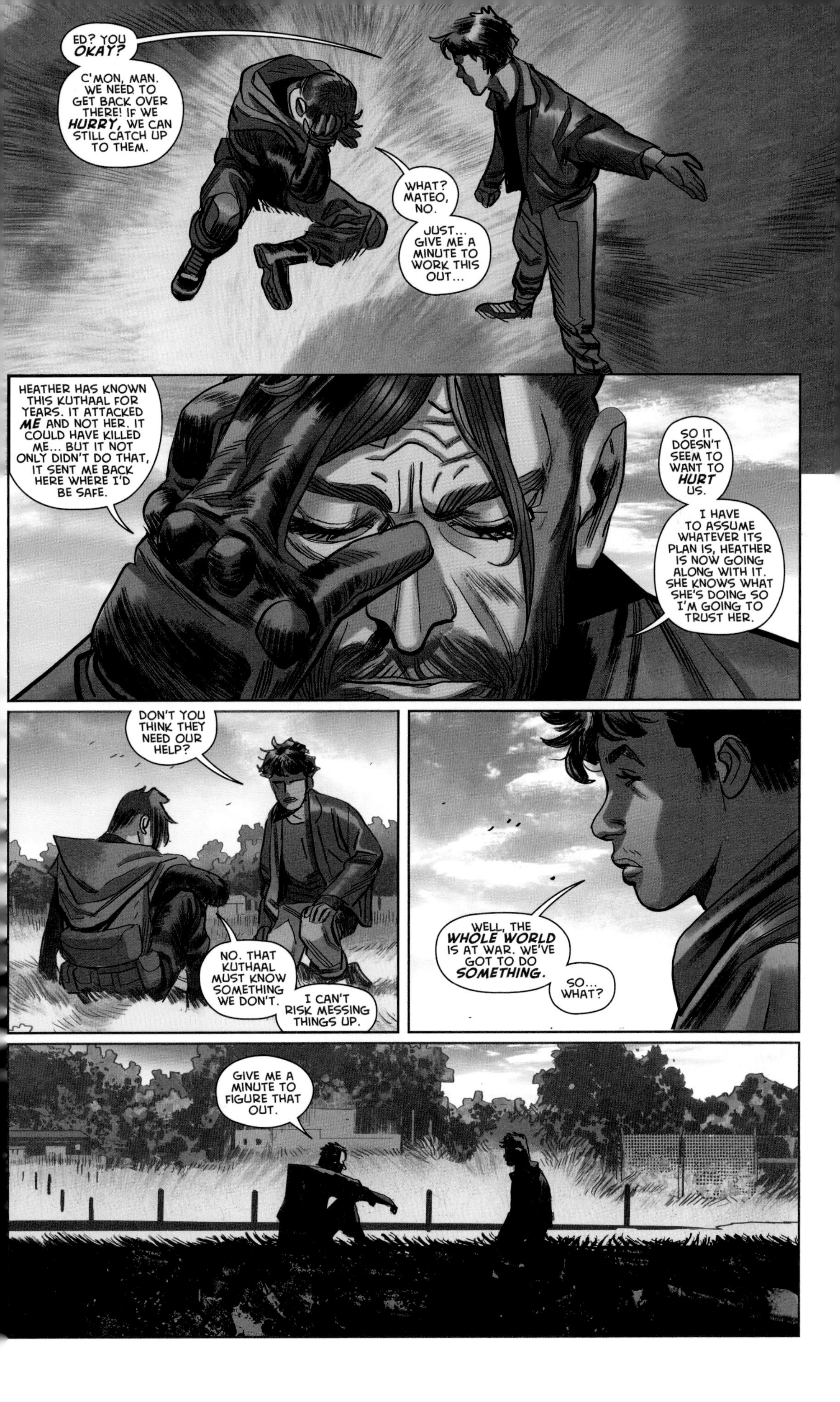
ED? YOU OKAY?
C'MON, MAN. WE NEED TO GET BACK OVER THERE! IF WE HURRY, WE CAN STILL CATCH UP TO THEM.
WHAT? MATEO, NO.
JUST... GIVE ME A MINUTE TO WORK THIS OUT...
HEATHER HAS KNOWN THIS KUTHAAL FOR YEARS. IT ATTACKED ME AND NOT HER. IT COULD HAVE KILLED ME... BUT IT NOT ONLY DIDN'T DO THAT, IT SENT ME BACK HERE WHERE I'D BE SAFE.
SO IT DOESN'T SEEM TO WANT TO HURT US.
I HAVE TO ASSUME WHATEVER ITS PLAN IS, HEATHER IS NOW GOING ALONG WITH IT. SHE KNOWS WHAT SHE'S DOING SO I'M GOING TO TRUST HER.
DON'T YOU THINK THEY NEED OUR HELP?
NO. THAT KUTHAAL MUST KNOW SOMETHING WE DON'T.
I CAN'T RISK MESSING THINGS UP.
WELL, THE WHOLE WORLD IS AT WAR. WE'VE GOT TO DO SOMETHING.
SO... WHAT?
GIVE ME A MINUTE TO FIGURE THAT OUT.

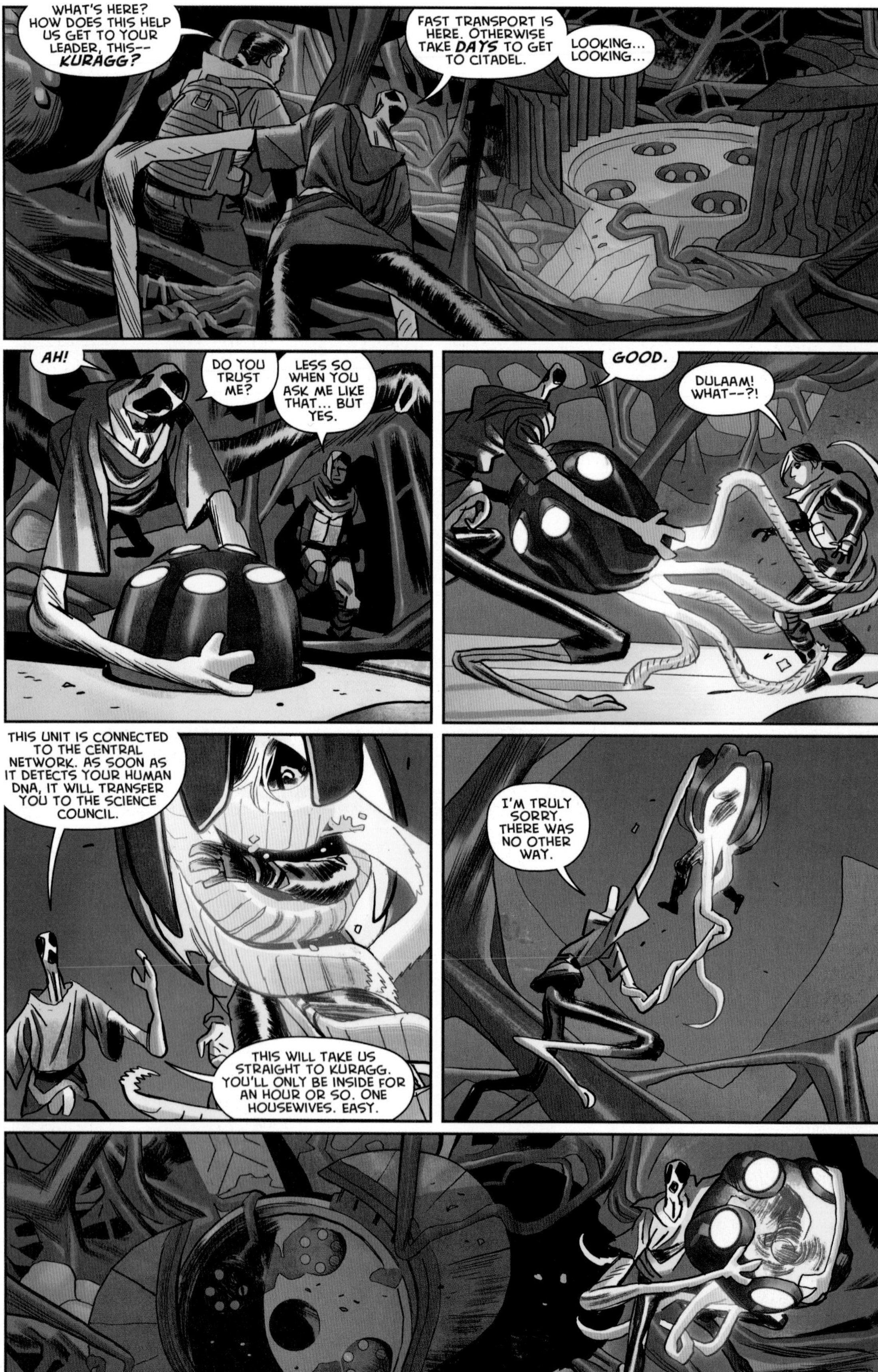
WHAT'S HERE? HOW DOES THIS HELP US GET TO YOUR LEADER, THIS-- KURAGG?
FAST TRANSPORT IS HERE. OTHERWISE TAKE DAYS TO GET TO CITADEL.
LOOKING... LOOKING...
AH!
DO YOU TRUST ME?
LESS SO WHEN YOU ASK ME LIKE THAT... BUT YES.
GOOD.
DULAAM! WHAT--?!
THIS UNIT IS CONNECTED TO THE CENTRAL NETWORK. AS SOON AS IT DETECTS YOUR HUMAN DNA, IT WILL TRANSFER YOU TO THE SCIENCE COUNCIL.
THIS WILL TAKE US STRAIGHT TO KURAGG. YOU'LL ONLY BE INSIDE FOR AN HOUR OR SO. ONE HOUSEWIVES. EASY.
I'M TRULY SORRY. THERE WAS NO OTHER WAY.

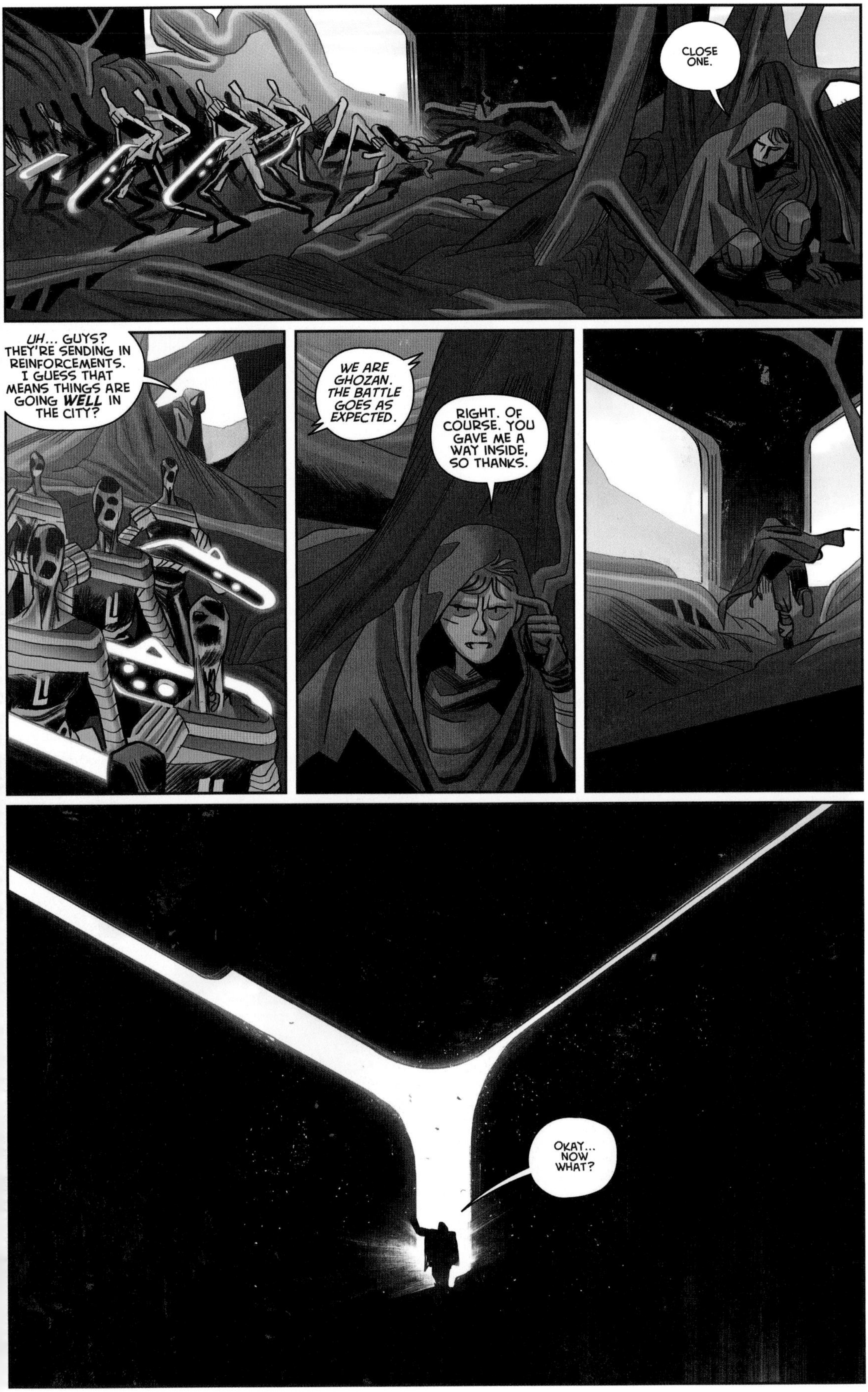
CLOSE ONE.
UH... GUYS? THEY'RE SENDING IN REINFORCEMENTS. I GUESS THAT MEANS THINGS ARE GOING WELL IN THE CITY?
WE ARE GHOZAN. THE BATTLE GOES AS EXPECTED.
RIGHT. OF COURSE. YOU GAVE ME A WAY INSIDE, SO THANKS.
OKAY... NOW WHAT?

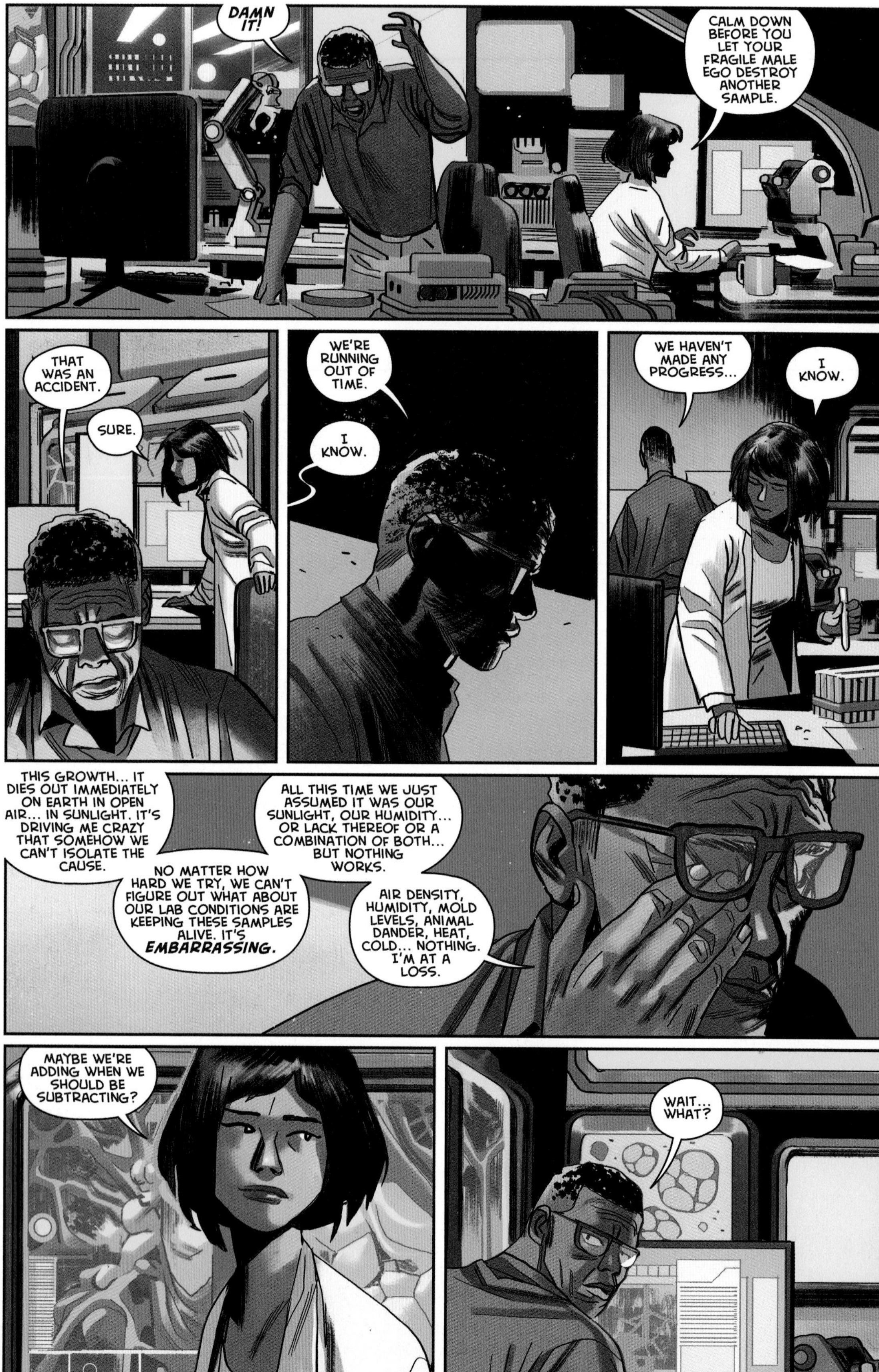
DAMN IT!
CALM DOWN BEFORE YOU LET YOUR FRAGILE MALE EGO DESTROY ANOTHER SAMPLE.
THAT WAS AN ACCIDENT.
SURE.
WE'RE RUNNING OUT OF TIME.
I KNOW.
WE HAVEN'T MADE ANY PROGRESS...
I KNOW.
THIS GROWTH... IT DIES OUT IMMEDIATELY ON EARTH IN OPEN AIR... IN SUNLIGHT. IT'S DRIVING ME CRAZY THAT SOMEHOW WE CAN'T ISOLATE THE CAUSE.
NO MATTER HOW HARD WE TRY, WE CAN'T FIGURE OUT WHAT ABOUT OUR LAB CONDITIONS ARE KEEPING THESE SAMPLES ALIVE. IT'S *EMBARRASSING.*
ALL THIS TIME WE JUST ASSUMED IT WAS OUR SUNLIGHT, OUR HUMIDITY... OR LACK THEREOF OR A COMBINATION OF BOTH... BUT NOTHING WORKS.
AIR DENSITY, HUMIDITY, MOLD LEVELS, ANIMAL DANDER, HEAT, COLD... NOTHING. I'M AT A LOSS.
MAYBE WE'RE ADDING WHEN WE SHOULD BE SUBTRACTING?
WAIT... WHAT?

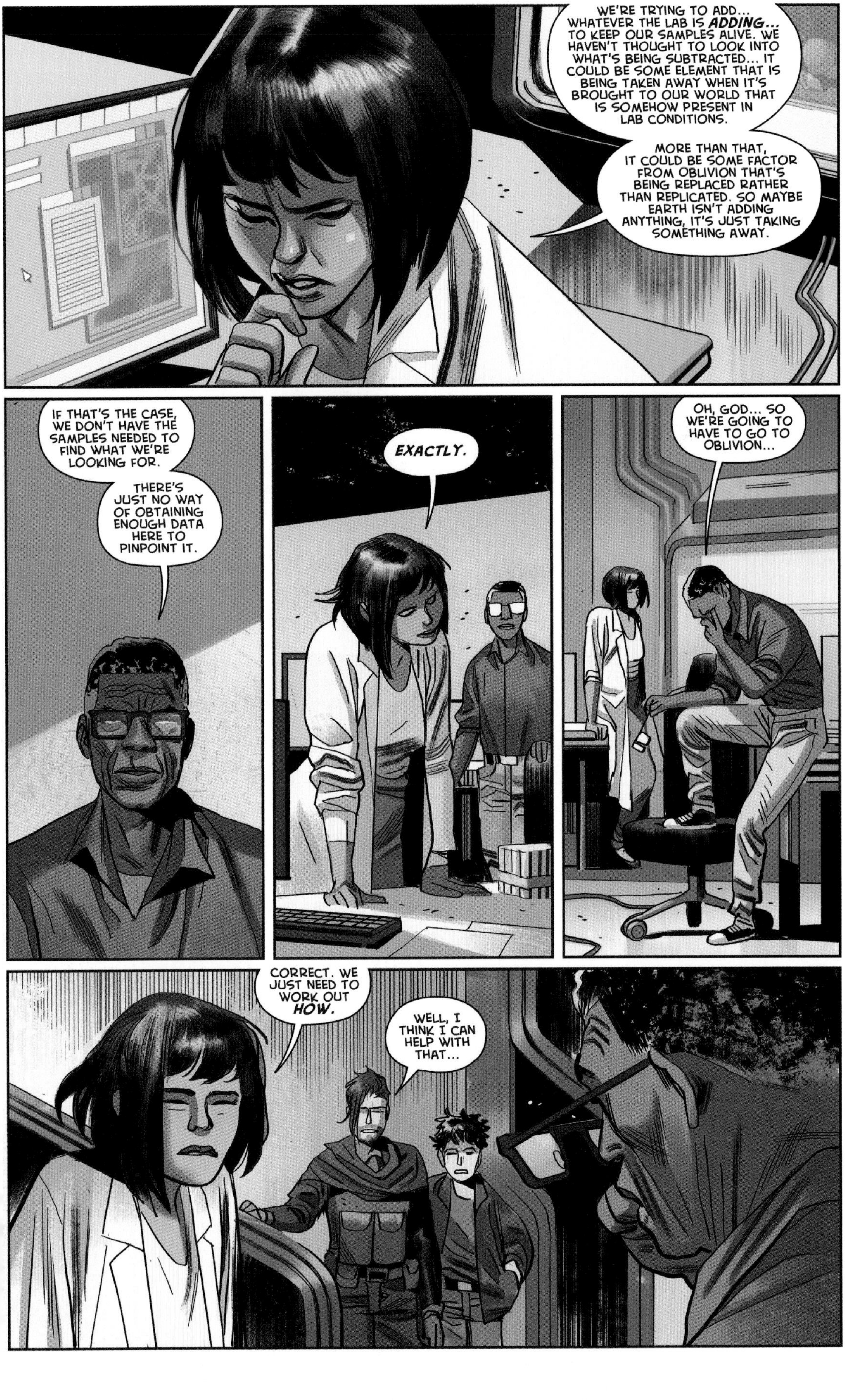
WE'RE TRYING TO ADD... WHATEVER THE LAB IS ADDING... TO KEEP OUR SAMPLES ALIVE. WE HAVEN'T THOUGHT TO LOOK INTO WHAT'S BEING SUBTRACTED... IT COULD BE SOME ELEMENT THAT IS BEING TAKEN AWAY WHEN IT'S BROUGHT TO OUR WORLD THAT IS SOMEHOW PRESENT IN LAB CONDITIONS.
MORE THAN THAT, IT COULD BE SOME FACTOR FROM OBLIVION THAT'S BEING REPLACED RATHER THAN REPLICATED. SO MAYBE EARTH ISN'T ADDING ANYTHING, IT'S JUST TAKING SOMETHING AWAY.
IF THAT'S THE CASE, WE DON'T HAVE THE SAMPLES NEEDED TO FIND WHAT WE'RE LOOKING FOR.
THERE'S JUST NO WAY OF OBTAINING ENOUGH DATA HERE TO PINPOINT IT.
EXACTLY.
OH, GOD... SO WE'RE GOING TO HAVE TO GO TO OBLIVION...
CORRECT. WE JUST NEED TO WORK OUT HOW.
WELL, I THINK I CAN HELP WITH THAT...

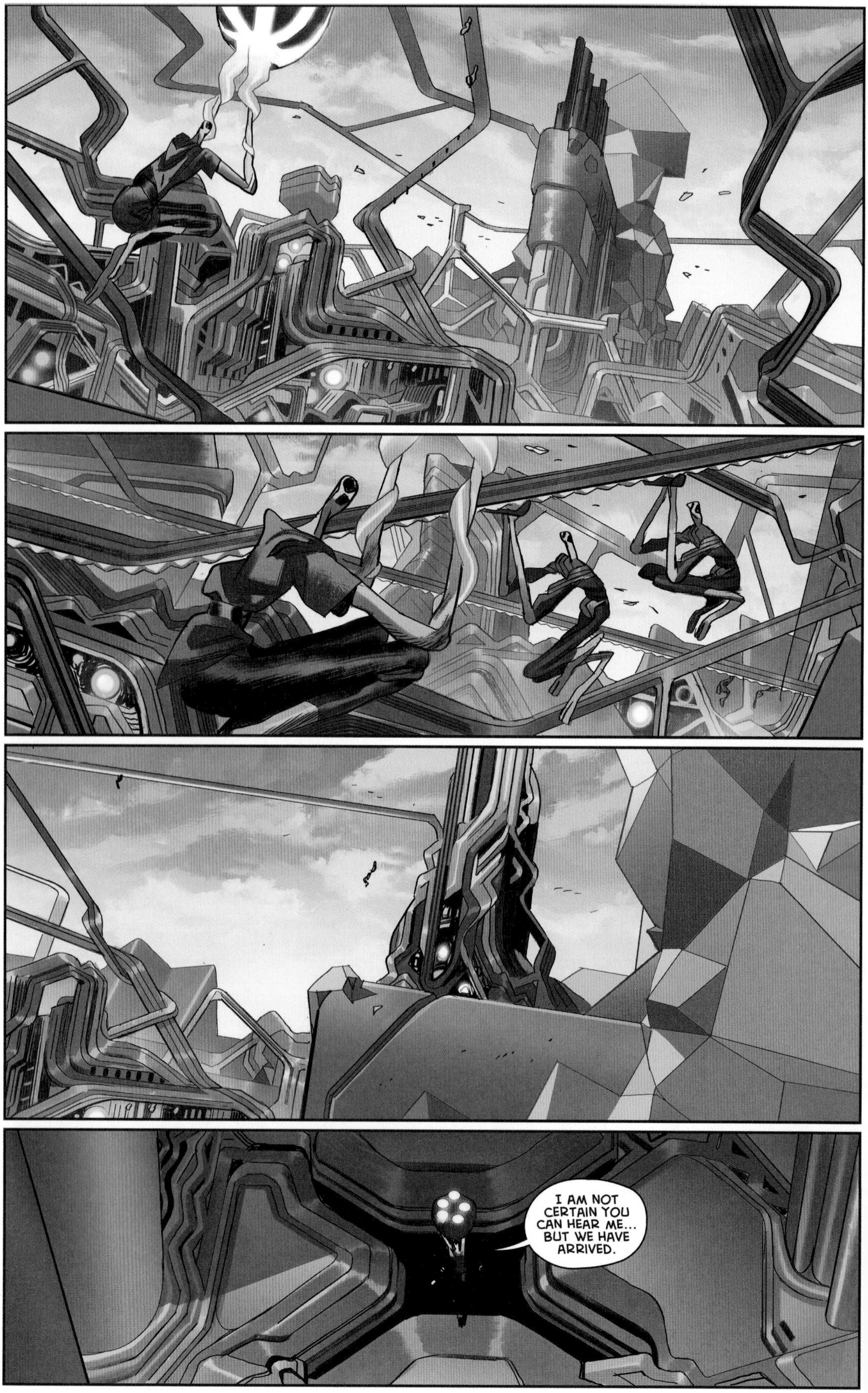
I AM NOT CERTAIN YOU CAN HEAR ME... BUT WE HAVE ARRIVED.

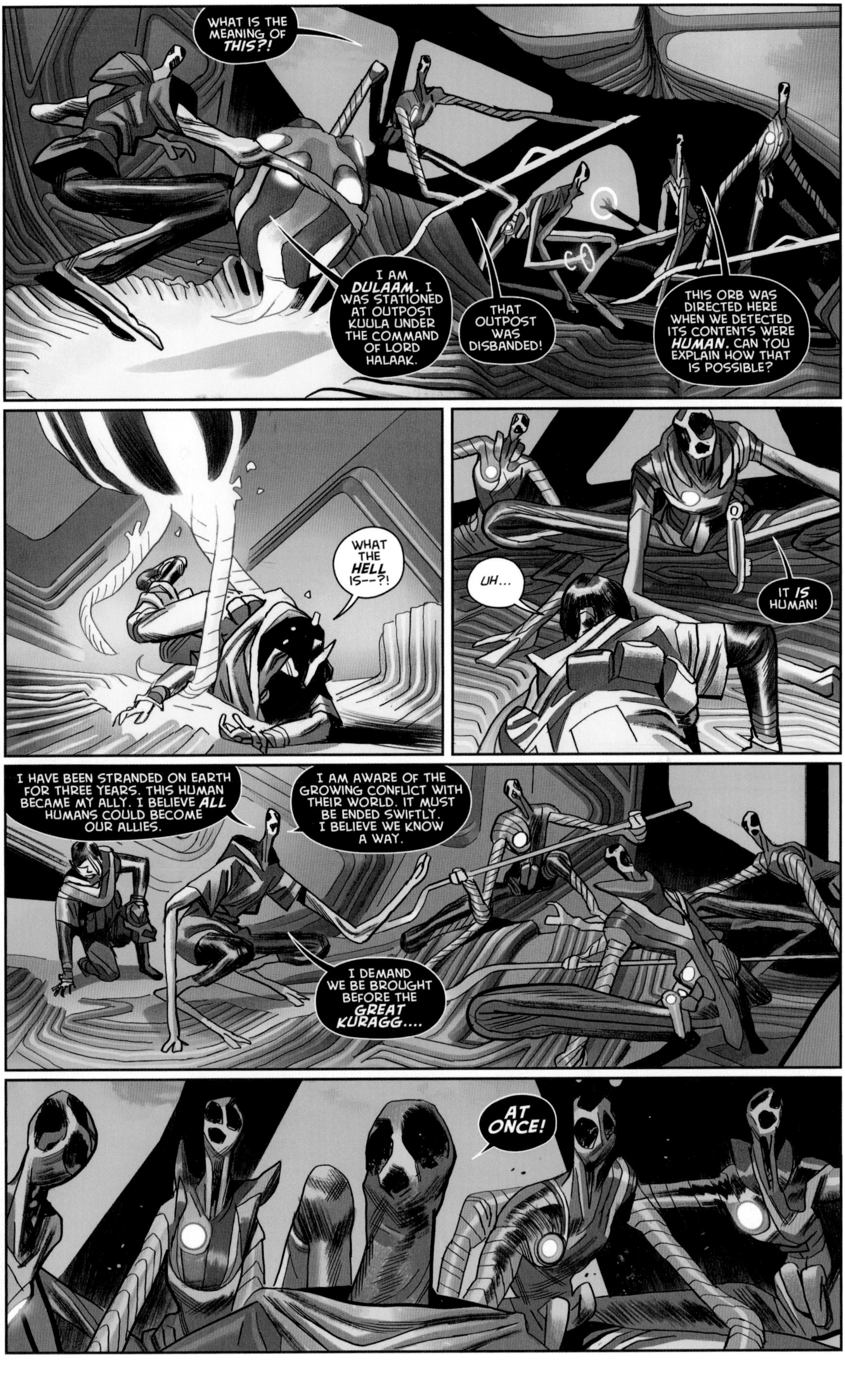
WHAT IS THE MEANING OF THIS?!
I AM DULAAM. I WAS STATIONED AT OUTPOST KUULA UNDER THE COMMAND OF LORD HALAAK.
THAT OUTPOST WAS DISBANDED!
THIS ORB WAS DIRECTED HERE WHEN WE DETECTED ITS CONTENTS WERE HUMAN. CAN YOU EXPLAIN HOW THAT IS POSSIBLE?
WHAT THE HELL IS--?!
UH...
IT IS HUMAN!
I HAVE BEEN STRANDED ON EARTH FOR THREE YEARS. THIS HUMAN BECAME MY ALLY. I BELIEVE ALL HUMANS COULD BECOME OUR ALLIES.
I AM AWARE OF THE GROWING CONFLICT WITH THEIR WORLD. IT MUST BE ENDED SWIFTLY. I BELIEVE WE KNOW A WAY.
I DEMAND WE BE BROUGHT BEFORE THE GREAT KURAGG....
AT ONCE!

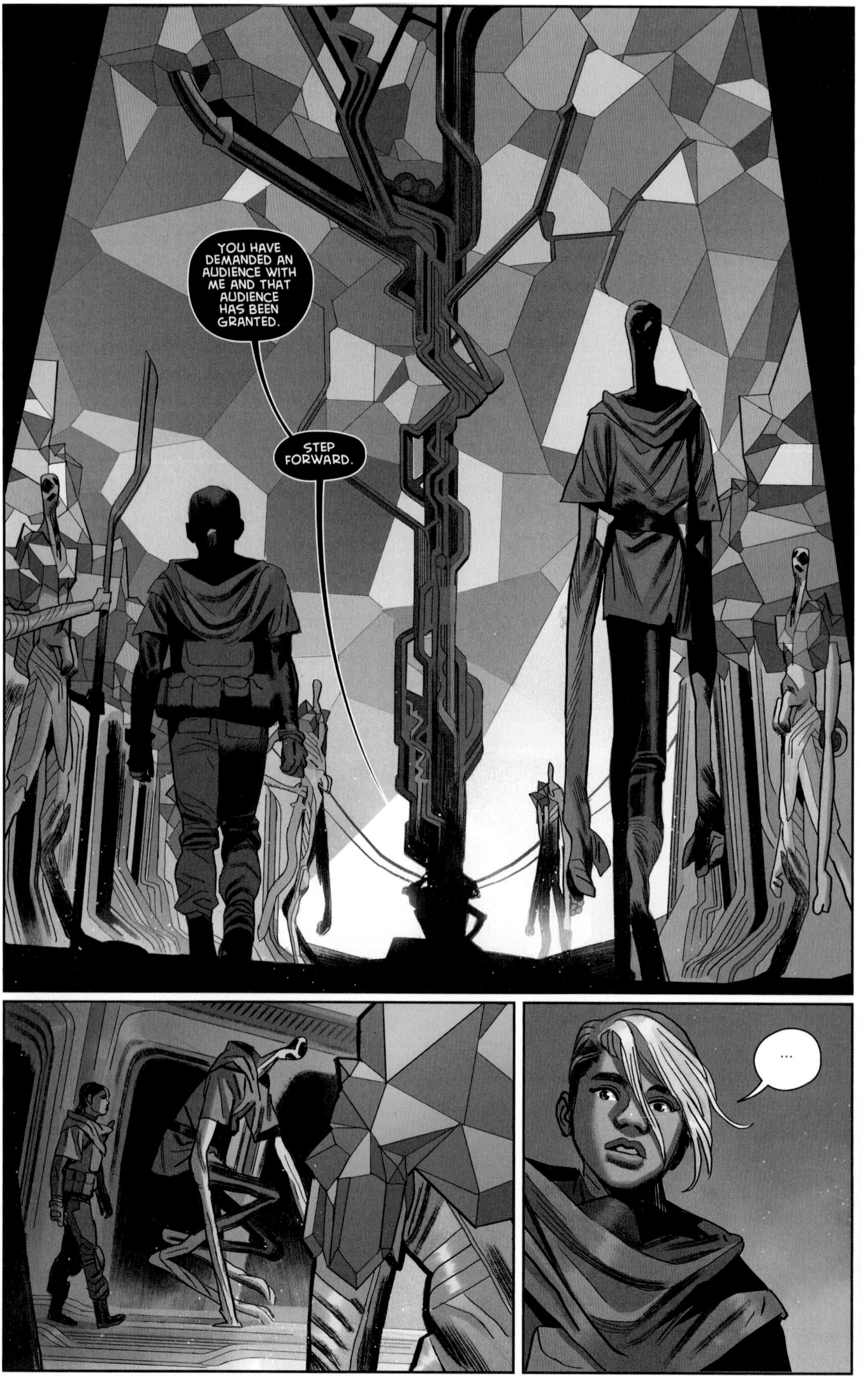
YOU HAVE DEMANDED AN AUDIENCE WITH ME AND THAT AUDIENCE HAS BEEN GRANTED.
STEP FORWARD.
...

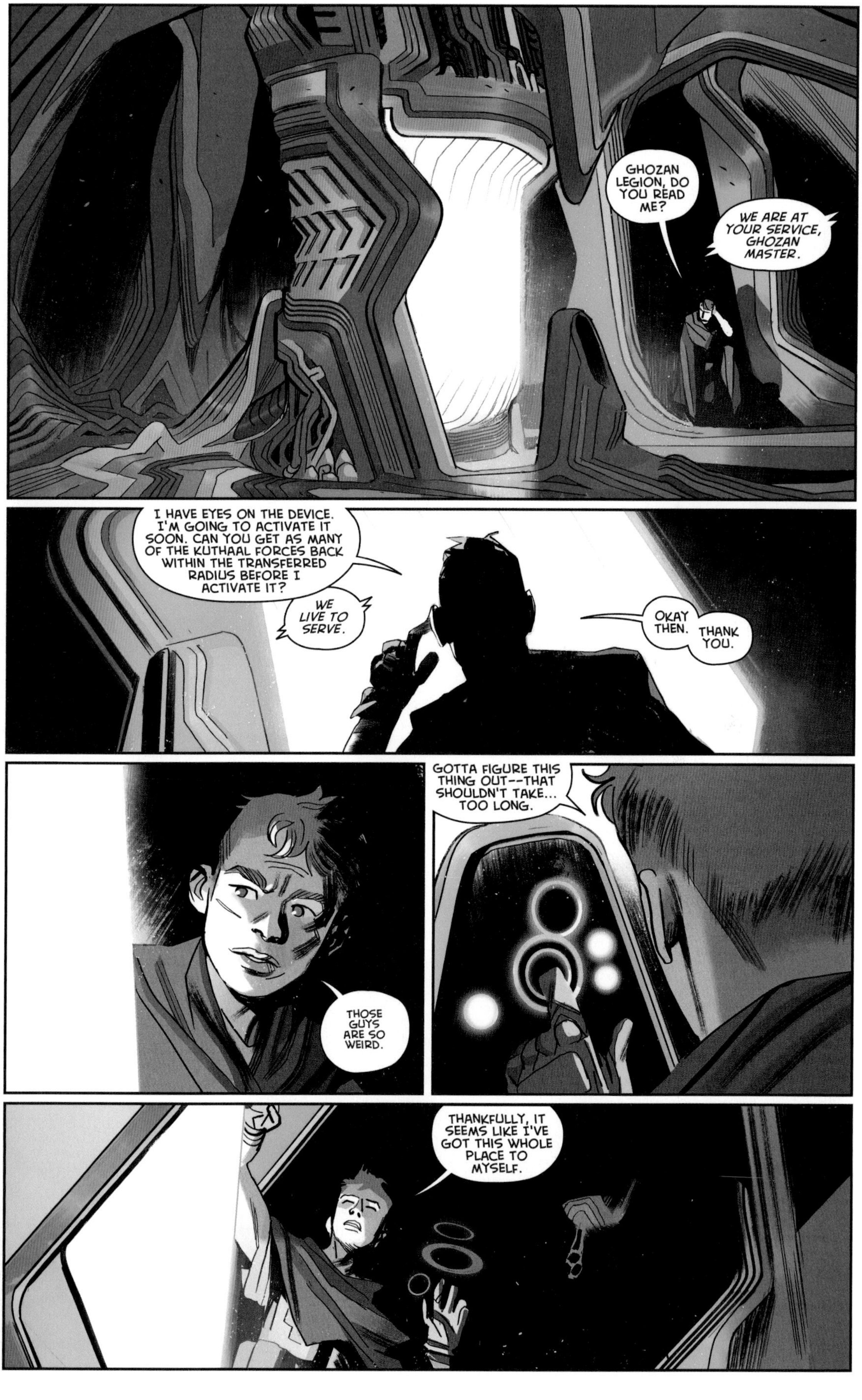
GHOZAN LEGION, DO YOU READ ME?
WE ARE AT YOUR SERVICE, GHOZAN MASTER.
I HAVE EYES ON THE DEVICE. I'M GOING TO ACTIVATE IT SOON. CAN YOU GET AS MANY OF THE KUTHAAL FORCES BACK WITHIN THE TRANSFERRED RADIUS BEFORE I ACTIVATE IT?
WE LIVE TO SERVE.
OKAY THEN.
THANK YOU.
THOSE GUYS ARE SO WEIRD.
GOTTA FIGURE THIS THING OUT--THAT SHOULDN'T TAKE... TOO LONG.
THANKFULLY, IT SEEMS LIKE I'VE GOT THIS WHOLE PLACE TO MYSELF.

I AM TOLD YOU HAVE LIVED AMONG THEM IN THE YEARS SINCE YOUR DISAPPEARANCE FROM OUTPOST KUULA.

HALAAK'S GREAT FAILURE.

YES, GREAT KURAGG.

HE HAS BEEN SAFE WITH MY PERSON. I TOOK HIM IN AND LEARNED HIM OUR WAYS. HE, IN TURN, TAUGHT ME YOURS. WE MEAN YOUR PEOPLE NO DAMAGE.

PLEASE KNOW, MY GOAL IS ONLY TO BRING PEACE TO OUR WORLDS. I WISH YOUR PEOPLE AND MINE CAN FORM ALLIES. THE SAME AS DULAAM AND I HAVE.

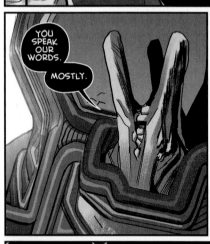

YOU SPEAK OUR WORDS.

MOSTLY.

I HAD A GOOD TEACHER.

I HAVE LEARNED OF YOUR GROWTH... THE DANGER IT BRINGS YOU... HOW *DIRE* THINGS ARE IN YOUR WORLD.

I URGE YOU TO RECALL THAT IT WAS *OUR PEOPLE* WHO DISCOVER THE HOW TO ACCESS YOUR WORLD IN THE FIRST.

YOUR FIGHT ON OUR HOME IS *UNNECESSARY.* IF YOU CEASE THIS FIGHT IMMEDIATELY, I CAN TALK MY PEOPLE INTO WORKING *WITH* YOU.

THE GROWTH CAN'T LIVE ON OUR PLANET. WITH TIME AND ACCESS TO YOUR WORLD, WE CAN WORK *TOGETHER* TO DISCOVER *WHY...*

...AND MAKE YOUR WORLD LIVABLE AGAIN.

YOU JUST NEED TO *TRUST* US.

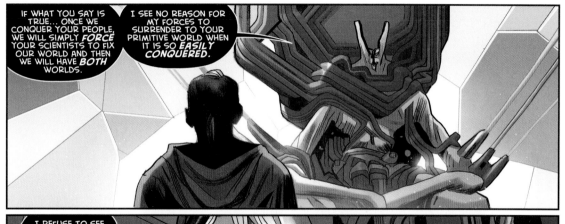

IF WHAT YOU SAY IS TRUE... ONCE WE CONQUER YOUR PEOPLE, WE WILL SIMPLY **FORCE** YOUR SCIENTISTS TO FIX OUR WORLD AND THEN WE WILL HAVE **BOTH** WORLDS.

I SEE NO REASON FOR MY FORCES TO SURRENDER TO YOUR PRIMITIVE WORLD WHEN IT IS SO **EASILY** CONQUERED.

I REFUSE TO SEE YOUR DESPERATION AS ANYTHING ELSE. YOU ARE **NOT** A SINISTER FORCE.

DULAAM HAS TOLD ME THE STORIES OF YOUR PEOPLE... YOUR UNIFICATION... YOUR CENTURIES OF PEACE THAT WERE ONLY BROKEN AS THE GROWTH CONSUMED YOUR RESOURCES.

YOU ARE **NOT** A WARRING PEOPLE. YOU'RE **BETTER** THAN THIS.

I **KNOW** IT.

SO...

WHAT DO YOU PROPOSE I DO... IF WE ARE TO HAVE PEACE BETWEEN OUR PEOPLE?

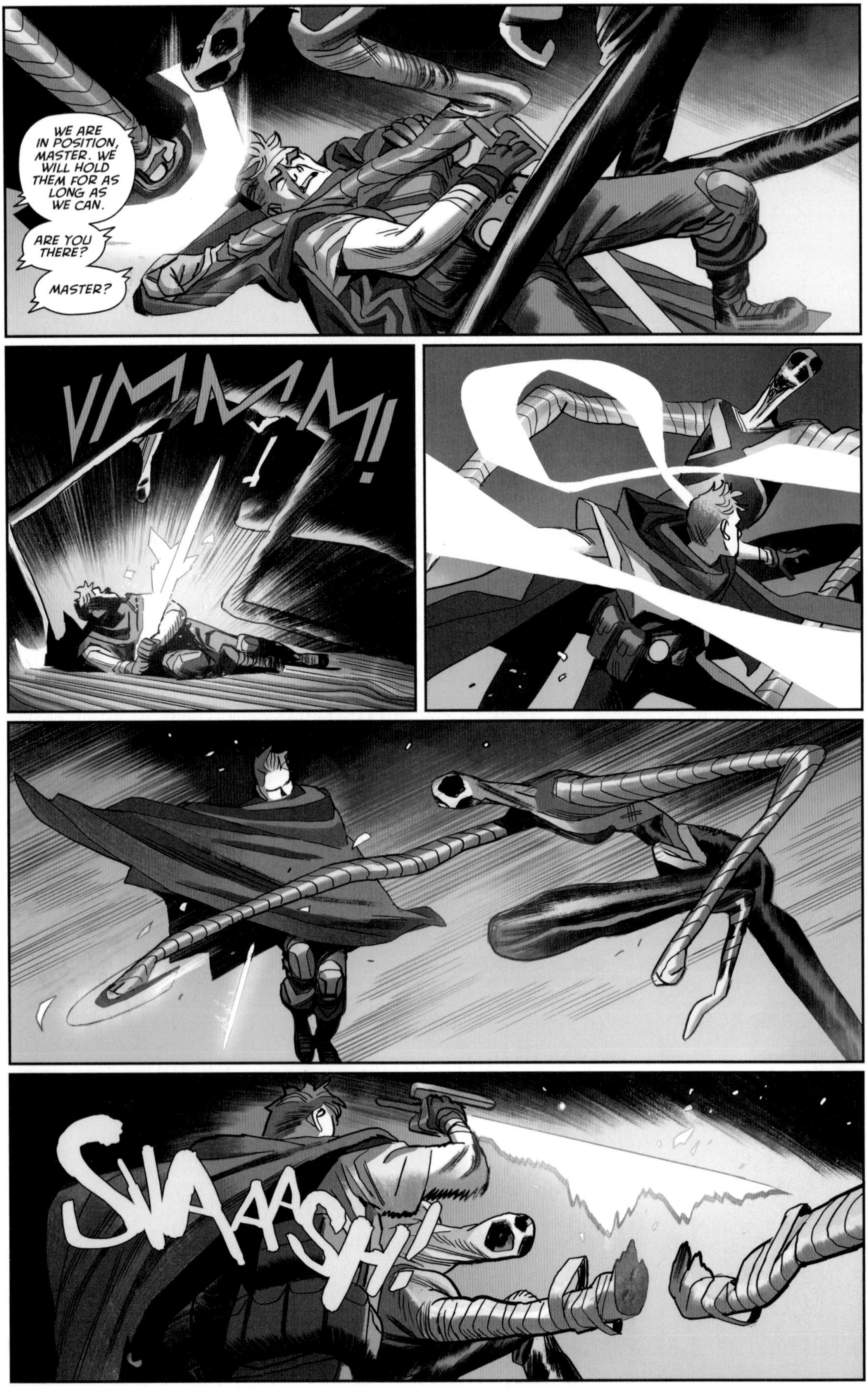
WE ARE IN POSITION, MASTER. WE WILL HOLD THEM FOR AS LONG AS WE CAN.
ARE YOU THERE?
MASTER?
VMMM!!
SHAAASH!

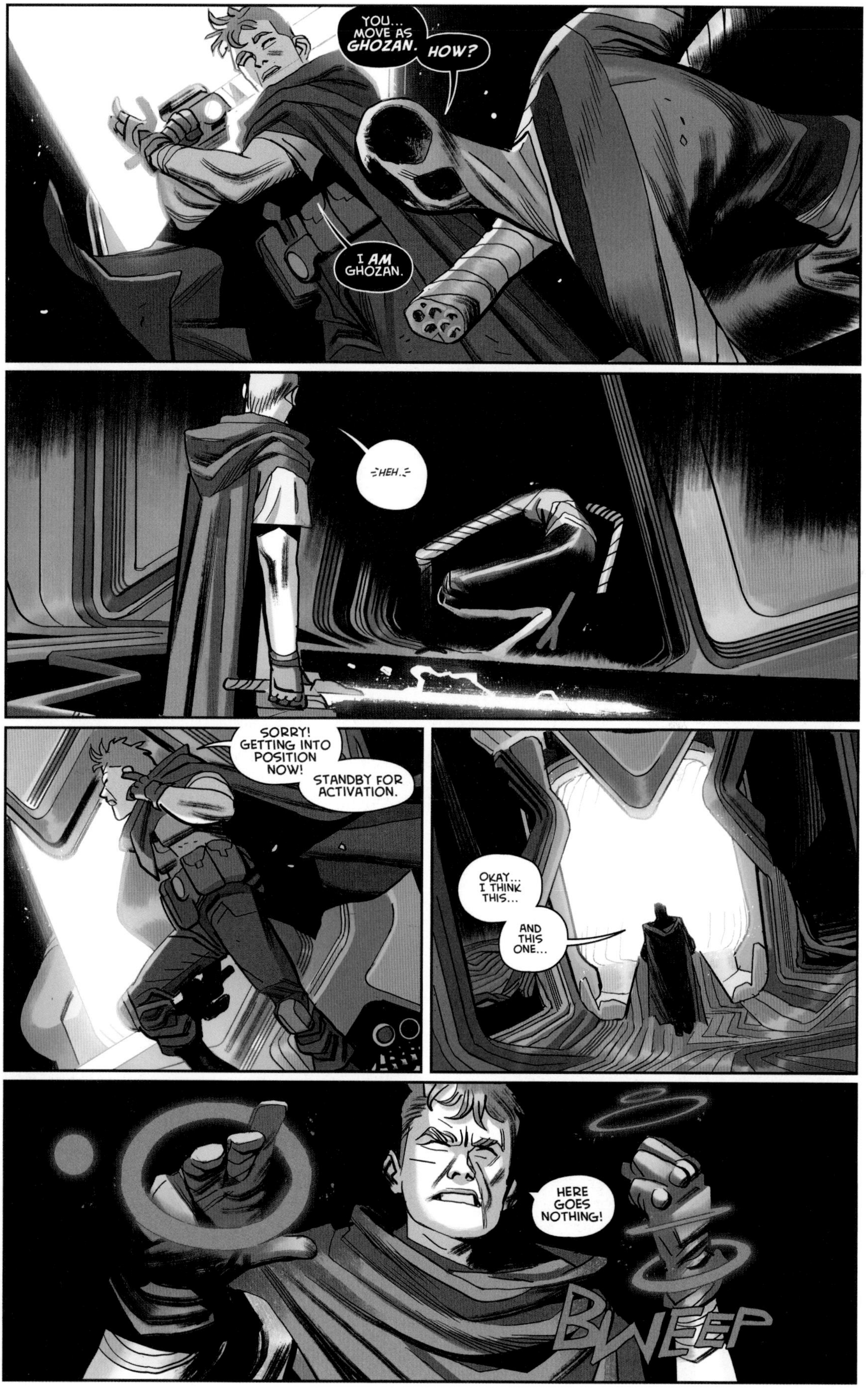
YOU... MOVE AS GHOZAN.
HOW?
I AM GHOZAN.
HEH.
SORRY! GETTING INTO POSITION NOW!
STANDBY FOR ACTIVATION.
OKAY... I THINK THIS...
AND THIS ONE...
HERE GOES NOTHING!
BWEEP

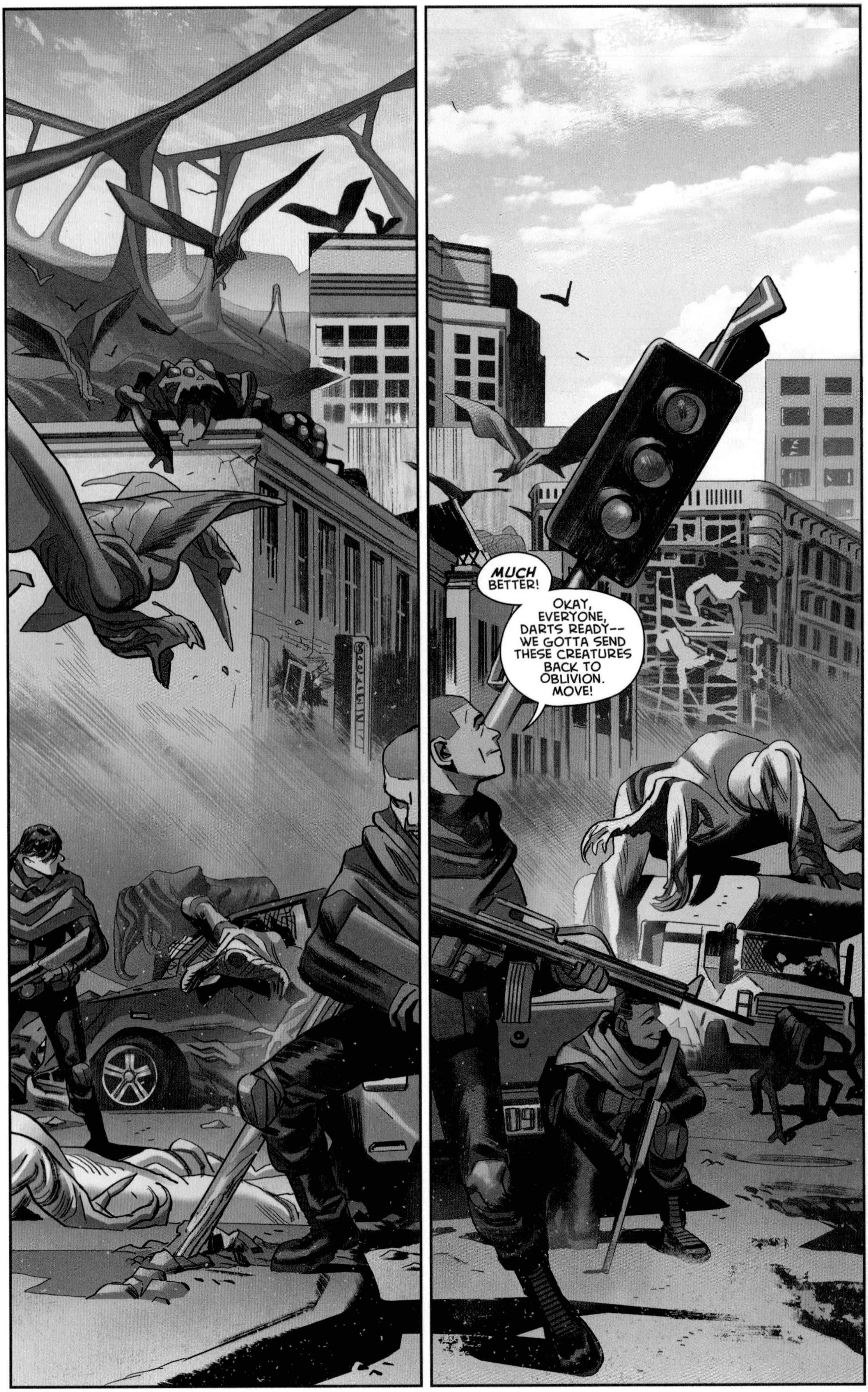
MUCH BETTER!
OKAY, EVERYONE, DARTS READY-- WE GOTTA SEND THESE CREATURES BACK TO OBLIVION. MOVE!

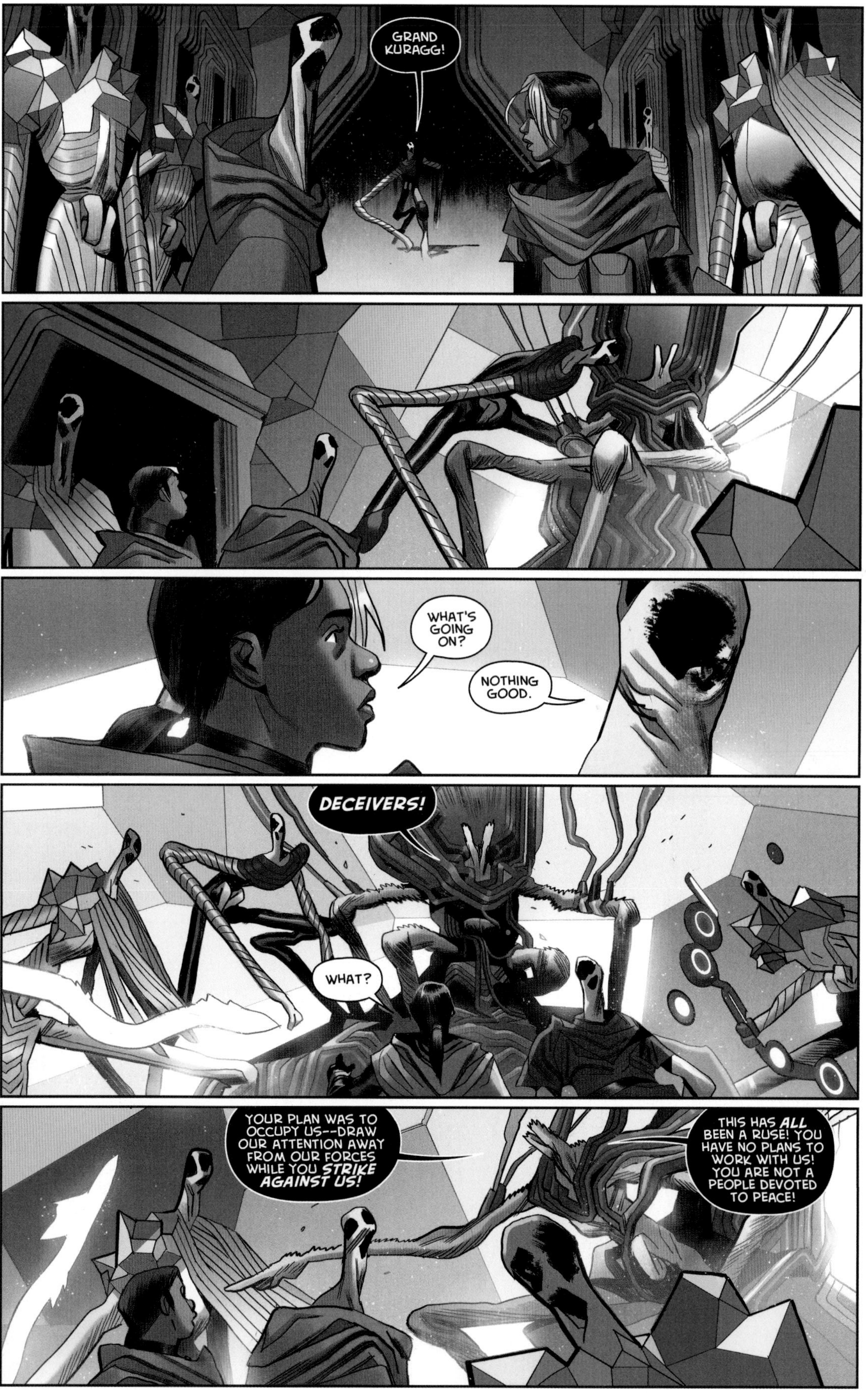

GRAND KURAGG!
WHAT'S GOING ON?
NOTHING GOOD.
DECEIVERS!
WHAT?
YOUR PLAN WAS TO OCCUPY US--DRAW OUR ATTENTION AWAY FROM OUR FORCES WHILE YOU STRIKE AGAINST US!
THIS HAS ALL BEEN A RUSE! YOU HAVE NO PLANS TO WORK WITH US! YOU ARE NOT A PEOPLE DEVOTED TO PEACE!

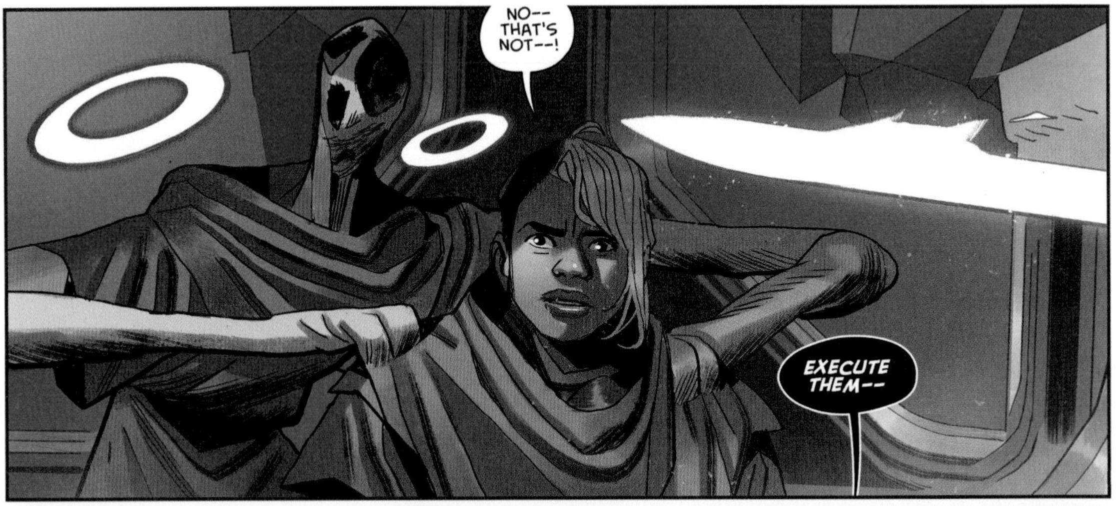
NO-- THAT'S NOT--!
EXECUTE THEM--

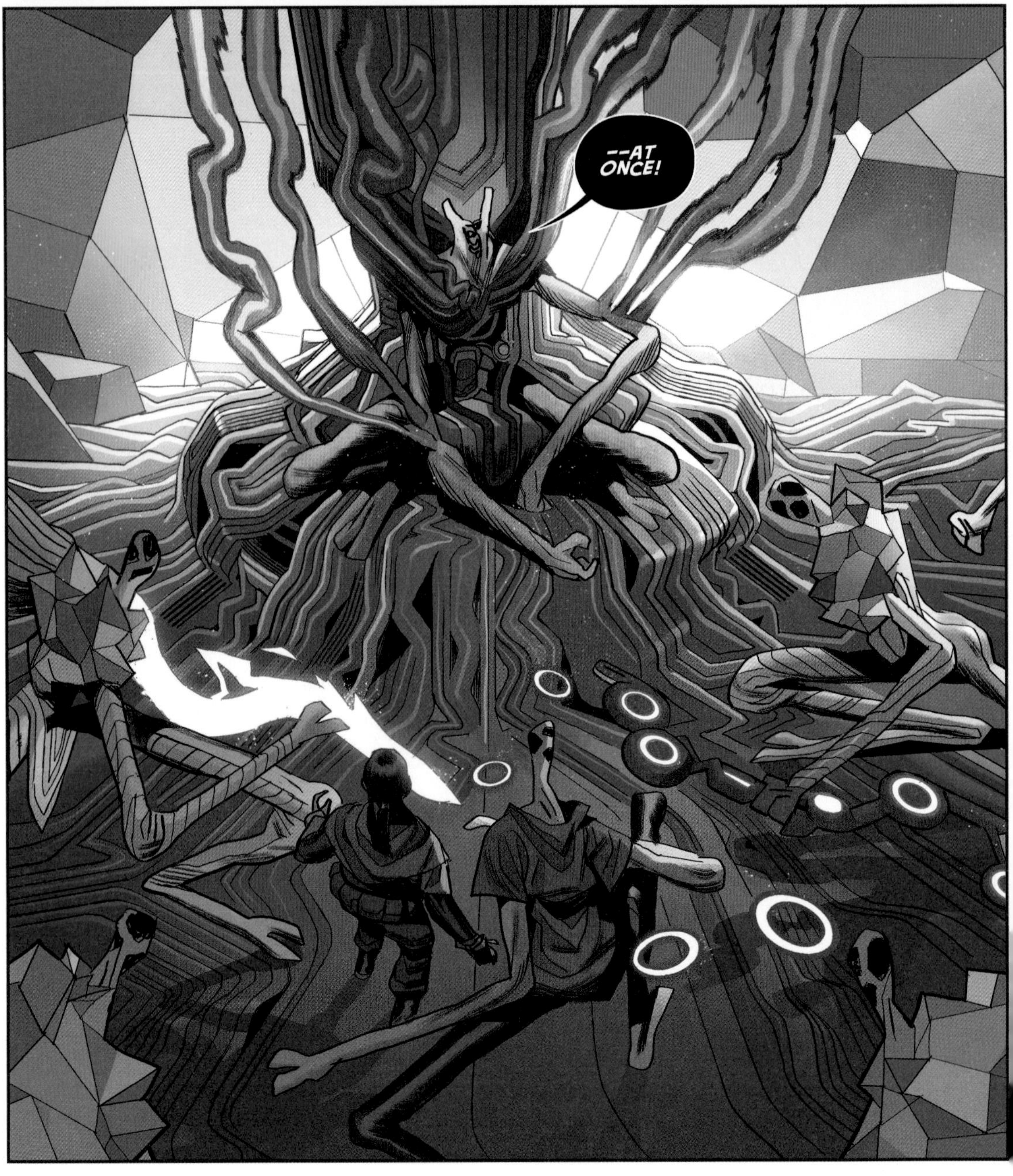
--AT ONCE!

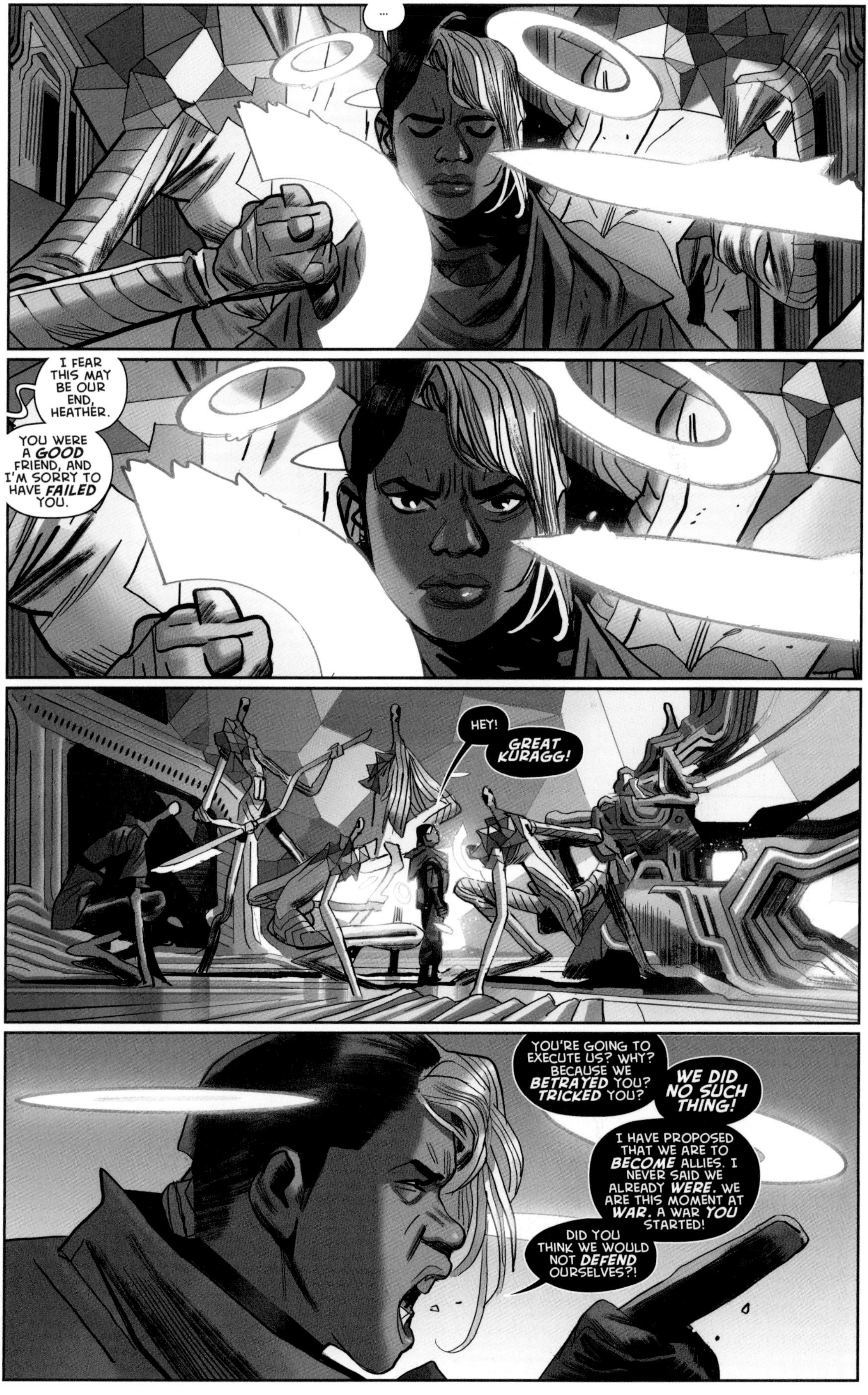
...
I FEAR THIS MAY BE OUR END, HEATHER.
YOU WERE A GOOD FRIEND, AND I'M SORRY TO HAVE FAILED YOU.
HEY!
GREAT KURAGG!
YOU'RE GOING TO EXECUTE US? WHY? BECAUSE WE BETRAYED YOU? TRICKED YOU?
WE DID NO SUCH THING!
I HAVE PROPOSED THAT WE ARE TO BECOME ALLIES. I NEVER SAID WE ALREADY WERE. WE ARE THIS MOMENT AT WAR. A WAR YOU STARTED!
DID YOU THINK WE WOULD NOT DEFEND OURSELVES?!

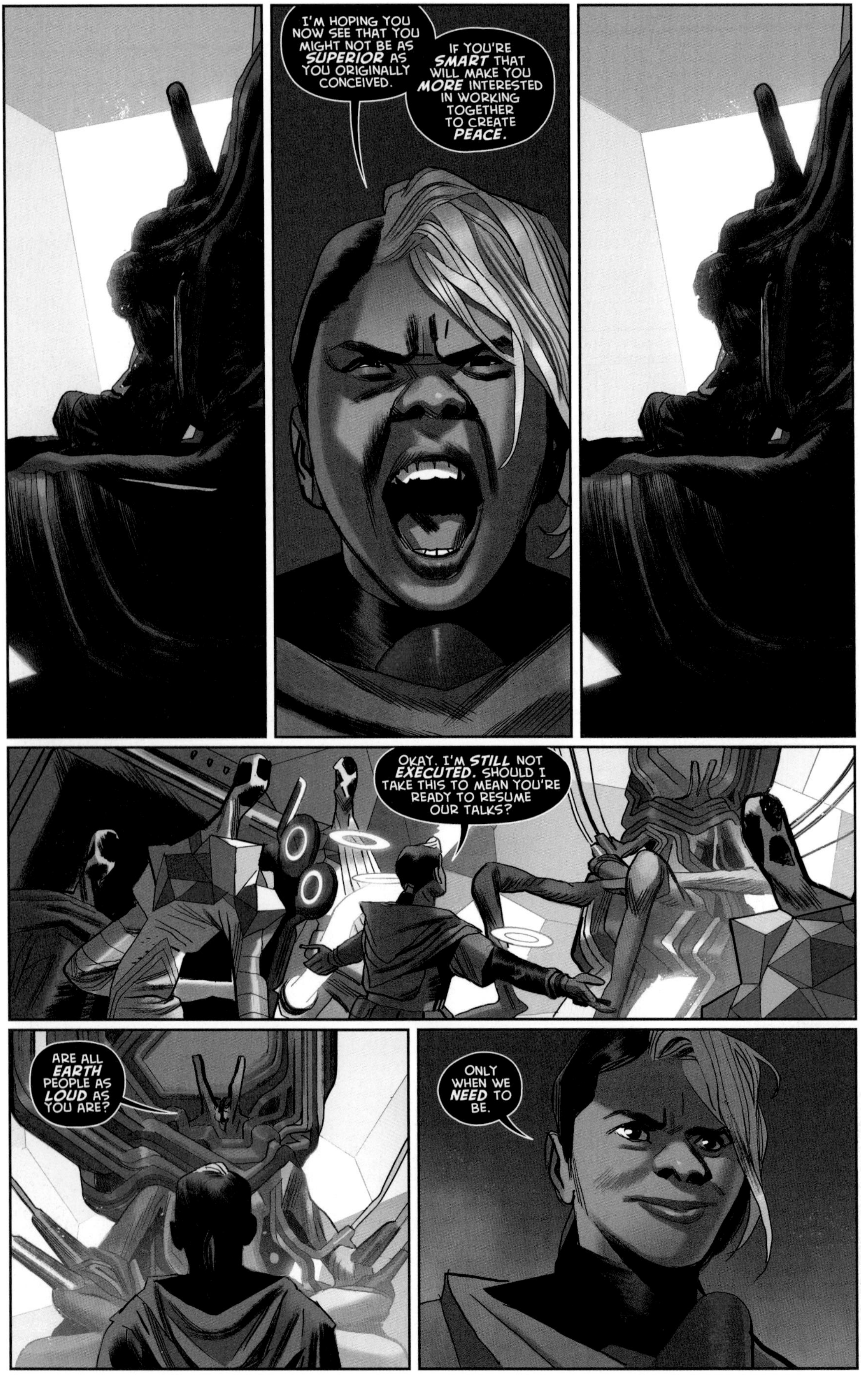

I'M HOPING YOU NOW SEE THAT YOU MIGHT NOT BE AS *SUPERIOR* AS YOU ORIGINALLY CONCEIVED.
IF YOU'RE *SMART* THAT WILL MAKE YOU *MORE* INTERESTED IN WORKING TOGETHER TO CREATE *PEACE.*
OKAY. I'M *STILL* NOT *EXECUTED.* SHOULD I TAKE THIS TO MEAN YOU'RE READY TO RESUME OUR TALKS?
ARE ALL *EARTH* PEOPLE AS *LOUD* AS YOU ARE?
ONLY WHEN WE *NEED* TO BE.

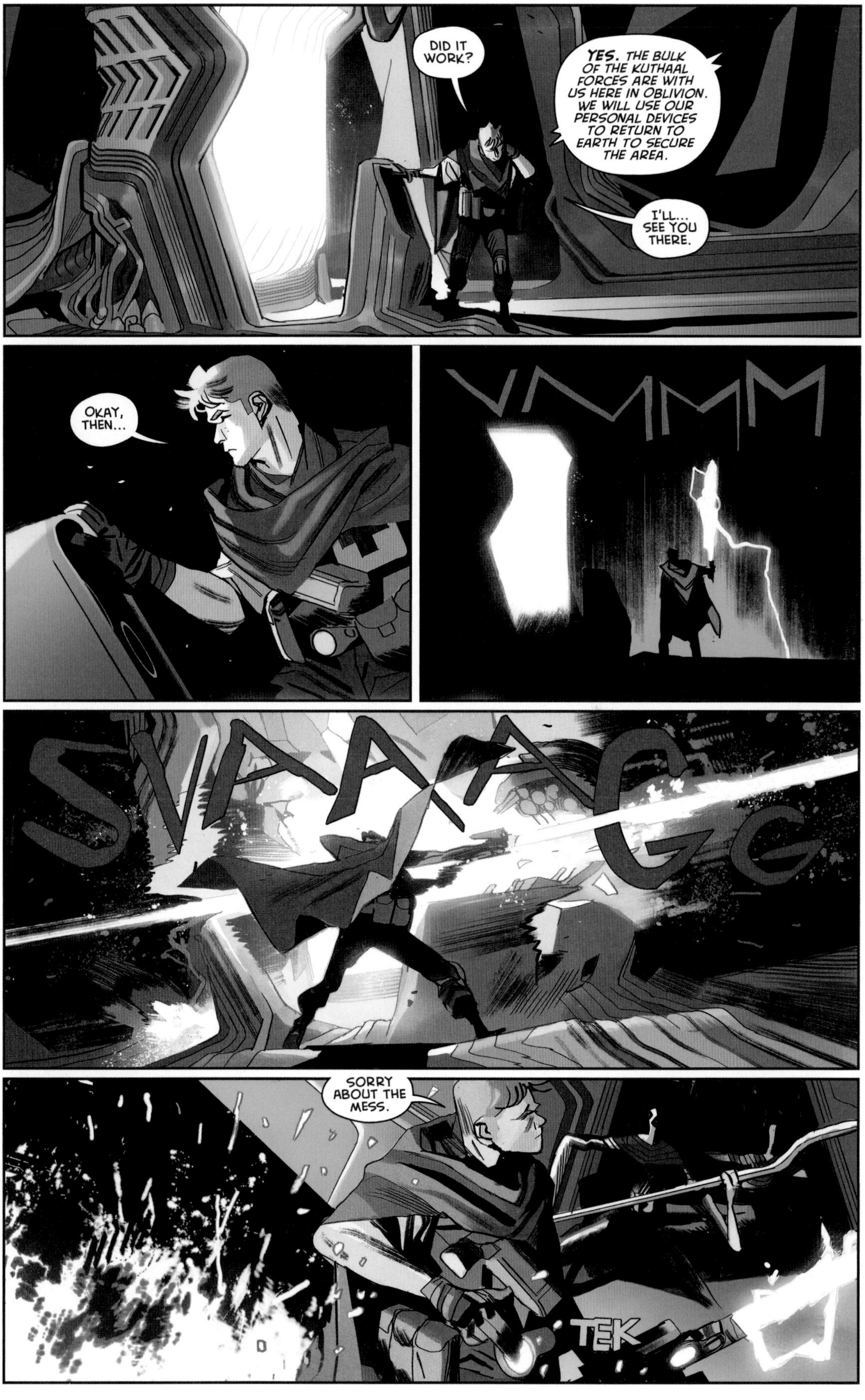
DID IT WORK?
YES. THE BULK OF THE KUTHAAL FORCES ARE WITH US HERE IN OBLIVION. WE WILL USE OUR PERSONAL DEVICES TO RETURN TO EARTH TO SECURE THE AREA.
I'LL... SEE YOU THERE.
OKAY, THEN...
VMMM
SVAAAGG
SORRY ABOUT THE MESS.
TEK

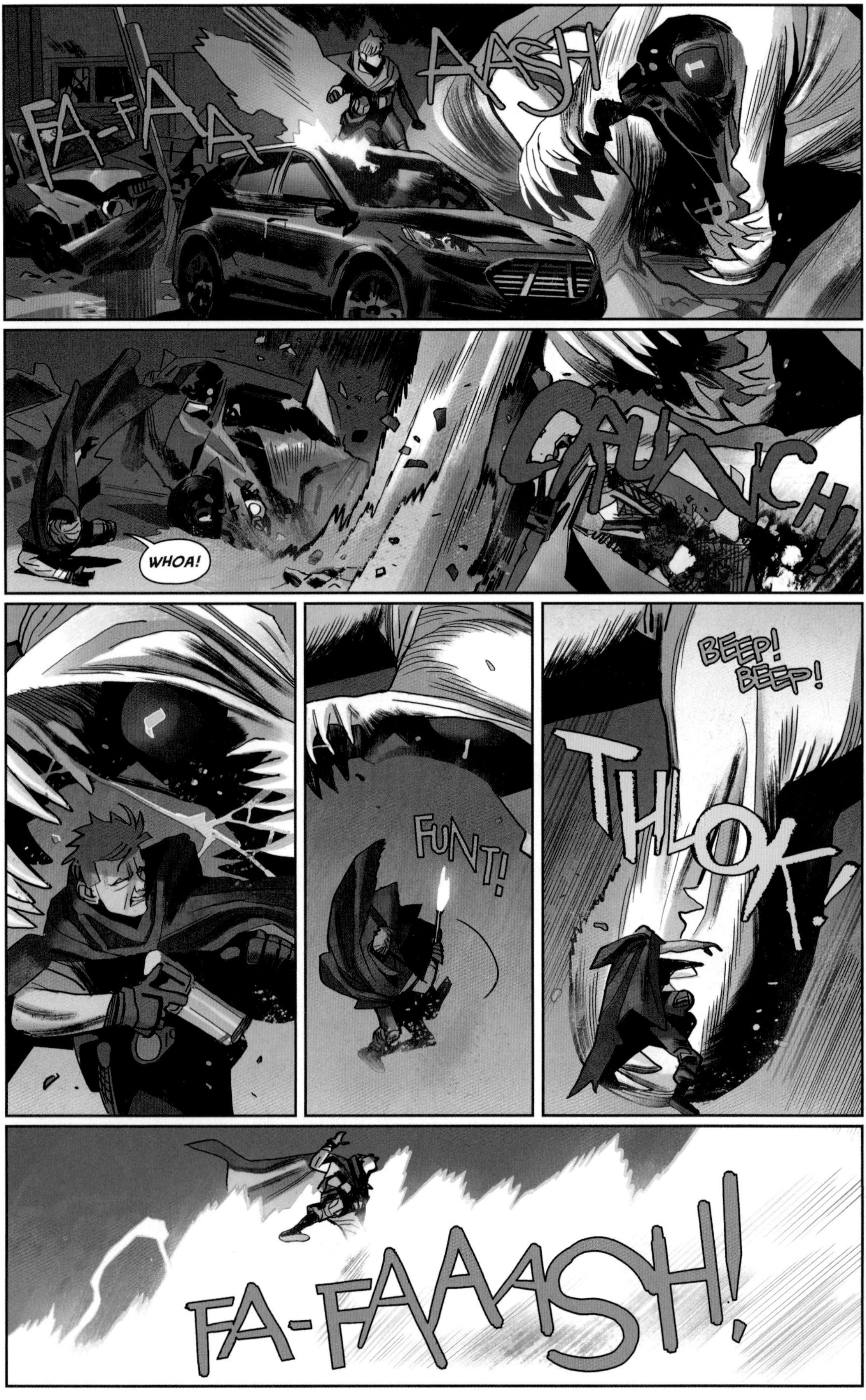
FA-FAA
AASH
CRUNCH!
WHOA!
FUNT!
BEEP! BEEP!
THLOK!
FA-FAAASH!

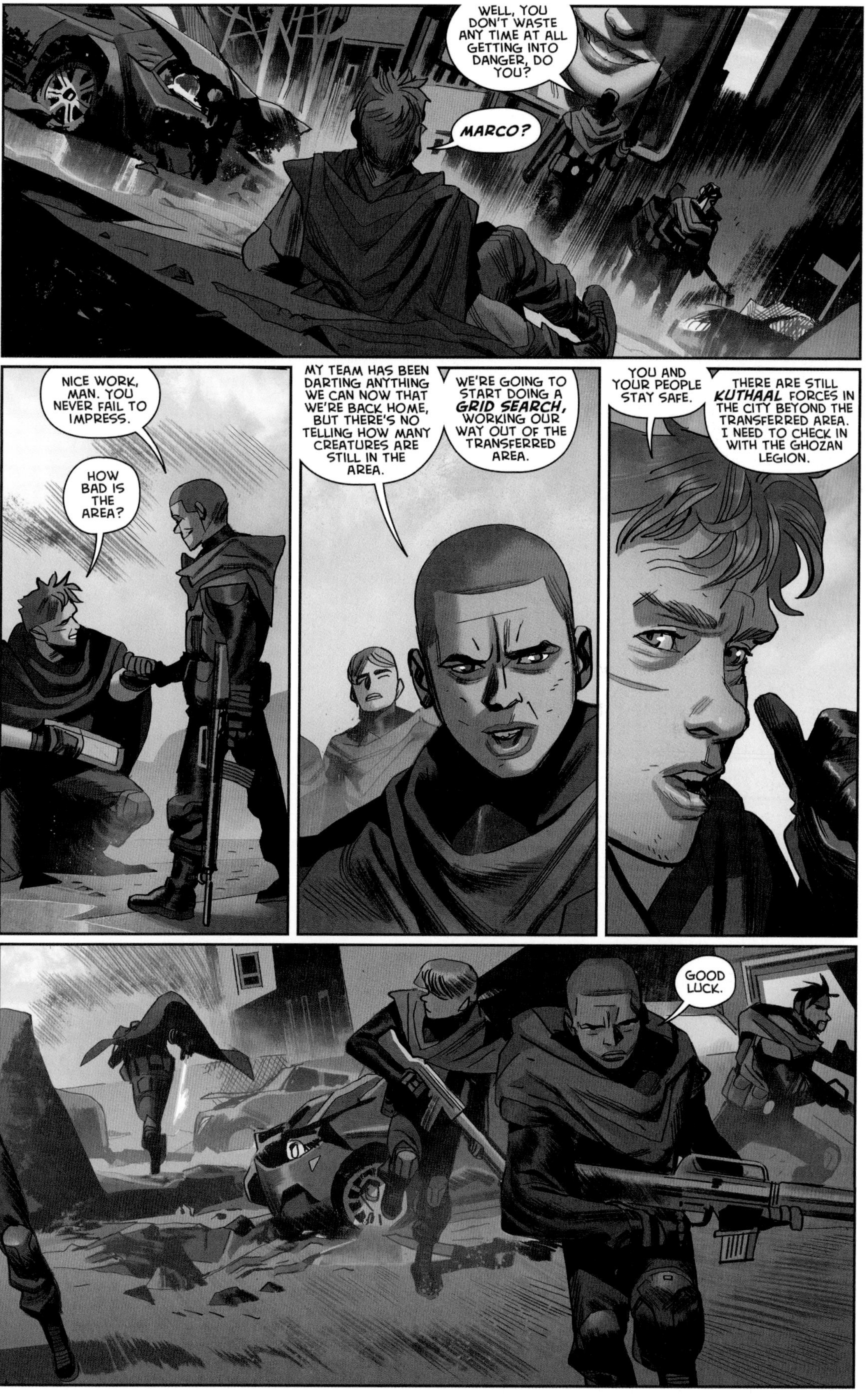
WELL, YOU DON'T WASTE ANY TIME AT ALL GETTING INTO DANGER, DO YOU?
MARCO?
NICE WORK, MAN. YOU NEVER FAIL TO IMPRESS.
HOW BAD IS THE AREA?
MY TEAM HAS BEEN DARTING ANYTHING WE CAN NOW THAT WE'RE BACK HOME, BUT THERE'S NO TELLING HOW MANY CREATURES ARE STILL IN THE AREA.
WE'RE GOING TO START DOING A GRID SEARCH, WORKING OUR WAY OUT OF THE TRANSFERRED AREA.
YOU AND YOUR PEOPLE STAY SAFE.
THERE ARE STILL KUTHAAL FORCES IN THE CITY BEYOND THE TRANSFERRED AREA. I NEED TO CHECK IN WITH THE GHOZAN LEGION.
GOOD LUCK.

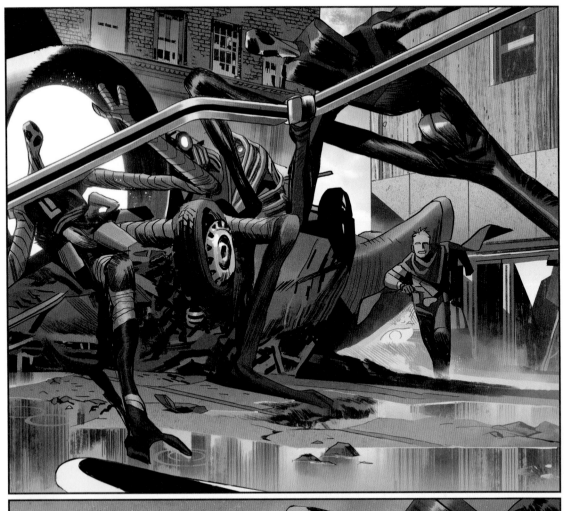

NO--
GHOZAN!
STOP!

THIS ONE HAS **KILLED HUMANS** IN THE BATTLE. IS HE NOT YOUR ENEMY?

THE BATTLE IS **OVER.** THERE'S... NO NEED FOR MORE BLOODSHED.

I CAN SEND HIM BACK. YOU DON'T HAVE TO KILL HIM.

FUNT

BEEP
BEEP

FA-FAAAASH!

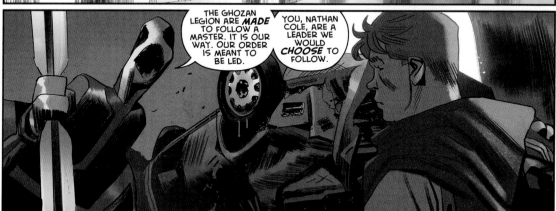

THE GHOZAN LEGION ARE *MADE* TO FOLLOW A MASTER. IT IS OUR WAY. OUR ORDER IS MEANT TO BE LED.

YOU, NATHAN COLE, ARE A LEADER WE WOULD *CHOOSE* TO FOLLOW.

COME. THERE IS STILL MUCH TO DO.

YOU LEAD--WE FOLLOW.

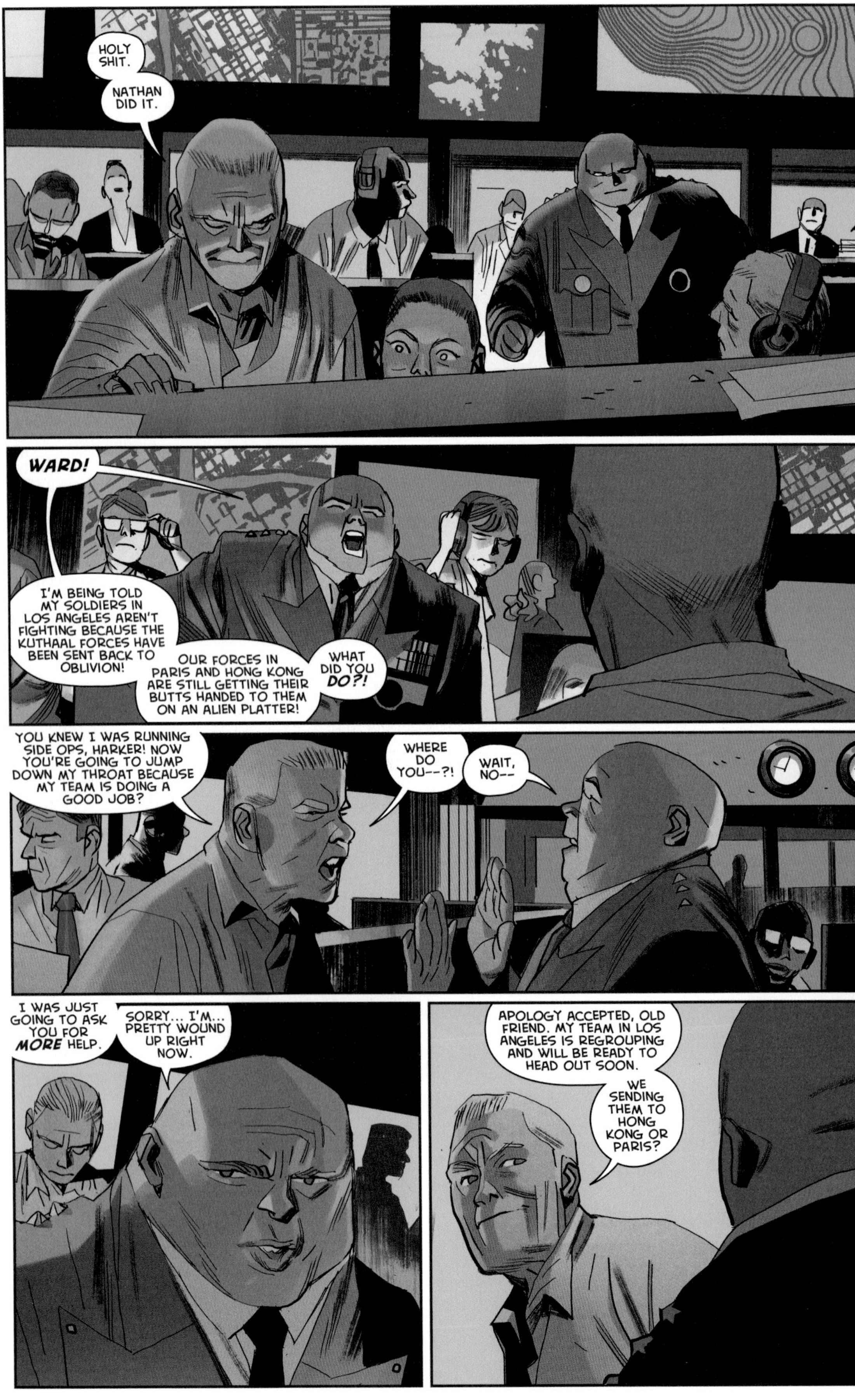
HOLY SHIT.
NATHAN DID IT.
WARD!
I'M BEING TOLD MY SOLDIERS IN LOS ANGELES AREN'T FIGHTING BECAUSE THE KUTHAAL FORCES HAVE BEEN SENT BACK TO OBLIVION!
OUR FORCES IN PARIS AND HONG KONG ARE STILL GETTING THEIR BUTTS HANDED TO THEM ON AN ALIEN PLATTER!
WHAT DID YOU DO?!
YOU KNEW I WAS RUNNING SIDE OPS, HARKER! NOW YOU'RE GOING TO JUMP DOWN MY THROAT BECAUSE MY TEAM IS DOING A GOOD JOB?
WHERE DO YOU--?!
WAIT, NO--
I WAS JUST GOING TO ASK YOU FOR MORE HELP.
SORRY... I'M... PRETTY WOUND UP RIGHT NOW.
APOLOGY ACCEPTED, OLD FRIEND. MY TEAM IN LOS ANGELES IS REGROUPING AND WILL BE READY TO HEAD OUT SOON.
WE SENDING THEM TO HONG KONG OR PARIS?

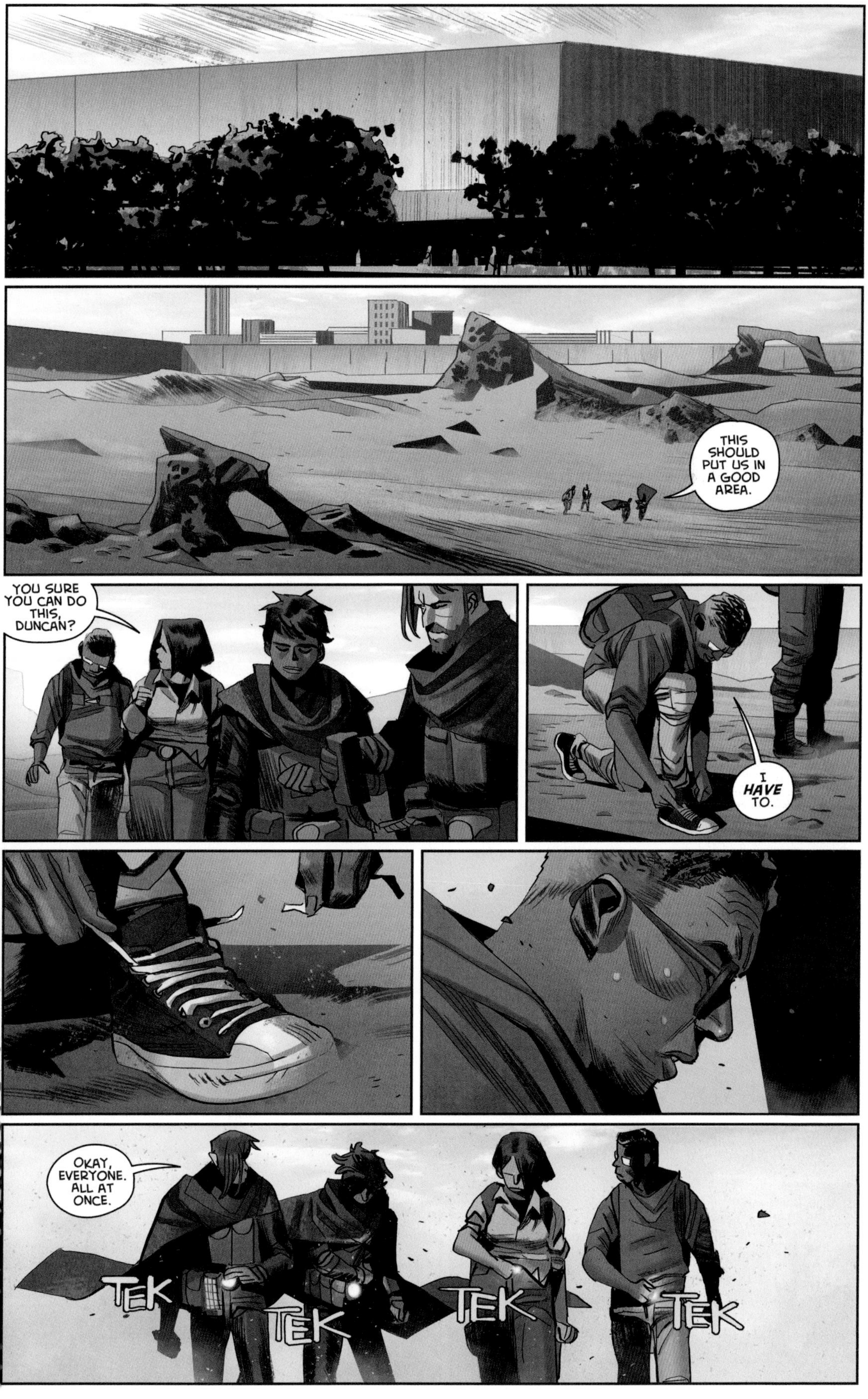

THIS SHOULD PUT US IN A GOOD AREA.
YOU SURE YOU CAN DO THIS, DUNCAN?
I *HAVE* TO.
OKAY, EVERYONE. ALL AT ONCE.
TEK
TEK
TEK
TEK

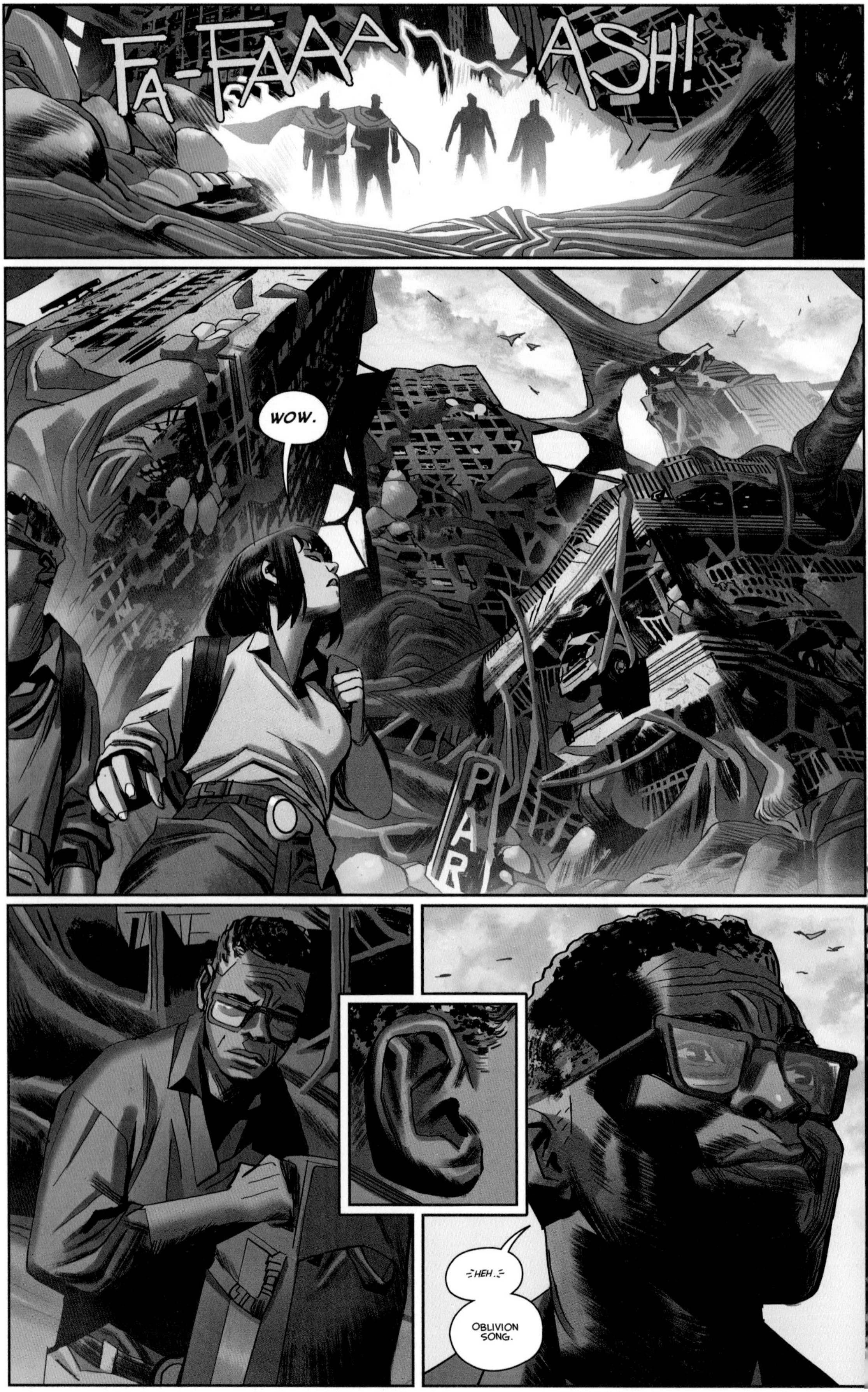
FA-FAAAA--ASH!
WOW.
HEH.
OBLIVION SONG.

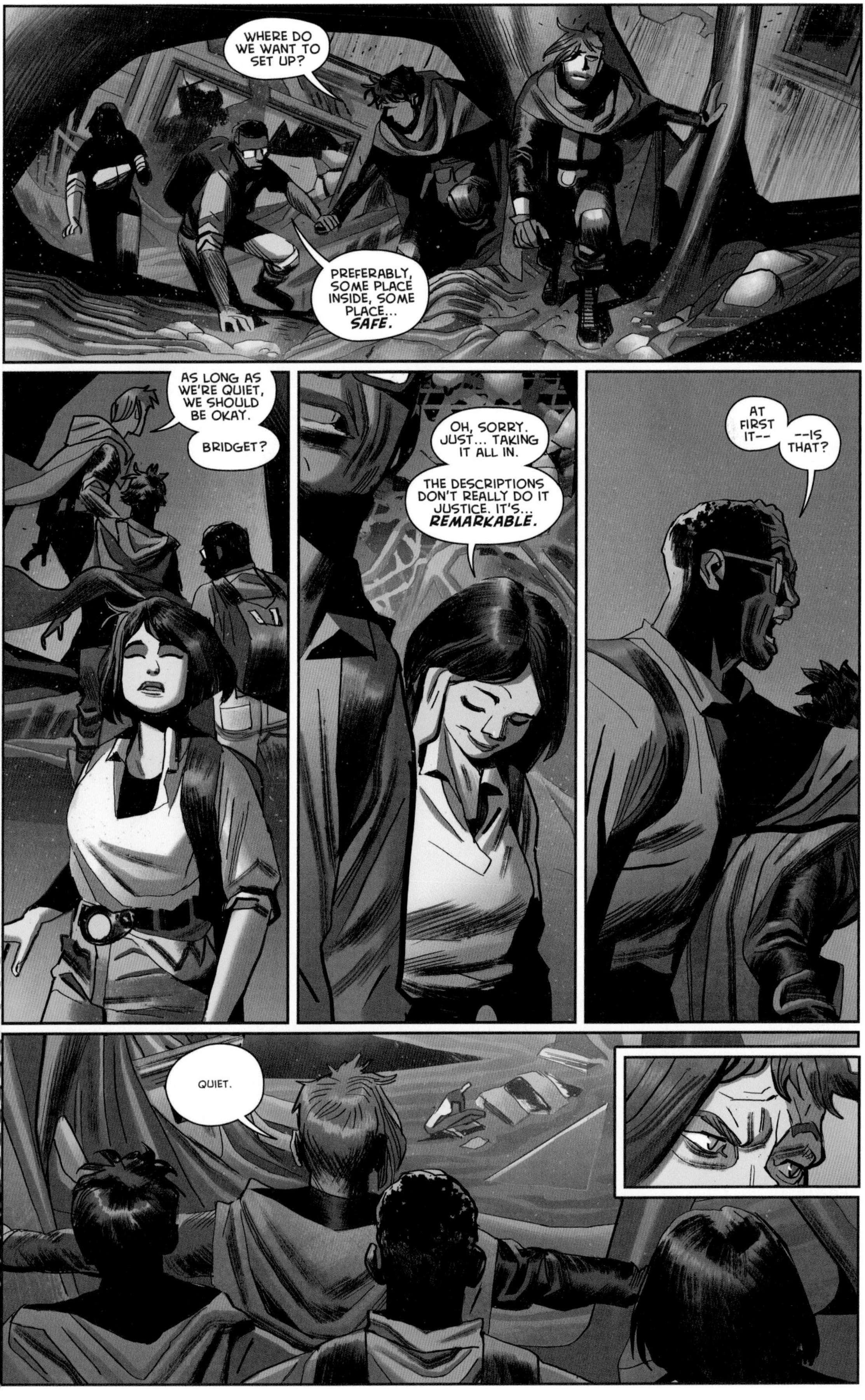
WHERE DO WE WANT TO SET UP?
PREFERABLY, SOME PLACE INSIDE, SOME PLACE... SAFE.
AS LONG AS WE'RE QUIET, WE SHOULD BE OKAY.
BRIDGET?
OH, SORRY. JUST... TAKING IT ALL IN.
THE DESCRIPTIONS DON'T REALLY DO IT JUSTICE. IT'S... REMARKABLE.
AT FIRST IT--
--IS THAT?
QUIET.

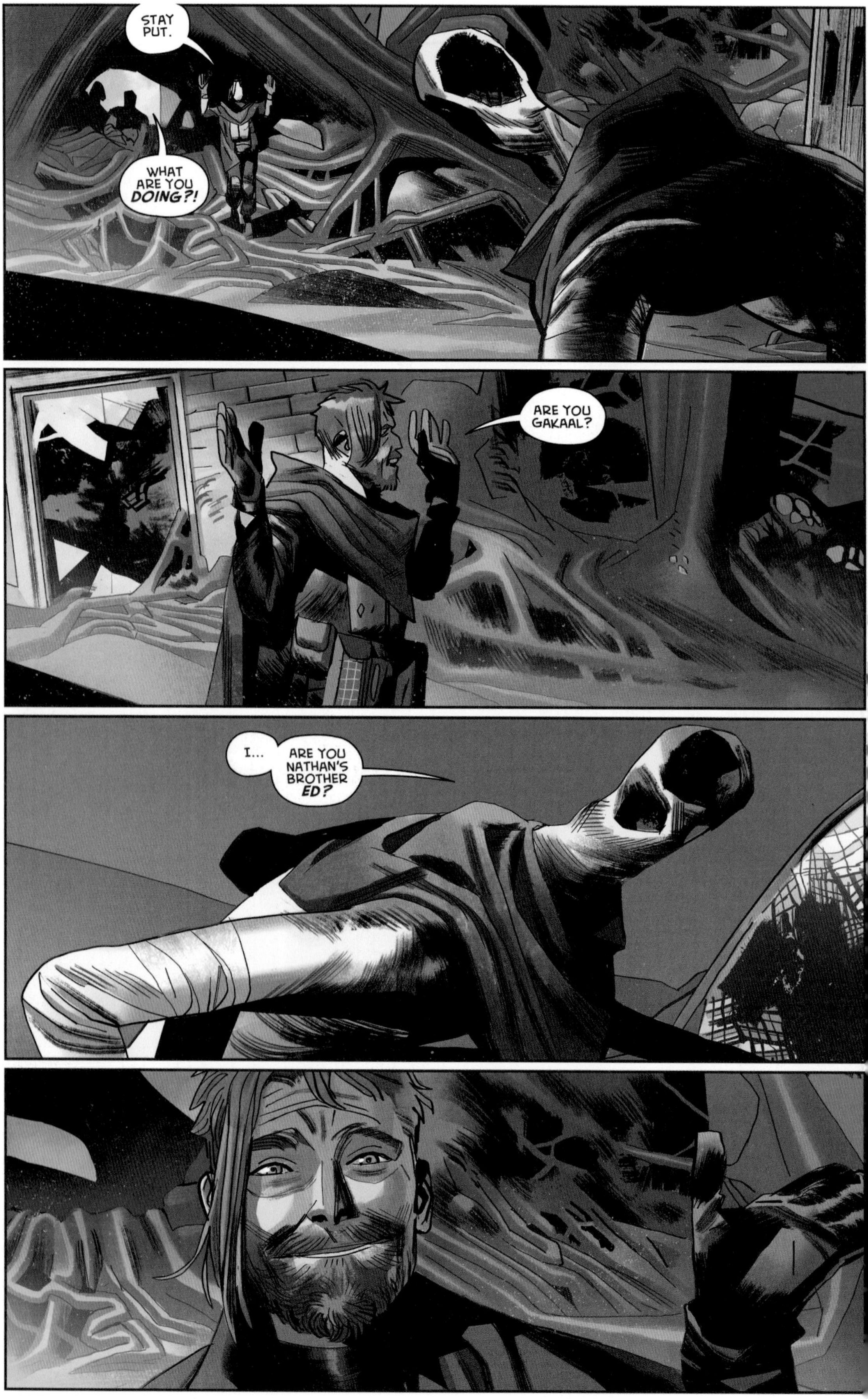
STAY PUT.
WHAT ARE YOU DOING?!
ARE YOU GAKAAL?
I...
ARE YOU NATHAN'S BROTHER ED?

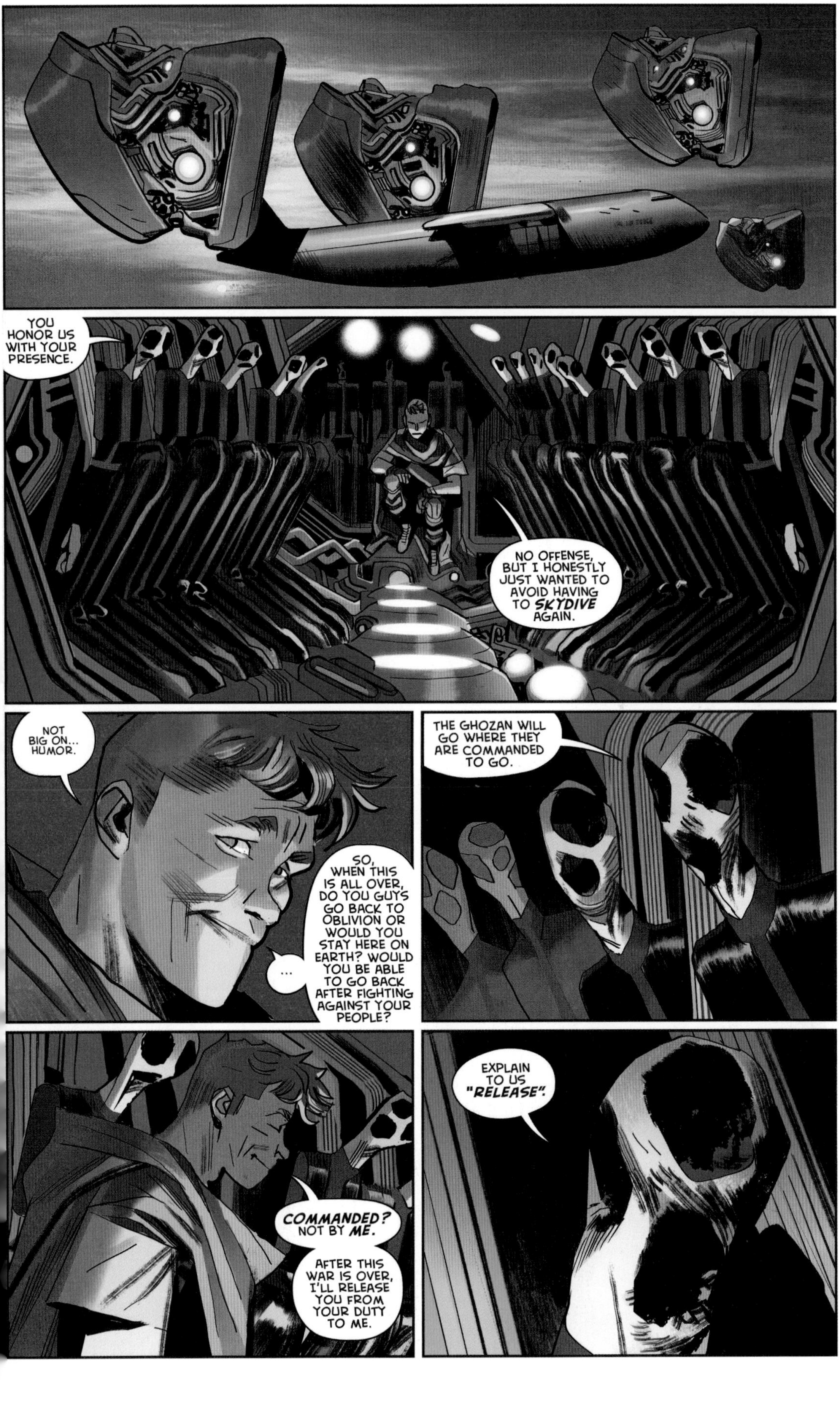
YOU HONOR US WITH YOUR PRESENCE.
NO OFFENSE, BUT I HONESTLY JUST WANTED TO AVOID HAVING TO SKYDIVE AGAIN.
NOT BIG ON... HUMOR.
SO, WHEN THIS IS ALL OVER, DO YOU GUYS GO BACK TO OBLIVION OR WOULD YOU STAY HERE ON EARTH? WOULD YOU BE ABLE TO GO BACK AFTER FIGHTING AGAINST YOUR PEOPLE?
...
THE GHOZAN WILL GO WHERE THEY ARE COMMANDED TO GO.
COMMANDED? NOT BY ME.
AFTER THIS WAR IS OVER, I'LL RELEASE YOU FROM YOUR DUTY TO ME.
EXPLAIN TO US "RELEASE".

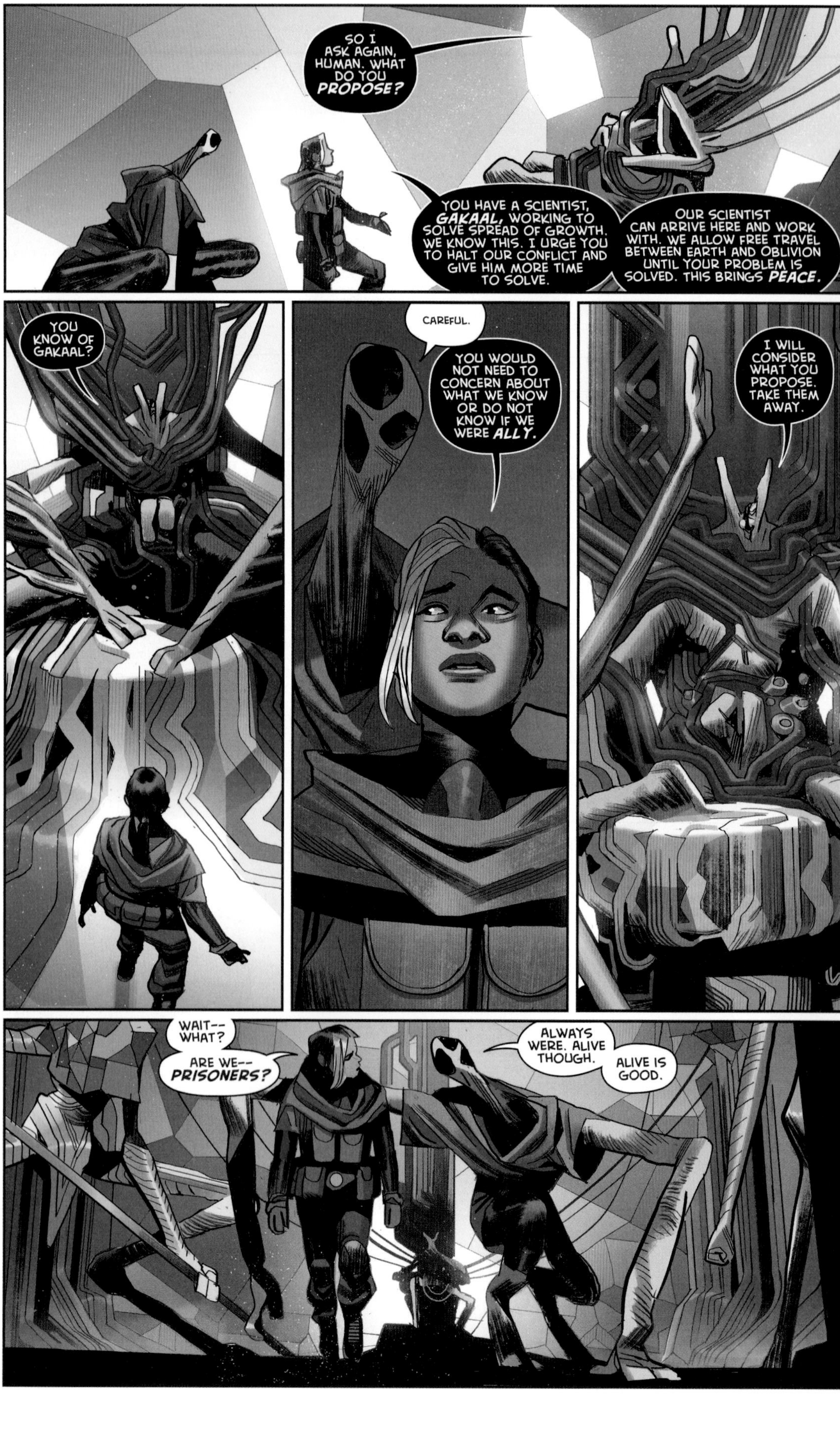
SO I ASK AGAIN, HUMAN. WHAT DO YOU PROPOSE?
YOU HAVE A SCIENTIST, GAKAAL, WORKING TO SOLVE SPREAD OF GROWTH. WE KNOW THIS. I URGE YOU TO HALT OUR CONFLICT AND GIVE HIM MORE TIME TO SOLVE.
OUR SCIENTIST CAN ARRIVE HERE AND WORK WITH. WE ALLOW FREE TRAVEL BETWEEN EARTH AND OBLIVION UNTIL YOUR PROBLEM IS SOLVED. THIS BRINGS PEACE.
YOU KNOW OF GAKAAL?
CAREFUL.
YOU WOULD NOT NEED TO CONCERN ABOUT WHAT WE KNOW OR DO NOT KNOW IF WE WERE ALLY.
I WILL CONSIDER WHAT YOU PROPOSE. TAKE THEM AWAY.
WAIT-- WHAT?
ARE WE-- PRISONERS?
ALWAYS WERE. ALIVE THOUGH.
ALIVE IS GOOD.

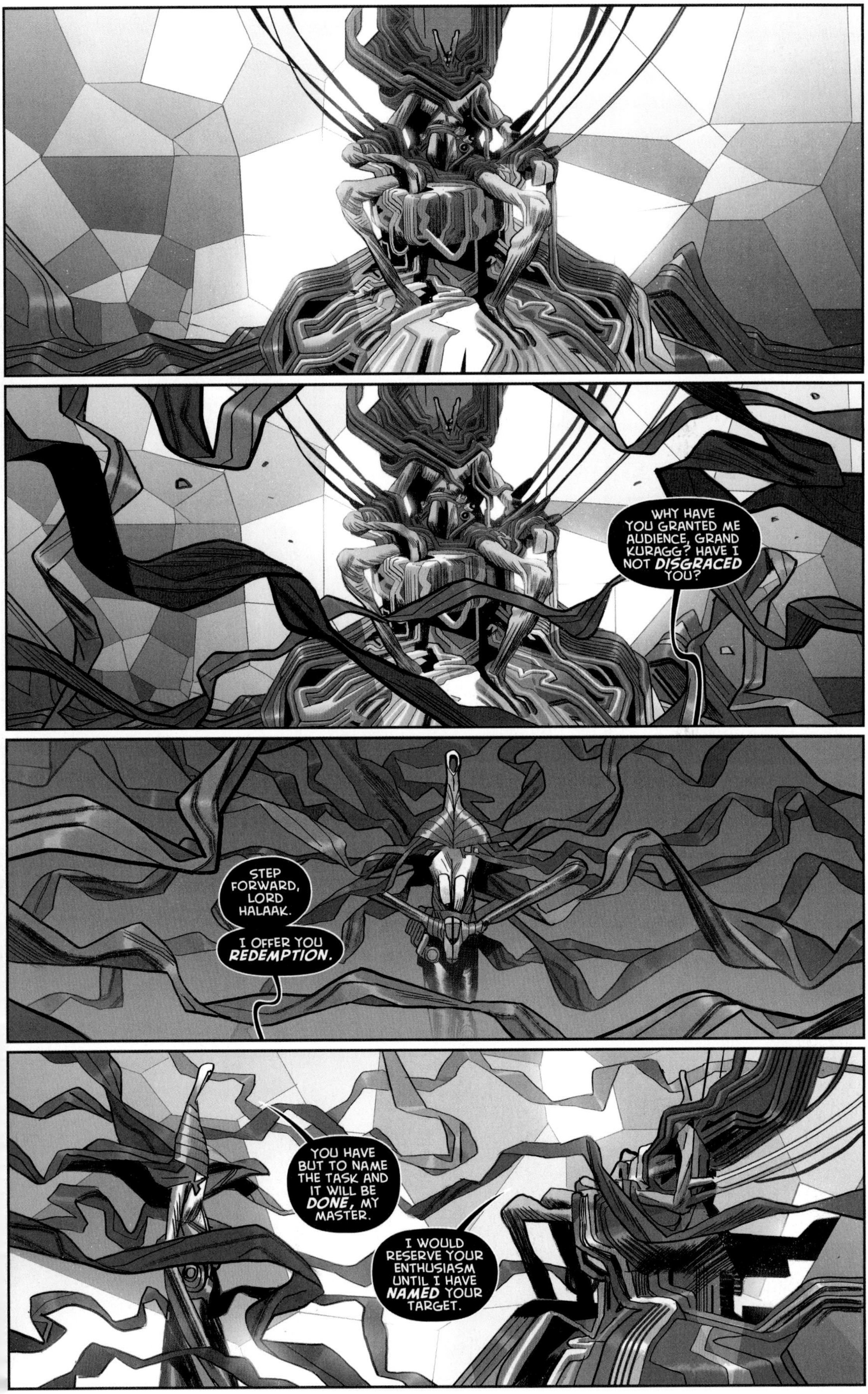
WHY HAVE YOU GRANTED ME AUDIENCE, GRAND KURAGG? HAVE I NOT DISGRACED YOU?
STEP FORWARD, LORD HALAAK.
I OFFER YOU REDEMPTION.
YOU HAVE BUT TO NAME THE TASK AND IT WILL BE DONE, MY MASTER.
I WOULD RESERVE YOUR ENTHUSIASM UNTIL I HAVE NAMED YOUR TARGET.

THE DISGRACED GHOZAN, *GAKAAL*, HAS BEEN WORKING FOR US IN SECRET, WORKING TO END THE GROWTH. FEW AMONG US KNOW THIS.

A *HUMAN* KNOWS THIS.

I NOW BELIEVE GAKAAL TO BE WORKING WITH THE HUMANS OF EARTH AGAINST US.

DISGRACED OR NOT, TO INVITE CONFLICT WITH GAKAAL IS TO ENSURE YOUR OWN *DEATH*.

IS *REDEMPTION* NOT WORTH YOUR LIFE?

IT IS.

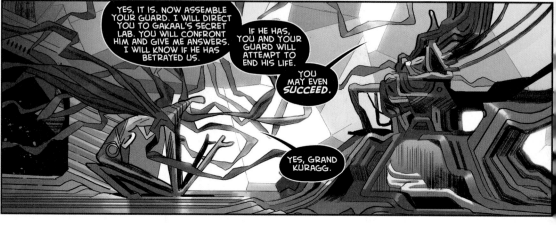

YES, IT IS. NOW ASSEMBLE YOUR GUARD. I WILL DIRECT YOU TO GAKAAL'S SECRET LAB. YOU WILL CONFRONT HIM AND GIVE ME ANSWERS. I WILL KNOW IF HE HAS BETRAYED US.

IF HE HAS, YOU AND YOUR GUARD WILL ATTEMPT TO END HIS LIFE.

YOU MAY EVEN *SUCCEED.*

YES, GRAND KURAGG.

KRA-KOOM

BRAKKA!
BRAKKA!
BRAKKA!

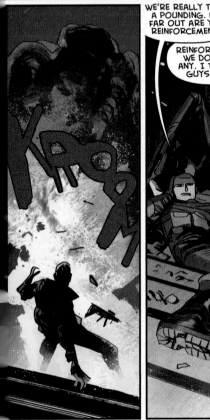

KRA

WE'RE REALLY TAKING A POUNDING. HOW FAR OUT ARE YOUR REINFORCEMENTS?

REINFORCEMENTS? WE DON'T HAVE ANY. I THINK YOU GUYS ARE *IT*.

NATHAN? YOU THERE?

THINGS ARE FAR MORE DIRE THAN THEY EVER WERE IN LOS ANGELES. YOU'RE GOING TO BE ABLE TO DO YOUR THING *FASTER* THIS TIME, RIGHT?

YEAH. I'M ALMOST IN. SHOULD BE A BREEZE NOW THAT I KNOW WHAT I'M DOING. I'M--

NATHAN? YOU CUT OUT. YOU STILL THERE?

NATHAN?

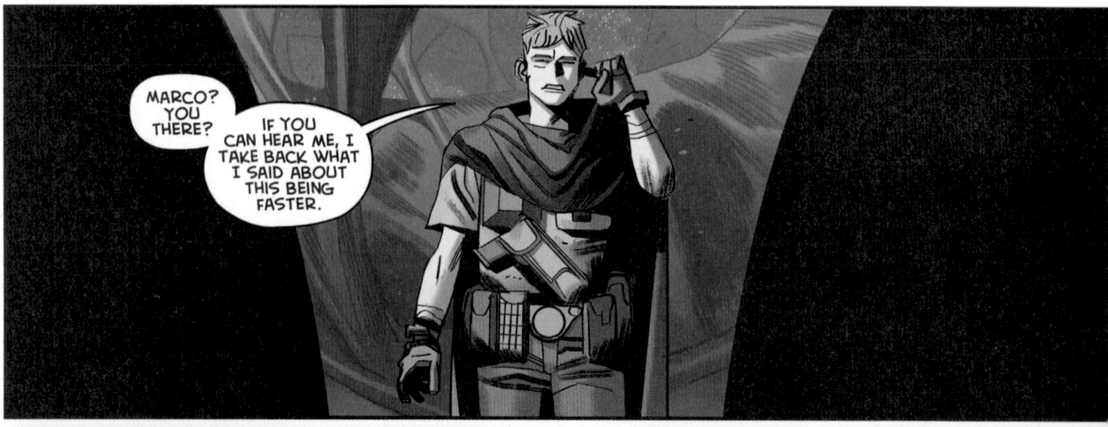
MARCO? YOU THERE?
IF YOU CAN HEAR ME, I TAKE BACK WHAT I SAID ABOUT THIS BEING FASTER.
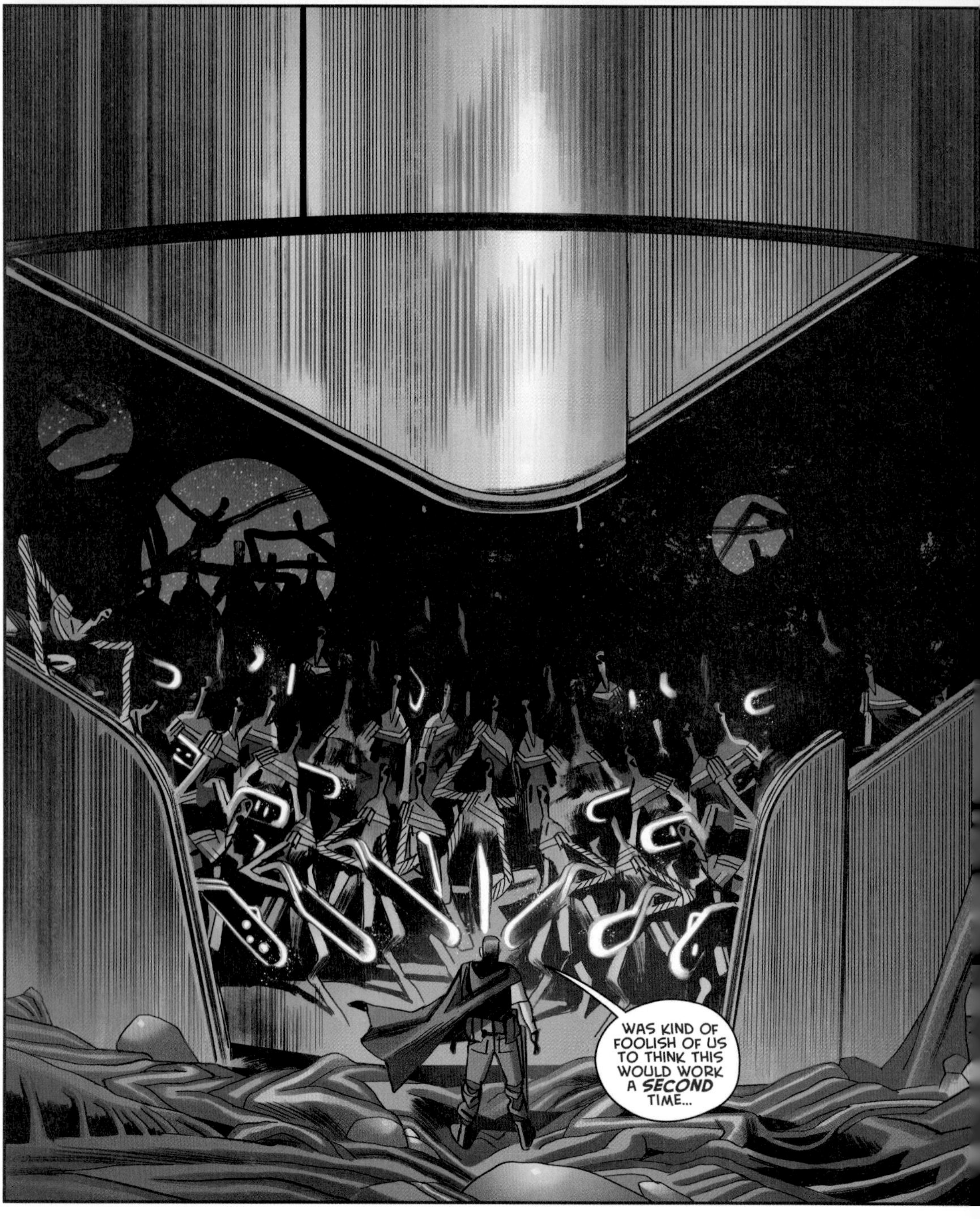
WAS KIND OF FOOLISH OF US TO THINK THIS WOULD WORK A *SECOND* TIME...

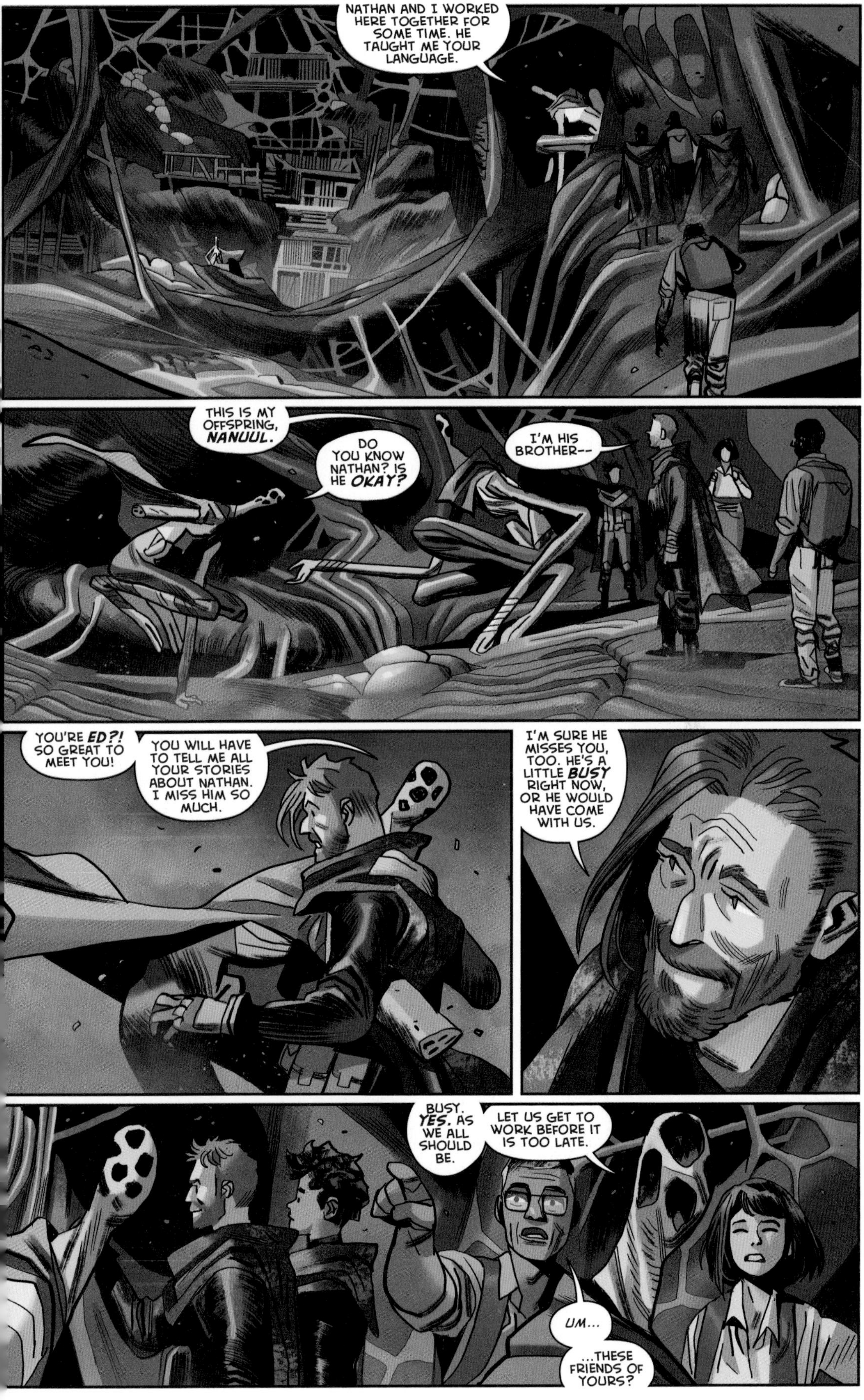
NATHAN AND I WORKED HERE TOGETHER FOR SOME TIME. HE TAUGHT ME YOUR LANGUAGE.
THIS IS MY OFFSPRING, NANUUL.
DO YOU KNOW NATHAN? IS HE OKAY?
I'M HIS BROTHER--
YOU'RE ED?! SO GREAT TO MEET YOU!
YOU WILL HAVE TO TELL ME ALL YOUR STORIES ABOUT NATHAN. I MISS HIM SO MUCH.
I'M SURE HE MISSES YOU, TOO. HE'S A LITTLE BUSY RIGHT NOW, OR HE WOULD HAVE COME WITH US.
BUSY. YES. AS WE ALL SHOULD BE.
LET US GET TO WORK BEFORE IT IS TOO LATE.
UM...
...THESE FRIENDS OF YOURS?

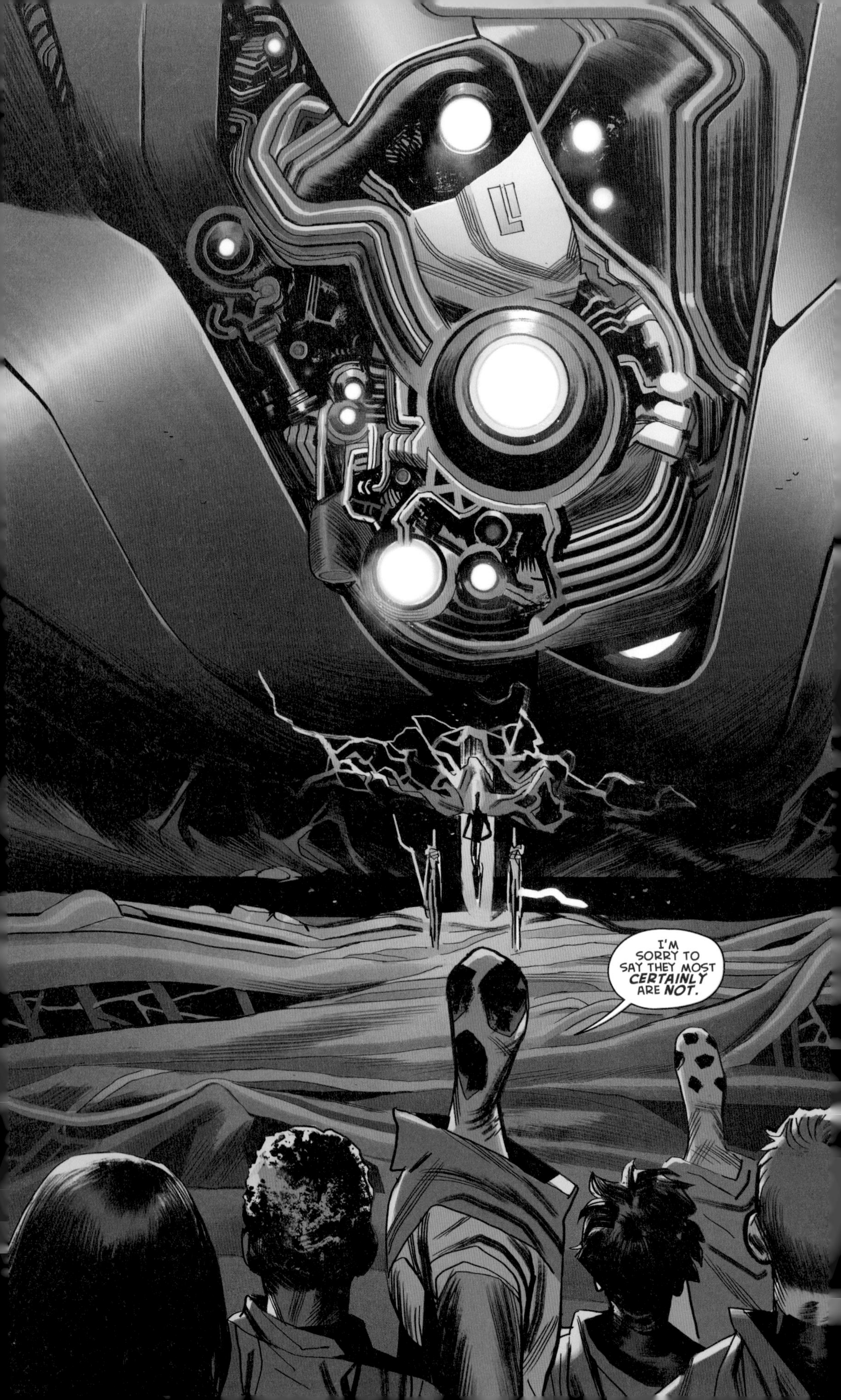
I'M SORRY TO SAY THEY MOST *CERTAINLY* ARE *NOT*.

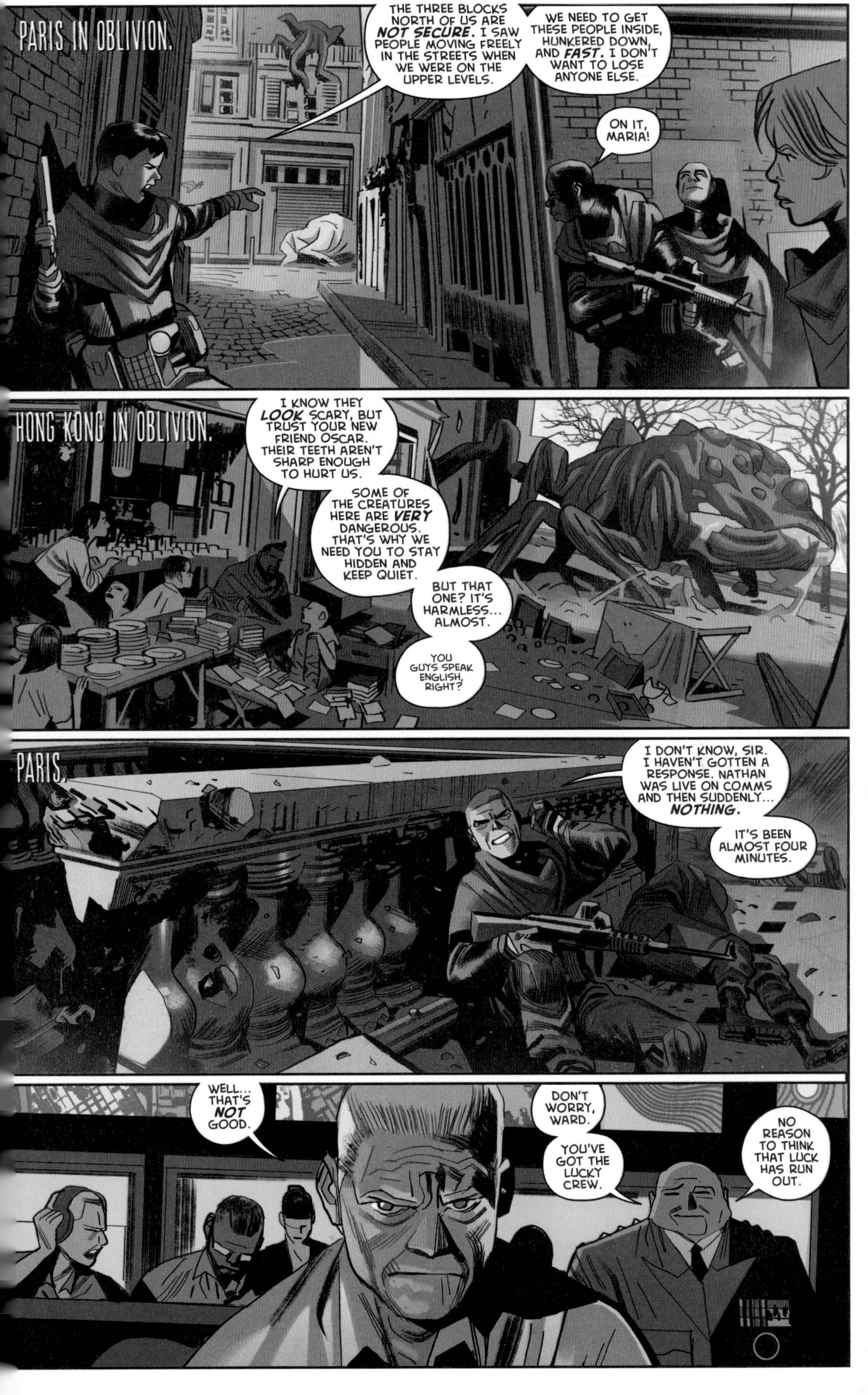
PARIS IN OBLIVION.
THE THREE BLOCKS NORTH OF US ARE NOT SECURE. I SAW PEOPLE MOVING FREELY IN THE STREETS WHEN WE WERE ON THE UPPER LEVELS.
WE NEED TO GET THESE PEOPLE INSIDE, HUNKERED DOWN, AND FAST. I DON'T WANT TO LOSE ANYONE ELSE.
ON IT, MARIA!
HONG KONG IN OBLIVION.
I KNOW THEY LOOK SCARY, BUT TRUST YOUR NEW FRIEND OSCAR. THEIR TEETH AREN'T SHARP ENOUGH TO HURT US.
SOME OF THE CREATURES HERE ARE VERY DANGEROUS. THAT'S WHY WE NEED YOU TO STAY HIDDEN AND KEEP QUIET.
BUT THAT ONE? IT'S HARMLESS... ALMOST.
YOU GUYS SPEAK ENGLISH, RIGHT?
PARIS.
I DON'T KNOW, SIR. I HAVEN'T GOTTEN A RESPONSE. NATHAN WAS LIVE ON COMMS AND THEN SUDDENLY... NOTHING.
IT'S BEEN ALMOST FOUR MINUTES.
WELL... THAT'S NOT GOOD.
DON'T WORRY, WARD.
YOU'VE GOT THE LUCKY CREW.
NO REASON TO THINK THAT LUCK HAS RUN OUT.

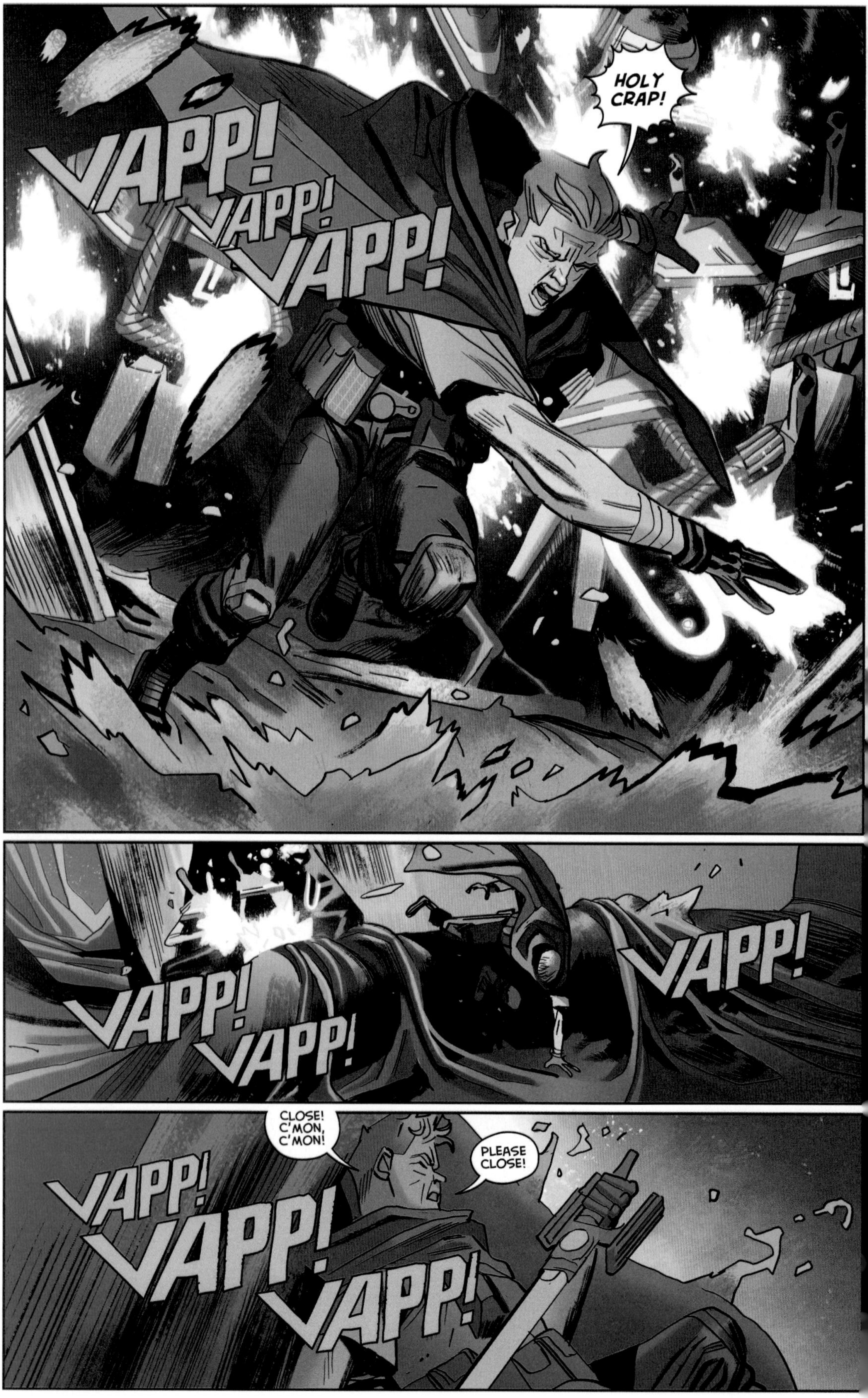
HOLY CRAP!
VAPP! VAPP! VAPP!
VAPP! VAPP!
VAPP!
CLOSE! C'MON, C'MON!
PLEASE CLOSE!
VAPP! VAPP! VAPP!

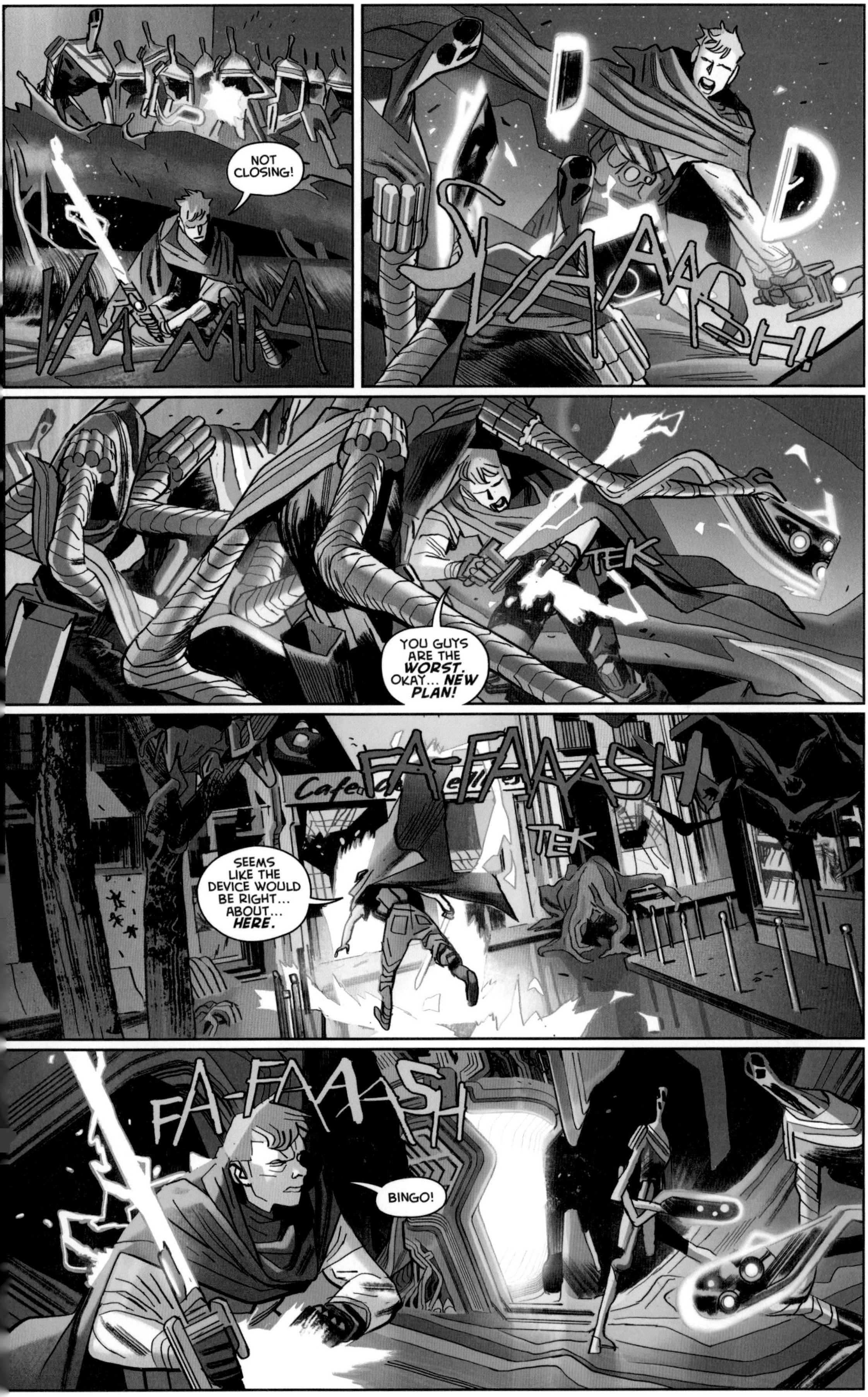
NOT CLOSING!
VMMM
SVAAASH!
TEK
YOU GUYS ARE THE WORST. OKAY... NEW PLAN!
FA-FAAASH
Cafe
TEK
SEEMS LIKE THE DEVICE WOULD BE RIGHT... ABOUT... HERE.
FA-FAAASH
BINGO!

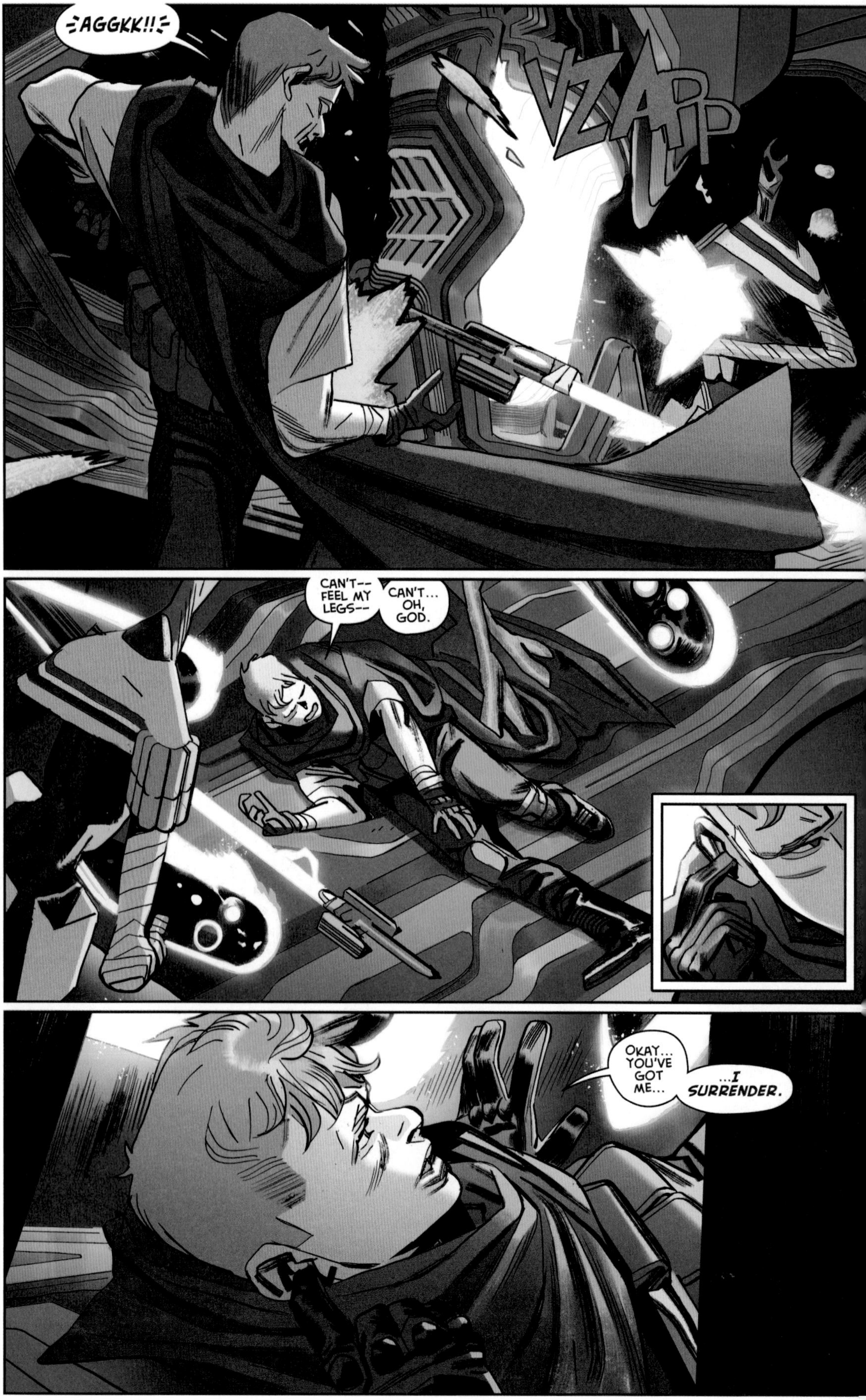
AGGKK!!
VZAPP
CAN'T-- FEEL MY LEGS--
CAN'T... OH, GOD.
OKAY... YOU'VE GOT ME...
...I SURRENDER.

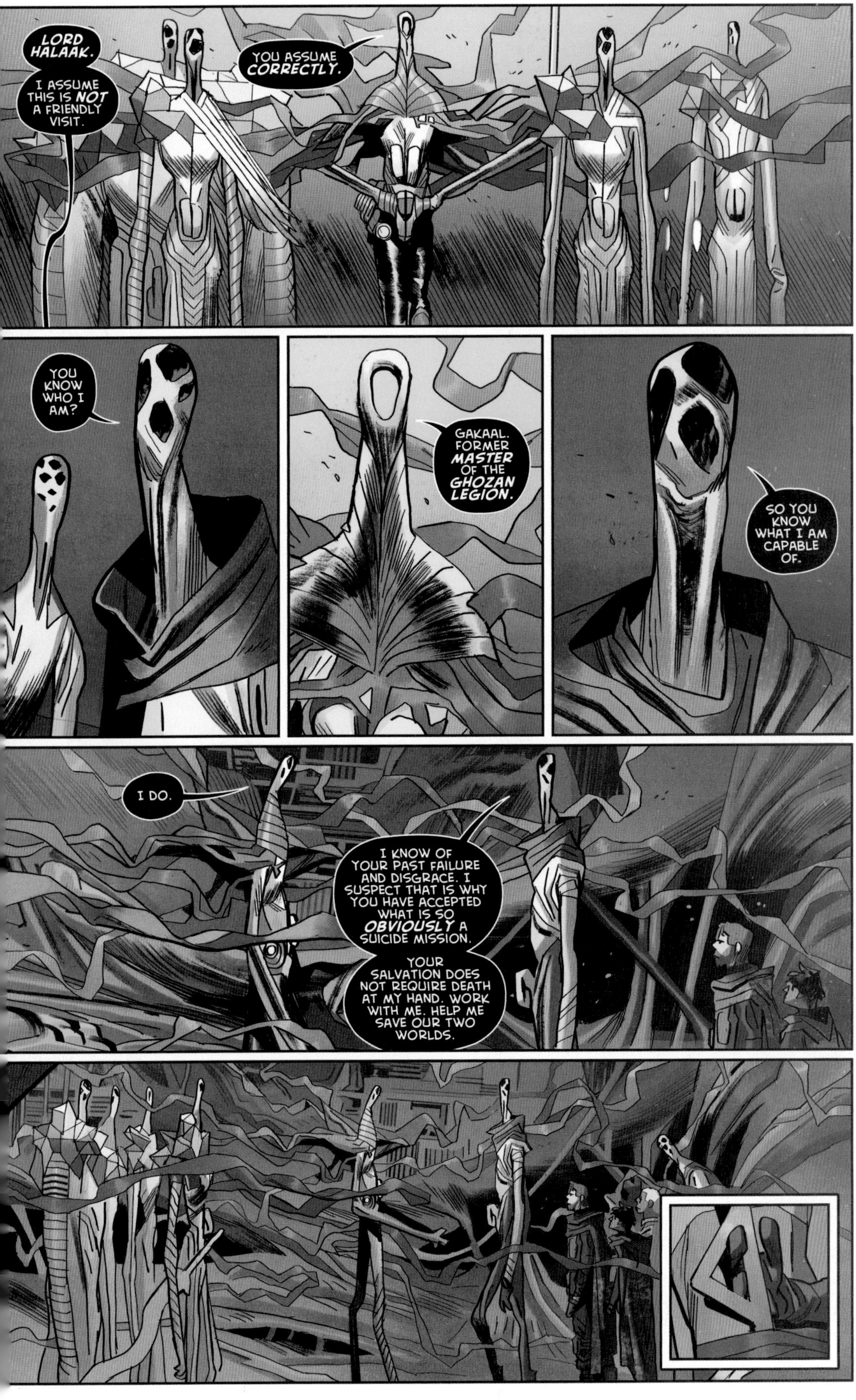

LORD HALAAK.
I ASSUME THIS IS NOT A FRIENDLY VISIT.
YOU ASSUME CORRECTLY.
YOU KNOW WHO I AM?
GAKAAL. FORMER MASTER OF THE GHOZAN LEGION.
SO YOU KNOW WHAT I AM CAPABLE OF.
I DO.
I KNOW OF YOUR PAST FAILURE AND DISGRACE. I SUSPECT THAT IS WHY YOU HAVE ACCEPTED WHAT IS SO OBVIOUSLY A SUICIDE MISSION.
YOUR SALVATION DOES NOT REQUIRE DEATH AT MY HAND. WORK WITH ME. HELP ME SAVE OUR TWO WORLDS.

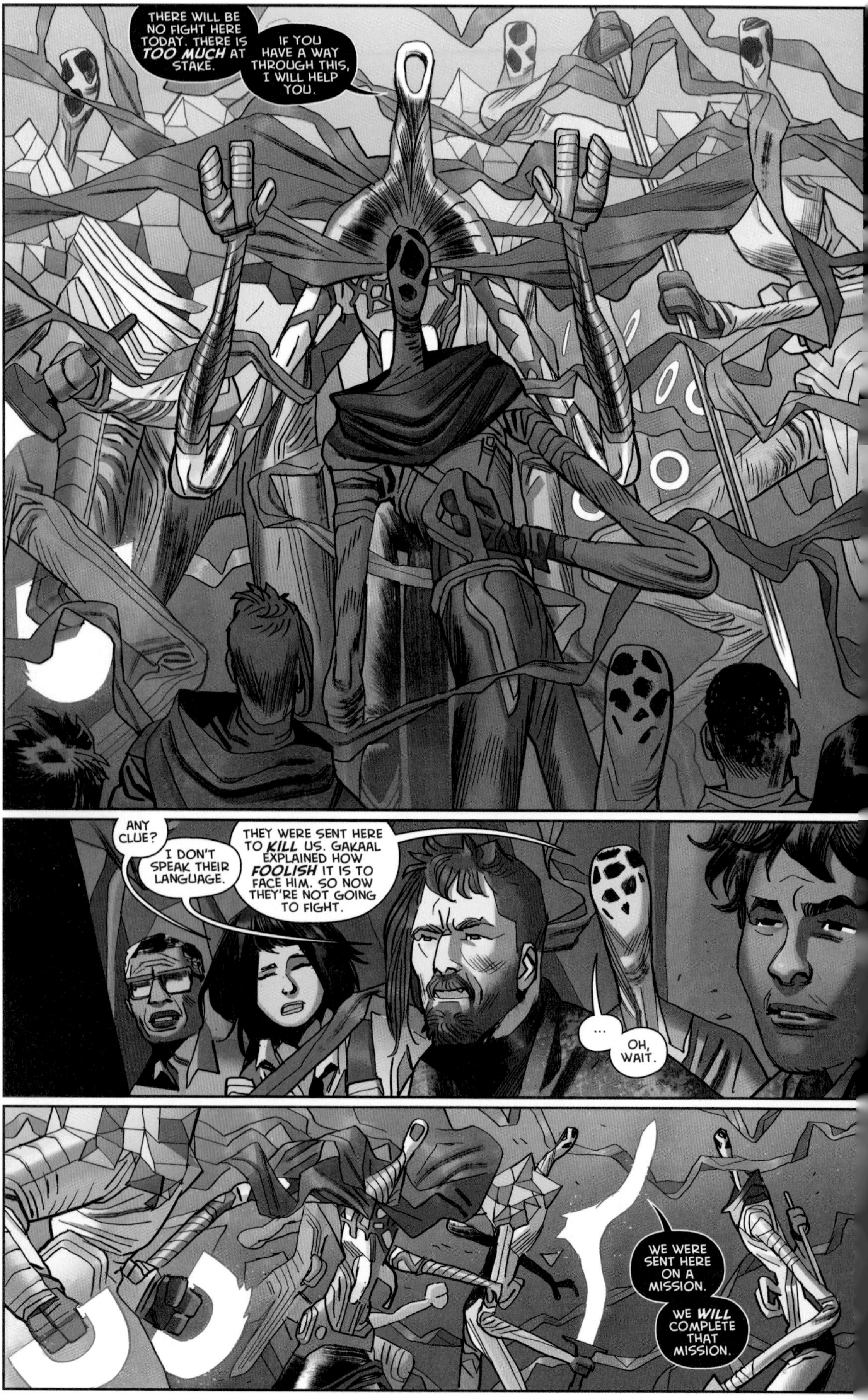
THERE WILL BE NO FIGHT HERE TODAY. THERE IS TOO MUCH AT STAKE.
IF YOU HAVE A WAY THROUGH THIS, I WILL HELP YOU.
ANY CLUE?
I DON'T SPEAK THEIR LANGUAGE.
THEY WERE SENT HERE TO KILL US. GAKAAL EXPLAINED HOW FOOLISH IT IS TO FACE HIM. SO NOW THEY'RE NOT GOING TO FIGHT.
...
OH, WAIT.
WE WERE SENT HERE ON A MISSION.
WE WILL COMPLETE THAT MISSION.

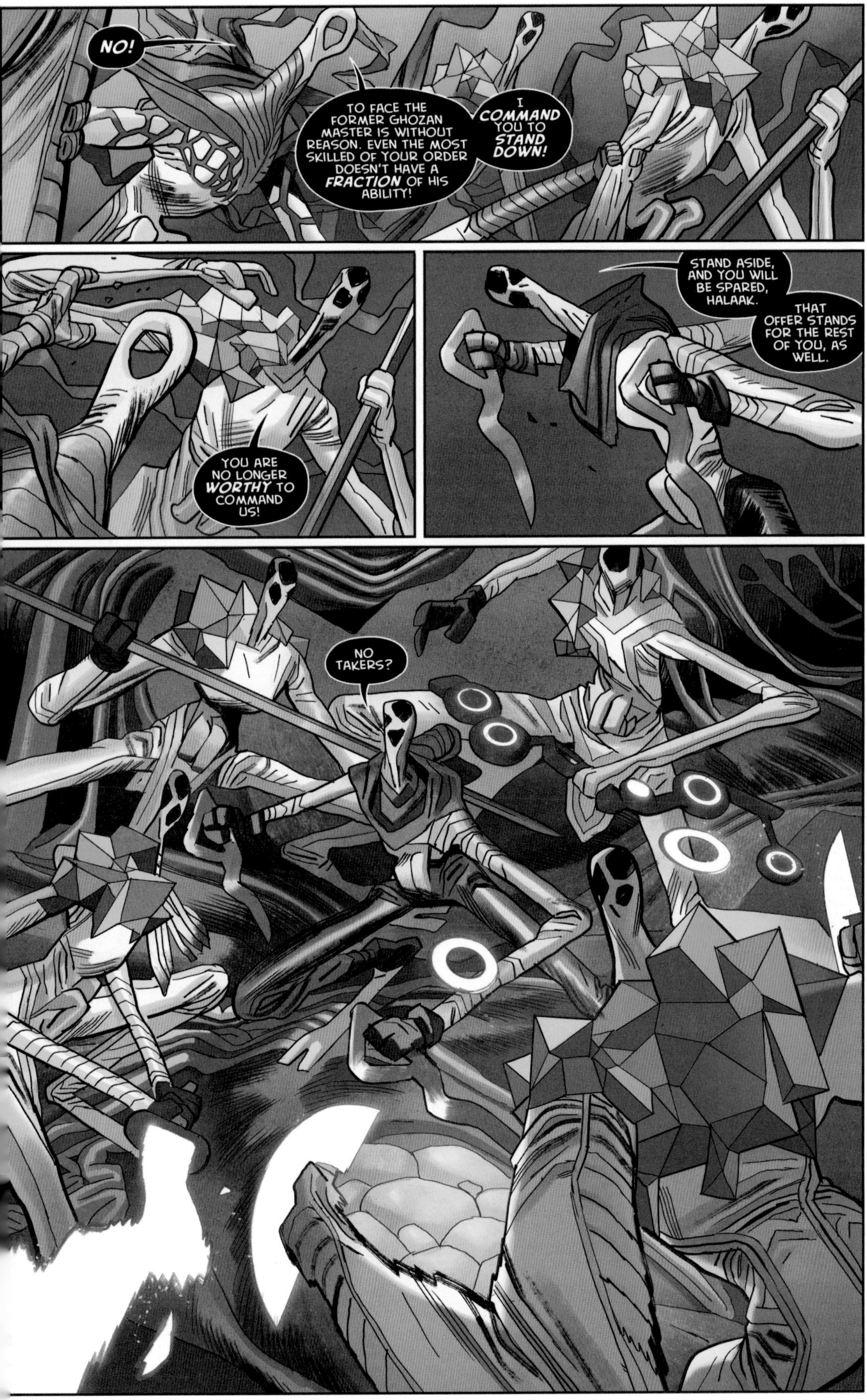
NO!
TO FACE THE FORMER GHOZAN MASTER IS WITHOUT REASON. EVEN THE MOST SKILLED OF YOUR ORDER DOESN'T HAVE A FRACTION OF HIS ABILITY!
I COMMAND YOU TO STAND DOWN!
YOU ARE NO LONGER WORTHY TO COMMAND US!
STAND ASIDE, AND YOU WILL BE SPARED, HALAAK.
THAT OFFER STANDS FOR THE REST OF YOU, AS WELL.
NO TAKERS?

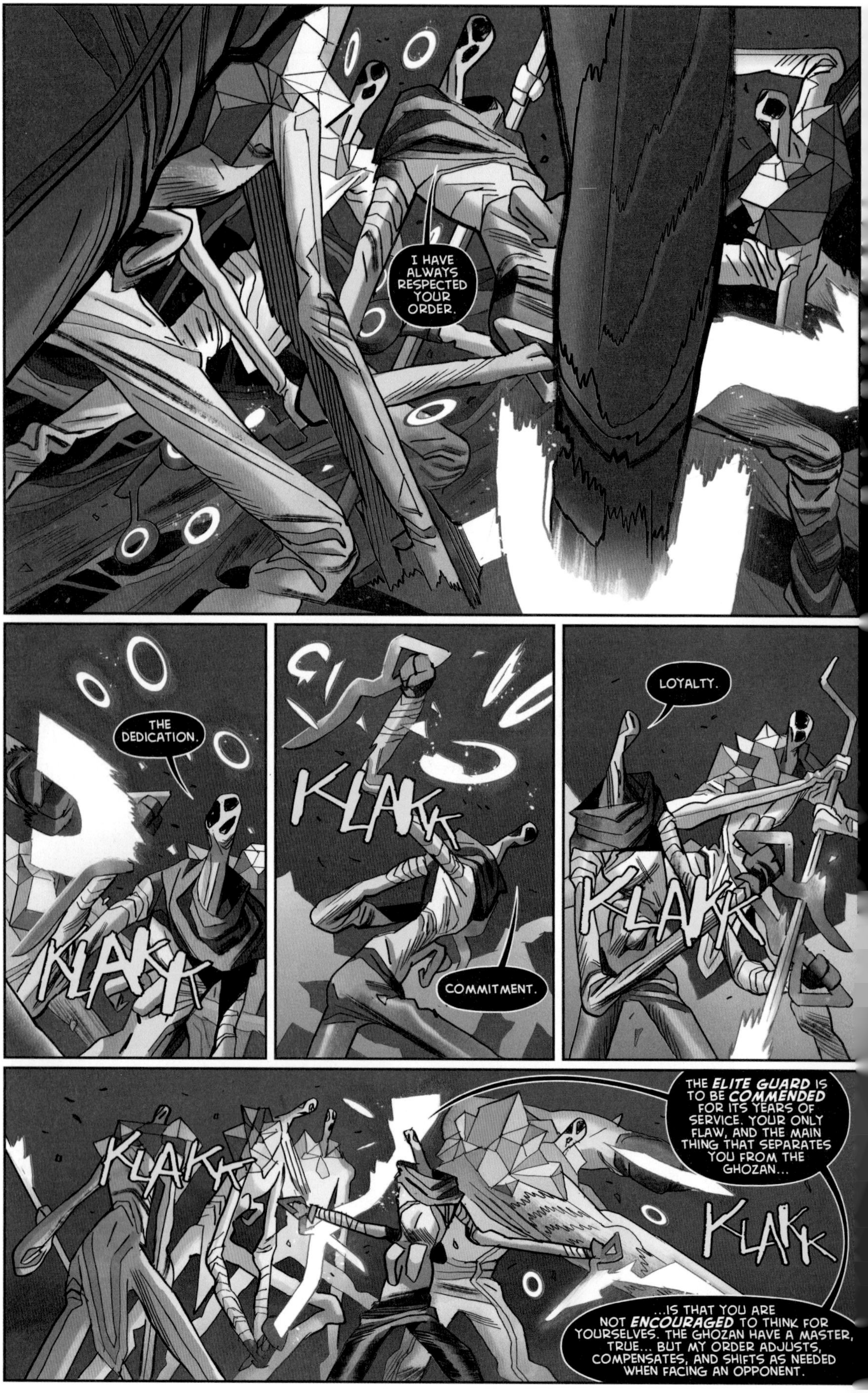

I HAVE ALWAYS RESPECTED YOUR ORDER.
THE DEDICATION.
KLAKK
KLAKK
COMMITMENT.
LOYALTY.
KLAKK
KLAKK
THE ELITE GUARD IS TO BE COMMENDED FOR ITS YEARS OF SERVICE. YOUR ONLY FLAW, AND THE MAIN THING THAT SEPARATES YOU FROM THE GHOZAN...
KLAKK
...IS THAT YOU ARE NOT ENCOURAGED TO THINK FOR YOURSELVES. THE GHOZAN HAVE A MASTER, TRUE... BUT MY ORDER ADJUSTS, COMPENSATES, AND SHIFTS AS NEEDED WHEN FACING AN OPPONENT.

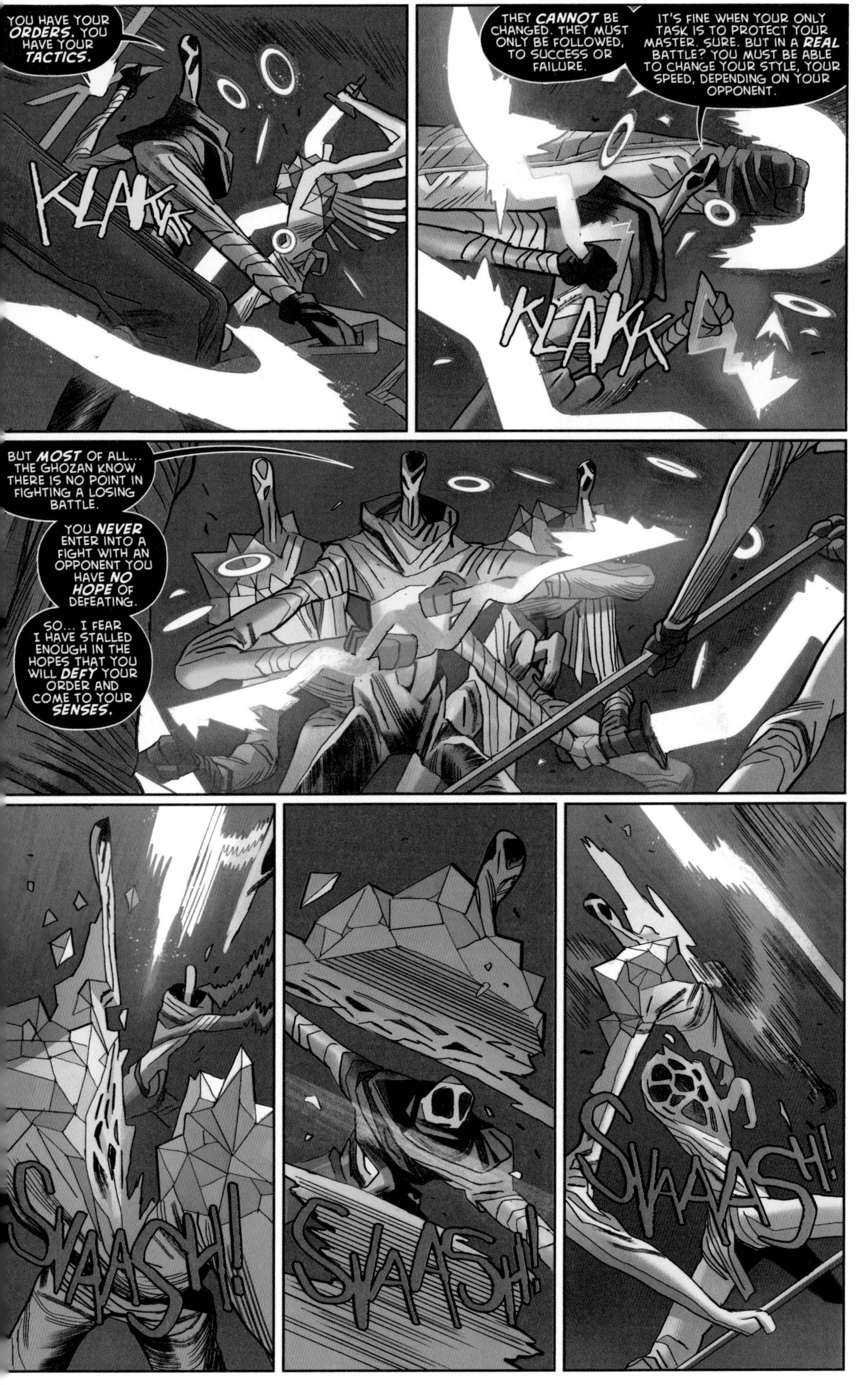

YOU HAVE YOUR ORDERS. YOU HAVE YOUR TACTICS.
KLAKKK
THEY CANNOT BE CHANGED. THEY MUST ONLY BE FOLLOWED, TO SUCCESS OR FAILURE.
IT'S FINE WHEN YOUR ONLY TASK IS TO PROTECT YOUR MASTER. SURE. BUT IN A REAL BATTLE? YOU MUST BE ABLE TO CHANGE YOUR STYLE, YOUR SPEED, DEPENDING ON YOUR OPPONENT.
KLAKK
BUT MOST OF ALL... THE GHOZAN KNOW THERE IS NO POINT IN FIGHTING A LOSING BATTLE.
YOU NEVER ENTER INTO A FIGHT WITH AN OPPONENT YOU HAVE NO HOPE OF DEFEATING.
SO... I FEAR I HAVE STALLED ENOUGH IN THE HOPES THAT YOU WILL DEFY YOUR ORDER AND COME TO YOUR SENSES.
SWASH!
SWASH!
SWAASH!

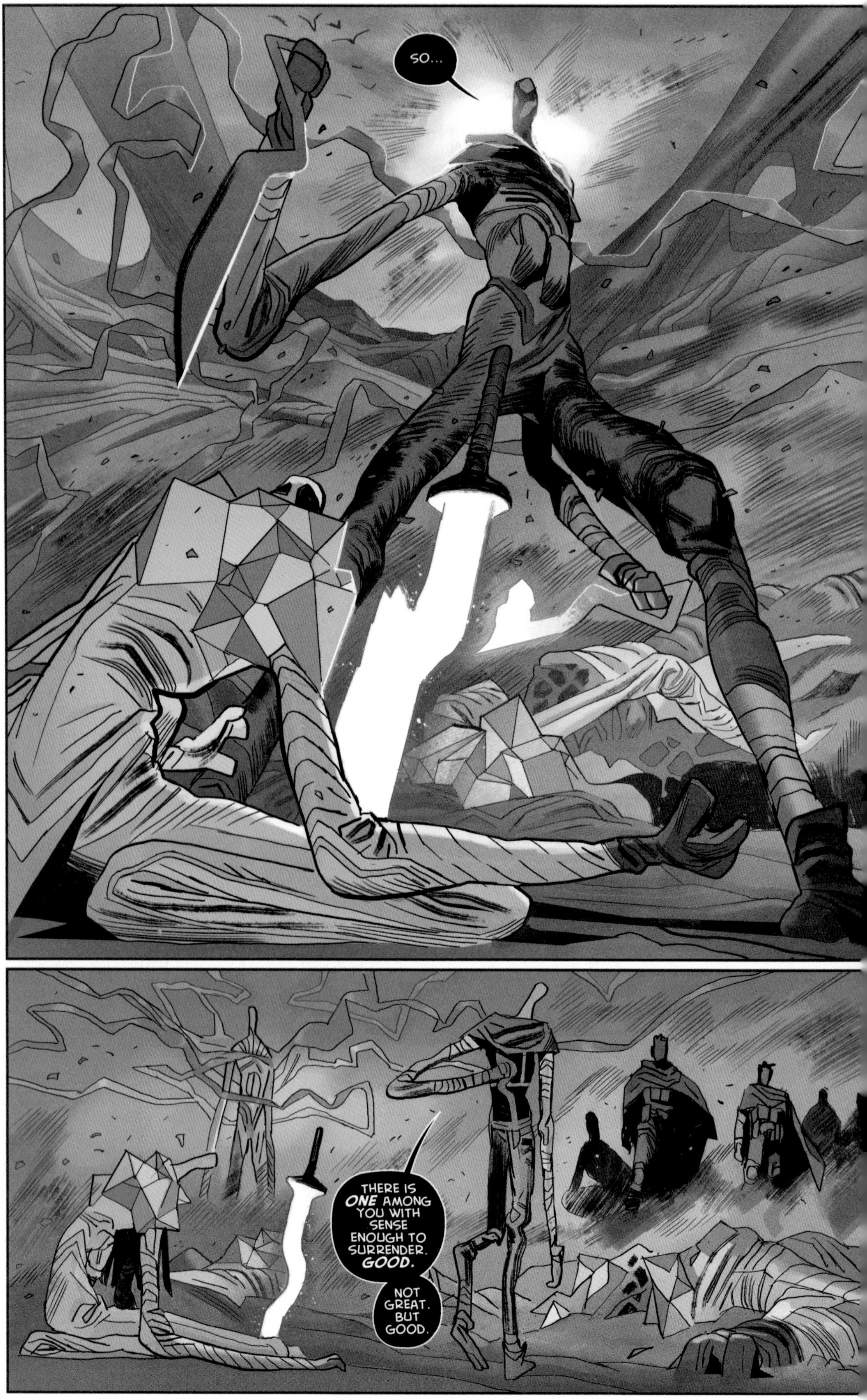
SO...
THERE IS ONE AMONG YOU WITH SENSE ENOUGH TO SURRENDER. GOOD.
NOT GREAT. BUT GOOD.

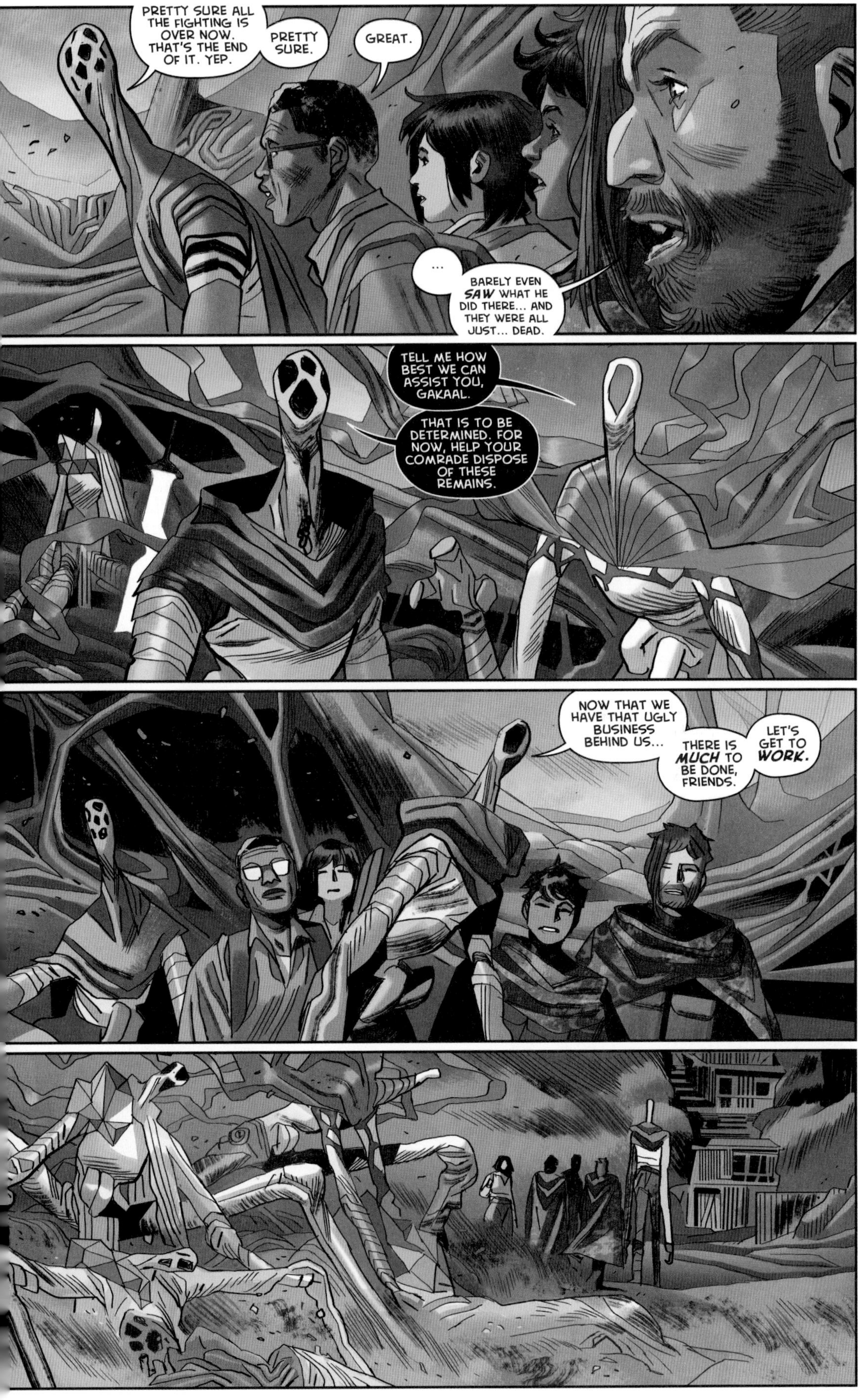
PRETTY SURE ALL THE FIGHTING IS OVER NOW. THAT'S THE END OF IT. YEP.
PRETTY SURE.
GREAT.
...
BARELY EVEN SAW WHAT HE DID THERE... AND THEY WERE ALL JUST... DEAD.
TELL ME HOW BEST WE CAN ASSIST YOU, GAKAAL.
THAT IS TO BE DETERMINED. FOR NOW, HELP YOUR COMRADE DISPOSE OF THESE REMAINS.
NOW THAT WE HAVE THAT UGLY BUSINESS BEHIND US...
THERE IS MUCH TO BE DONE, FRIENDS.
LET'S GET TO WORK.

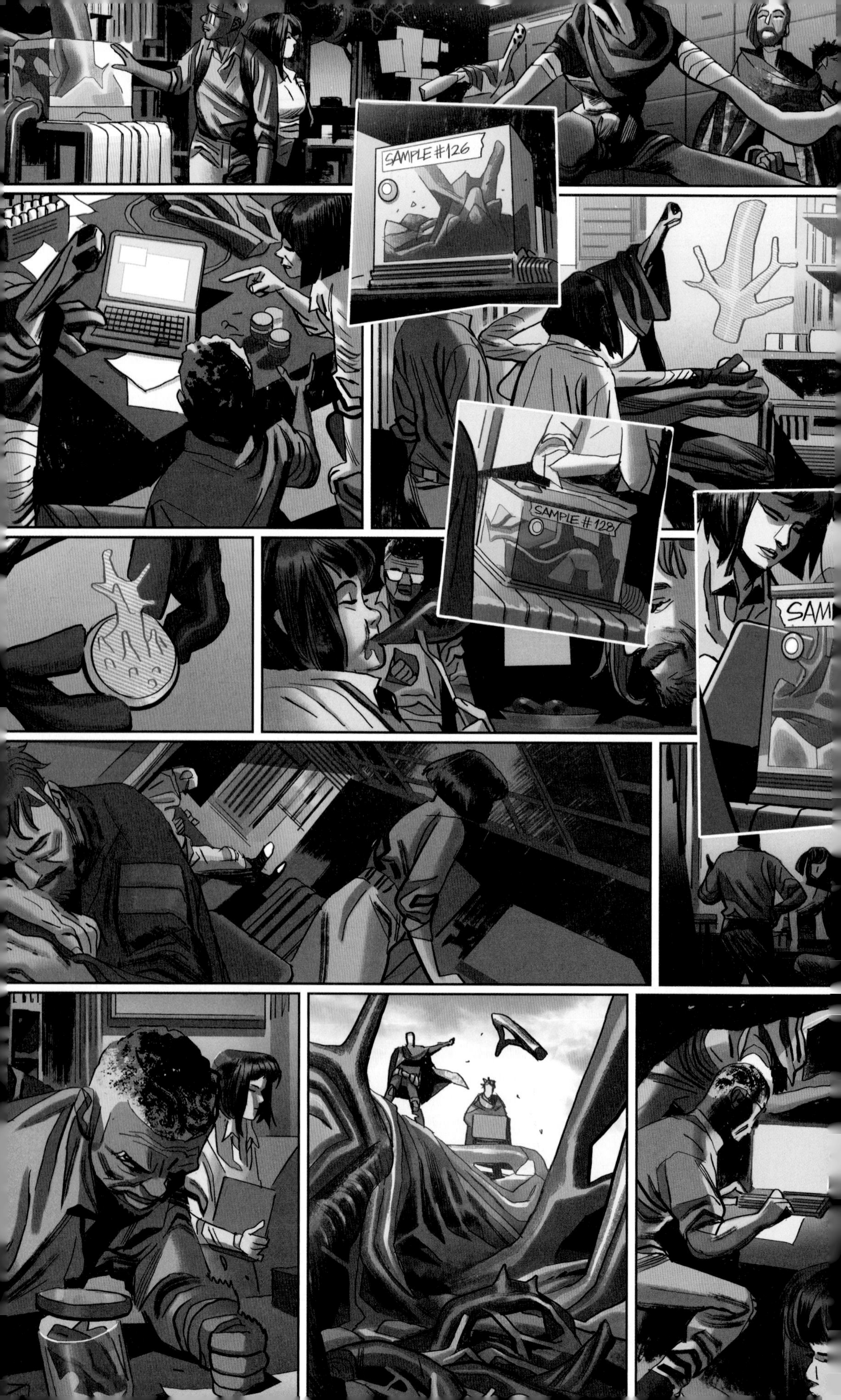
SAMPLE #126
SAMPLE #128

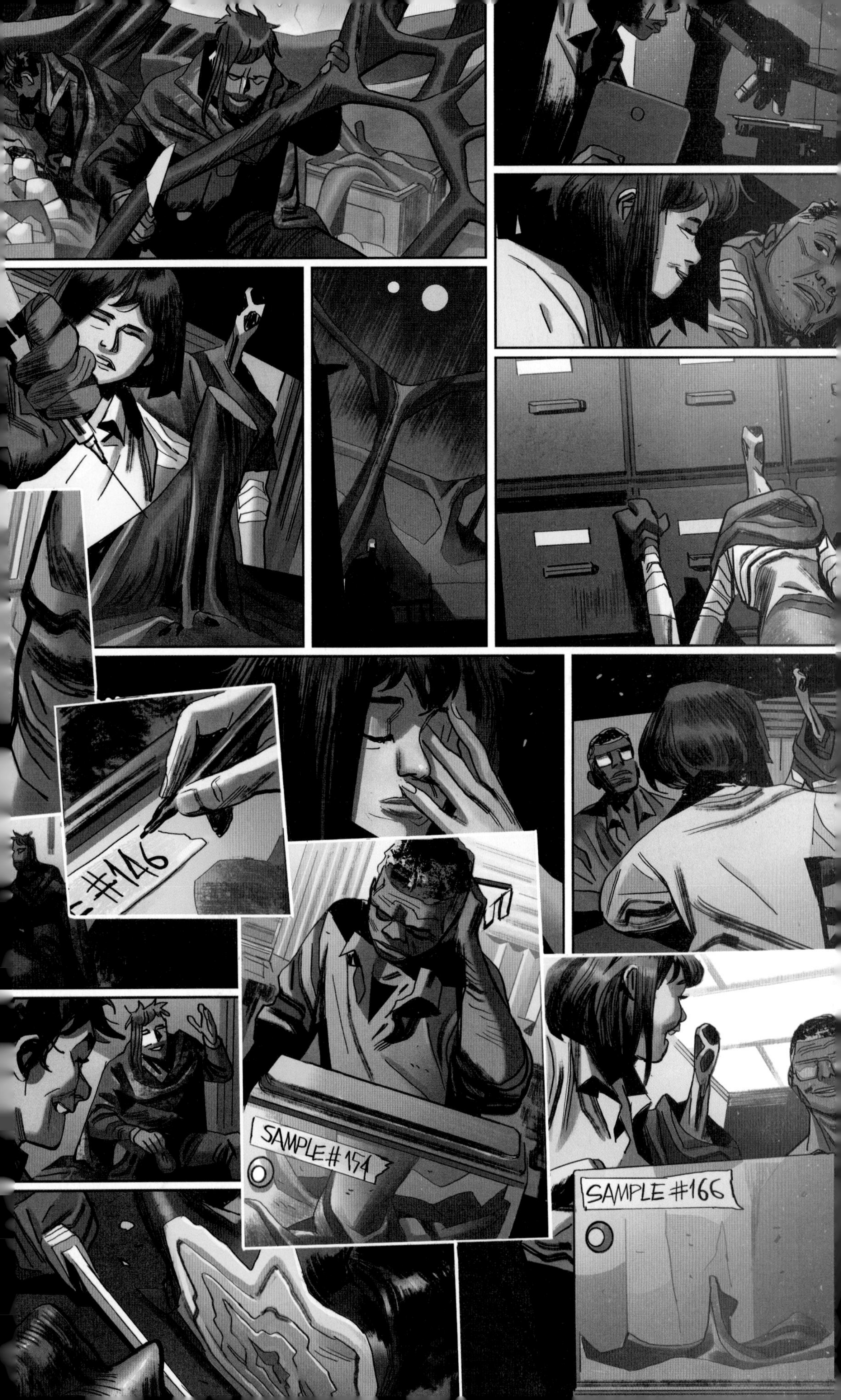
#146
SAMPLE #154
SAMPLE #166

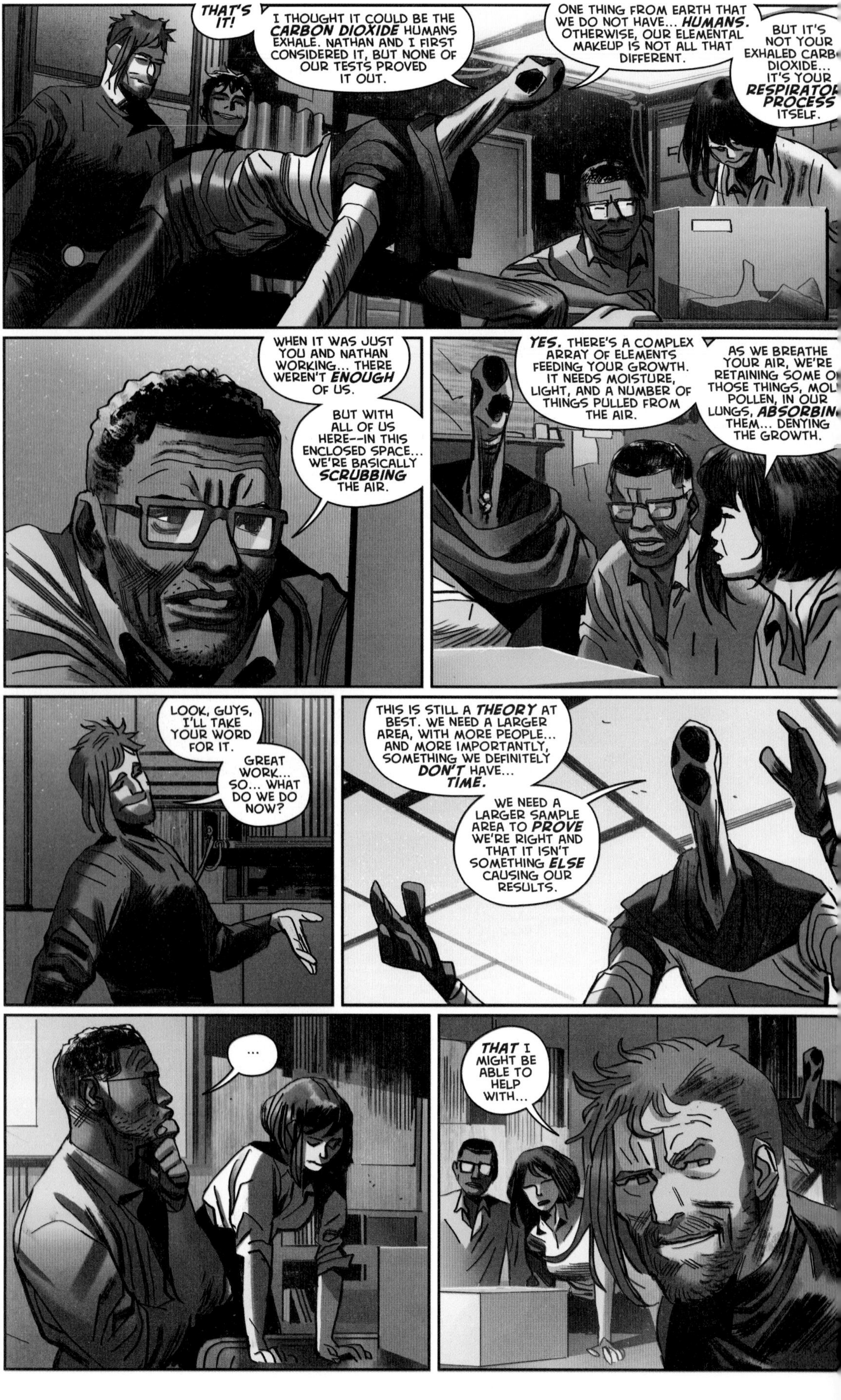
THAT'S IT!
I THOUGHT IT COULD BE THE CARBON DIOXIDE HUMANS EXHALE. NATHAN AND I FIRST CONSIDERED IT, BUT NONE OF OUR TESTS PROVED IT OUT.
ONE THING FROM EARTH THAT WE DO NOT HAVE... HUMANS. OTHERWISE, OUR ELEMENTAL MAKEUP IS NOT ALL THAT DIFFERENT.
BUT IT'S NOT YOUR EXHALED CARB DIOXIDE... IT'S YOUR RESPIRATOR PROCESS ITSELF.
WHEN IT WAS JUST YOU AND NATHAN WORKING... THERE WEREN'T ENOUGH OF US.
BUT WITH ALL OF US HERE--IN THIS ENCLOSED SPACE... WE'RE BASICALLY SCRUBBING THE AIR.
YES. THERE'S A COMPLEX ARRAY OF ELEMENTS FEEDING YOUR GROWTH. IT NEEDS MOISTURE, LIGHT, AND A NUMBER OF THINGS PULLED FROM THE AIR.
AS WE BREATHE YOUR AIR, WE'RE RETAINING SOME O THOSE THINGS, MOL POLLEN, IN OUR LUNGS, ABSORBIN THEM... DENYING THE GROWTH.
LOOK, GUYS, I'LL TAKE YOUR WORD FOR IT.
GREAT WORK... SO... WHAT DO WE DO NOW?
THIS IS STILL A THEORY AT BEST. WE NEED A LARGER AREA, WITH MORE PEOPLE... AND MORE IMPORTANTLY, SOMETHING WE DEFINITELY DON'T HAVE... TIME.
WE NEED A LARGER SAMPLE AREA TO PROVE WE'RE RIGHT AND THAT IT ISN'T SOMETHING ELSE CAUSING OUR RESULTS.
...
THAT I MIGHT BE ABLE TO HELP WITH...

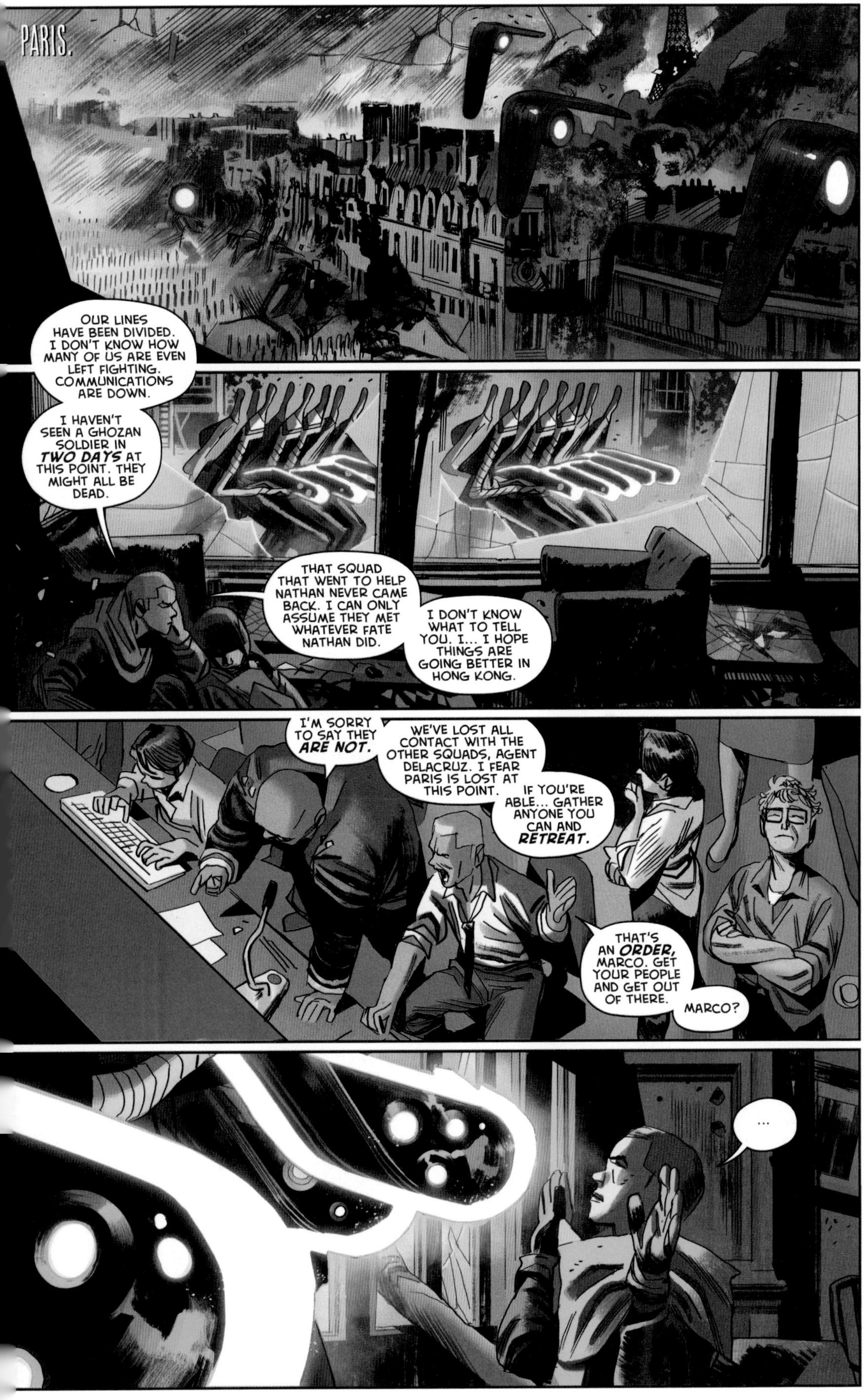
PARIS.
OUR LINES HAVE BEEN DIVIDED. I DON'T KNOW HOW MANY OF US ARE EVEN LEFT FIGHTING. COMMUNICATIONS ARE DOWN.
I HAVEN'T SEEN A GHOZAN SOLDIER IN **TWO DAYS** AT THIS POINT. THEY MIGHT ALL BE DEAD.
THAT SQUAD THAT WENT TO HELP NATHAN NEVER CAME BACK. I CAN ONLY ASSUME THEY MET WHATEVER FATE NATHAN DID.
I DON'T KNOW WHAT TO TELL YOU. I... I HOPE THINGS ARE GOING BETTER IN HONG KONG.
I'M SORRY TO SAY THEY **ARE NOT.**
WE'VE LOST ALL CONTACT WITH THE OTHER SQUADS, AGENT DELACRUZ. I FEAR PARIS IS LOST AT THIS POINT.
IF YOU'RE ABLE... GATHER ANYONE YOU CAN AND **RETREAT.**
THAT'S AN **ORDER,** MARCO. GET YOUR PEOPLE AND GET OUT OF THERE.
MARCO?
...

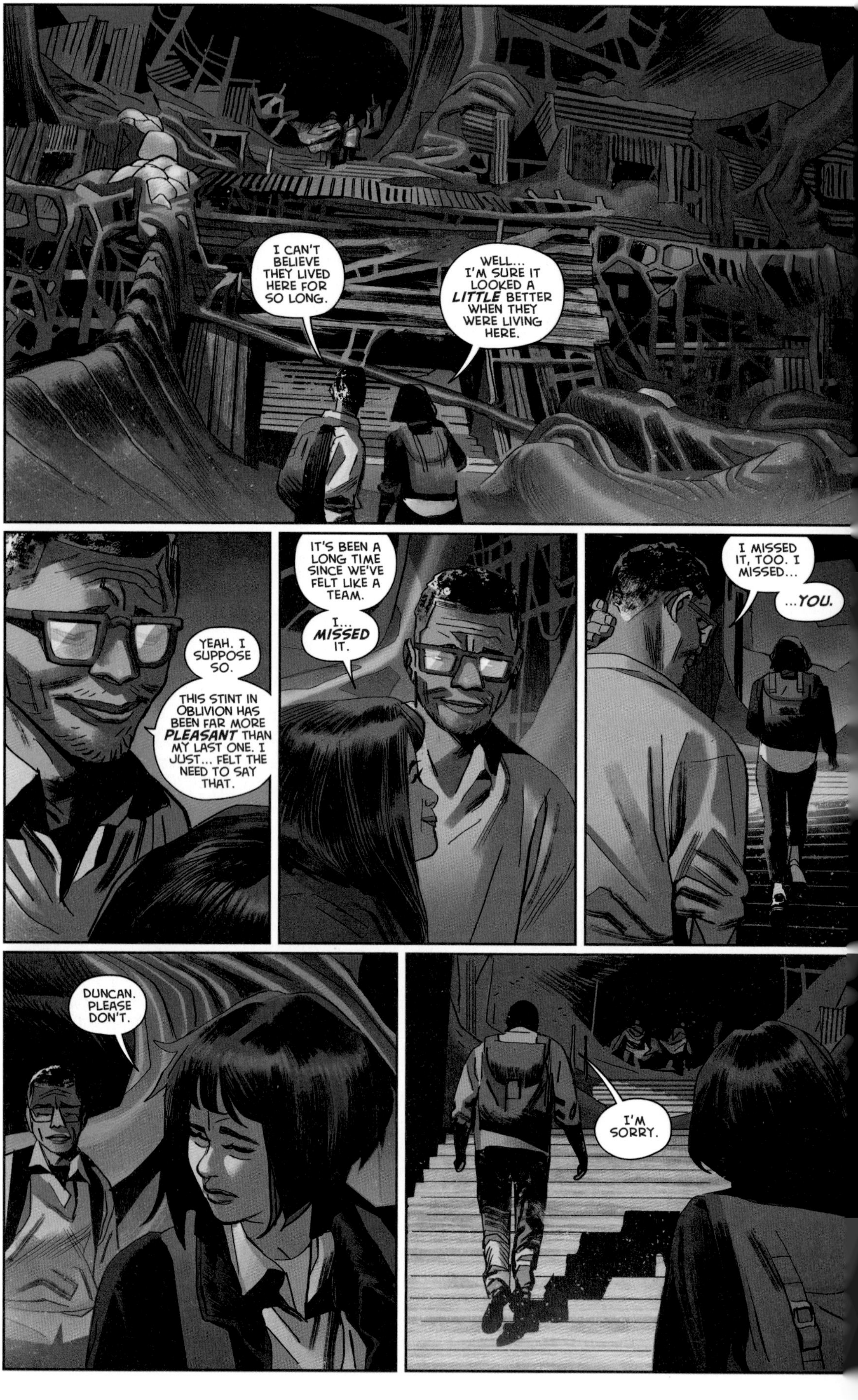
I CAN'T BELIEVE THEY LIVED HERE FOR SO LONG.
WELL... I'M SURE IT LOOKED A LITTLE BETTER WHEN THEY WERE LIVING HERE.
YEAH. I SUPPOSE SO.
THIS STINT IN OBLIVION HAS BEEN FAR MORE PLEASANT THAN MY LAST ONE. I JUST... FELT THE NEED TO SAY THAT.
IT'S BEEN A LONG TIME SINCE WE'VE FELT LIKE A TEAM.
I... MISSED IT.
I MISSED IT, TOO. I MISSED...
...YOU.
DUNCAN. PLEASE DON'T.
I'M SORRY.

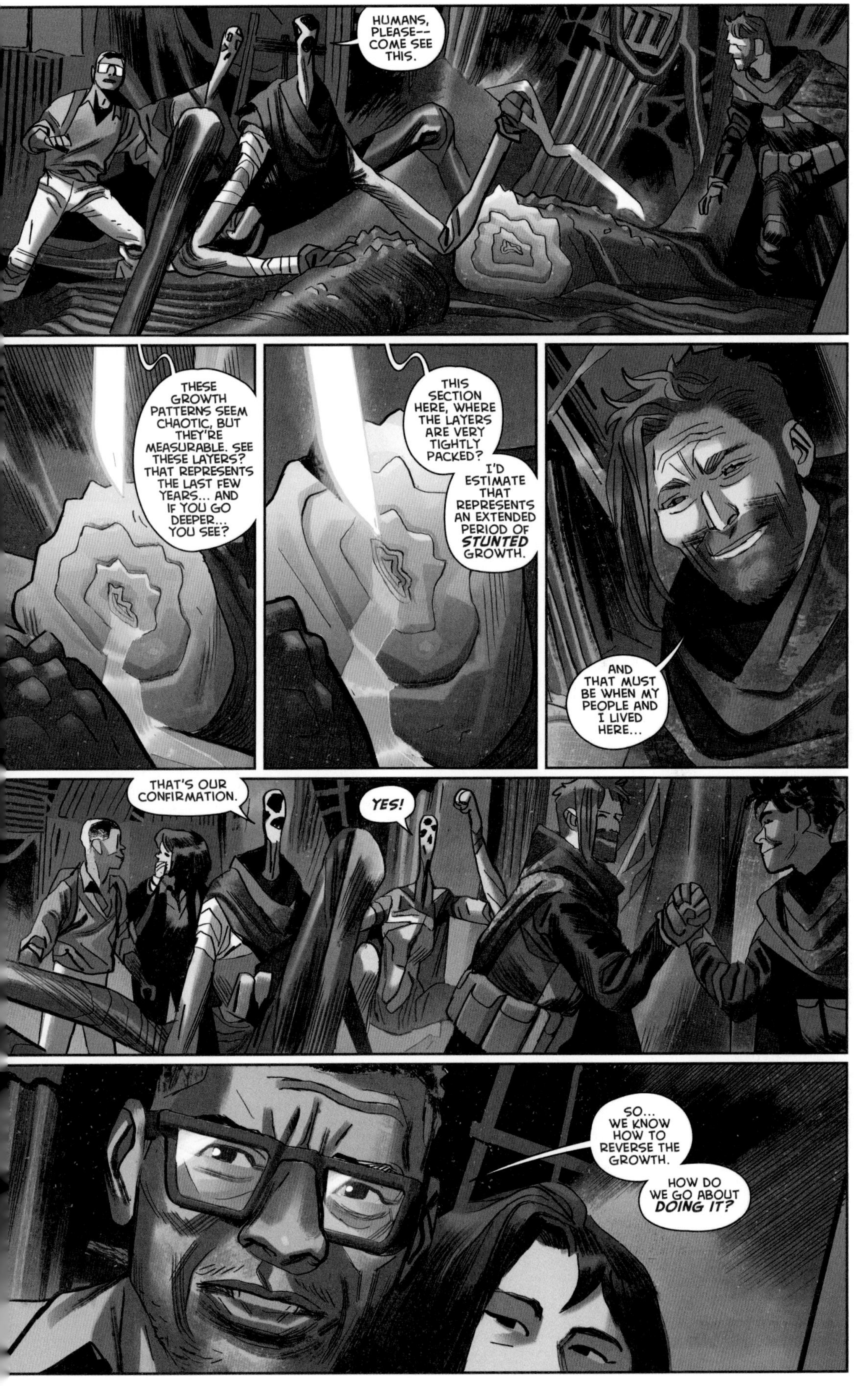
HUMANS, PLEASE-- COME SEE THIS.
THESE GROWTH PATTERNS SEEM CHAOTIC, BUT THEY'RE MEASURABLE. SEE THESE LAYERS? THAT REPRESENTS THE LAST FEW YEARS... AND IF YOU GO DEEPER... YOU SEE?
THIS SECTION HERE, WHERE THE LAYERS ARE VERY TIGHTLY PACKED?
I'D ESTIMATE THAT REPRESENTS AN EXTENDED PERIOD OF STUNTED GROWTH.
AND THAT MUST BE WHEN MY PEOPLE AND I LIVED HERE...
THAT'S OUR CONFIRMATION.
YES!
SO... WE KNOW HOW TO REVERSE THE GROWTH.
HOW DO WE GO ABOUT DOING IT?

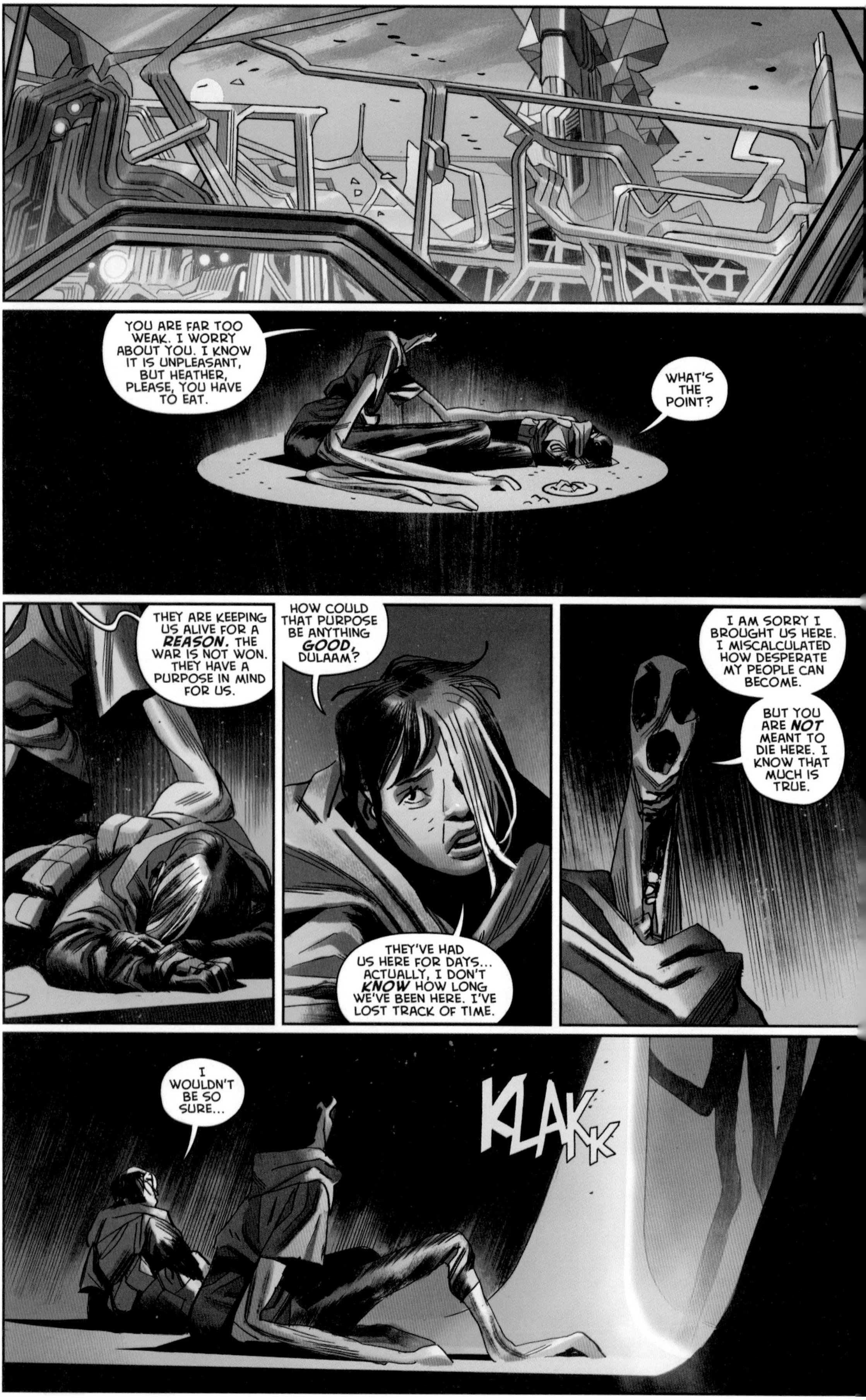

YOU ARE FAR TOO WEAK. I WORRY ABOUT YOU. I KNOW IT IS UNPLEASANT, BUT HEATHER, PLEASE, YOU HAVE TO EAT.
WHAT'S THE POINT?
THEY ARE KEEPING US ALIVE FOR A REASON. THE WAR IS NOT WON. THEY HAVE A PURPOSE IN MIND FOR US.
HOW COULD THAT PURPOSE BE ANYTHING GOOD, DULAAM?
THEY'VE HAD US HERE FOR DAYS... ACTUALLY, I DON'T KNOW HOW LONG WE'VE BEEN HERE. I'VE LOST TRACK OF TIME.
I AM SORRY I BROUGHT US HERE. I MISCALCULATED HOW DESPERATE MY PEOPLE CAN BECOME.
BUT YOU ARE NOT MEANT TO DIE HERE. I KNOW THAT MUCH IS TRUE.
I WOULDN'T BE SO SURE...
KLAKKK

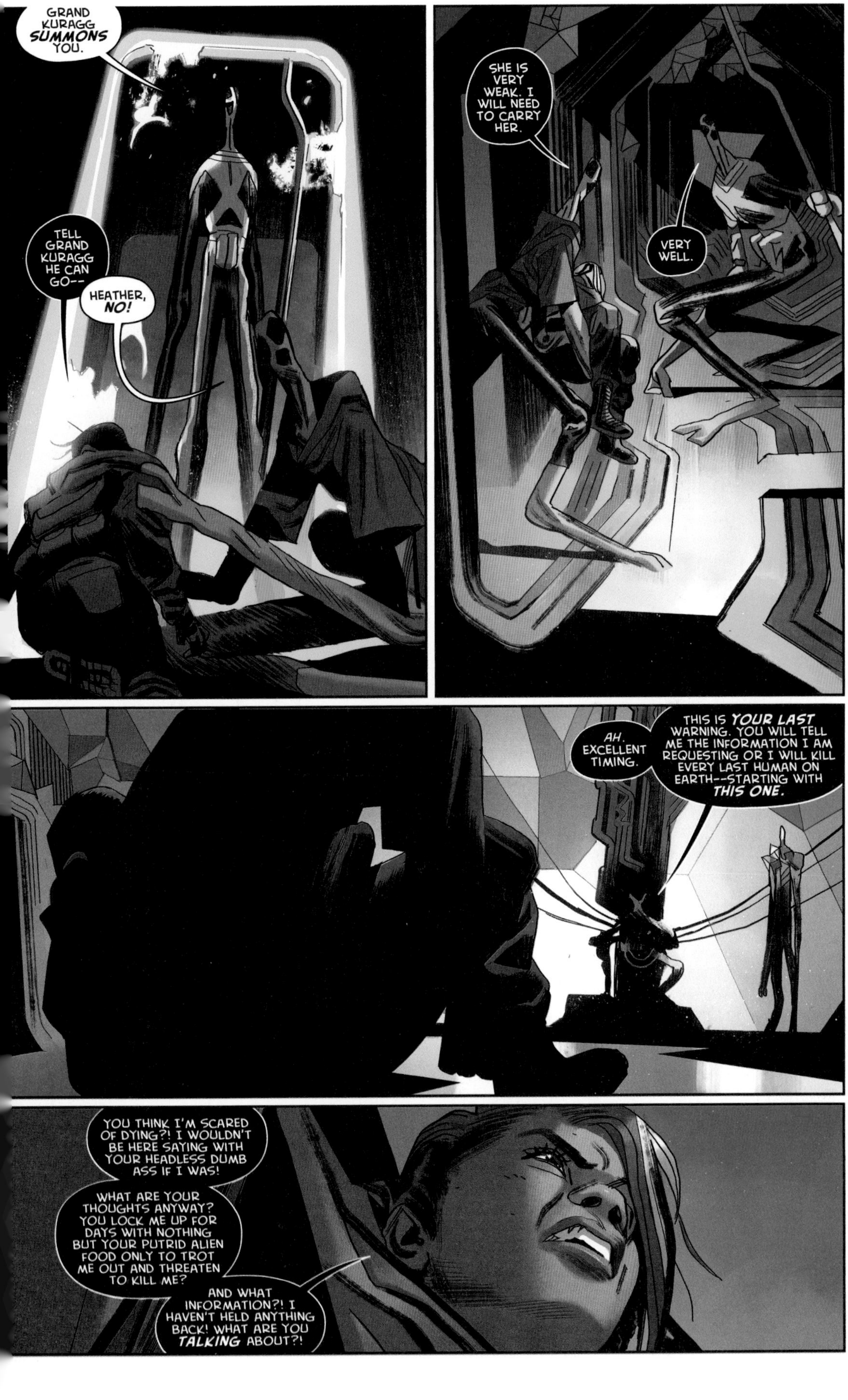
GRAND KURAGG SUMMONS YOU.
TELL GRAND KURAGG HE CAN GO--
HEATHER, NO!
SHE IS VERY WEAK. I WILL NEED TO CARRY HER.
VERY WELL.
AH. EXCELLENT TIMING.
THIS IS YOUR LAST WARNING. YOU WILL TELL ME THE INFORMATION I AM REQUESTING OR I WILL KILL EVERY LAST HUMAN ON EARTH--STARTING WITH THIS ONE.
YOU THINK I'M SCARED OF DYING?! I WOULDN'T BE HERE SAYING WITH YOUR HEADLESS DUMB ASS IF I WAS!
WHAT ARE YOUR THOUGHTS ANYWAY? YOU LOCK ME UP FOR DAYS WITH NOTHING BUT YOUR PUTRID ALIEN FOOD ONLY TO TROT ME OUT AND THREATEN TO KILL ME?
AND WHAT INFORMATION?! I HAVEN'T HELD ANYTHING BACK! WHAT ARE YOU TALKING ABOUT?!

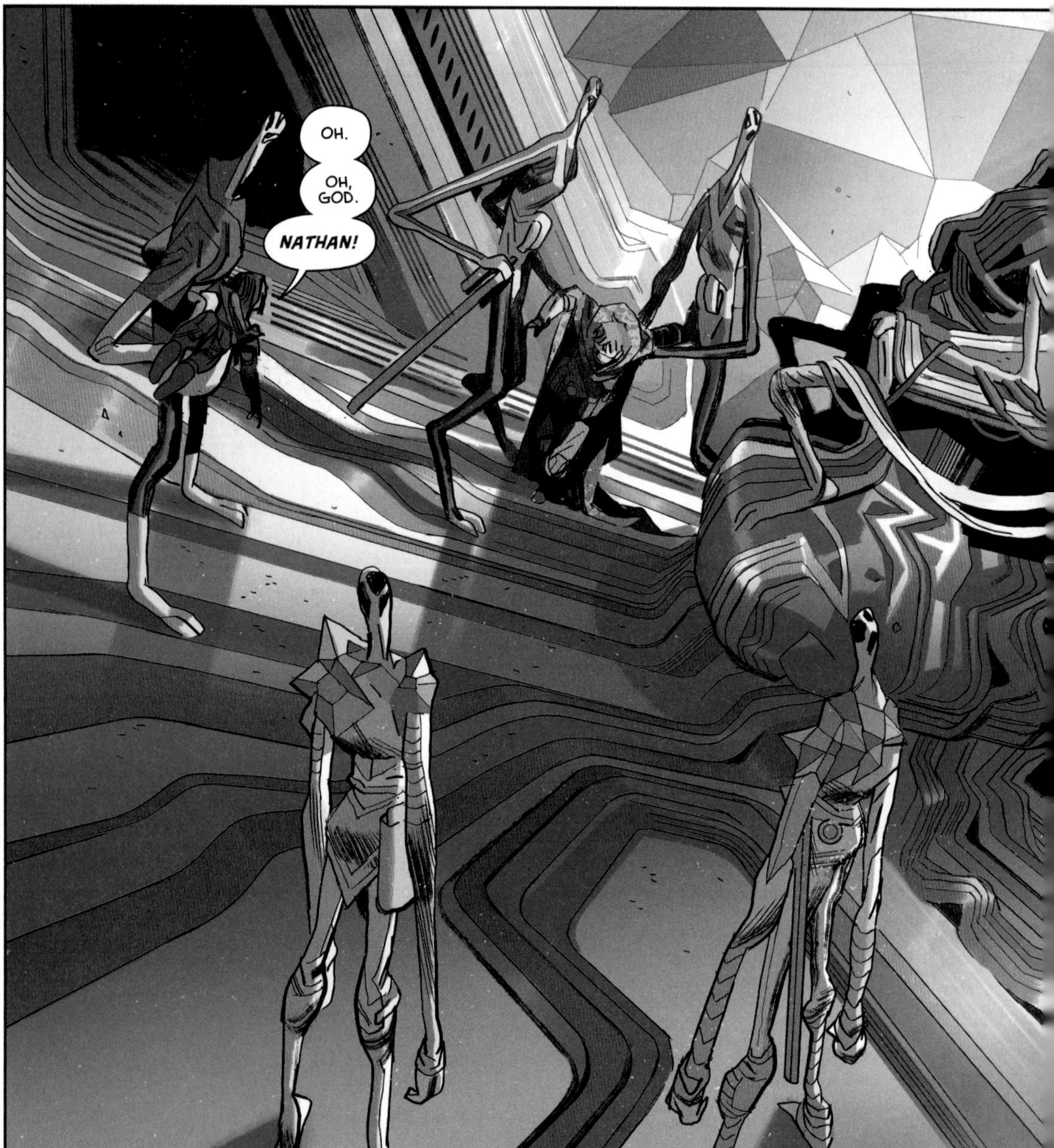
OH.
OH, GOD.
NATHAN!

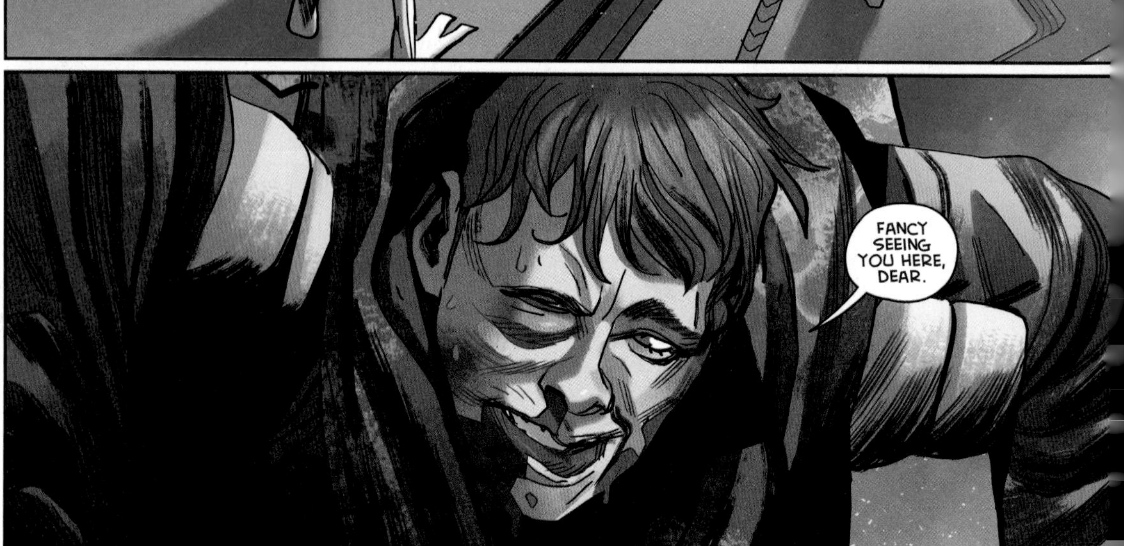
FANCY SEEING YOU HERE, DEAR.

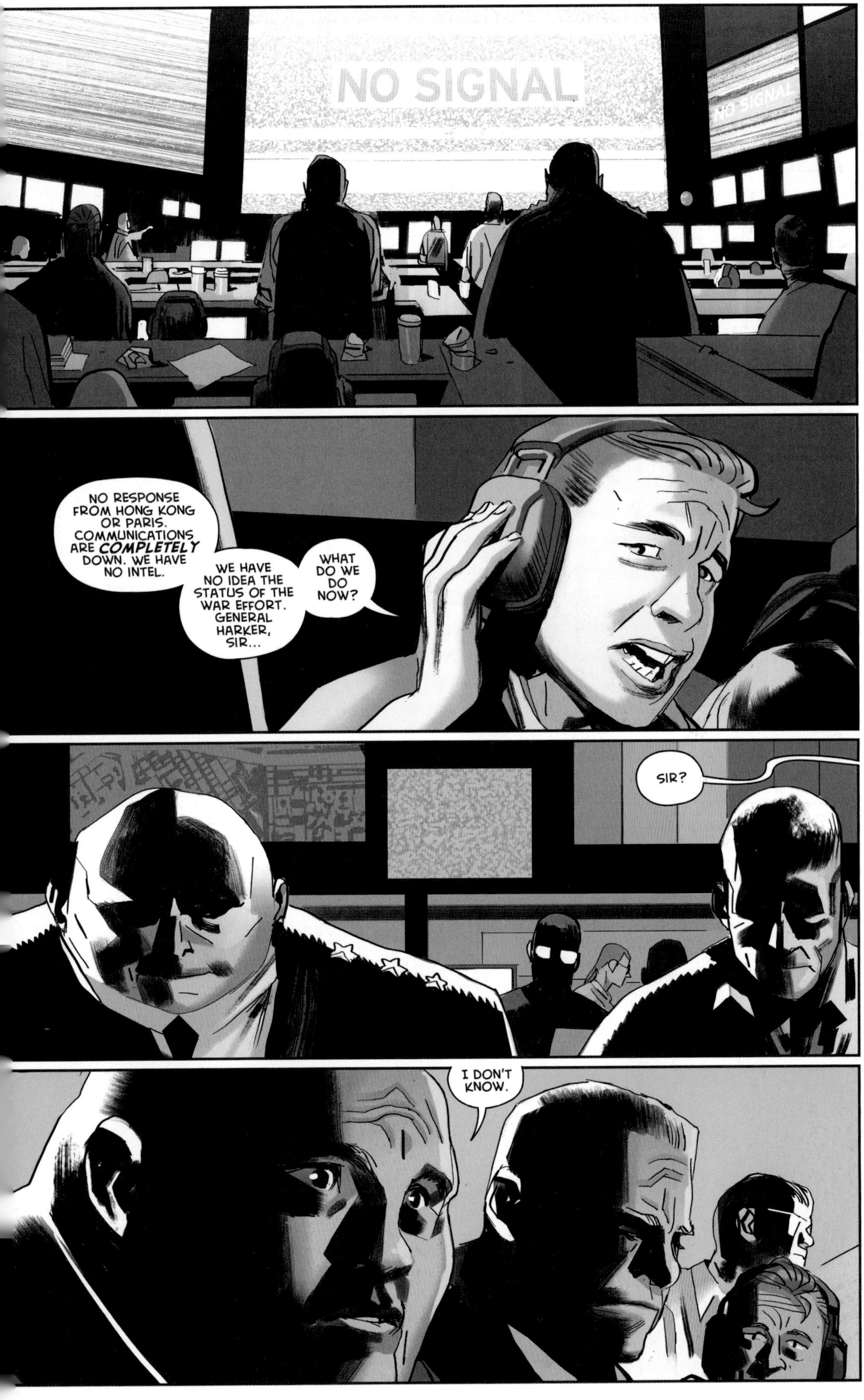
NO SIGNAL
NO SIGNAL
NO RESPONSE FROM HONG KONG OR PARIS. COMMUNICATIONS ARE COMPLETELY DOWN. WE HAVE NO INTEL.
WE HAVE NO IDEA THE STATUS OF THE WAR EFFORT. GENERAL HARKER, SIR...
WHAT DO WE DO NOW?
SIR?
I DON'T KNOW.

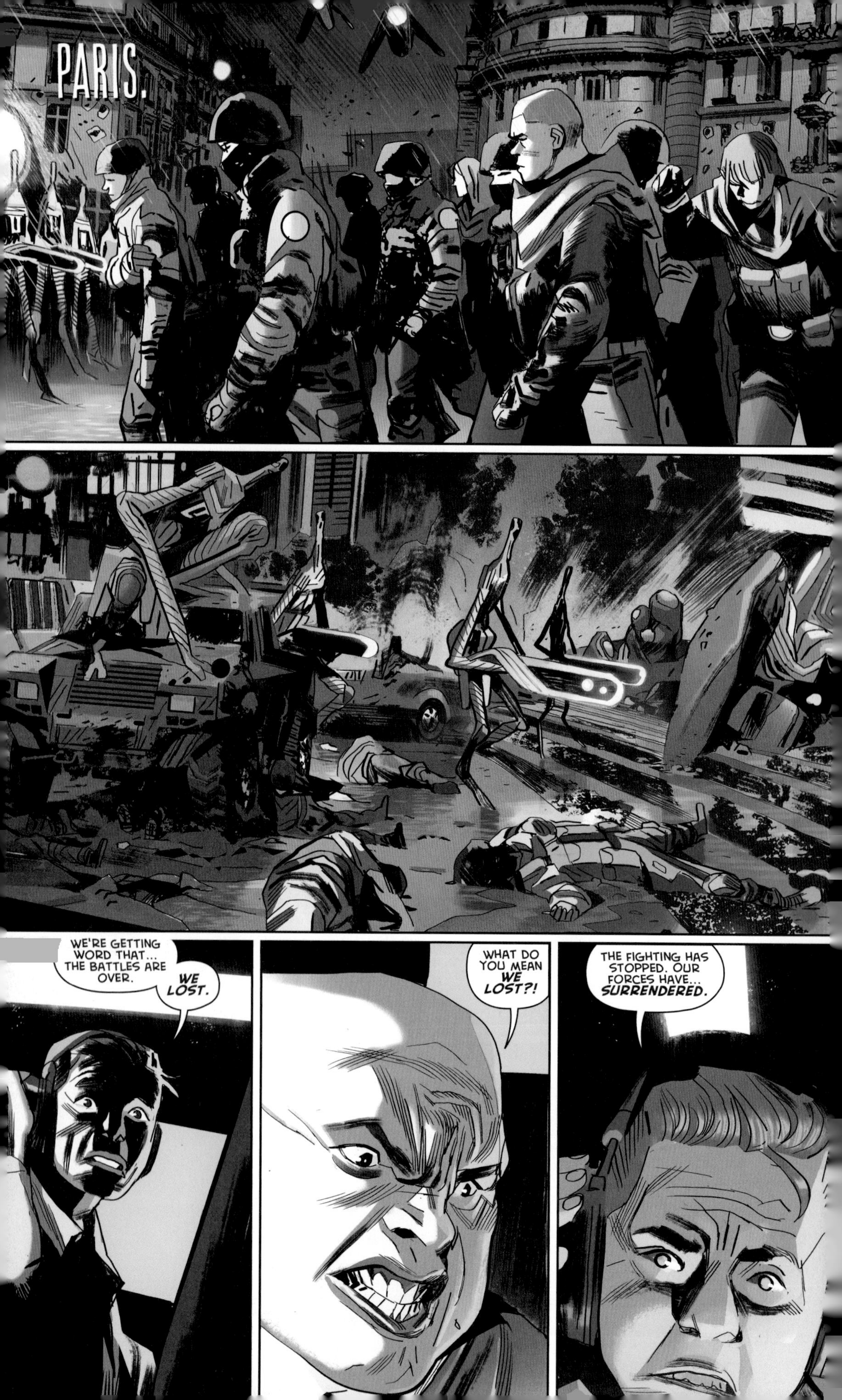
PARIS.
WE'RE GETTING WORD THAT... THE BATTLES ARE OVER.
WE LOST.
WHAT DO YOU MEAN WE LOST?!
THE FIGHTING HAS STOPPED. OUR FORCES HAVE... SURRENDERED.

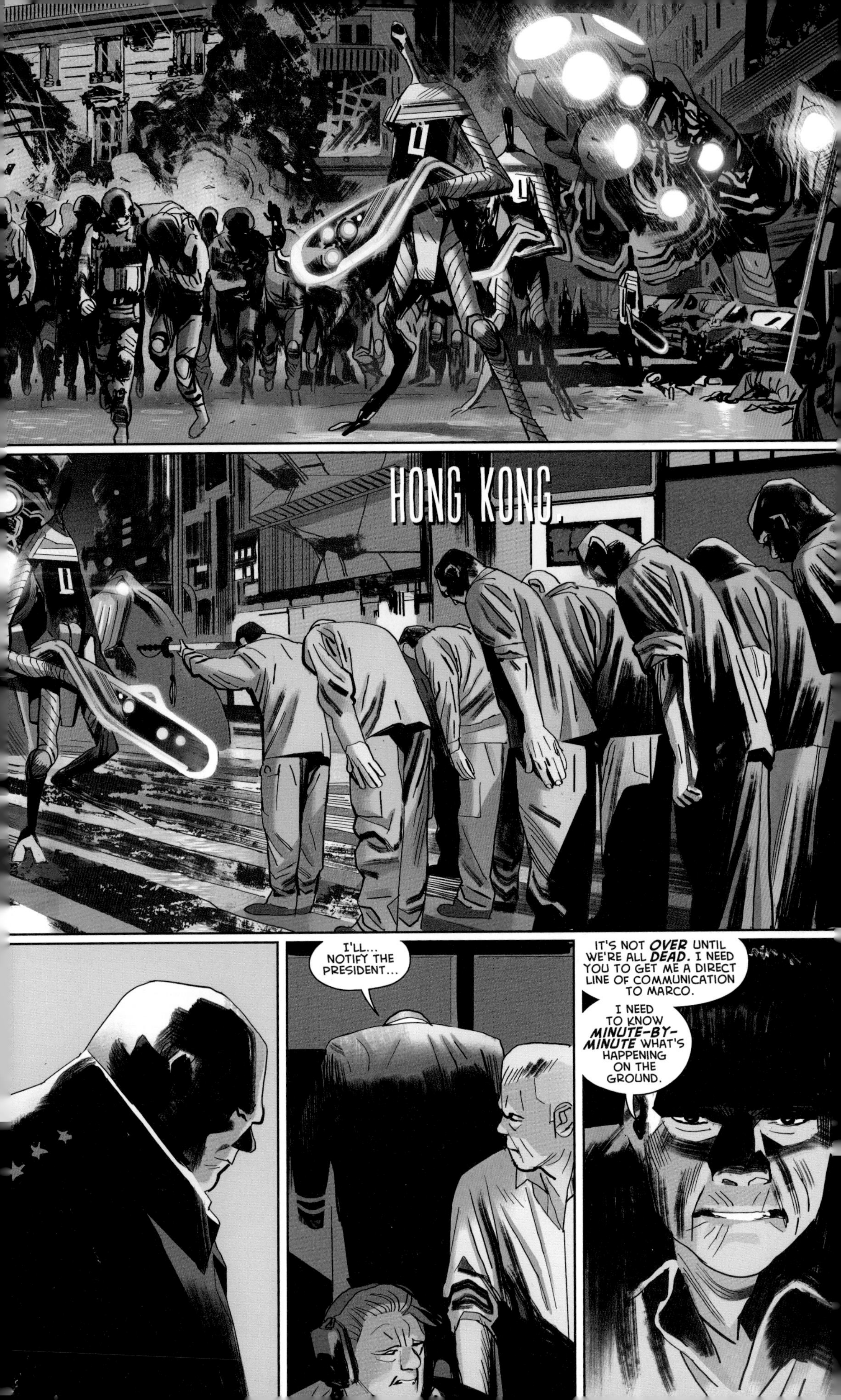
HONG KONG.
I'LL... NOTIFY THE PRESIDENT...
IT'S NOT OVER UNTIL WE'RE ALL DEAD. I NEED YOU TO GET ME A DIRECT LINE OF COMMUNICATION TO MARCO.
I NEED TO KNOW MINUTE-BY-MINUTE WHAT'S HAPPENING ON THE GROUND.

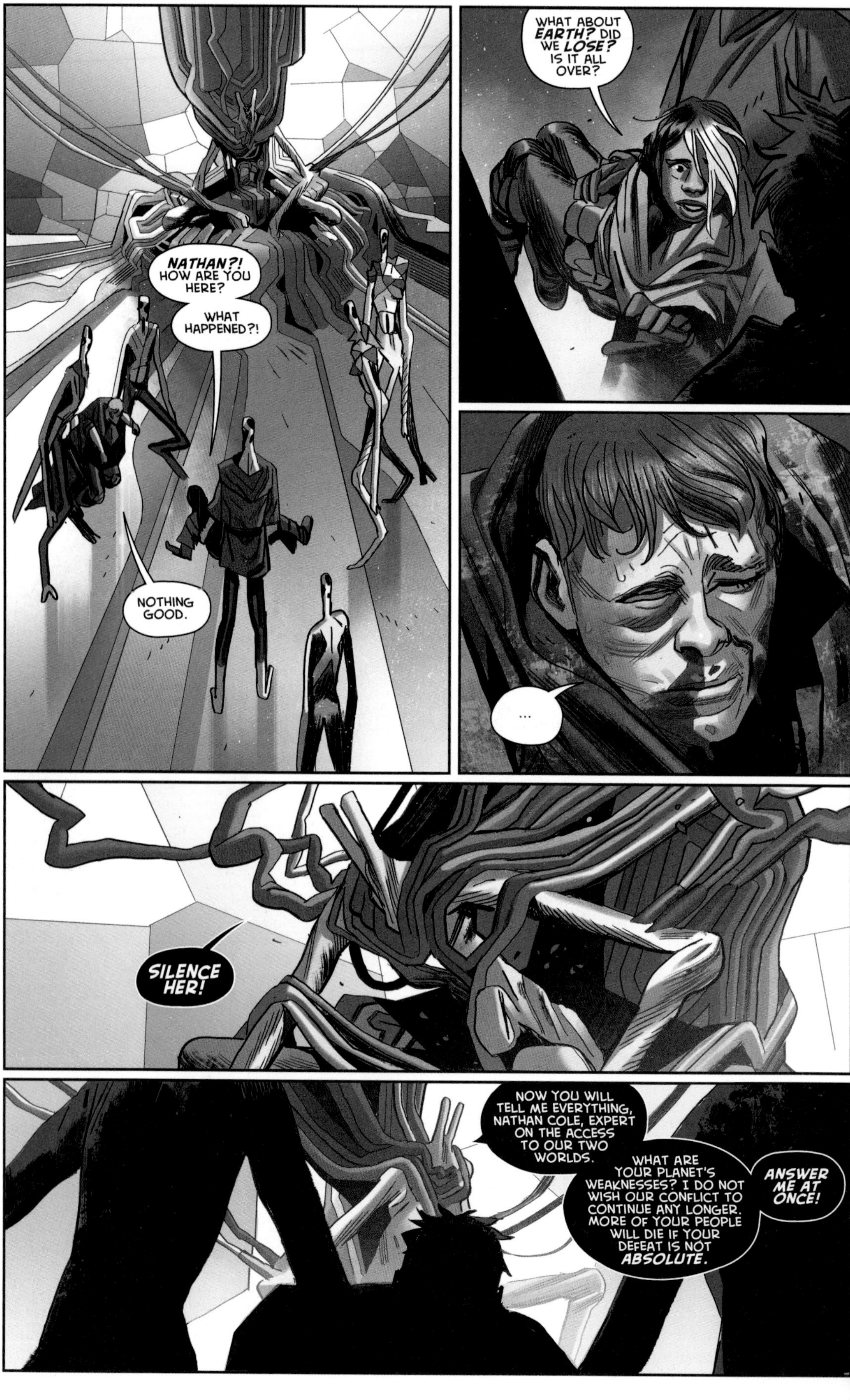
NATHAN?! HOW ARE YOU HERE?
WHAT HAPPENED?!
NOTHING GOOD.
WHAT ABOUT EARTH? DID WE LOSE? IS IT ALL OVER?
...
SILENCE HER!
NOW YOU WILL TELL ME EVERYTHING, NATHAN COLE, EXPERT ON THE ACCESS TO OUR TWO WORLDS.
WHAT ARE YOUR PLANET'S WEAKNESSES? I DO NOT WISH OUR CONFLICT TO CONTINUE ANY LONGER. MORE OF YOUR PEOPLE WILL DIE IF YOUR DEFEAT IS NOT ABSOLUTE.
ANSWER ME AT ONCE!

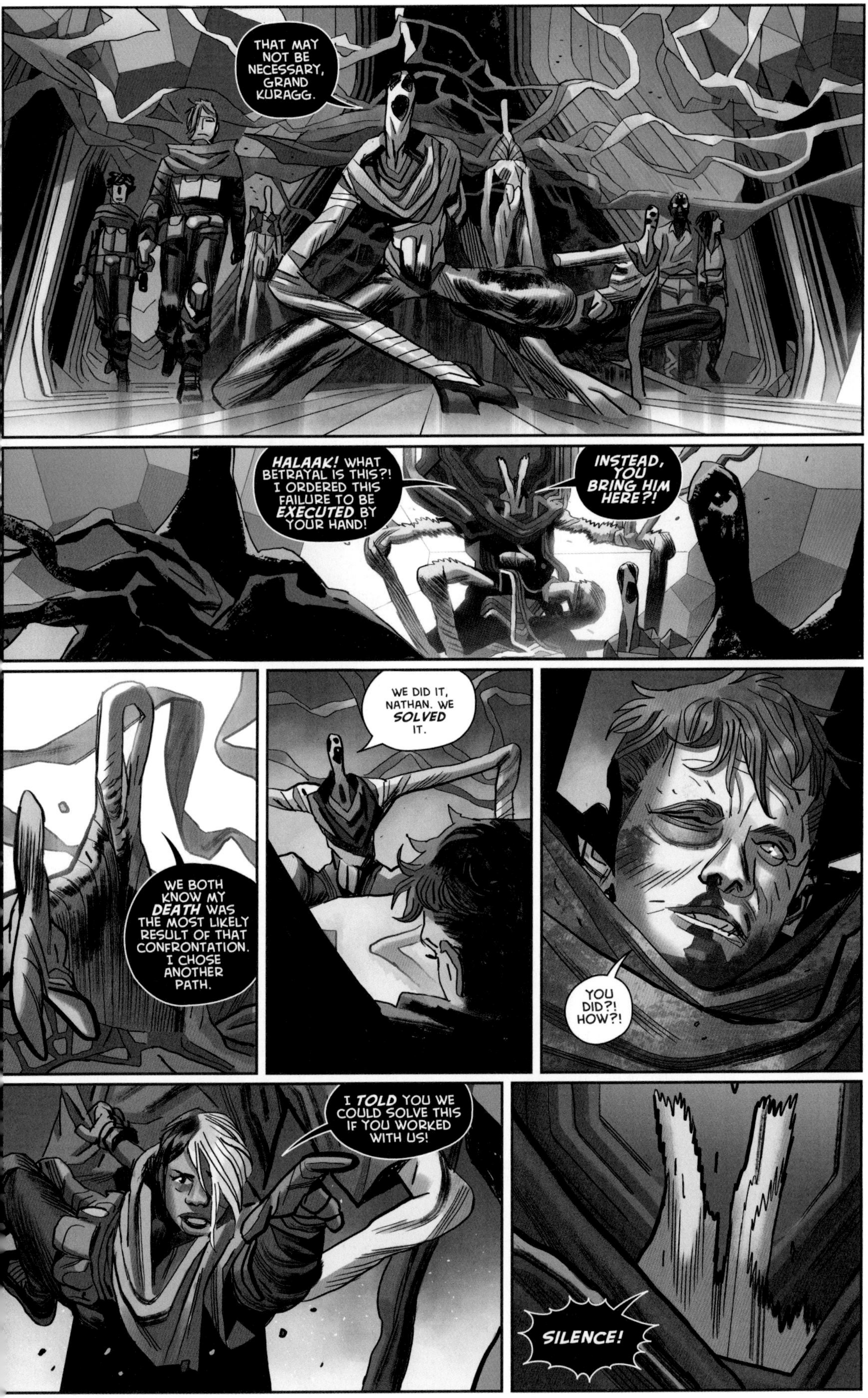
THAT MAY NOT BE NECESSARY, GRAND KURAGG.
HALAAK! WHAT BETRAYAL IS THIS?! I ORDERED THIS FAILURE TO BE EXECUTED BY YOUR HAND!
INSTEAD, YOU BRING HIM HERE?!
WE BOTH KNOW MY DEATH WAS THE MOST LIKELY RESULT OF THAT CONFRONTATION. I CHOSE ANOTHER PATH.
WE DID IT, NATHAN. WE SOLVED IT.
YOU DID?! HOW?!
I TOLD YOU WE COULD SOLVE THIS IF YOU WORKED WITH US!
SILENCE!

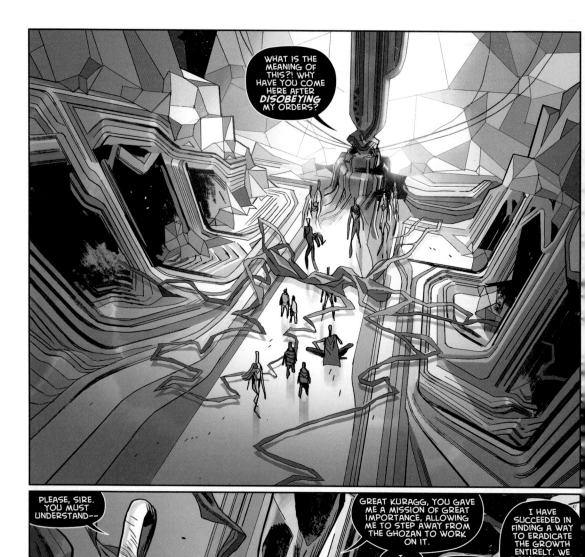

WHAT IS THE MEANING OF THIS?! WHY HAVE YOU COME HERE AFTER *DISOBEYING* MY ORDERS?

PLEASE, SIRE. YOU MUST UNDERSTAND--

GREAT KURAGG, YOU GAVE ME A MISSION OF GREAT IMPORTANCE, ALLOWING ME TO STEP AWAY FROM THE GHOZAN TO WORK ON IT.

I *FAILED* YOU.

I WAS UNABLE TO AVERT THIS WAR, BUT ALL IS NOT LOST. I DID NOT FAIL ENTIRELY. I COMPLETED MY TASK, ONLY LATE.

I HAVE SUCCEEDED IN FINDING A WAY TO ERADICATE THE GROWTH ENTIRELY. WE DON'T HAVE TO ABANDON OUR WORLD. WE DON'T HAVE TO CONQUER THEIRS.

WHAT IF THE CONQUERING HAS ALREADY BEEN *DONE?* OUR PEOPLE HAVE FOUGHT HARD AND SUCCEEDED. AM I TO SULLY THEIR VICTORY WITH SURRENDER AND RETREAT?

INSANITY.

YOU HAVE COME BEFORE THE GREAT KURAGG TO PROPOSE INSANITY!

YOU ATTACKED US TO SOLVE A PROBLEM THAT IS NOW SOLVED. IT IS *YOU* WHO ARE INSANE!

...

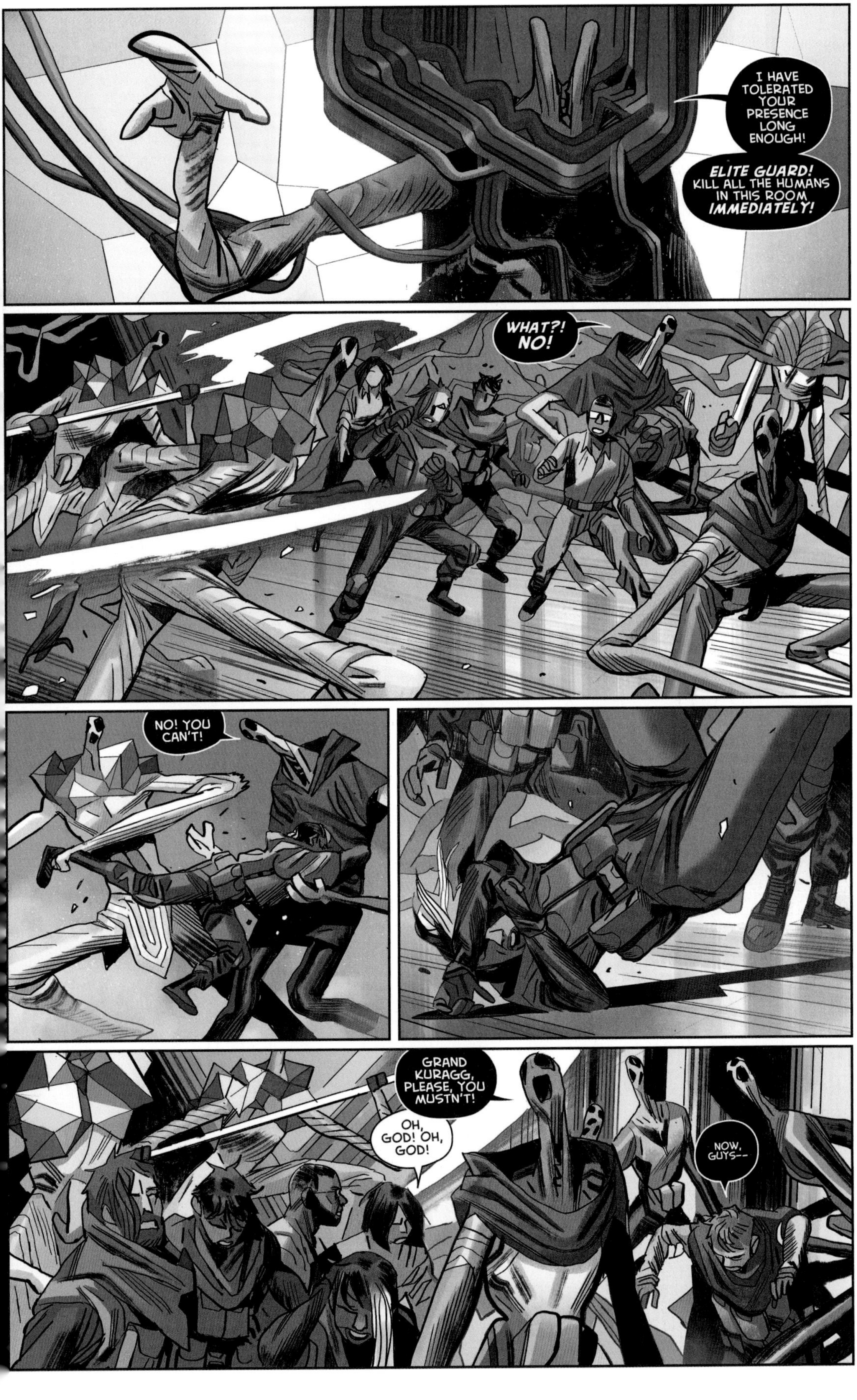
I HAVE TOLERATED YOUR PRESENCE LONG ENOUGH!
ELITE GUARD! KILL ALL THE HUMANS IN THIS ROOM IMMEDIATELY!
WHAT?! NO!
NO! YOU CAN'T!
GRAND KURAGG, PLEASE, YOU MUSTN'T!
OH, GOD! OH, GOD!
NOW, GUYS--

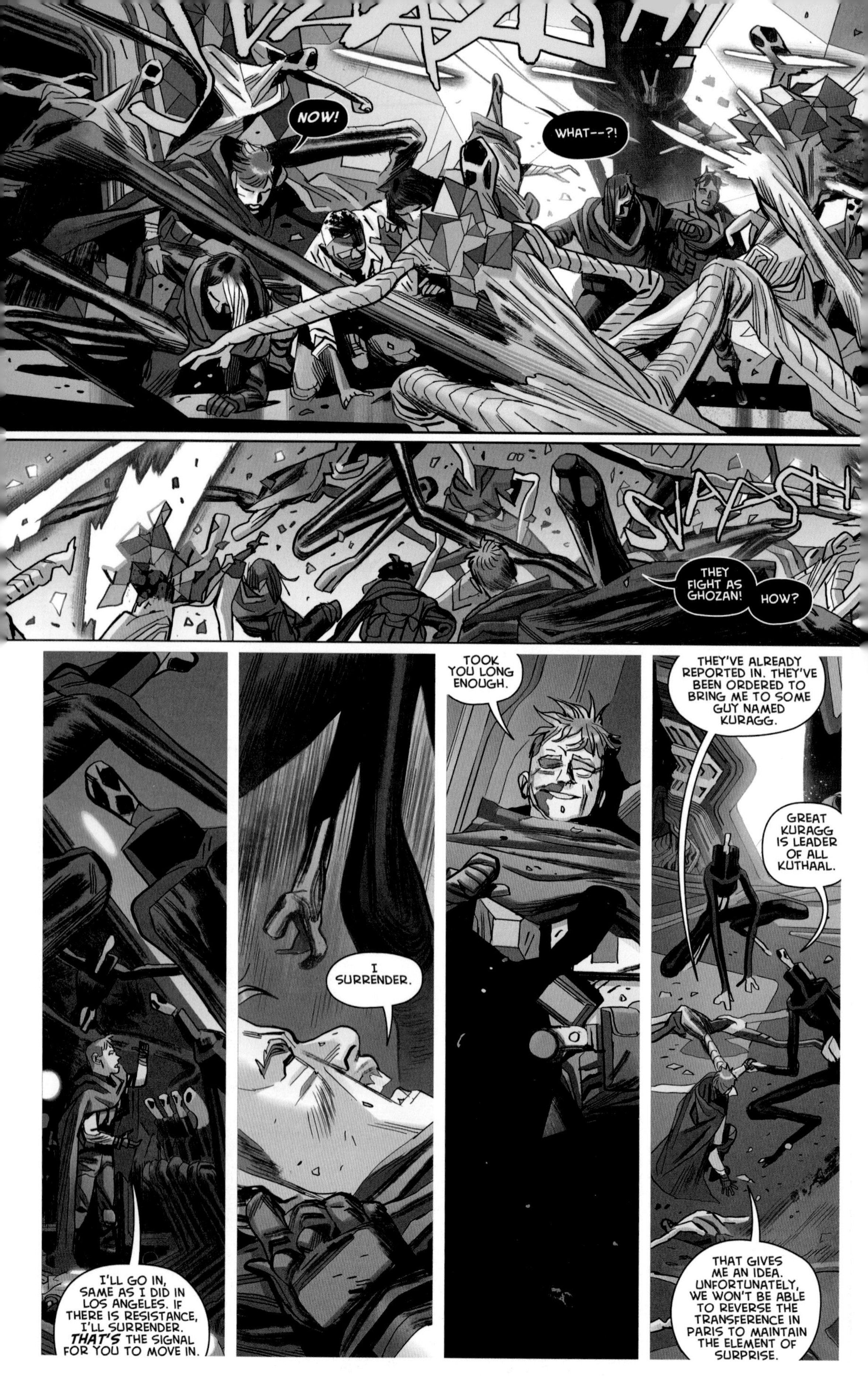
NOW!
WHAT--?!
SPLASH
THEY FIGHT AS GHOZAN!
HOW?
I'LL GO IN, SAME AS I DID IN LOS ANGELES. IF THERE IS RESISTANCE, I'LL SURRENDER. THAT'S THE SIGNAL FOR YOU TO MOVE IN.
I SURRENDER.
TOOK YOU LONG ENOUGH.
THEY'VE ALREADY REPORTED IN. THEY'VE BEEN ORDERED TO BRING ME TO SOME GUY NAMED KURAGG.
GREAT KURAGG IS LEADER OF ALL KUTHAAL.
THAT GIVES ME AN IDEA. UNFORTUNATELY, WE WON'T BE ABLE TO REVERSE THE TRANSFERENCE IN PARIS TO MAINTAIN THE ELEMENT OF SURPRISE.

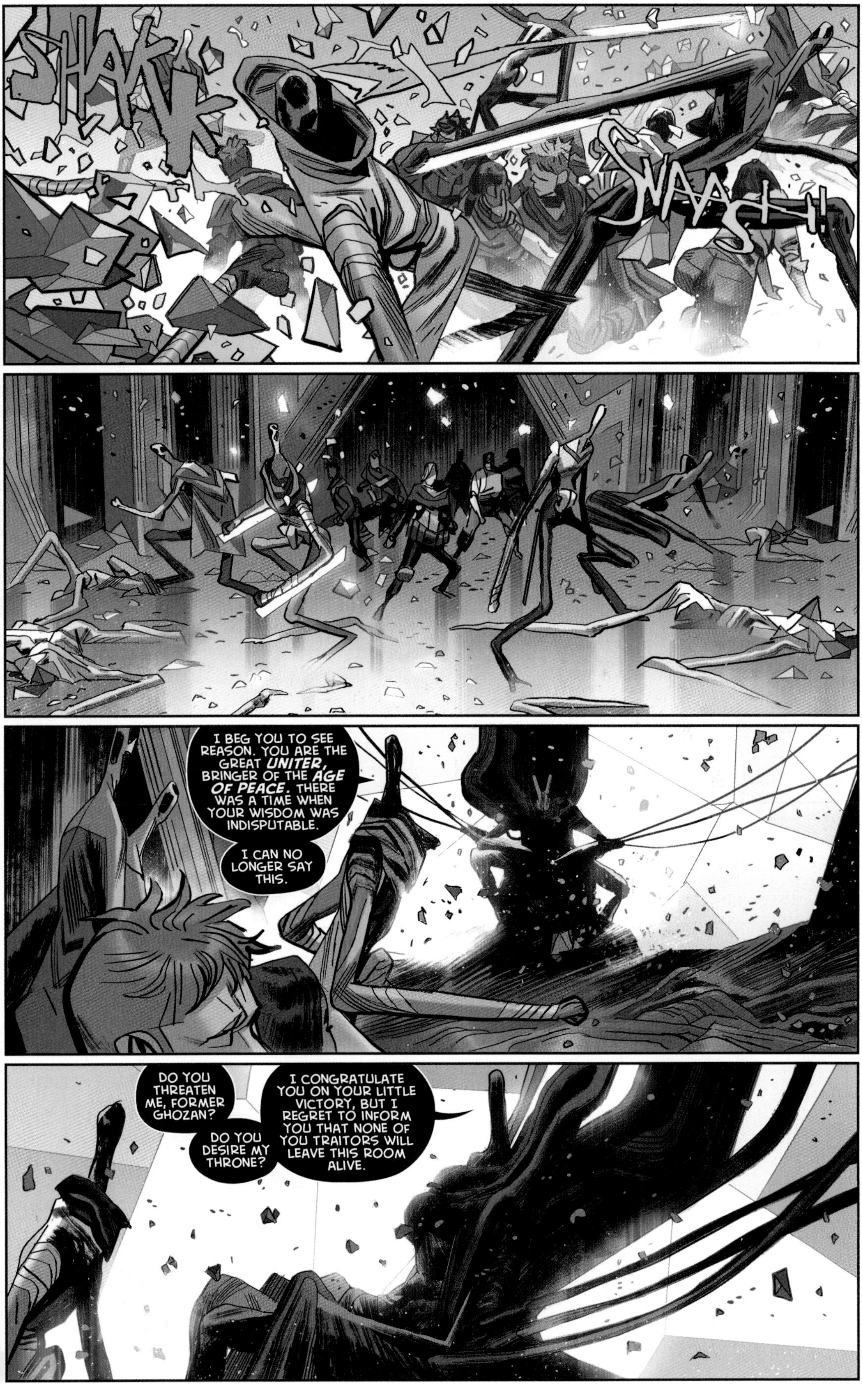
SHAKK
SWAASHH
I BEG YOU TO SEE REASON. YOU ARE THE GREAT UNITER, BRINGER OF THE AGE OF PEACE. THERE WAS A TIME WHEN YOUR WISDOM WAS INDISPUTABLE.
I CAN NO LONGER SAY THIS.
DO YOU THREATEN ME, FORMER GHOZAN?
DO YOU DESIRE MY THRONE?
I CONGRATULATE YOU ON YOUR LITTLE VICTORY, BUT I REGRET TO INFORM YOU THAT NONE OF YOU TRAITORS WILL LEAVE THIS ROOM ALIVE.

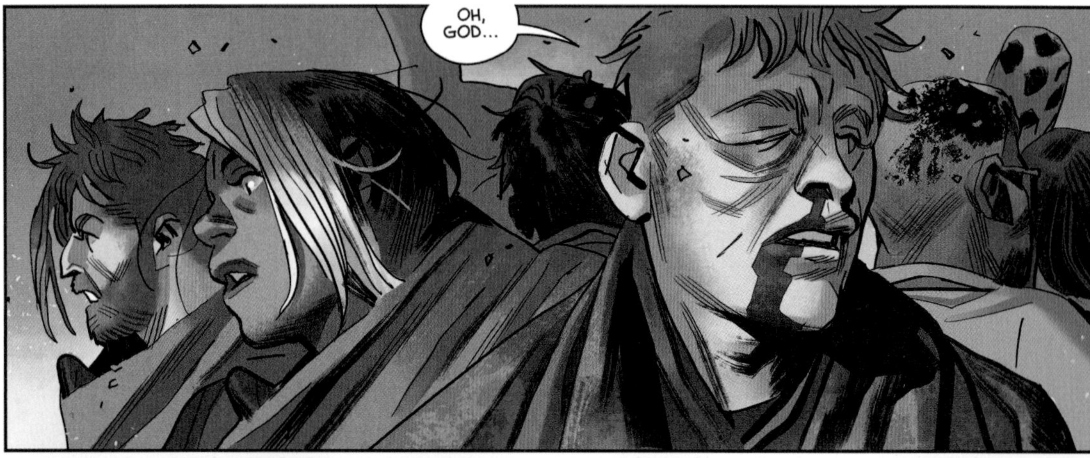
OH, GOD...

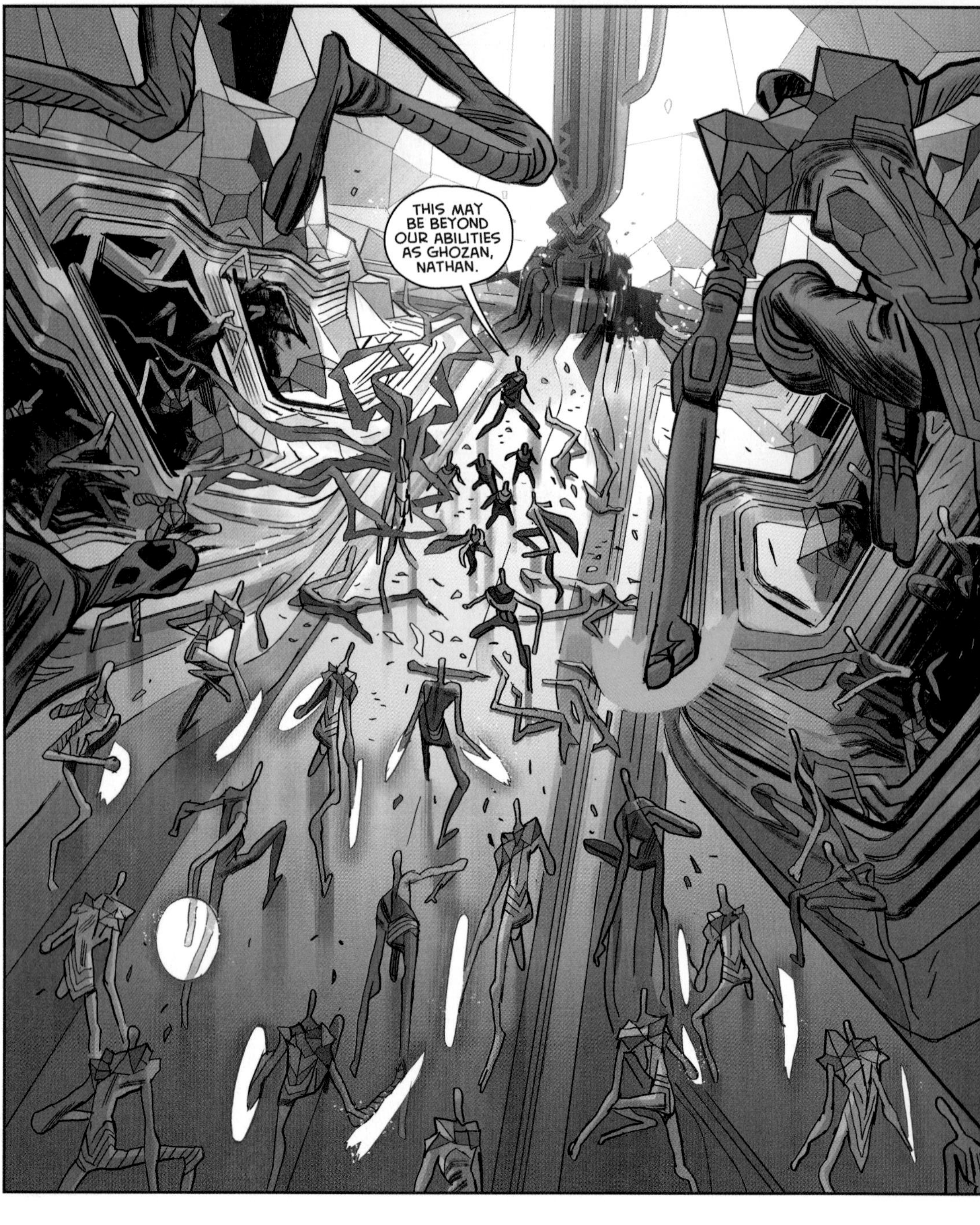
THIS MAY BE BEYOND OUR ABILITIES AS GHOZAN, NATHAN.

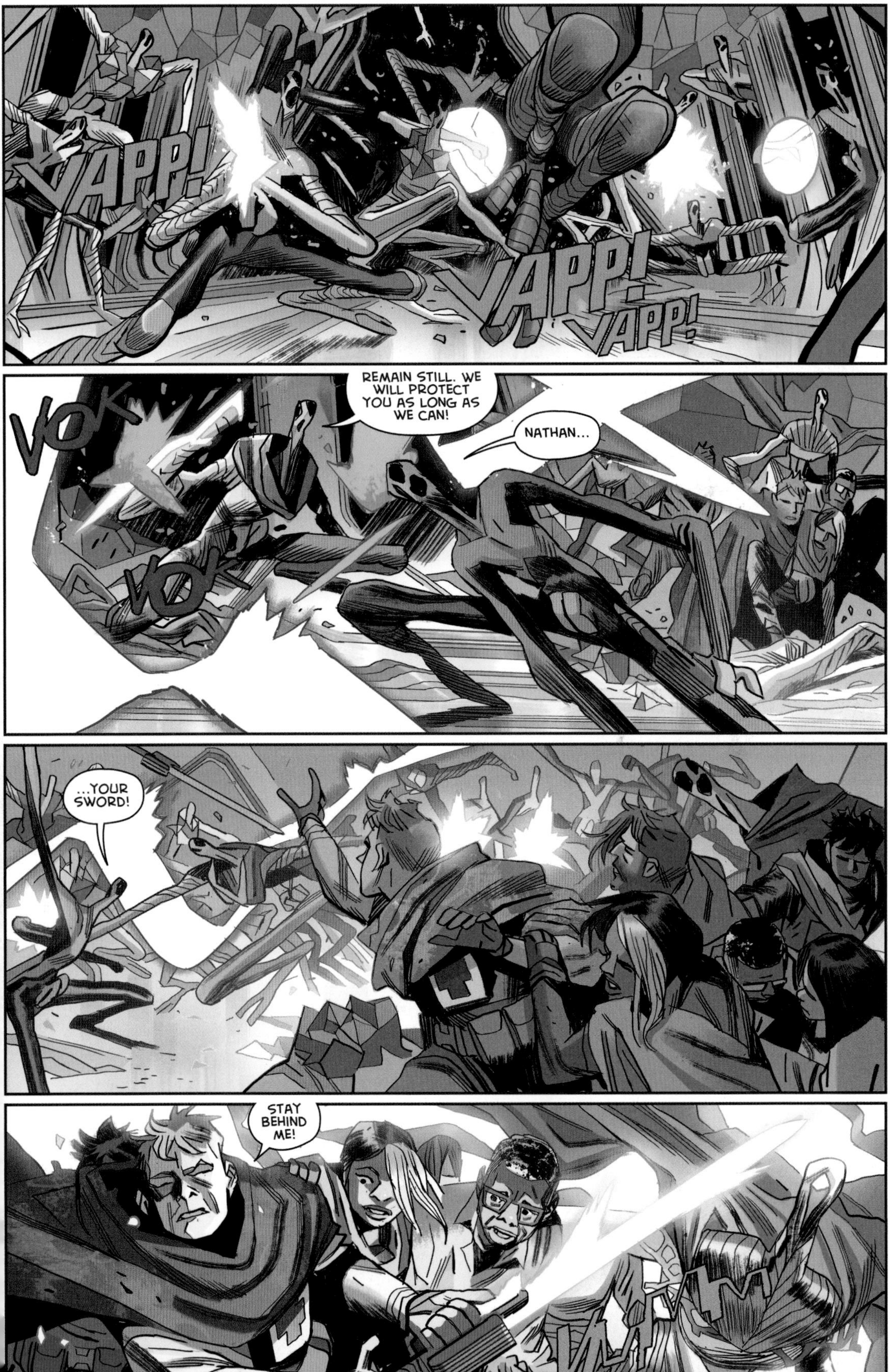
VAPP!
VAPP!
VAPP!
VOK
VOK
REMAIN STILL. WE WILL PROTECT YOU AS LONG AS WE CAN!
NATHAN...
...YOUR SWORD!
STAY BEHIND ME!

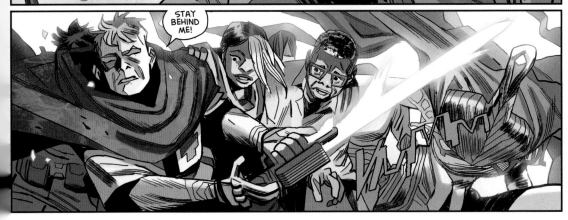

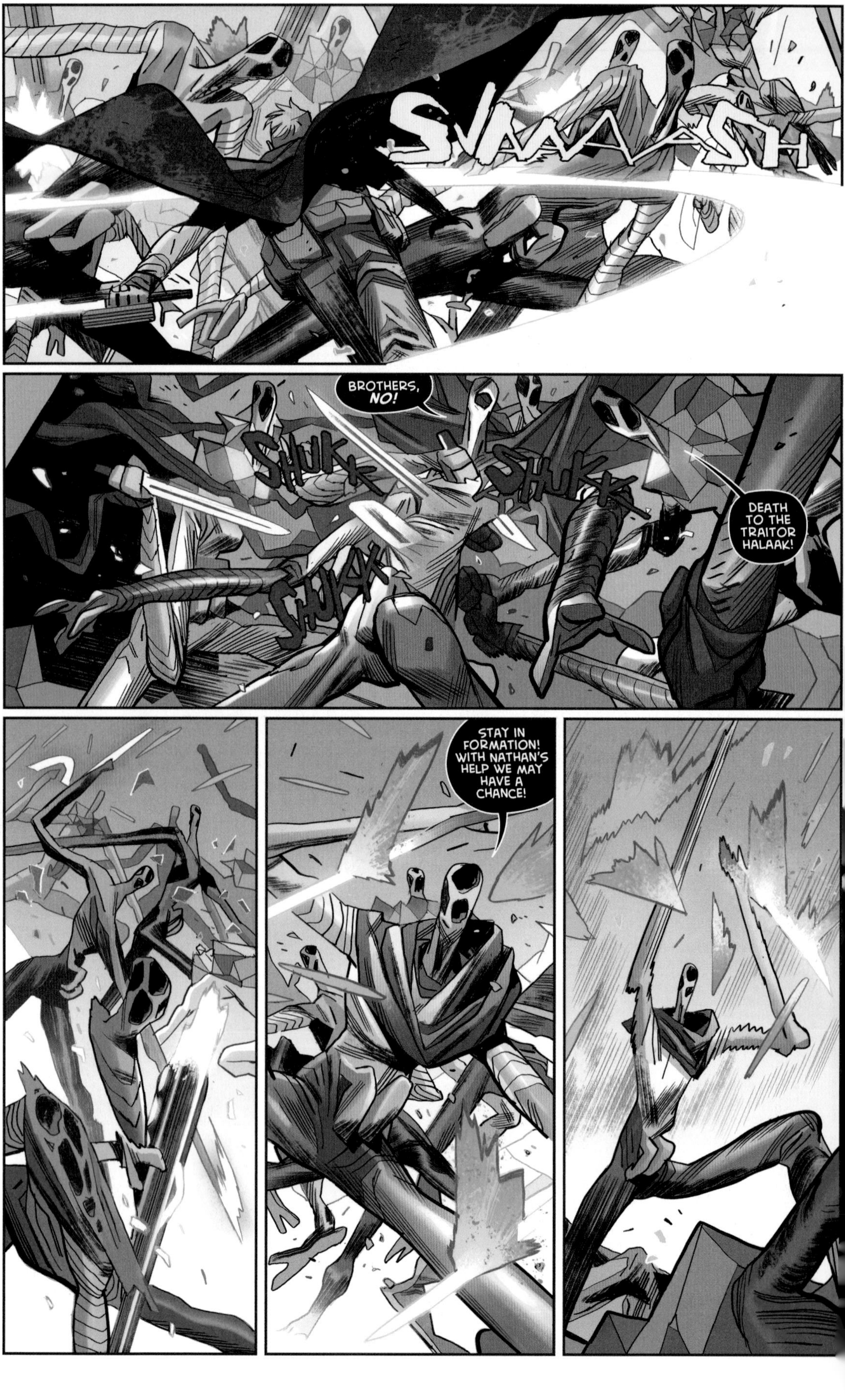
SWAAASH
BROTHERS, NO!
SHUKK
SHUKK
SHUKK
DEATH TO THE TRAITOR HALAAK!
STAY IN FORMATION! WITH NATHAN'S HELP WE MAY HAVE A CHANCE!

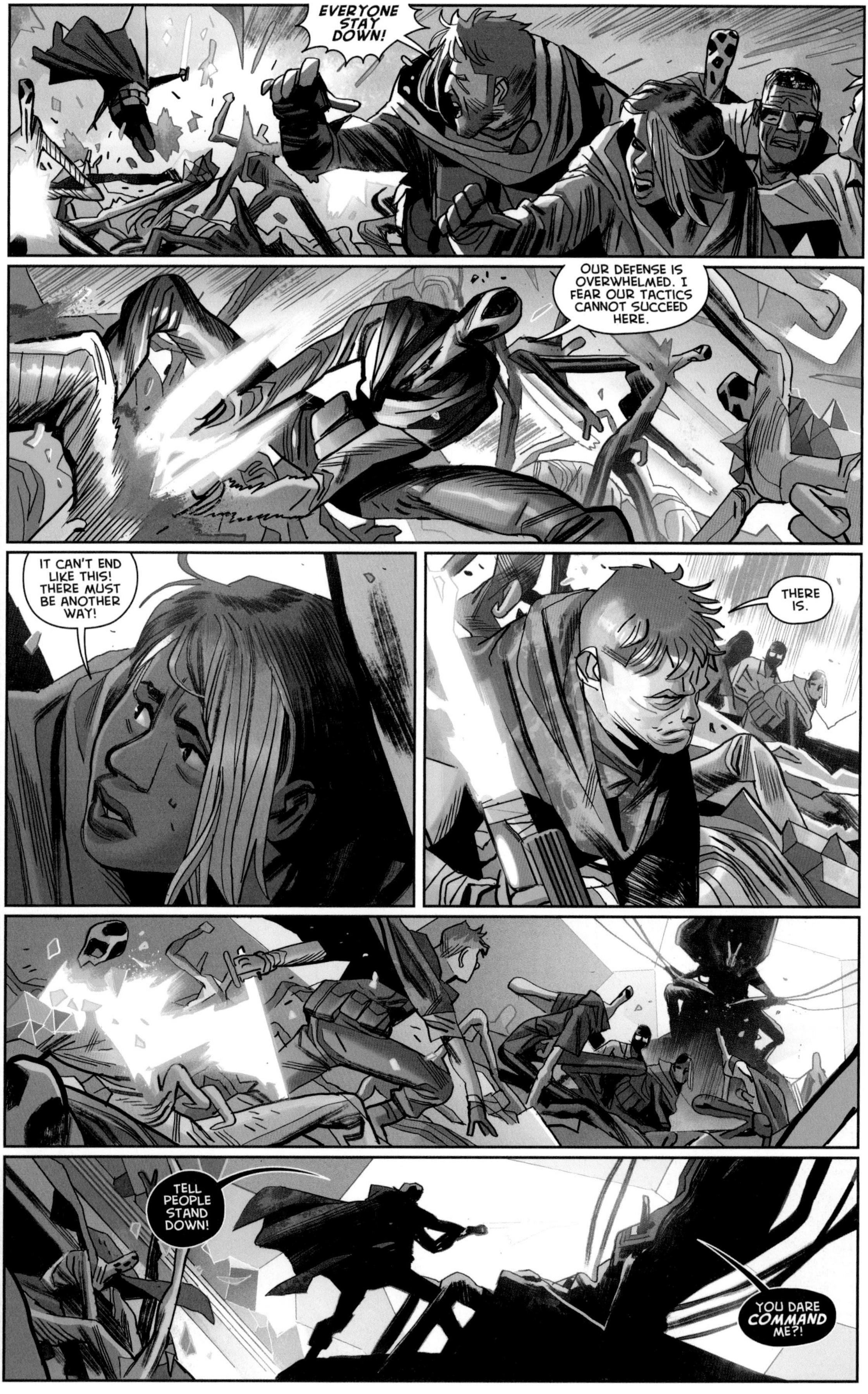
EVERYONE STAY DOWN!
OUR DEFENSE IS OVERWHELMED. I FEAR OUR TACTICS CANNOT SUCCEED HERE.
IT CAN'T END LIKE THIS! THERE MUST BE ANOTHER WAY!
THERE IS.
TELL PEOPLE STAND DOWN!
YOU DARE COMMAND ME?!

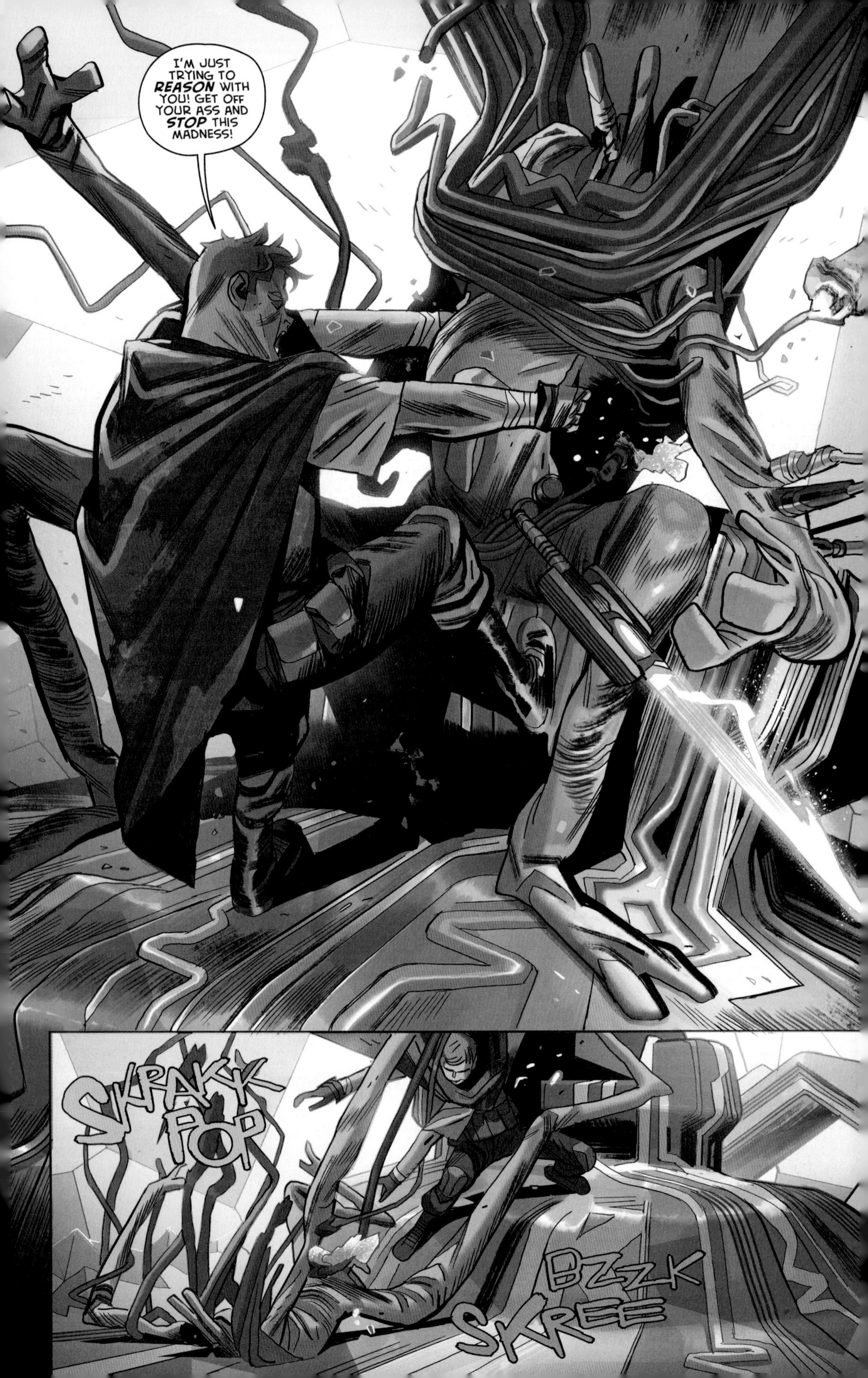
I'M JUST TRYING TO **REASON** WITH YOU! GET OFF YOUR ASS AND **STOP** THIS MADNESS!
SKRAKK
POP
BZZK
SKREE

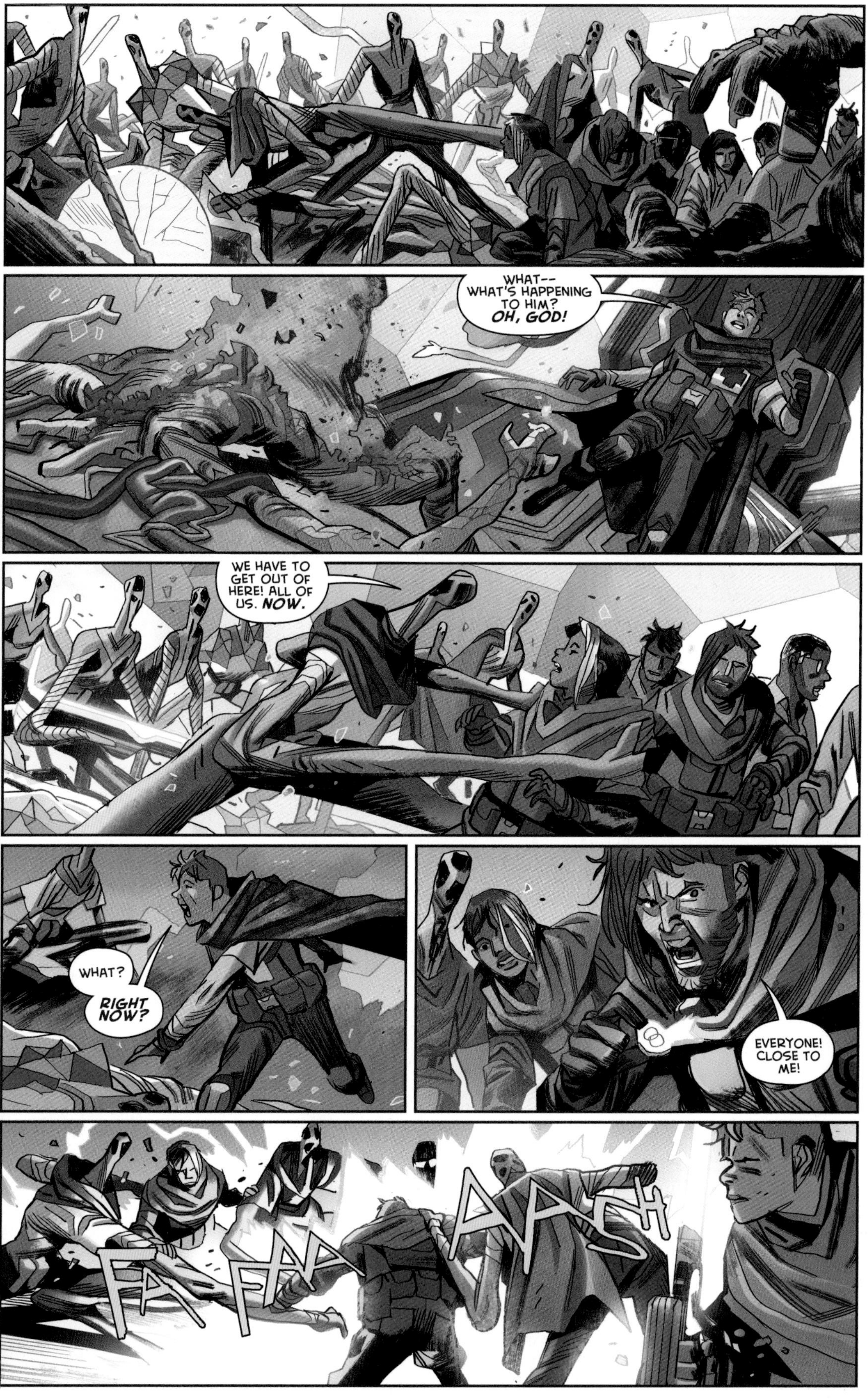
WHAT-- WHAT'S HAPPENING TO HIM? OH, GOD!
WE HAVE TO GET OUT OF HERE! ALL OF US. NOW.
WHAT?
RIGHT NOW?
EVERYONE! CLOSE TO ME!
FA FAA AAASH

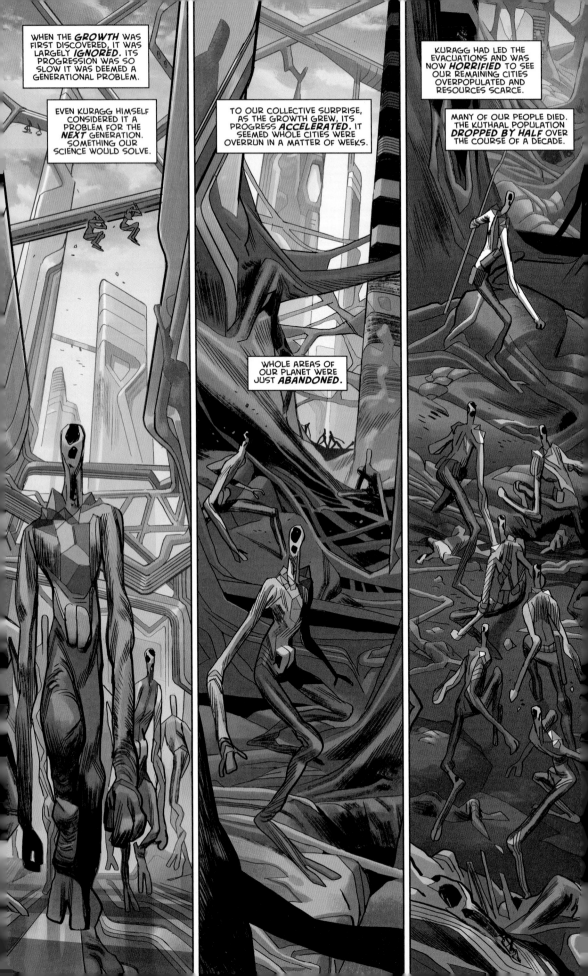

WHEN THE *GROWTH* WAS FIRST DISCOVERED, IT WAS LARGELY *IGNORED*. ITS PROGRESSION WAS SO SLOW IT WAS DEEMED A GENERATIONAL PROBLEM.

EVEN KURAGG HIMSELF CONSIDERED IT A PROBLEM FOR THE *NEXT* GENERATION. SOMETHING OUR SCIENCE WOULD SOLVE.

TO OUR COLLECTIVE SURPRISE, AS THE GROWTH GREW, ITS PROGRESS *ACCELERATED*. IT SEEMED WHOLE CITIES WERE OVERRUN IN A MATTER OF WEEKS.

WHOLE AREAS OF OUR PLANET WERE JUST *ABANDONED*.

KURAGG HAD LED THE EVACUATIONS AND WAS NOW *HORRIFIED* TO SEE OUR REMAINING CITIES OVERPOPULATED AND RESOURCES SCARCE.

MANY OF OUR PEOPLE DIED. THE KUTHAAL POPULATION *DROPPED BY HALF* OVER THE COURSE OF A DECADE.

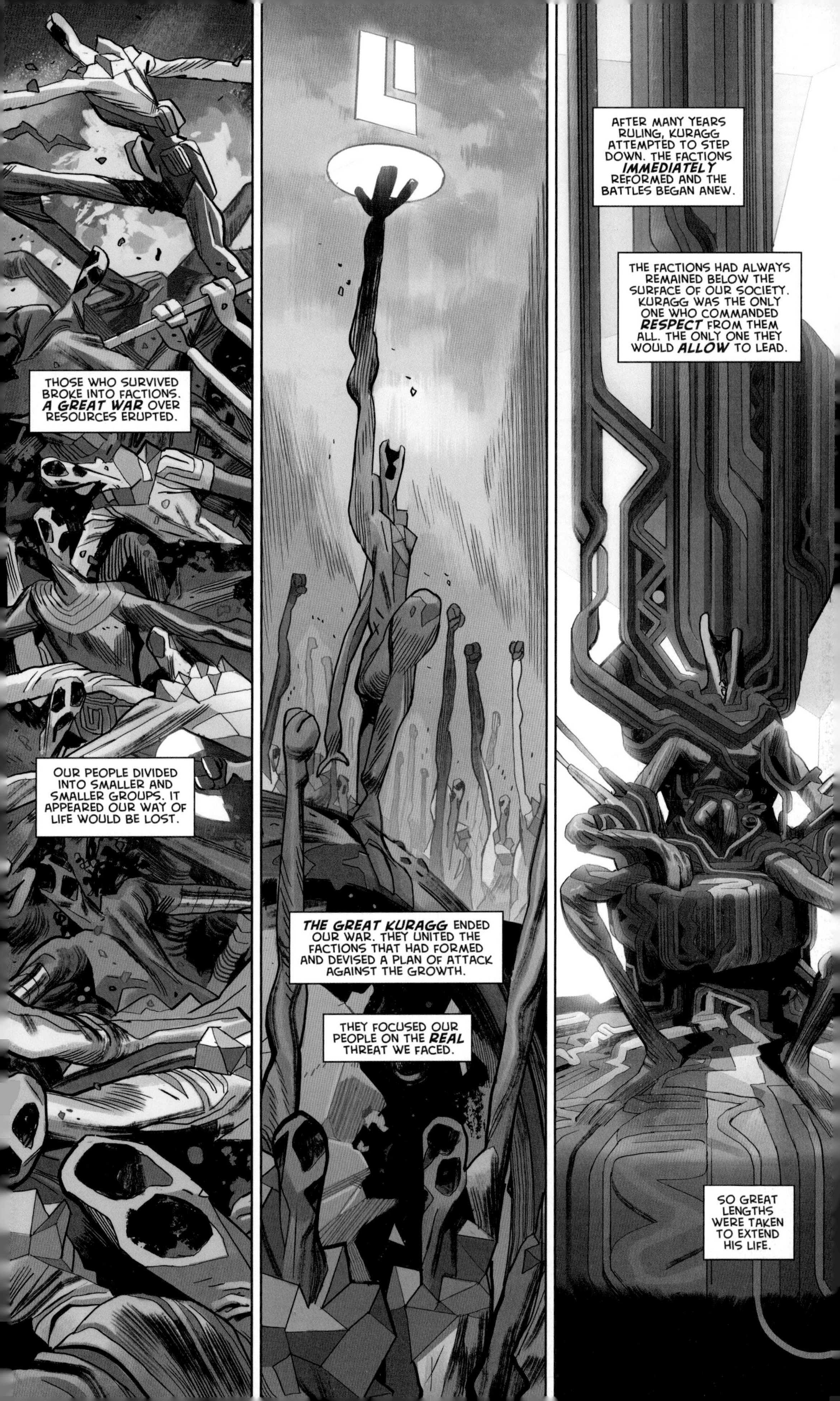
THOSE WHO SURVIVED BROKE INTO FACTIONS. ***A GREAT WAR*** OVER RESOURCES ERUPTED.
OUR PEOPLE DIVIDED INTO SMALLER AND SMALLER GROUPS. IT APPEARED OUR WAY OF LIFE WOULD BE LOST.
THE GREAT KURAGG ENDED OUR WAR. THEY UNITED THE FACTIONS THAT HAD FORMED AND DEVISED A PLAN OF ATTACK AGAINST THE GROWTH.
THEY FOCUSED OUR PEOPLE ON THE ***REAL*** THREAT WE FACED.
AFTER MANY YEARS RULING, KURAGG ATTEMPTED TO STEP DOWN. THE FACTIONS ***IMMEDIATELY*** REFORMED AND THE BATTLES BEGAN ANEW.
THE FACTIONS HAD ALWAYS REMAINED BELOW THE SURFACE OF OUR SOCIETY. KURAGG WAS THE ONLY ONE WHO COMMANDED ***RESPECT*** FROM THEM ALL. THE ONLY ONE THEY WOULD ***ALLOW*** TO LEAD.
SO GREAT LENGTHS WERE TAKEN TO EXTEND HIS LIFE.

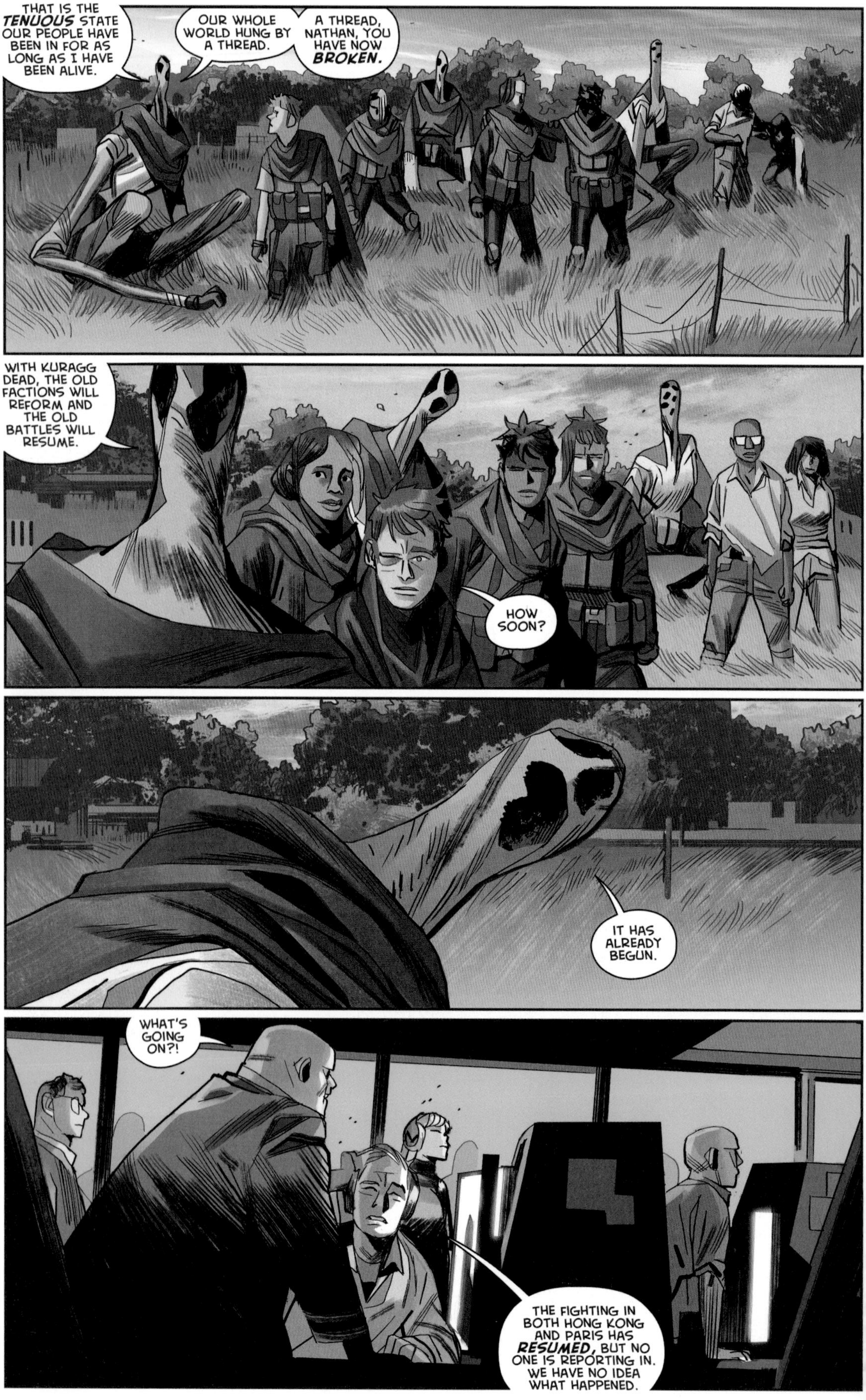
THAT IS THE TENUOUS STATE OUR PEOPLE HAVE BEEN IN FOR AS LONG AS I HAVE BEEN ALIVE.
OUR WHOLE WORLD HUNG BY A THREAD.
A THREAD, NATHAN, YOU HAVE NOW BROKEN.
WITH KURAGG DEAD, THE OLD FACTIONS WILL REFORM AND THE OLD BATTLES WILL RESUME.
HOW SOON?
IT HAS ALREADY BEGUN.
WHAT'S GOING ON?!
THE FIGHTING IN BOTH HONG KONG AND PARIS HAS RESUMED, BUT NO ONE IS REPORTING IN. WE HAVE NO IDEA WHAT HAPPENED.

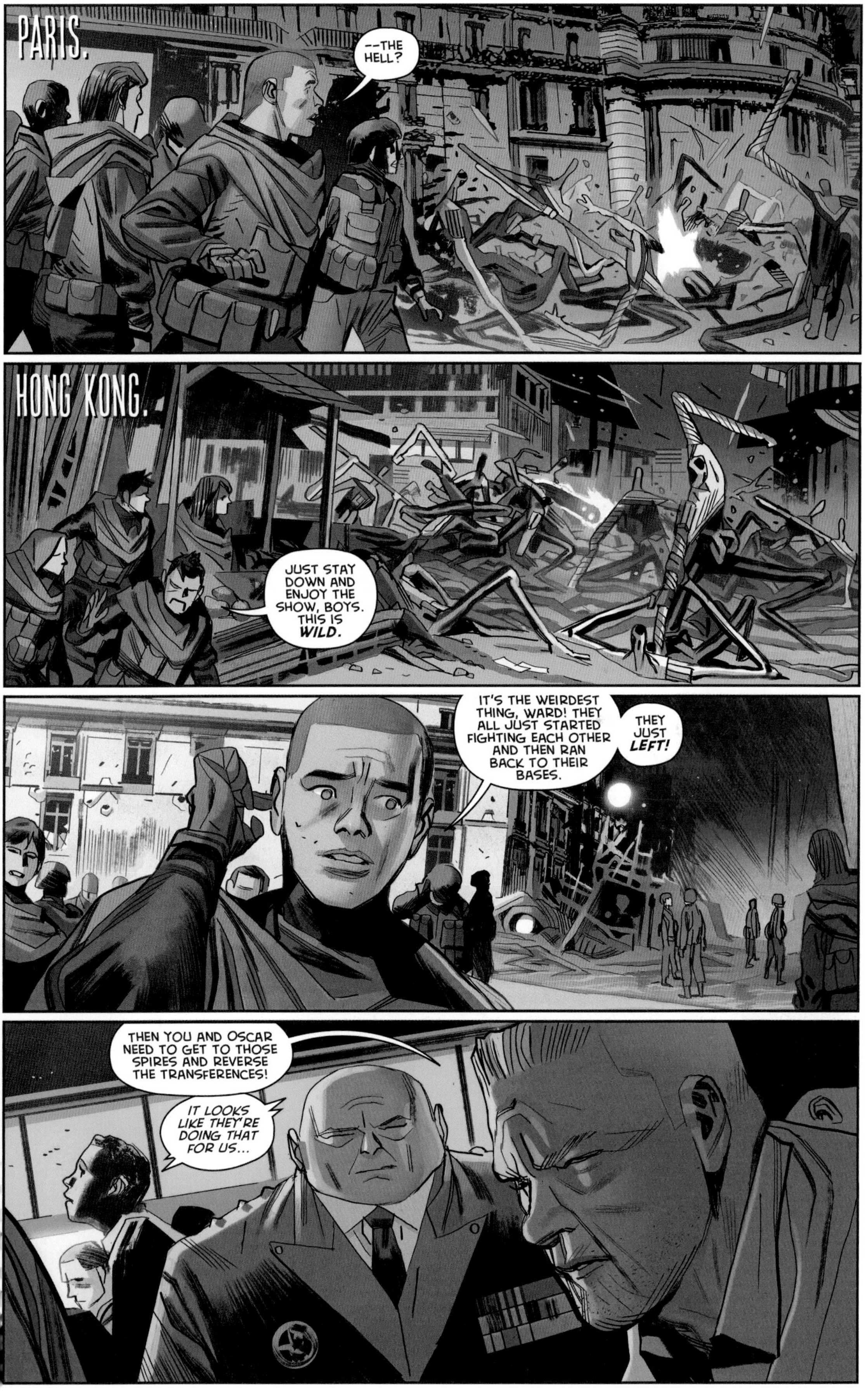
PARIS.
--THE HELL?
HONG KONG.
JUST STAY DOWN AND ENJOY THE SHOW, BOYS. THIS IS *WILD.*
IT'S THE WEIRDEST THING, WARD! THEY ALL JUST STARTED FIGHTING EACH OTHER AND THEN RAN BACK TO THEIR BASES.
THEY JUST *LEFT!*
THEN YOU AND OSCAR NEED TO GET TO THOSE SPIRES AND REVERSE THE TRANSFERENCES!
IT LOOKS LIKE THEY'RE DOING THAT FOR US...

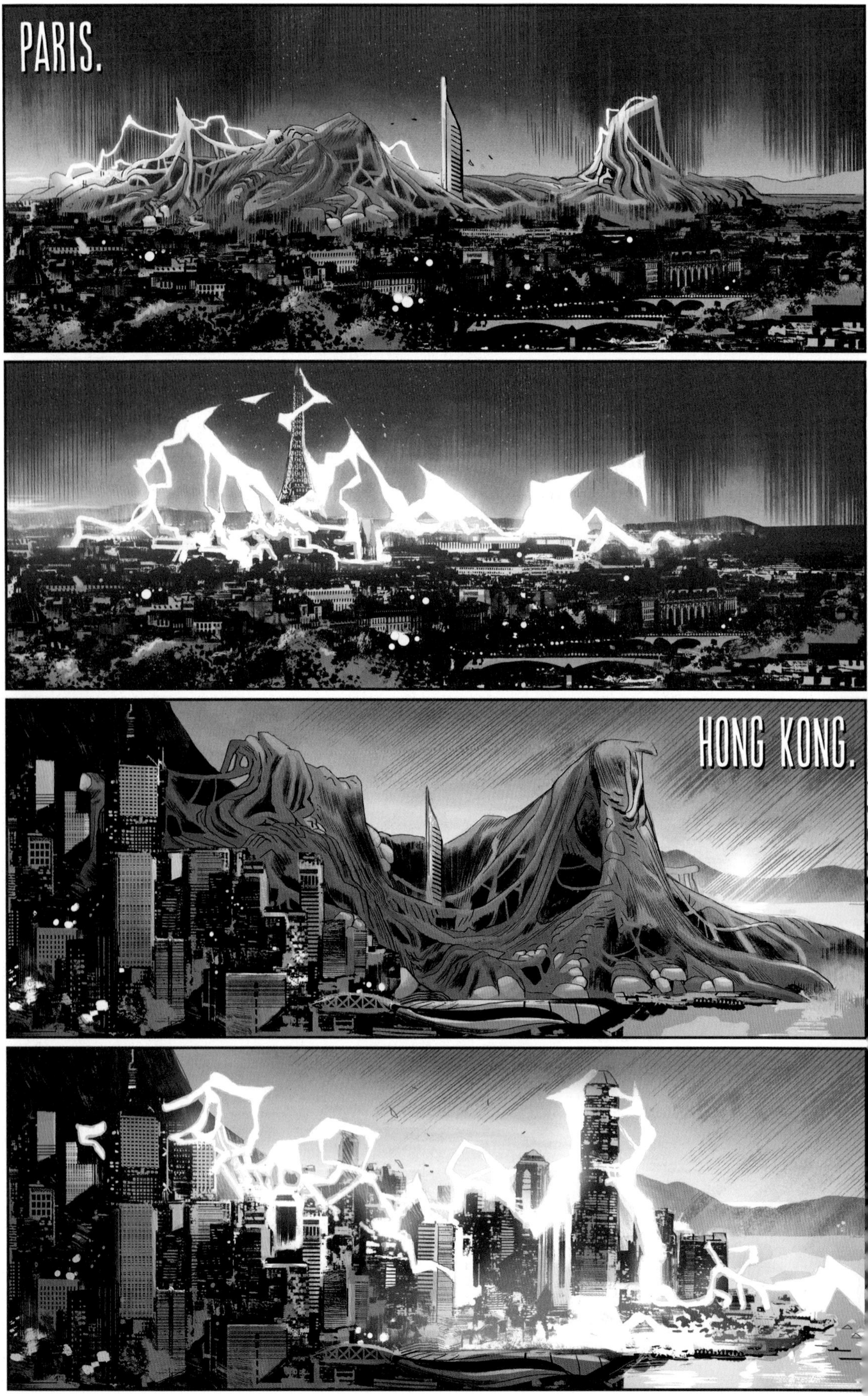
PARIS.
HONG KONG.

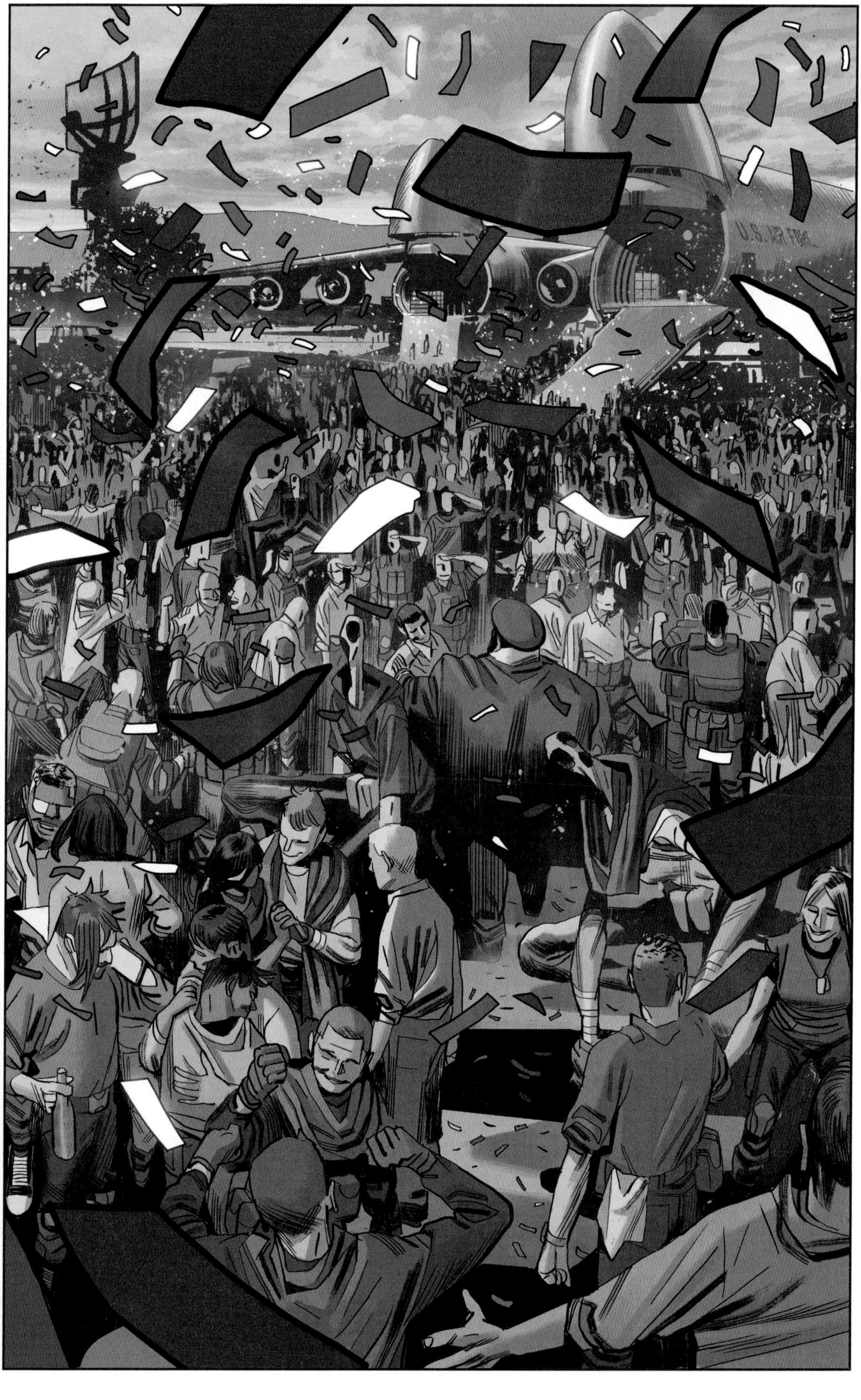
U.S. AIR

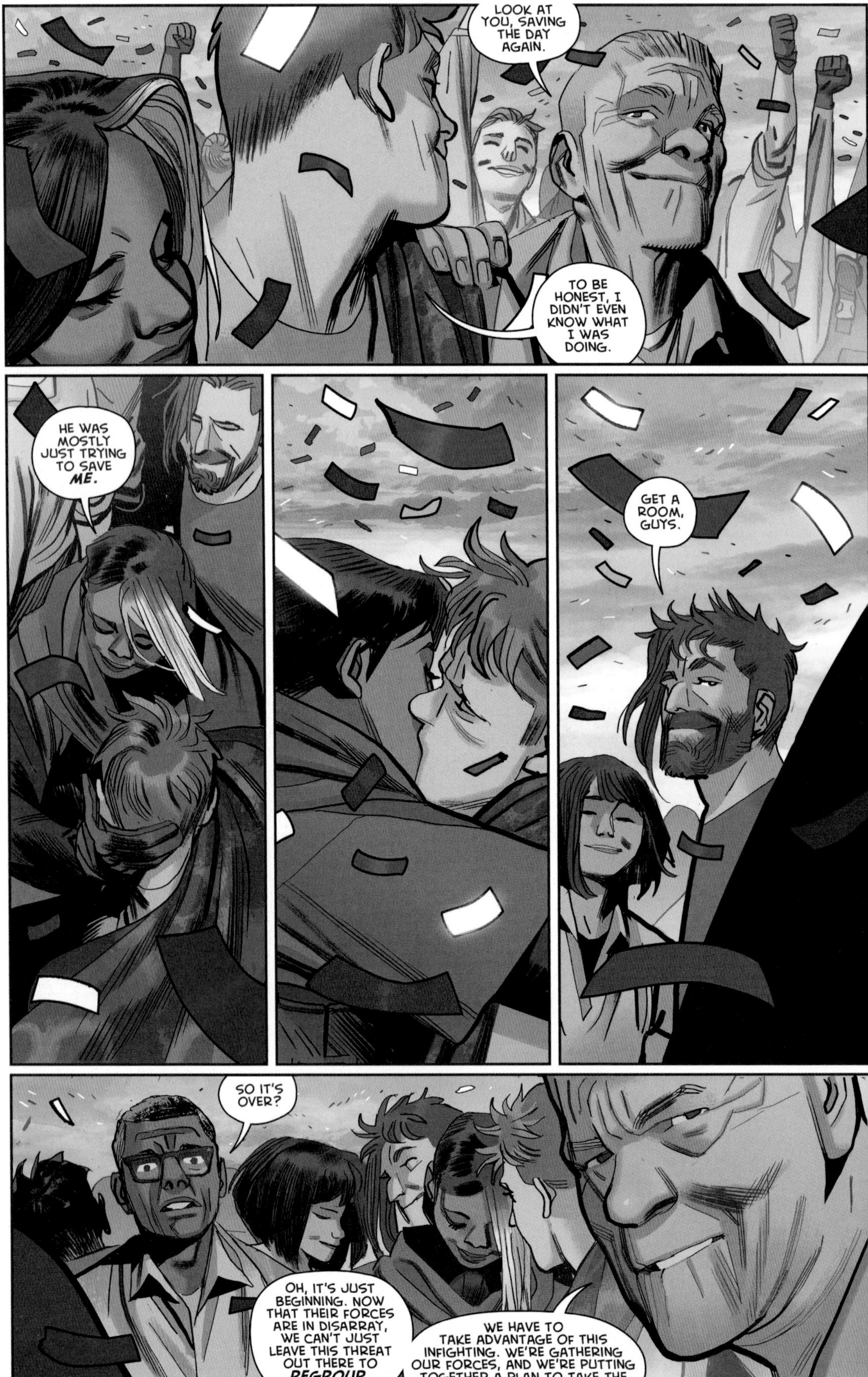
LOOK AT YOU, SAVING THE DAY AGAIN.
TO BE HONEST, I DIDN'T EVEN KNOW WHAT I WAS DOING.
HE WAS MOSTLY JUST TRYING TO SAVE *ME*.
GET A ROOM, GUYS.
SO IT'S OVER?
OH, IT'S JUST BEGINNING. NOW THAT THEIR FORCES ARE IN DISARRAY, WE CAN'T JUST LEAVE THIS THREAT OUT THERE TO *REGROUP*.
WE HAVE TO TAKE ADVANTAGE OF THIS INFIGHTING. WE'RE GATHERING OUR FORCES, AND WE'RE PUTTING TOGETHER A PLAN TO TAKE THE FIGHT TO *THEM* IN OBLIVION.

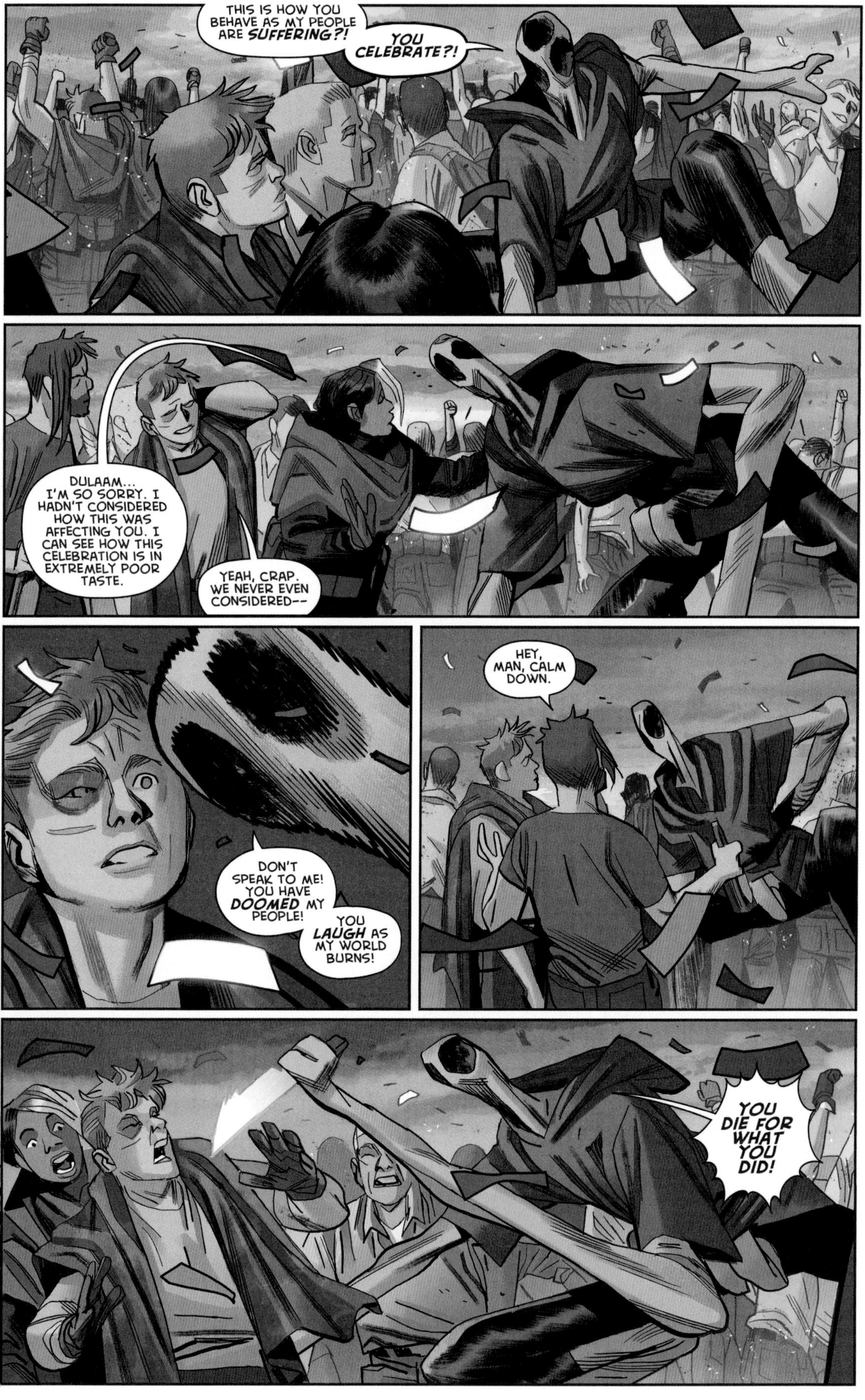
THIS IS HOW YOU BEHAVE AS MY PEOPLE ARE SUFFERING?!
YOU CELEBRATE?!
DULAAM... I'M SO SORRY. I HADN'T CONSIDERED HOW THIS WAS AFFECTING YOU. I CAN SEE HOW THIS CELEBRATION IS IN EXTREMELY POOR TASTE.
YEAH, CRAP. WE NEVER EVEN CONSIDERED--
DON'T SPEAK TO ME! YOU HAVE DOOMED MY PEOPLE!
YOU LAUGH AS MY WORLD BURNS!
HEY, MAN, CALM DOWN.
YOU DIE FOR WHAT YOU DID!

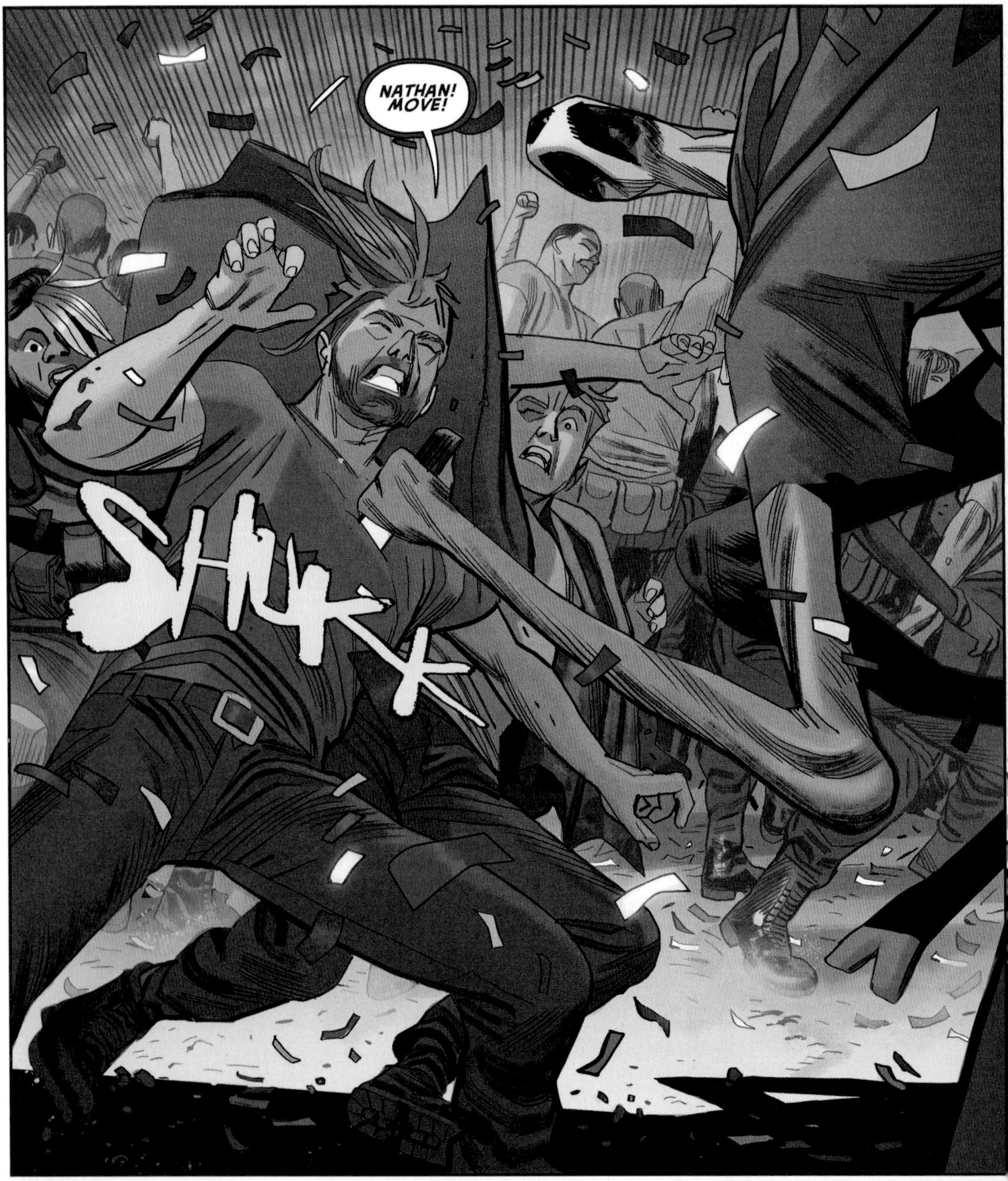
NATHAN! MOVE!
SHUK

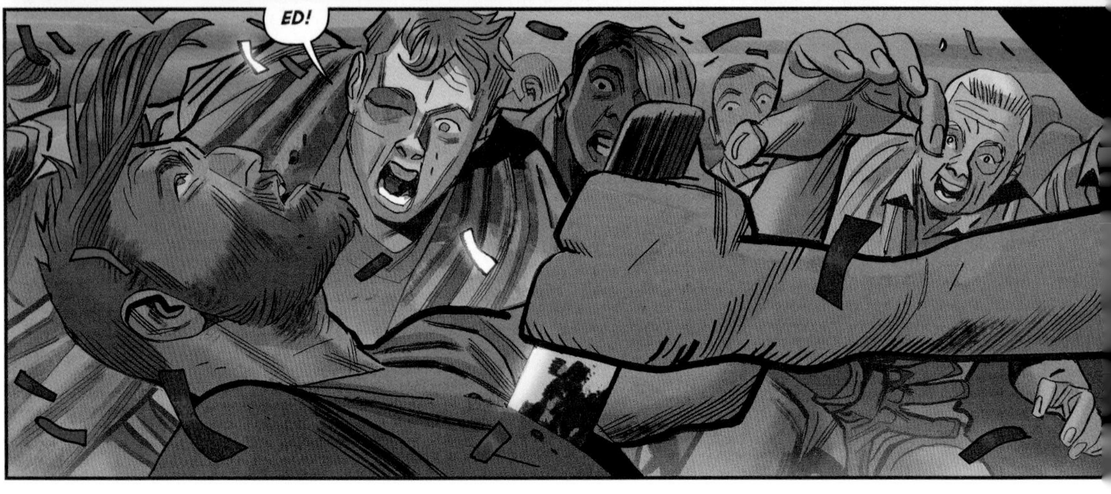
ED!

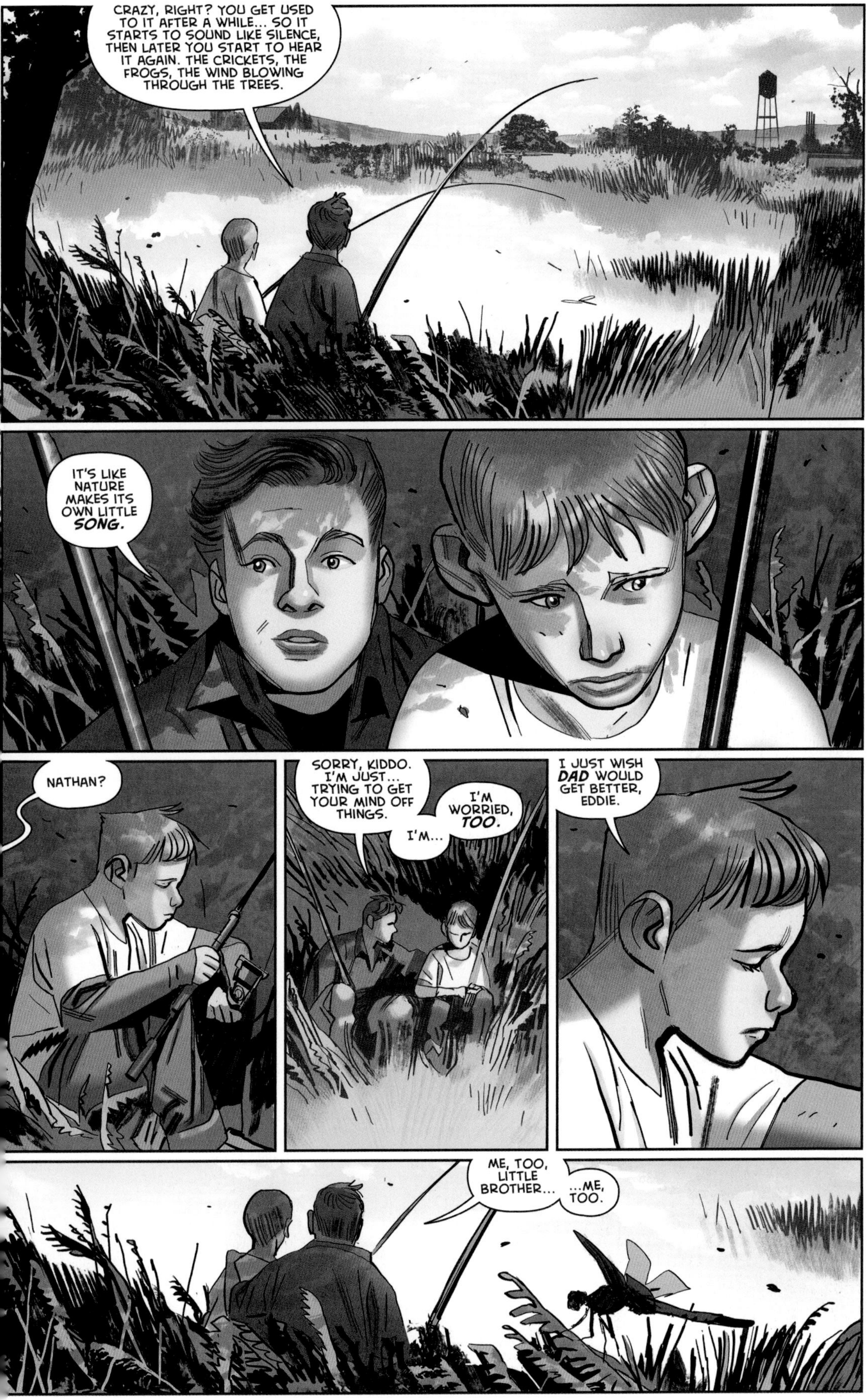
CRAZY, RIGHT? YOU GET USED TO IT AFTER A WHILE... SO IT STARTS TO SOUND LIKE SILENCE, THEN LATER YOU START TO HEAR IT AGAIN. THE CRICKETS, THE FROGS, THE WIND BLOWING THROUGH THE TREES.
IT'S LIKE NATURE MAKES ITS OWN LITTLE SONG.
NATHAN?
SORRY, KIDDO. I'M JUST... TRYING TO GET YOUR MIND OFF THINGS.
I'M...
I'M WORRIED, TOO.
I JUST WISH DAD WOULD GET BETTER, EDDIE.
ME, TOO, LITTLE BROTHER...
...ME, TOO.

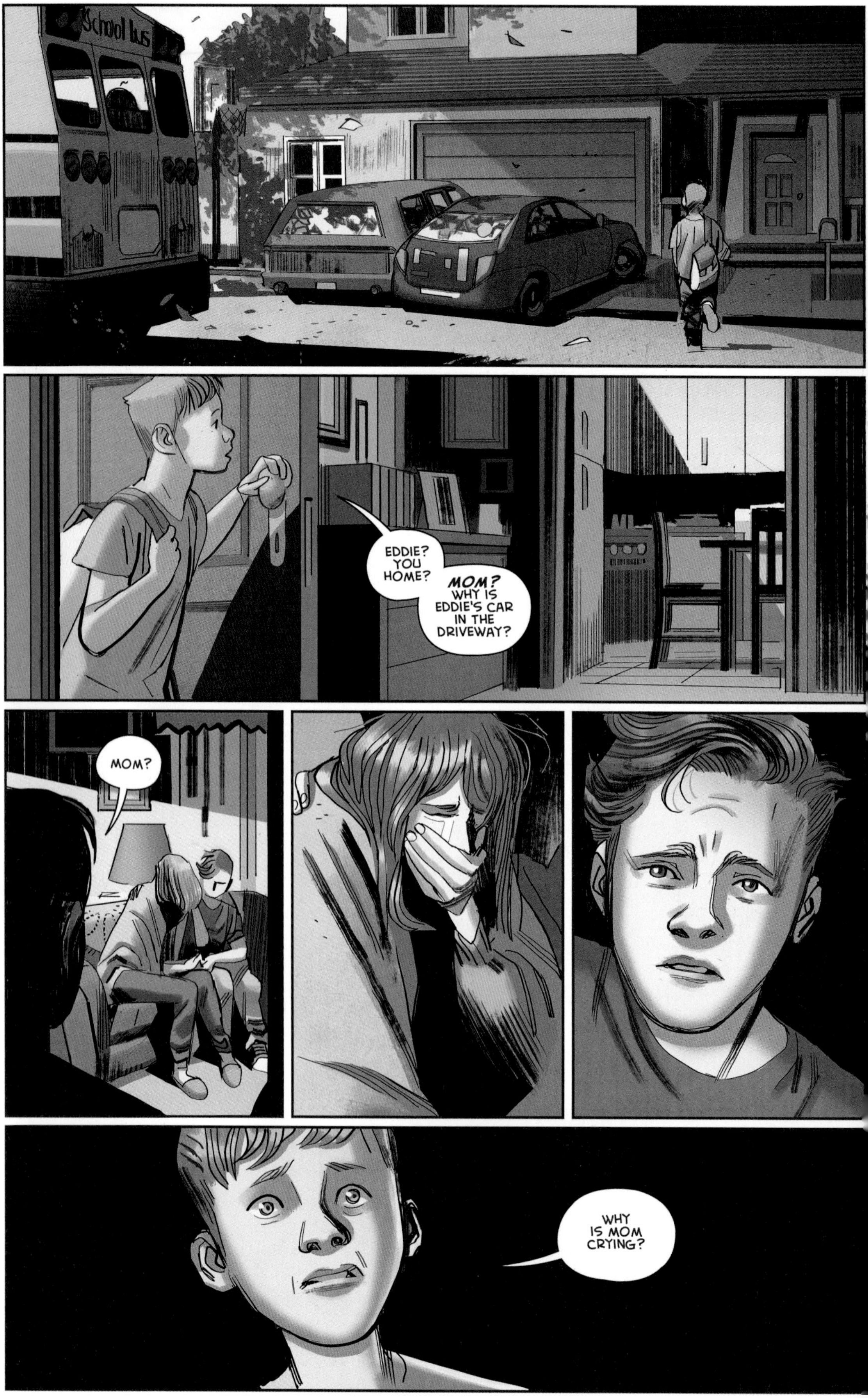
School bus
EDDIE? YOU HOME?
MOM? WHY IS EDDIE'S CAR IN THE DRIVEWAY?
MOM?
WHY IS MOM CRYING?

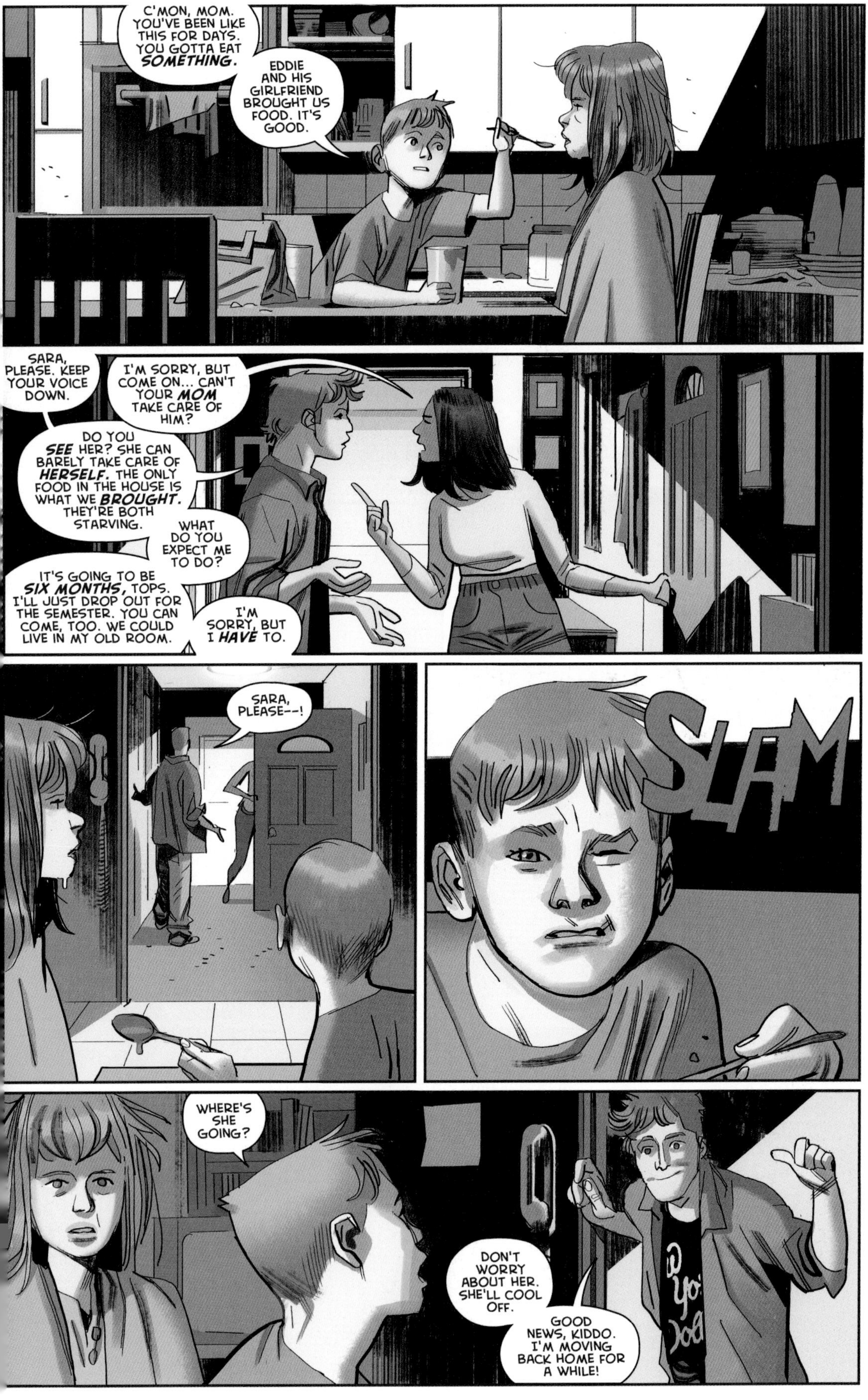
C'MON, MOM. YOU'VE BEEN LIKE THIS FOR DAYS. YOU GOTTA EAT SOMETHING.
EDDIE AND HIS GIRLFRIEND BROUGHT US FOOD. IT'S GOOD.
SARA, PLEASE. KEEP YOUR VOICE DOWN.
I'M SORRY, BUT COME ON... CAN'T YOUR MOM TAKE CARE OF HIM?
DO YOU SEE HER? SHE CAN BARELY TAKE CARE OF HERSELF. THE ONLY FOOD IN THE HOUSE IS WHAT WE BROUGHT. THEY'RE BOTH STARVING.
WHAT DO YOU EXPECT ME TO DO?
IT'S GOING TO BE SIX MONTHS, TOPS. I'LL JUST DROP OUT FOR THE SEMESTER. YOU CAN COME, TOO. WE COULD LIVE IN MY OLD ROOM.
I'M SORRY, BUT I HAVE TO.
SARA, PLEASE--!
SLAM
WHERE'S SHE GOING?
DON'T WORRY ABOUT HER. SHE'LL COOL OFF.
GOOD NEWS, KIDDO. I'M MOVING BACK HOME FOR A WHILE!

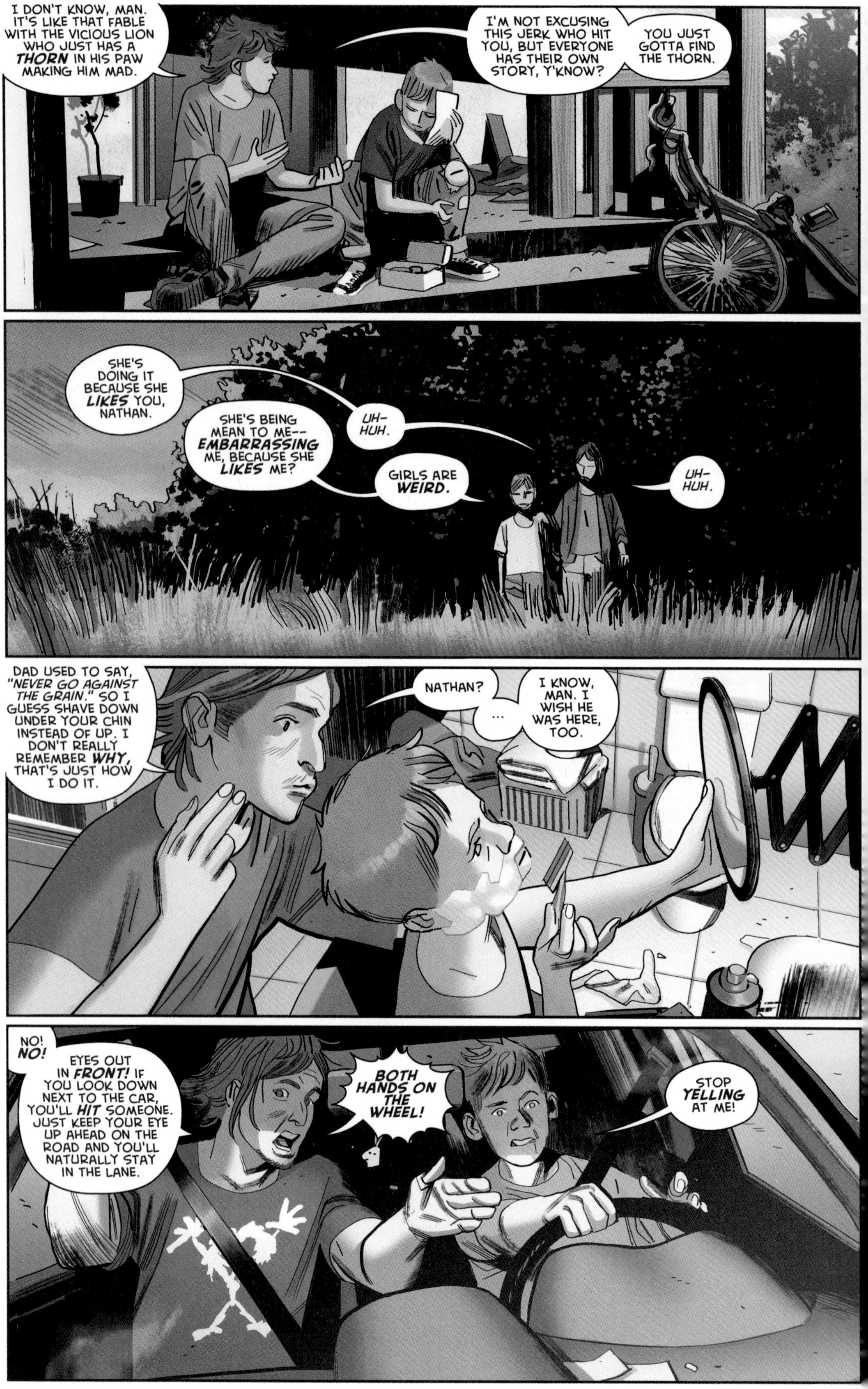
I DON'T KNOW, MAN. IT'S LIKE THAT FABLE WITH THE VICIOUS LION WHO JUST HAS A THORN IN HIS PAW MAKING HIM MAD.
I'M NOT EXCUSING THIS JERK WHO HIT YOU, BUT EVERYONE HAS THEIR OWN STORY, Y'KNOW?
YOU JUST GOTTA FIND THE THORN.
SHE'S DOING IT BECAUSE SHE LIKES YOU, NATHAN.
UH-HUH.
SHE'S BEING MEAN TO ME-- EMBARRASSING ME, BECAUSE SHE LIKES ME?
GIRLS ARE WEIRD.
UH-HUH.
DAD USED TO SAY, "NEVER GO AGAINST THE GRAIN." SO I GUESS SHAVE DOWN UNDER YOUR CHIN INSTEAD OF UP. I DON'T REALLY REMEMBER WHY, THAT'S JUST HOW I DO IT.
NATHAN?
...
I KNOW, MAN. I WISH HE WAS HERE, TOO.
NO! NO!
EYES OUT IN FRONT! IF YOU LOOK DOWN NEXT TO THE CAR, YOU'LL HIT SOMEONE. JUST KEEP YOUR EYE UP AHEAD ON THE ROAD AND YOU'LL NATURALLY STAY IN THE LANE.
BOTH HANDS ON THE WHEEL!
STOP YELLING AT ME!

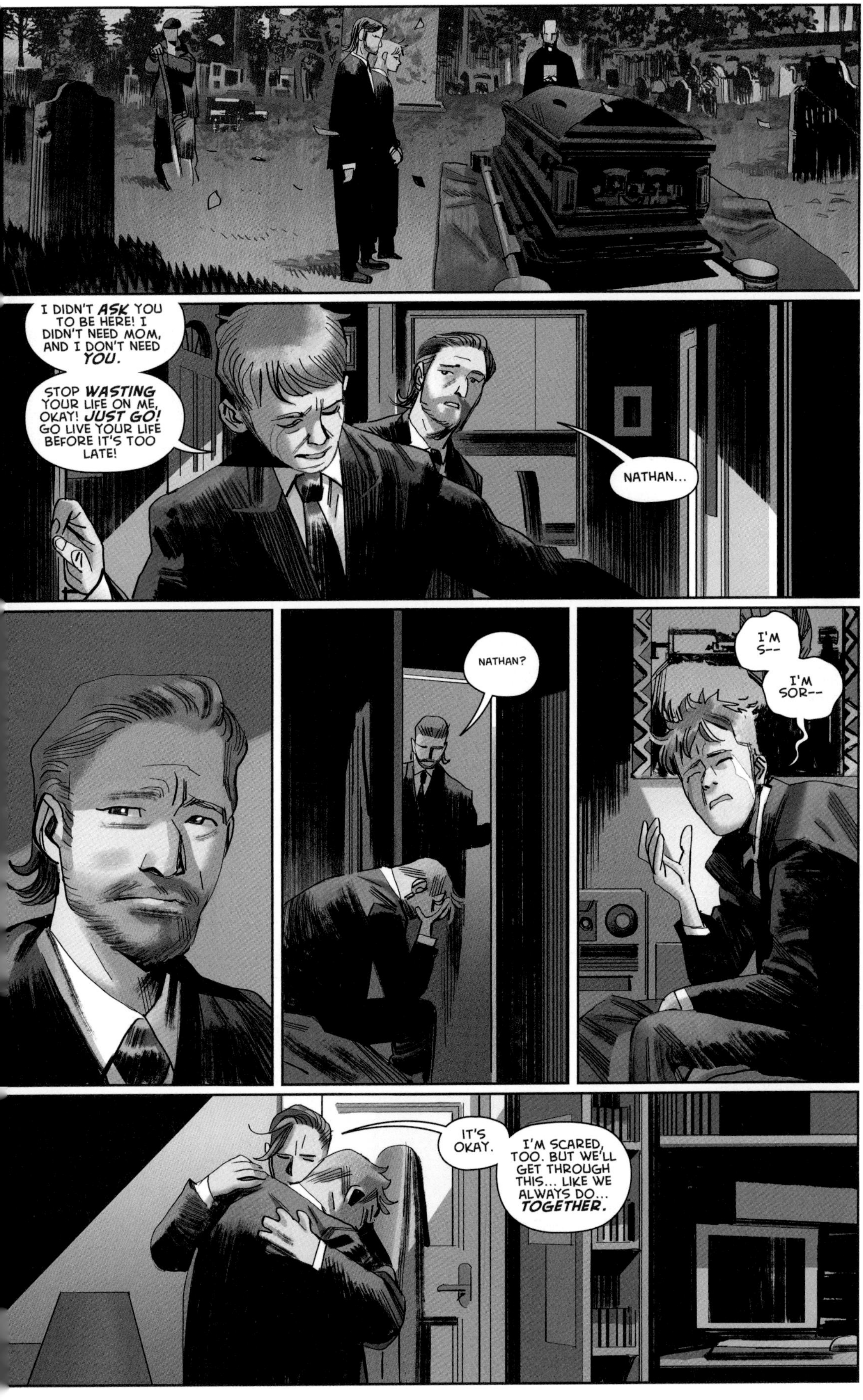
I DIDN'T ASK YOU TO BE HERE! I DIDN'T NEED MOM, AND I DON'T NEED YOU.
STOP WASTING YOUR LIFE ON ME, OKAY! JUST GO! GO LIVE YOUR LIFE BEFORE IT'S TOO LATE!
NATHAN...
NATHAN?
I'M S--
I'M SOR--
IT'S OKAY.
I'M SCARED, TOO. BUT WE'LL GET THROUGH THIS... LIKE WE ALWAYS DO... TOGETHER.

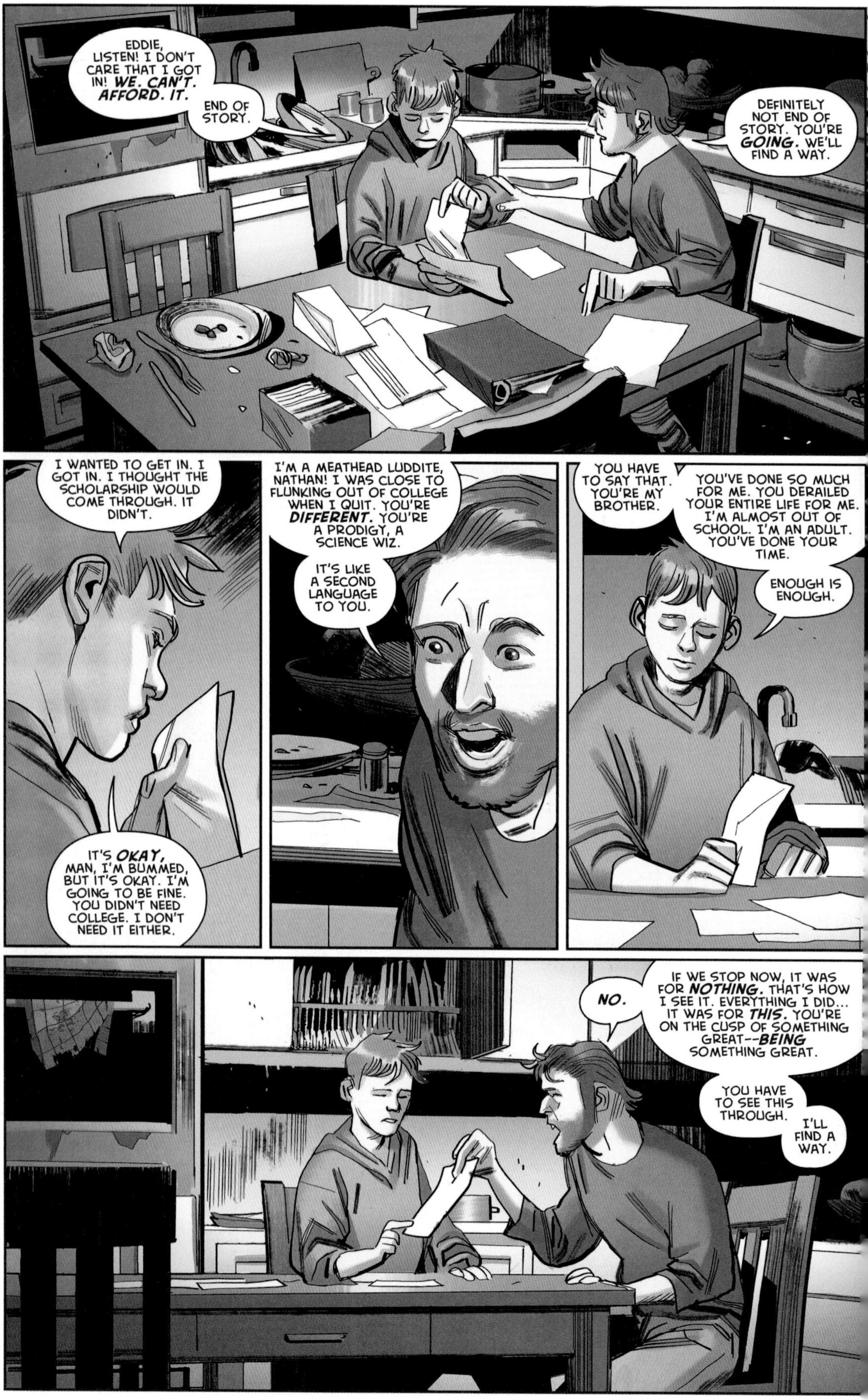

EDDIE, LISTEN! I DON'T CARE THAT I GOT IN! WE. CAN'T. AFFORD. IT.
END OF STORY.
DEFINITELY NOT END OF STORY. YOU'RE GOING. WE'LL FIND A WAY.
I WANTED TO GET IN. I GOT IN. I THOUGHT THE SCHOLARSHIP WOULD COME THROUGH. IT DIDN'T.
IT'S OKAY, MAN, I'M BUMMED, BUT IT'S OKAY. I'M GOING TO BE FINE. YOU DIDN'T NEED COLLEGE. I DON'T NEED IT EITHER.
I'M A MEATHEAD LUDDITE, NATHAN! I WAS CLOSE TO FLUNKING OUT OF COLLEGE WHEN I QUIT. YOU'RE DIFFERENT. YOU'RE A PRODIGY, A SCIENCE WIZ.
IT'S LIKE A SECOND LANGUAGE TO YOU.
YOU HAVE TO SAY THAT. YOU'RE MY BROTHER.
YOU'VE DONE SO MUCH FOR ME. YOU DERAILED YOUR ENTIRE LIFE FOR ME. I'M ALMOST OUT OF SCHOOL. I'M AN ADULT. YOU'VE DONE YOUR TIME.
ENOUGH IS ENOUGH.
NO.
IF WE STOP NOW, IT WAS FOR NOTHING. THAT'S HOW I SEE IT. EVERYTHING I DID... IT WAS FOR THIS. YOU'RE ON THE CUSP OF SOMETHING GREAT--BEING SOMETHING GREAT.
YOU HAVE TO SEE THIS THROUGH.
I'LL FIND A WAY.

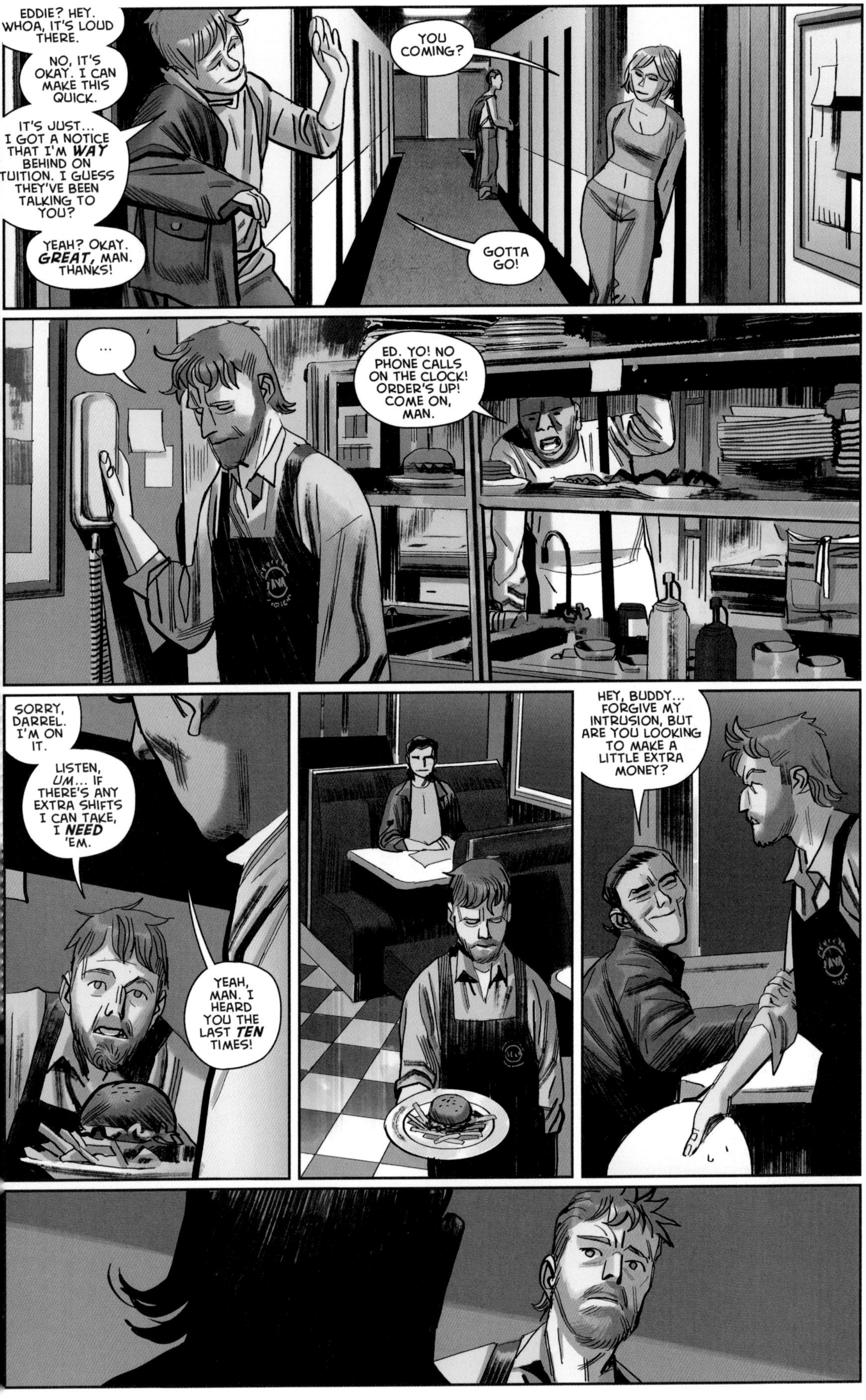
EDDIE? HEY. WHOA, IT'S LOUD THERE.
NO, IT'S OKAY. I CAN MAKE THIS QUICK.
IT'S JUST... I GOT A NOTICE THAT I'M *WAY* BEHIND ON TUITION. I GUESS THEY'VE BEEN TALKING TO YOU?
YEAH? OKAY. *GREAT,* MAN. THANKS!
YOU COMING?
GOTTA GO!
...
ED. YO! NO PHONE CALLS ON THE CLOCK! ORDER'S UP! COME ON, MAN.
SORRY, DARREL. I'M ON IT.
LISTEN, *UM*... IF THERE'S ANY EXTRA SHIFTS I CAN TAKE, I *NEED* 'EM.
YEAH, MAN. I HEARD YOU THE LAST *TEN* TIMES!
HEY, BUDDY... FORGIVE MY INTRUSION, BUT ARE YOU LOOKING TO MAKE A LITTLE EXTRA MONEY?

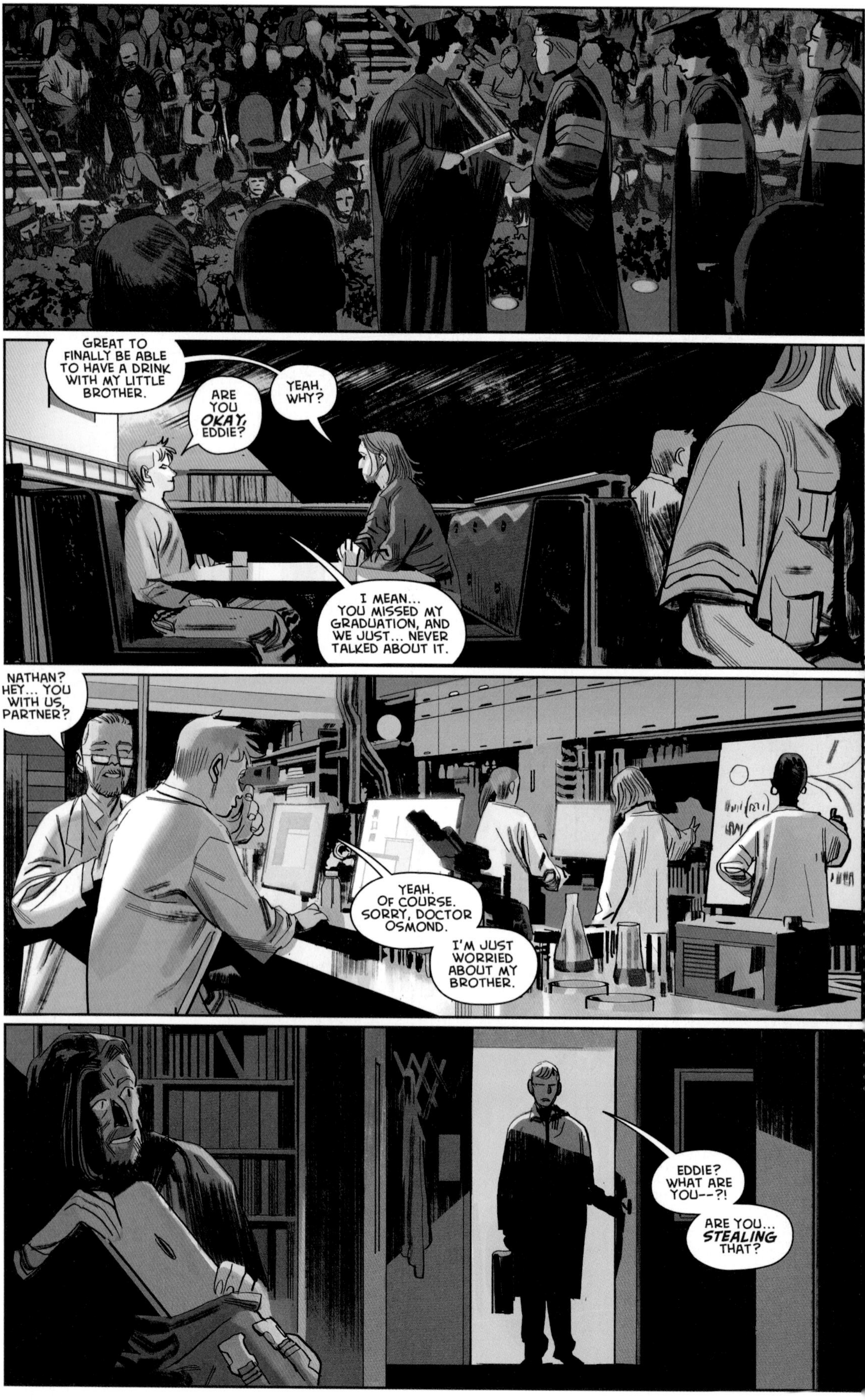

GREAT TO FINALLY BE ABLE TO HAVE A DRINK WITH MY LITTLE BROTHER.
ARE YOU OKAY, EDDIE?
YEAH. WHY?
I MEAN... YOU MISSED MY GRADUATION, AND WE JUST... NEVER TALKED ABOUT IT.
NATHAN? HEY... YOU WITH US, PARTNER?
YEAH. OF COURSE. SORRY, DOCTOR OSMOND.
I'M JUST WORRIED ABOUT MY BROTHER.
EDDIE? WHAT ARE YOU--?!
ARE YOU... STEALING THAT?

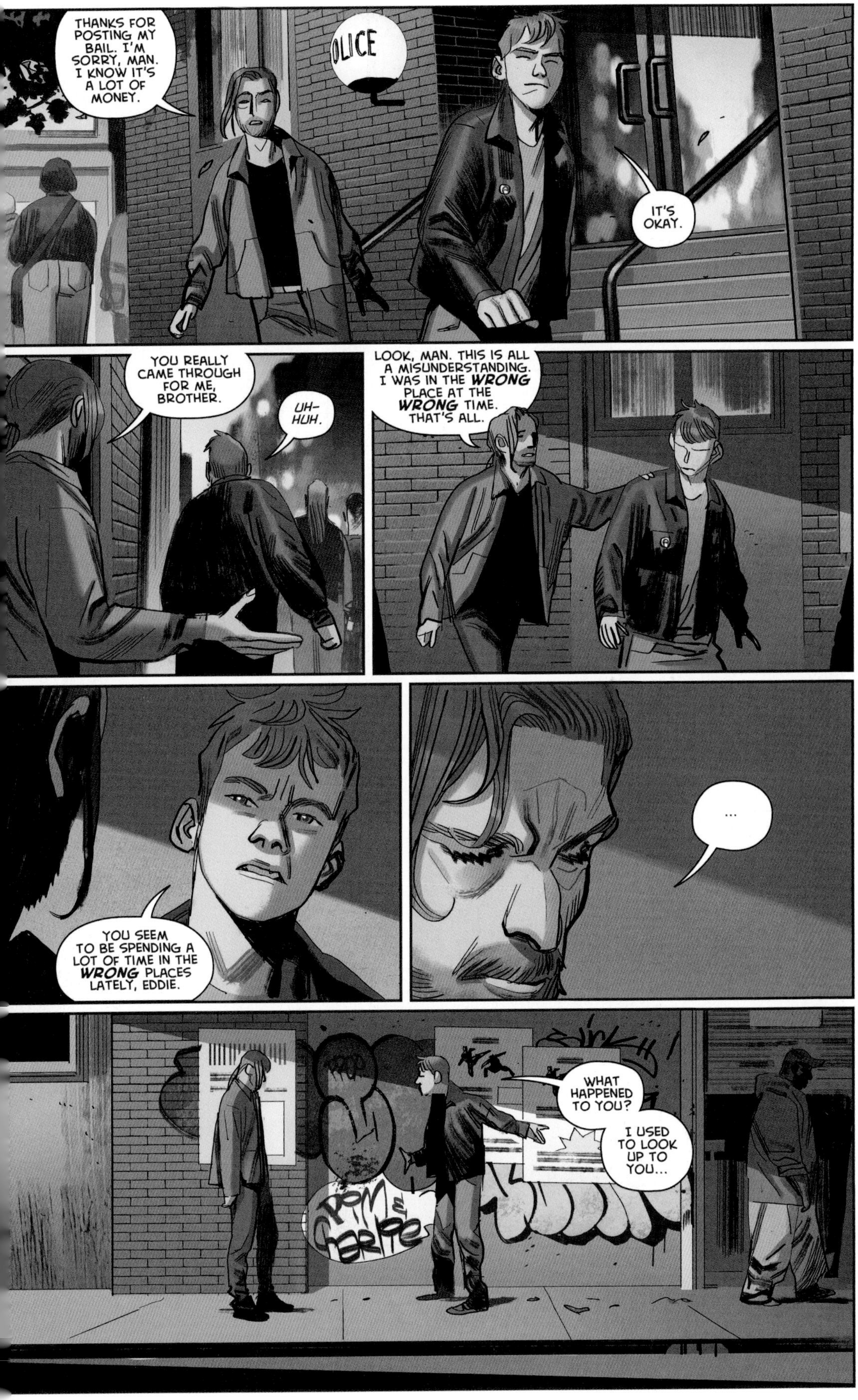
THANKS FOR POSTING MY BAIL. I'M SORRY, MAN. I KNOW IT'S A LOT OF MONEY.
OLICE
IT'S OKAY.
YOU REALLY CAME THROUGH FOR ME, BROTHER.
UH-HUH.
LOOK, MAN. THIS IS ALL A MISUNDERSTANDING. I WAS IN THE WRONG PLACE AT THE WRONG TIME. THAT'S ALL.
YOU SEEM TO BE SPENDING A LOT OF TIME IN THE WRONG PLACES LATELY, EDDIE.
...
WHAT HAPPENED TO YOU?
I USED TO LOOK UP TO YOU...

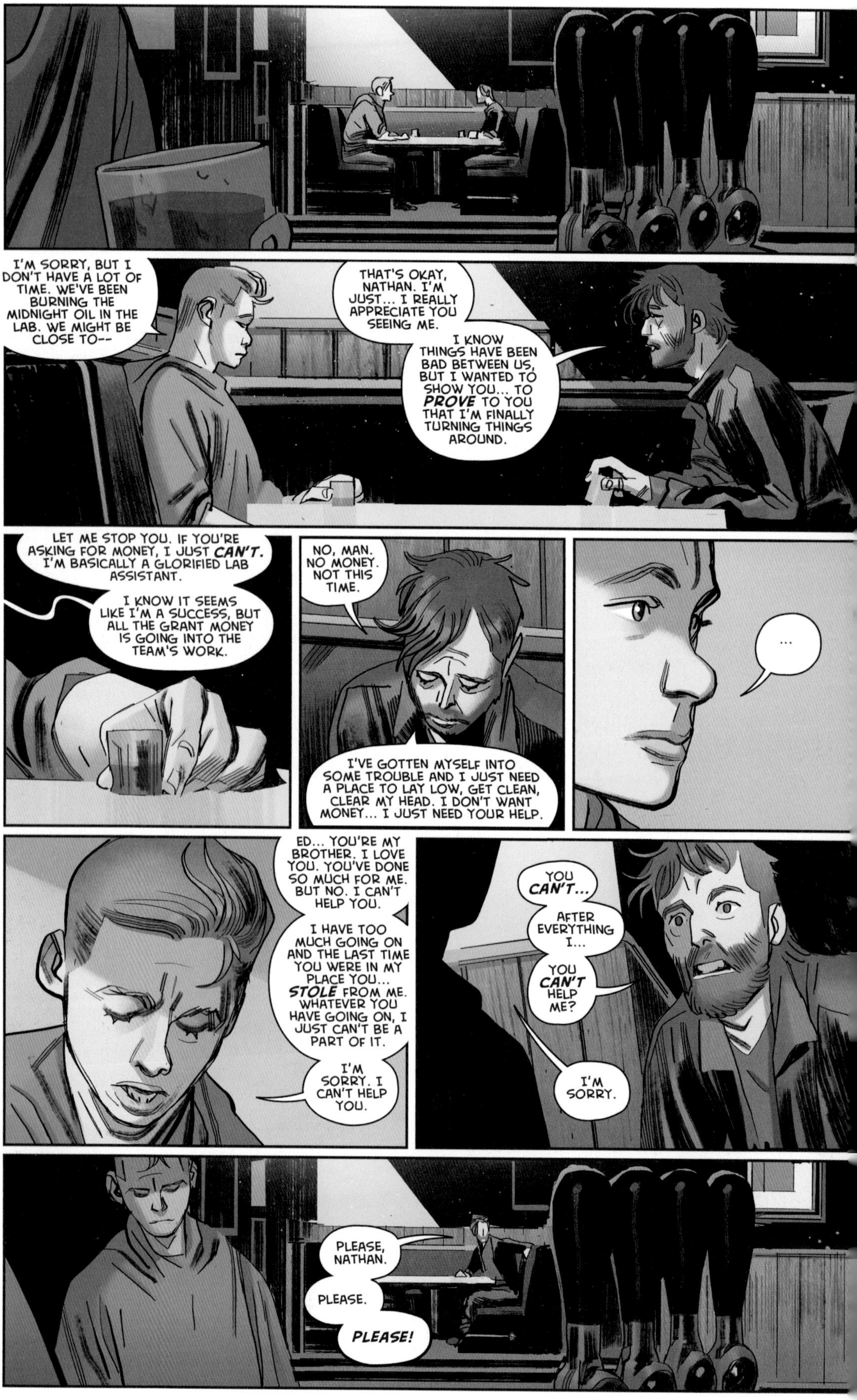
I'M SORRY, BUT I DON'T HAVE A LOT OF TIME. WE'VE BEEN BURNING THE MIDNIGHT OIL IN THE LAB. WE MIGHT BE CLOSE TO--
THAT'S OKAY, NATHAN. I'M JUST... I REALLY APPRECIATE YOU SEEING ME.
I KNOW THINGS HAVE BEEN BAD BETWEEN US, BUT I WANTED TO SHOW YOU... TO PROVE TO YOU THAT I'M FINALLY TURNING THINGS AROUND.
LET ME STOP YOU. IF YOU'RE ASKING FOR MONEY, I JUST CAN'T. I'M BASICALLY A GLORIFIED LAB ASSISTANT.
I KNOW IT SEEMS LIKE I'M A SUCCESS, BUT ALL THE GRANT MONEY IS GOING INTO THE TEAM'S WORK.
NO, MAN. NO MONEY. NOT THIS TIME.
I'VE GOTTEN MYSELF INTO SOME TROUBLE AND I JUST NEED A PLACE TO LAY LOW, GET CLEAN, CLEAR MY HEAD. I DON'T WANT MONEY... I JUST NEED YOUR HELP.
...
ED... YOU'RE MY BROTHER. I LOVE YOU. YOU'VE DONE SO MUCH FOR ME. BUT NO. I CAN'T HELP YOU.
I HAVE TOO MUCH GOING ON AND THE LAST TIME YOU WERE IN MY PLACE YOU... STOLE FROM ME. WHATEVER YOU HAVE GOING ON, I JUST CAN'T BE A PART OF IT.
I'M SORRY. I CAN'T HELP YOU.
YOU CAN'T...
AFTER EVERYTHING I...
YOU CAN'T HELP ME?
I'M SORRY.
PLEASE, NATHAN.
PLEASE.
PLEASE!

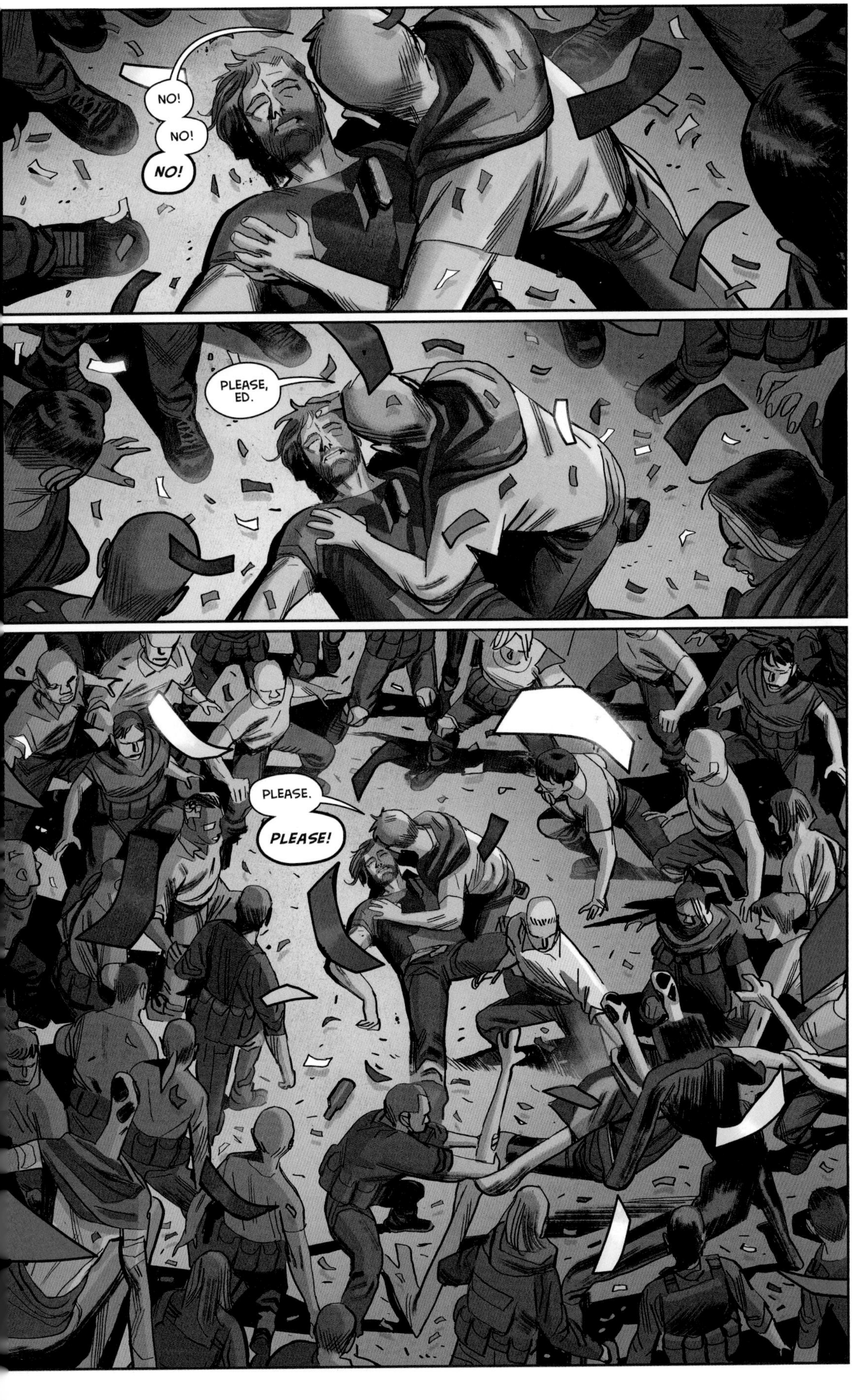
NO!
NO!
NO!
PLEASE, ED.
PLEASE.
PLEASE!

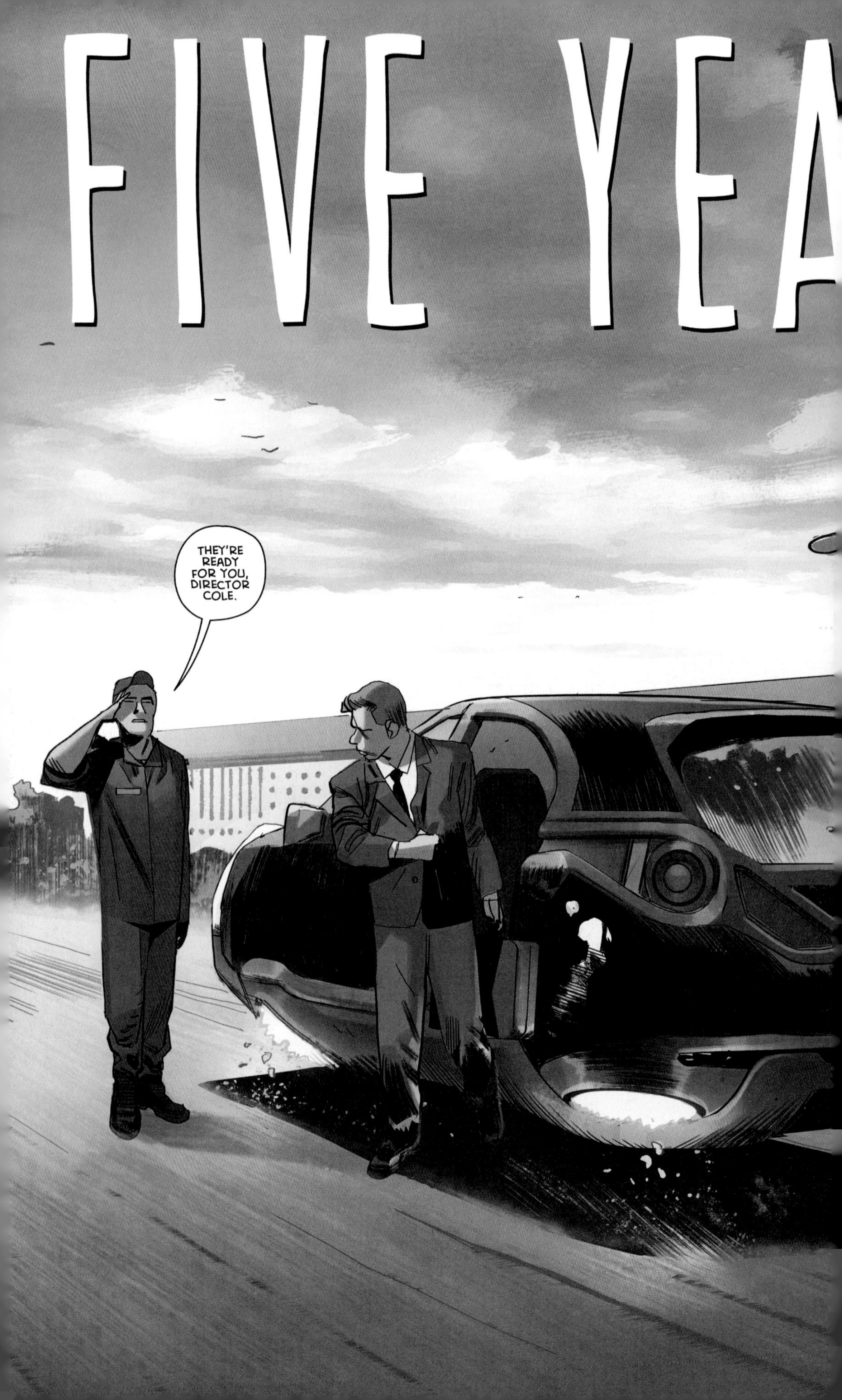
FIVE YEA
THEY'RE READY FOR YOU, DIRECTOR COLE.

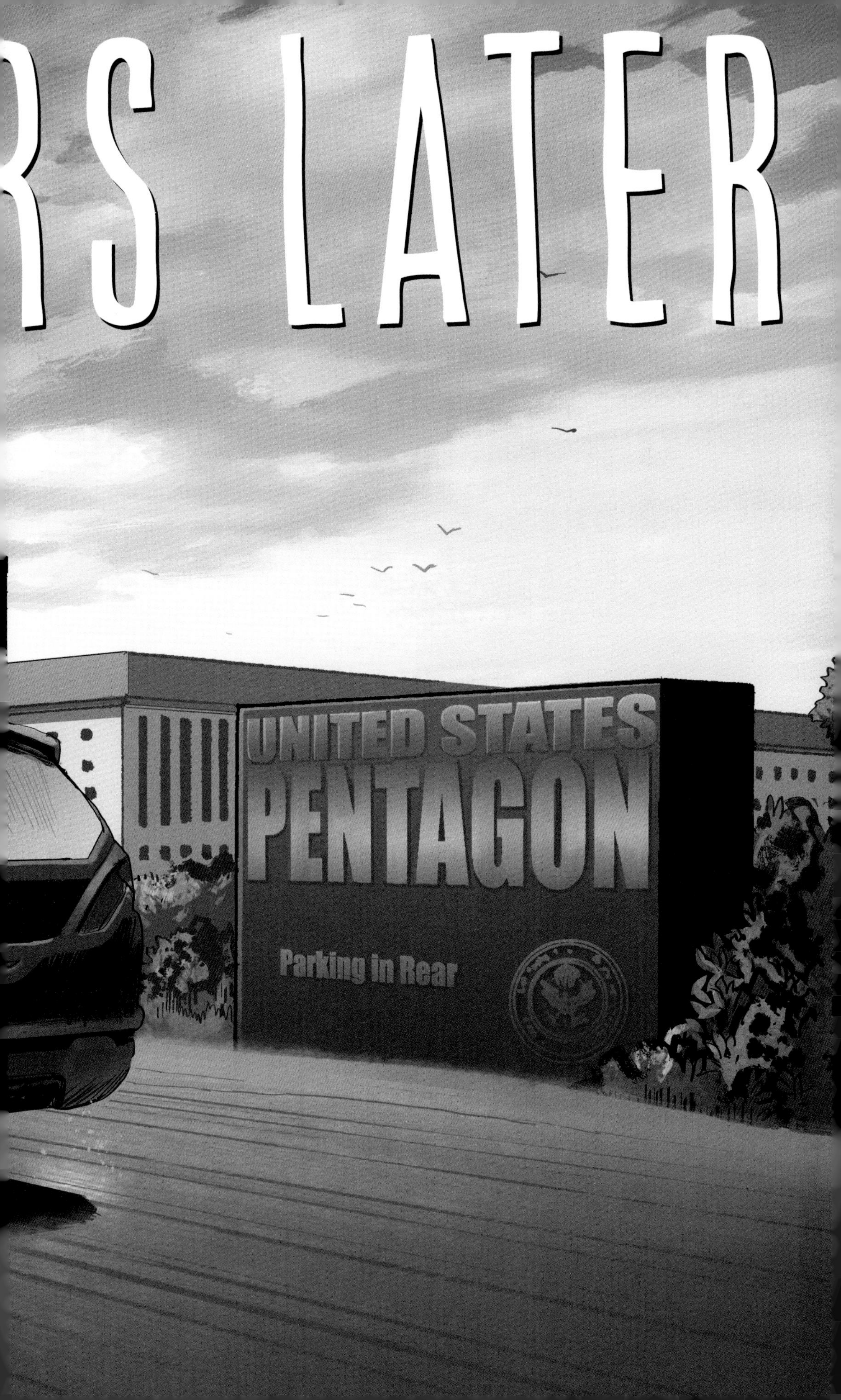
RS LATER
UNITED STATES
PENTAGON
Parking in Rear

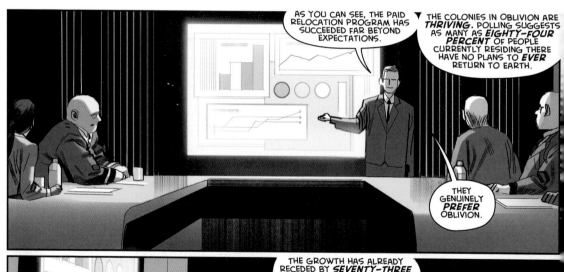

AS YOU CAN SEE, THE PAID RELOCATION PROGRAM HAS SUCCEEDED FAR BEYOND EXPECTATIONS.

▼ THE COLONIES IN OBLIVION ARE *THRIVING*. POLLING SUGGESTS AS MANY AS *EIGHTY-FOUR PERCENT* OF PEOPLE CURRENTLY RESIDING THERE HAVE NO PLANS TO *EVER* RETURN TO EARTH.

THEY GENUINELY *PREFER* OBLIVION.

THE GROWTH HAS ALREADY RECEDED BY *SEVENTY-THREE PERCENT*, PROVIDING OUR COLONIES WITH MORE THAN ENOUGH UNOCCUPIED LANDMASS TO CONTINUE *EXPANDING*.

GOOD. *GOOD*.

THE KUTHAAL THEMSELVES ARE *THRIVING*. WITH OUR SUPPORT, THE ALLIANCE BETWEEN THE FACTIONS HAS ONLY GROWN STRONGER.

GRAND GHOZAN GAKAAL HAS EARNED THE RESPECT OF THE VAST MAJORITY OF HIS PEOPLE. THE LITTLE IN-FIGHTING THAT REMAINS HAS NOT BEEN TOO DISRUPTIVE TO OUR GOALS.

YOUR PLAN WORKED, DIRECTOR WARD.

CREDIT WHERE CREDIT IS DUE, SON...

...AND I'LL *TAKE* IT.

WHILE WE'RE ALL KISSING OUR OWN ASSES, LET ME TAKE A TURN.

▼ OUR GEOLOGICAL SURVEYS CAME BACK AND IT'S BETTER THAN WE COULD HAVE HOPED.

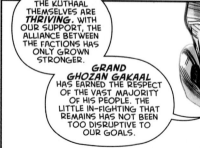

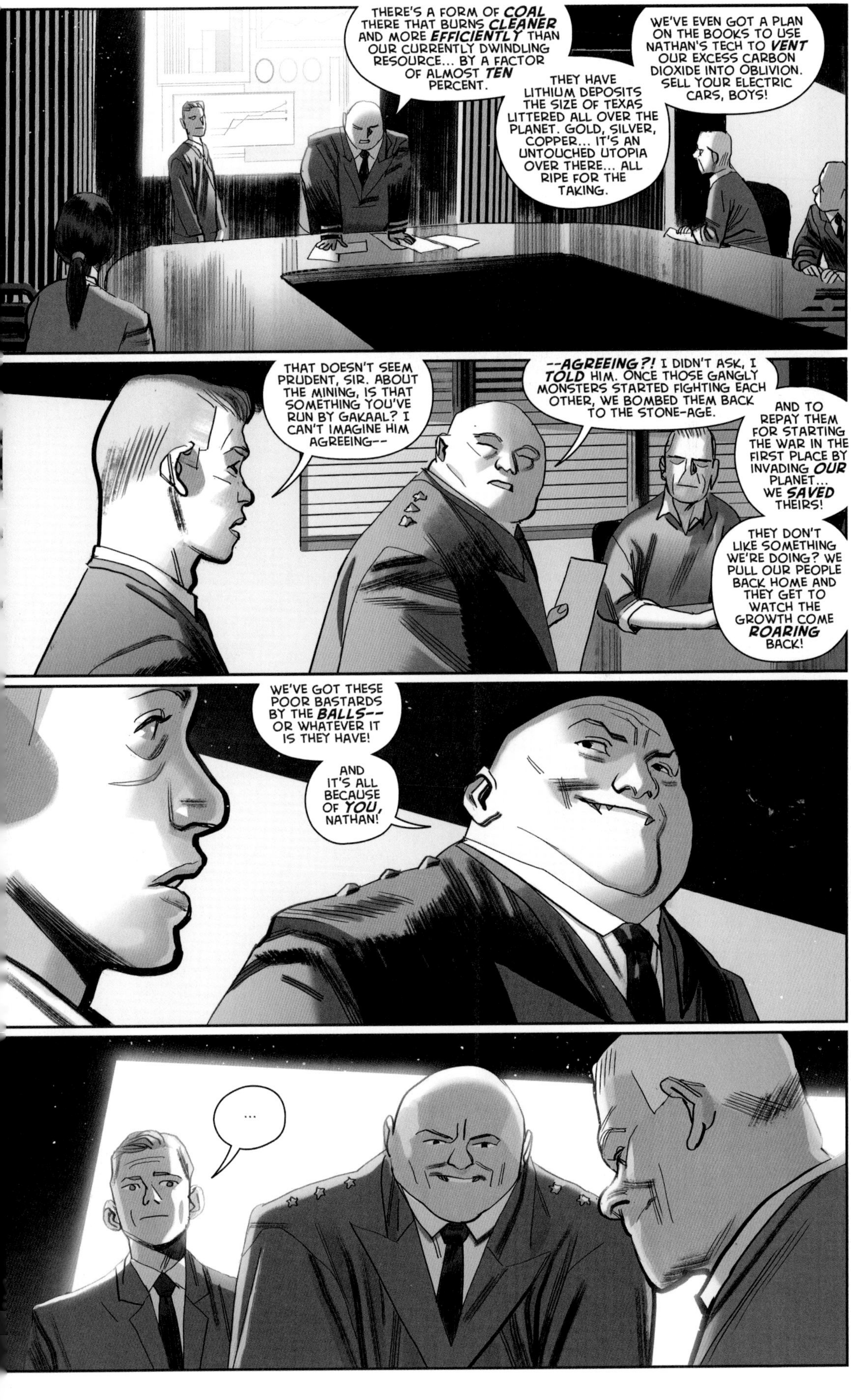
THERE'S A FORM OF COAL THERE THAT BURNS CLEANER AND MORE EFFICIENTLY THAN OUR CURRENTLY DWINDLING RESOURCE... BY A FACTOR OF ALMOST TEN PERCENT.
THEY HAVE LITHIUM DEPOSITS THE SIZE OF TEXAS LITTERED ALL OVER THE PLANET. GOLD, SILVER, COPPER... IT'S AN UNTOUCHED UTOPIA OVER THERE... ALL RIPE FOR THE TAKING.
WE'VE EVEN GOT A PLAN ON THE BOOKS TO USE NATHAN'S TECH TO VENT OUR EXCESS CARBON DIOXIDE INTO OBLIVION. SELL YOUR ELECTRIC CARS, BOYS!
THAT DOESN'T SEEM PRUDENT, SIR. ABOUT THE MINING, IS THAT SOMETHING YOU'VE RUN BY GAKAAL? I CAN'T IMAGINE HIM AGREEING--
--AGREEING?! I DIDN'T ASK, I TOLD HIM. ONCE THOSE GANGLY MONSTERS STARTED FIGHTING EACH OTHER, WE BOMBED THEM BACK TO THE STONE-AGE.
AND TO REPAY THEM FOR STARTING THE WAR IN THE FIRST PLACE BY INVADING OUR PLANET... WE SAVED THEIRS!
THEY DON'T LIKE SOMETHING WE'RE DOING? WE PULL OUR PEOPLE BACK HOME AND THEY GET TO WATCH THE GROWTH COME ROARING BACK!
WE'VE GOT THESE POOR BASTARDS BY THE BALLS-- OR WHATEVER IT IS THEY HAVE!
AND IT'S ALL BECAUSE OF YOU, NATHAN!
...

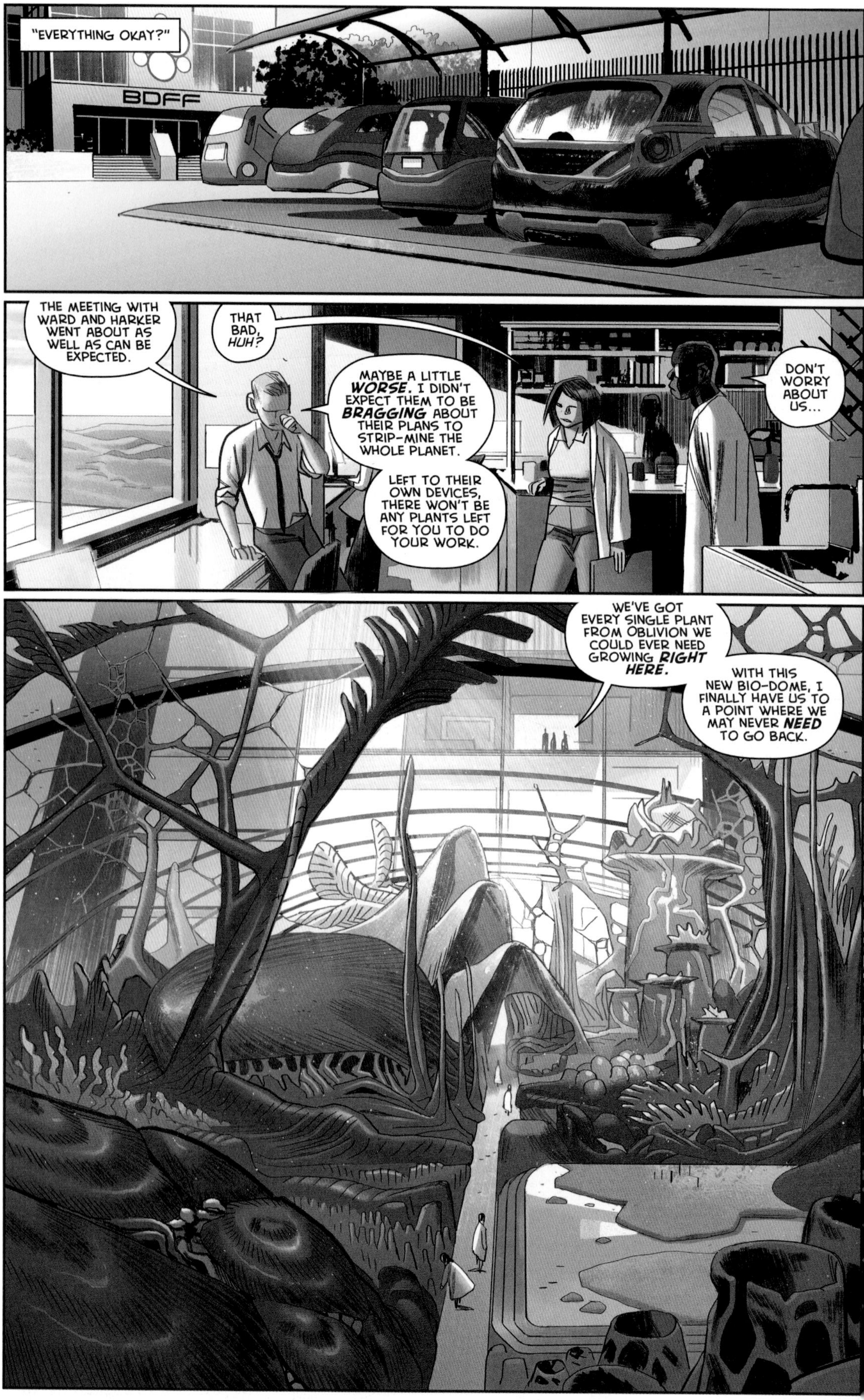
"EVERYTHING OKAY?"
BDFF
THE MEETING WITH WARD AND HARKER WENT ABOUT AS WELL AS CAN BE EXPECTED.
THAT BAD, HUH?
MAYBE A LITTLE WORSE. I DIDN'T EXPECT THEM TO BE BRAGGING ABOUT THEIR PLANS TO STRIP-MINE THE WHOLE PLANET.
LEFT TO THEIR OWN DEVICES, THERE WON'T BE ANY PLANTS LEFT FOR YOU TO DO YOUR WORK.
DON'T WORRY ABOUT US...
WE'VE GOT EVERY SINGLE PLANT FROM OBLIVION WE COULD EVER NEED GROWING RIGHT HERE.
WITH THIS NEW BIO-DOME, I FINALLY HAVE US TO A POINT WHERE WE MAY NEVER NEED TO GO BACK.

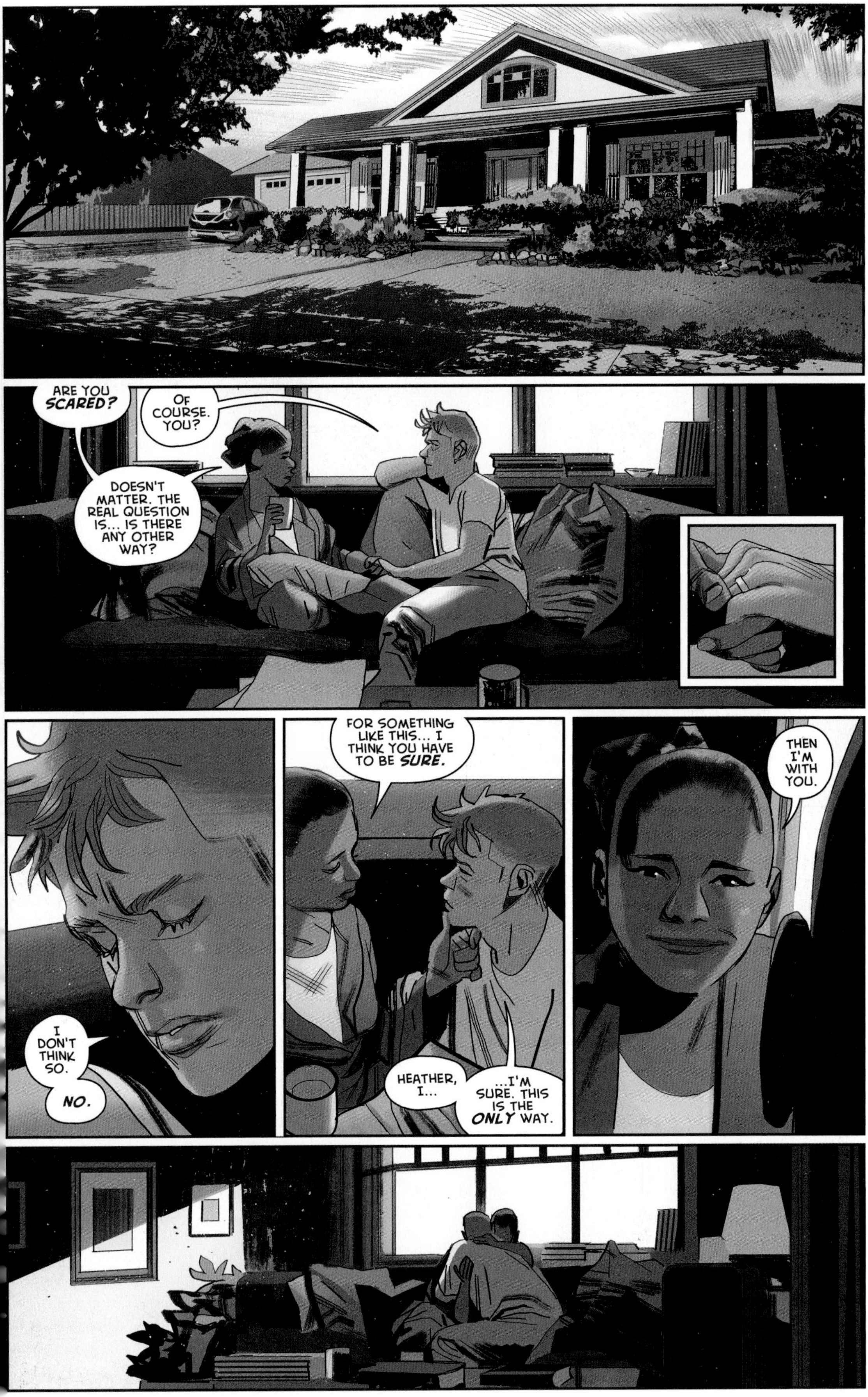

ARE YOU SCARED?
OF COURSE. YOU?
DOESN'T MATTER. THE REAL QUESTION IS... IS THERE ANY OTHER WAY?
I DON'T THINK SO.
NO.
FOR SOMETHING LIKE THIS... I THINK YOU HAVE TO BE SURE.
HEATHER, I...
...I'M SURE. THIS IS THE ONLY WAY.
THEN I'M WITH YOU.

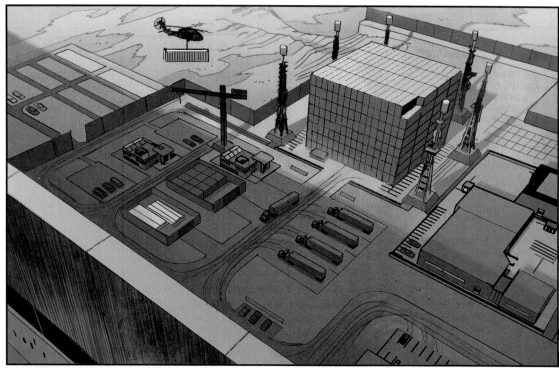

FA-FFAYAYA-AASH!

HEY, YOU!

WHAT ARE YOU *DOING* UP THERE?!

OH, SORRY.

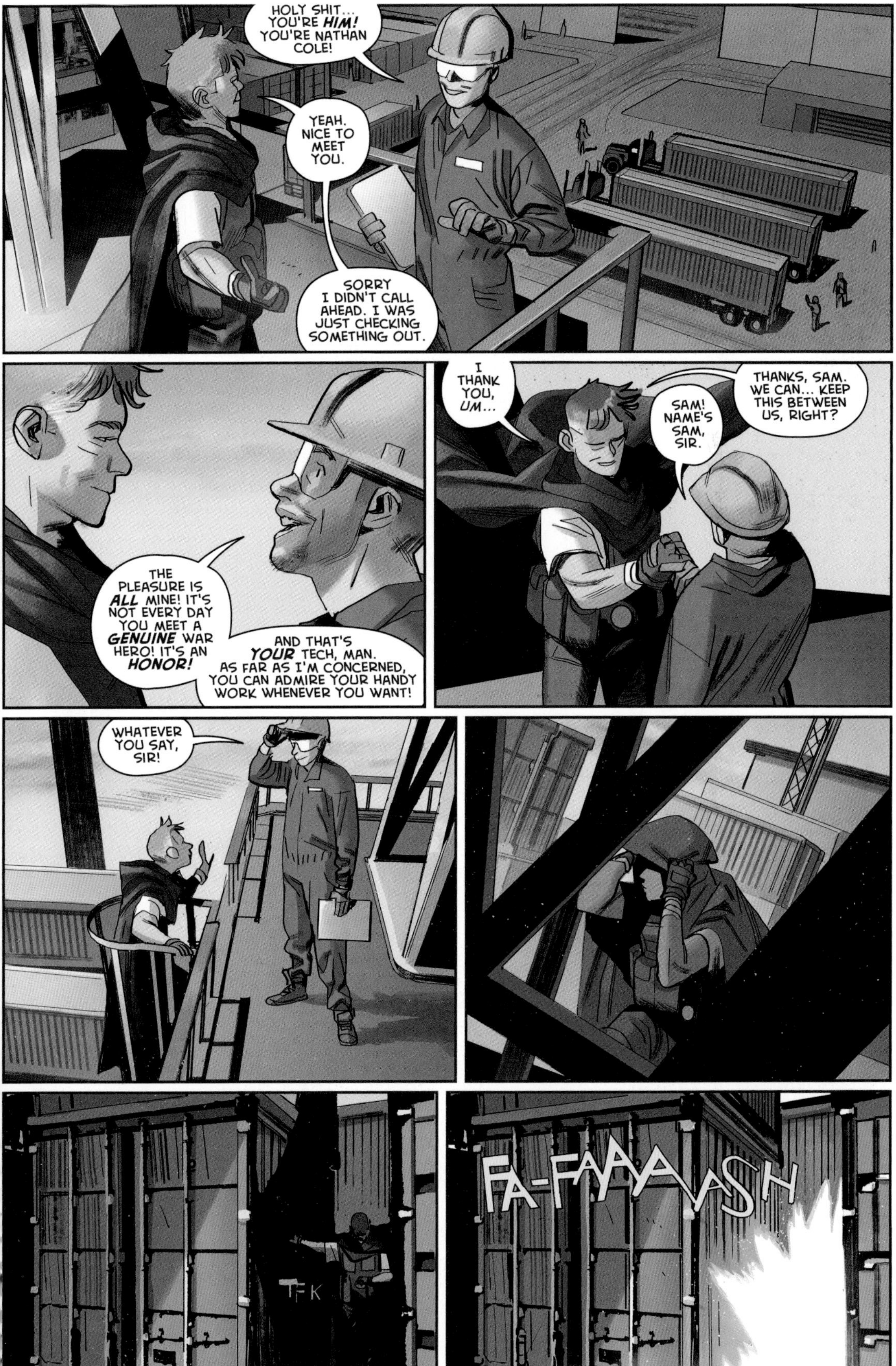
HOLY SHIT... YOU'RE HIM! YOU'RE NATHAN COLE!
YEAH. NICE TO MEET YOU.
SORRY I DIDN'T CALL AHEAD. I WAS JUST CHECKING SOMETHING OUT.
THE PLEASURE IS ALL MINE! IT'S NOT EVERY DAY YOU MEET A GENUINE WAR HERO! IT'S AN HONOR!
AND THAT'S YOUR TECH, MAN. AS FAR AS I'M CONCERNED, YOU CAN ADMIRE YOUR HANDY WORK WHENEVER YOU WANT!
I THANK YOU, UM...
SAM! NAME'S SAM, SIR.
THANKS, SAM. WE CAN... KEEP THIS BETWEEN US, RIGHT?
WHATEVER YOU SAY, SIR!
TFK
FA-FAAAASH

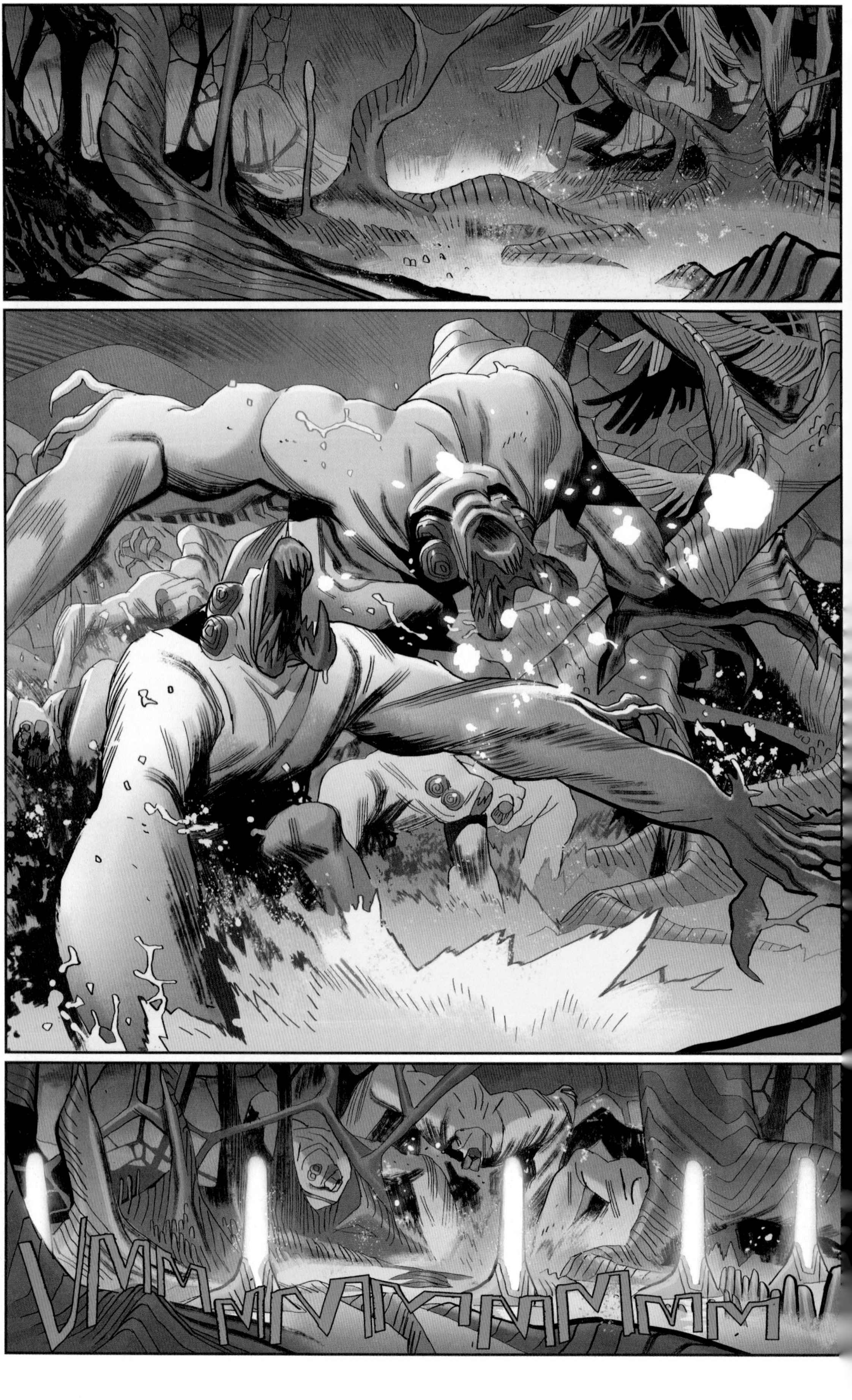

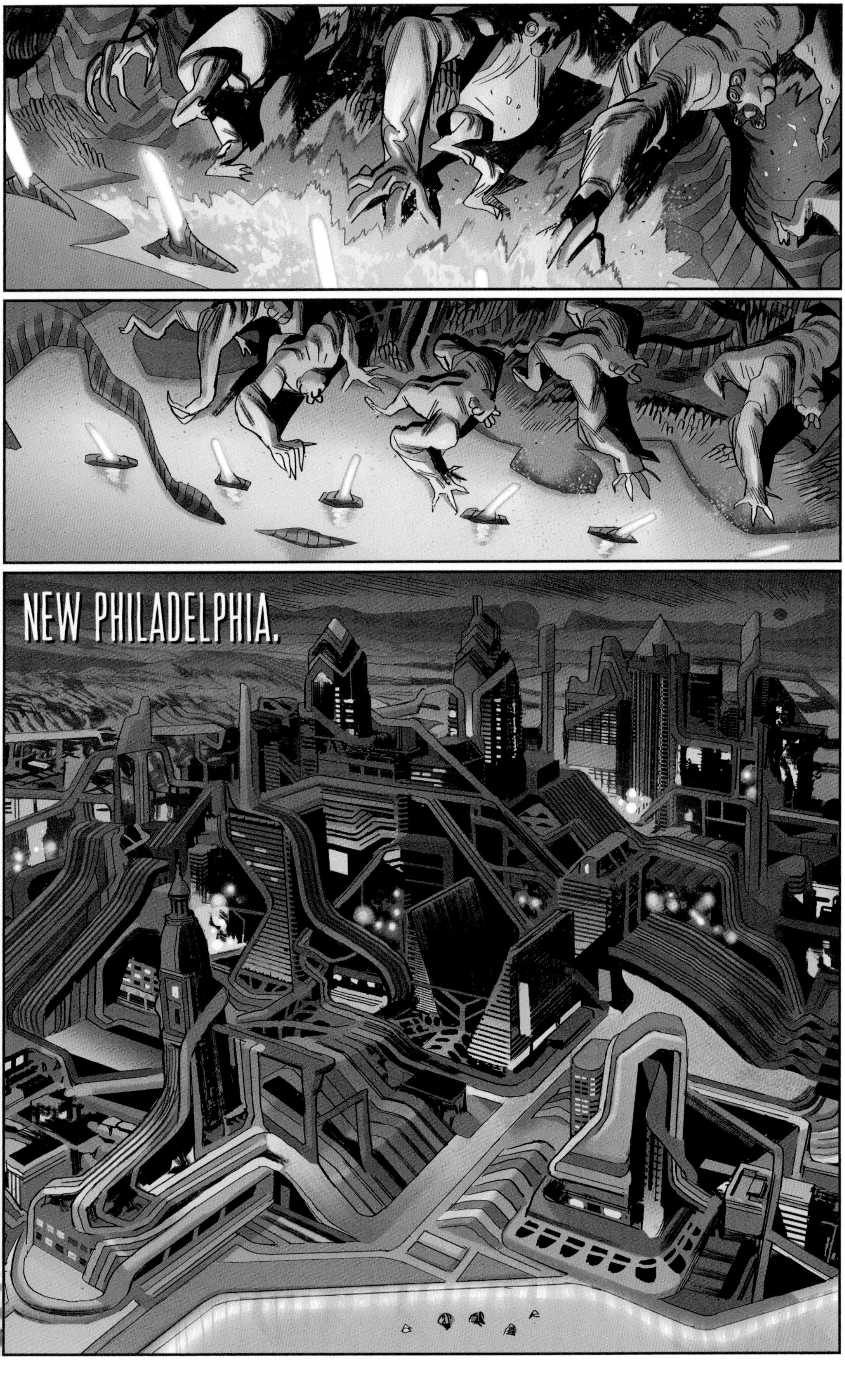
NEW PHILADELPHIA.

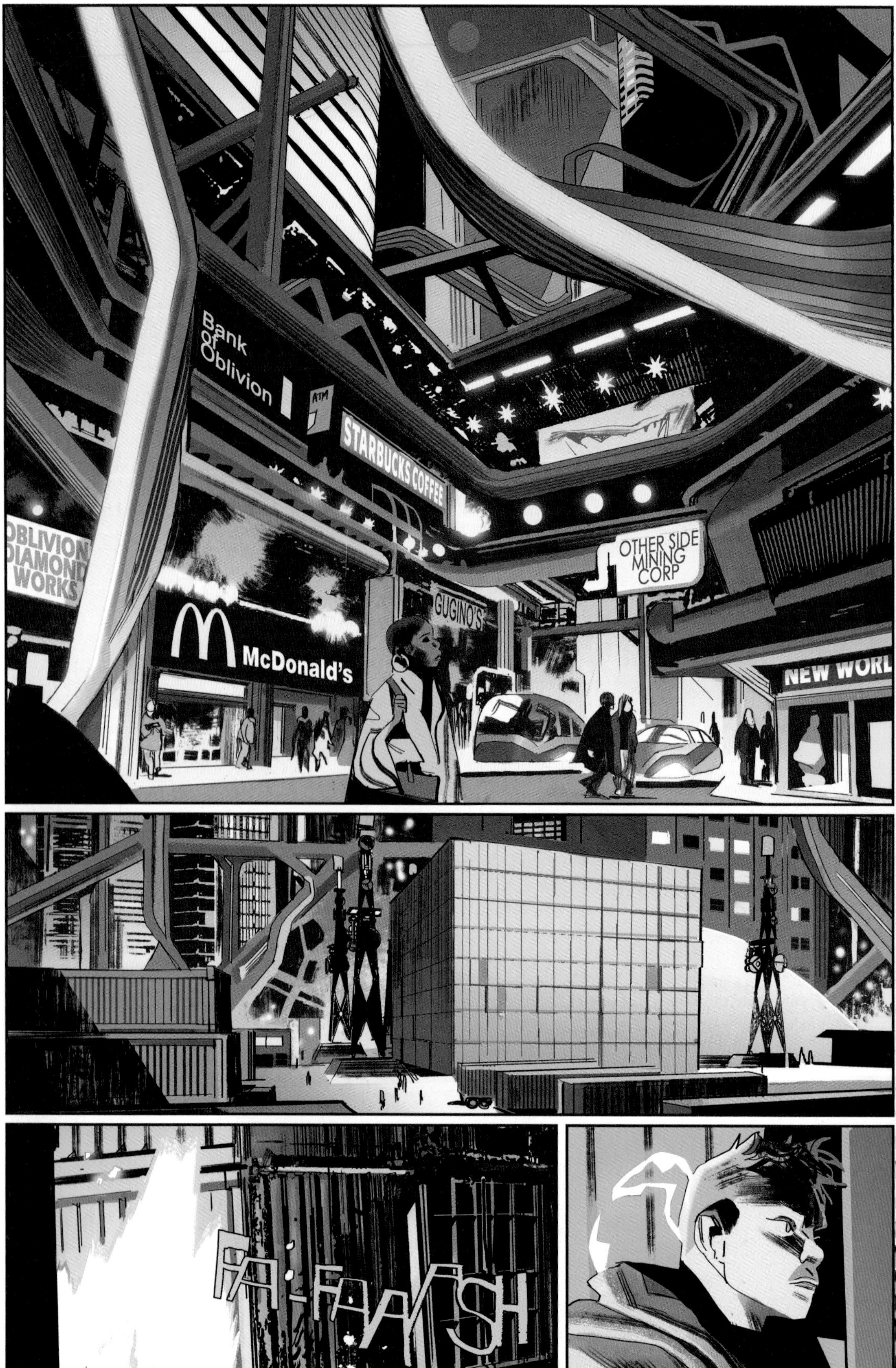
Bank of Oblivion
ATM
STARBUCKS COFFEE
OBLIVION DIAMOND WORKS
McDonald's
GUGINO'S
OTHER SIDE MINING CORP
NEW WORL
FA-FAASH

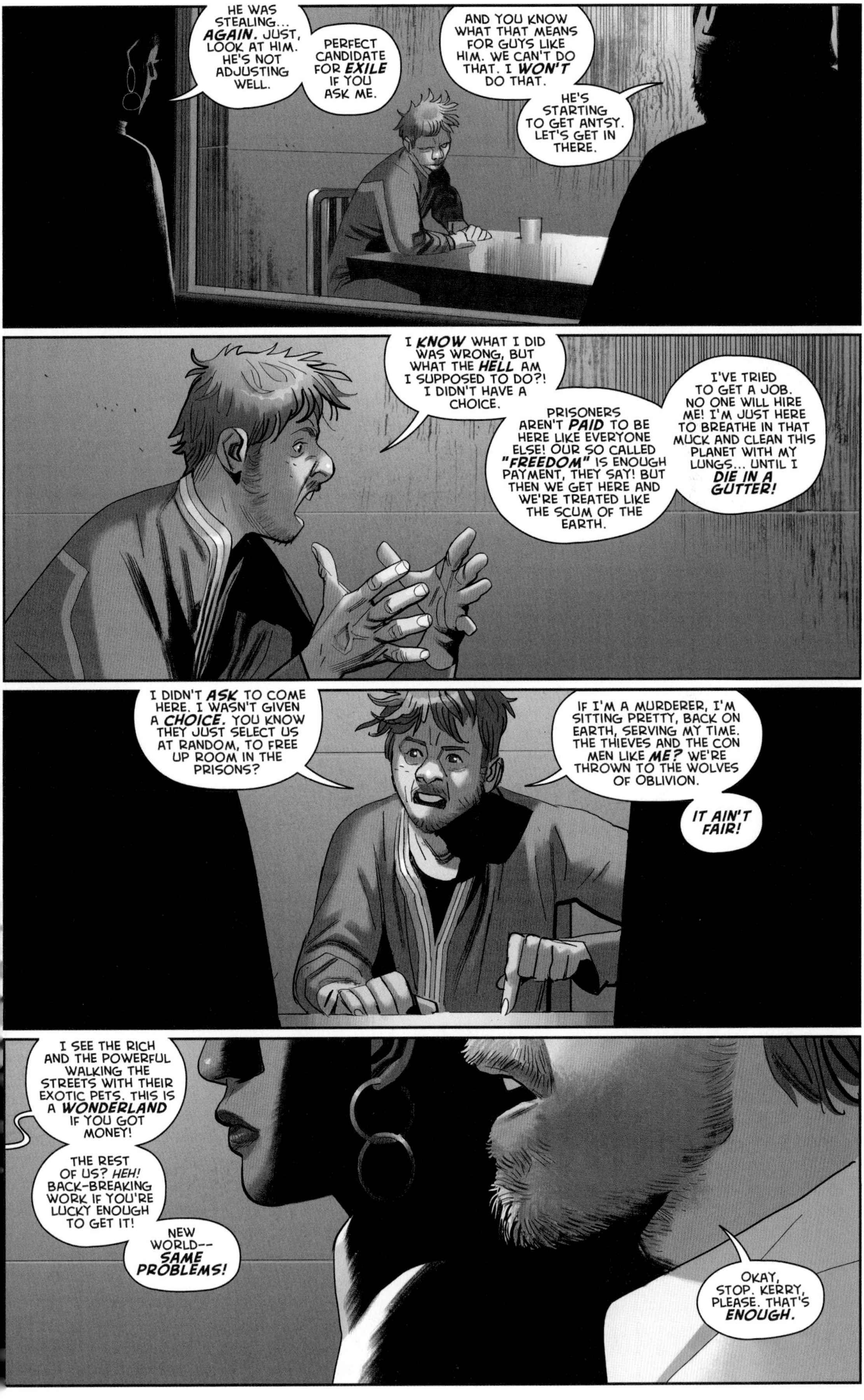

HE WAS STEALING... AGAIN. JUST, LOOK AT HIM. HE'S NOT ADJUSTING WELL.
PERFECT CANDIDATE FOR EXILE IF YOU ASK ME.
AND YOU KNOW WHAT THAT MEANS FOR GUYS LIKE HIM. WE CAN'T DO THAT. I WON'T DO THAT.
HE'S STARTING TO GET ANTSY. LET'S GET IN THERE.
I KNOW WHAT I DID WAS WRONG, BUT WHAT THE HELL AM I SUPPOSED TO DO?! I DIDN'T HAVE A CHOICE.
PRISONERS AREN'T PAID TO BE HERE LIKE EVERYONE ELSE! OUR SO CALLED "FREEDOM" IS ENOUGH PAYMENT, THEY SAY! BUT THEN WE GET HERE AND WE'RE TREATED LIKE THE SCUM OF THE EARTH.
I'VE TRIED TO GET A JOB. NO ONE WILL HIRE ME! I'M JUST HERE TO BREATHE IN THAT MUCK AND CLEAN THIS PLANET WITH MY LUNGS... UNTIL I DIE IN A GUTTER!
I DIDN'T ASK TO COME HERE. I WASN'T GIVEN A CHOICE. YOU KNOW THEY JUST SELECT US AT RANDOM, TO FREE UP ROOM IN THE PRISONS?
IF I'M A MURDERER, I'M SITTING PRETTY, BACK ON EARTH, SERVING MY TIME. THE THIEVES AND THE CON MEN LIKE ME? WE'RE THROWN TO THE WOLVES OF OBLIVION.
IT AIN'T FAIR!
I SEE THE RICH AND THE POWERFUL WALKING THE STREETS WITH THEIR EXOTIC PETS. THIS IS A WONDERLAND IF YOU GOT MONEY!
THE REST OF US? HEH! BACK-BREAKING WORK IF YOU'RE LUCKY ENOUGH TO GET IT!
NEW WORLD-- SAME PROBLEMS!
OKAY, STOP. KERRY, PLEASE. THAT'S ENOUGH.

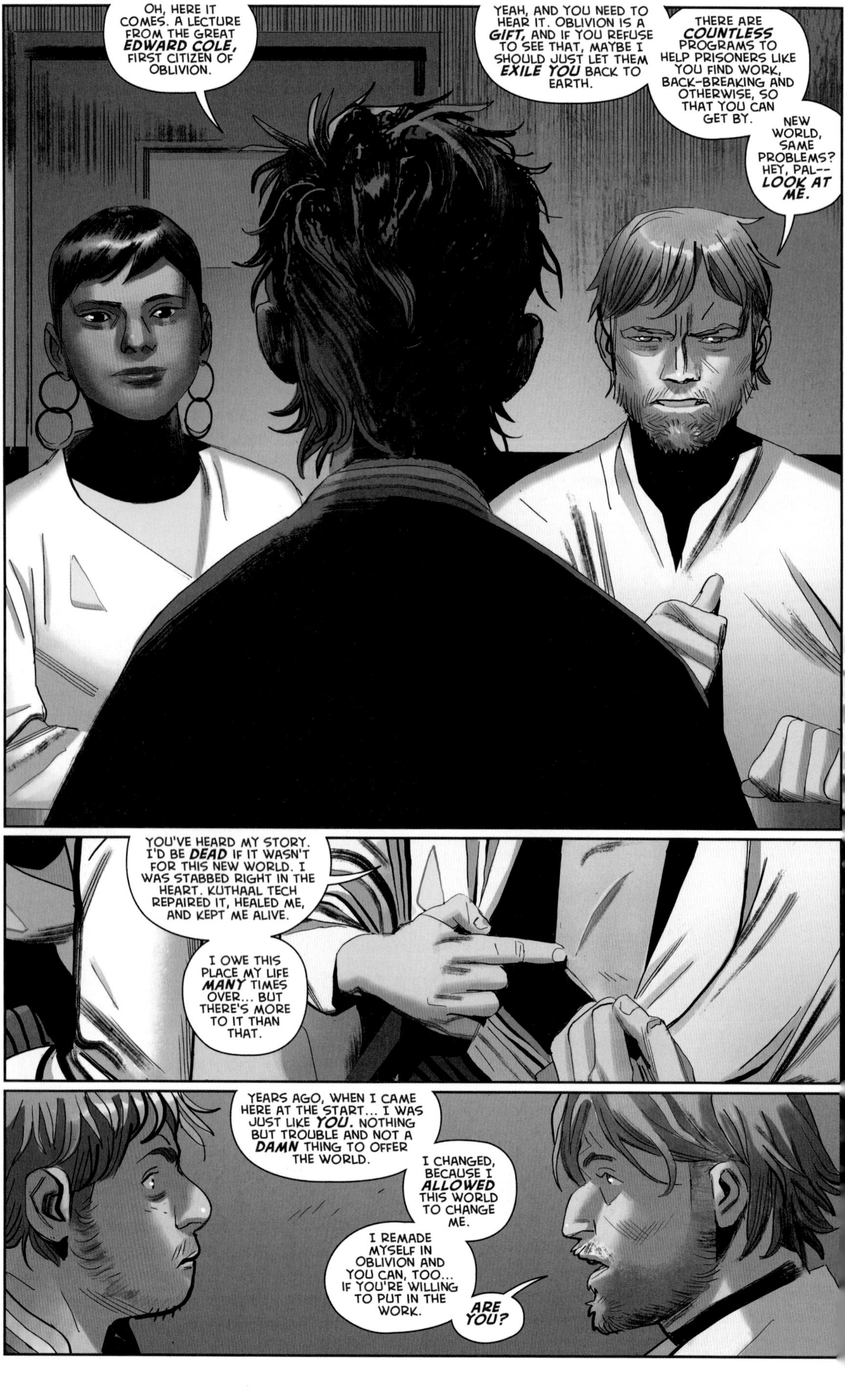
OH, HERE IT COMES. A LECTURE FROM THE GREAT EDWARD COLE, FIRST CITIZEN OF OBLIVION.
YEAH, AND YOU NEED TO HEAR IT. OBLIVION IS A GIFT, AND IF YOU REFUSE TO SEE THAT, MAYBE I SHOULD JUST LET THEM EXILE YOU BACK TO EARTH.
THERE ARE COUNTLESS PROGRAMS TO HELP PRISONERS LIKE YOU FIND WORK, BACK-BREAKING AND OTHERWISE, SO THAT YOU CAN GET BY.
NEW WORLD, SAME PROBLEMS? HEY, PAL-- LOOK AT ME.
YOU'VE HEARD MY STORY. I'D BE DEAD IF IT WASN'T FOR THIS NEW WORLD. I WAS STABBED RIGHT IN THE HEART. KUTHAAL TECH REPAIRED IT, HEALED ME, AND KEPT ME ALIVE.
I OWE THIS PLACE MY LIFE MANY TIMES OVER... BUT THERE'S MORE TO IT THAN THAT.
YEARS AGO, WHEN I CAME HERE AT THE START... I WAS JUST LIKE YOU. NOTHING BUT TROUBLE AND NOT A DAMN THING TO OFFER THE WORLD.
I CHANGED, BECAUSE I ALLOWED THIS WORLD TO CHANGE ME.
I REMADE MYSELF IN OBLIVION AND YOU CAN, TOO... IF YOU'RE WILLING TO PUT IN THE WORK.
ARE YOU?

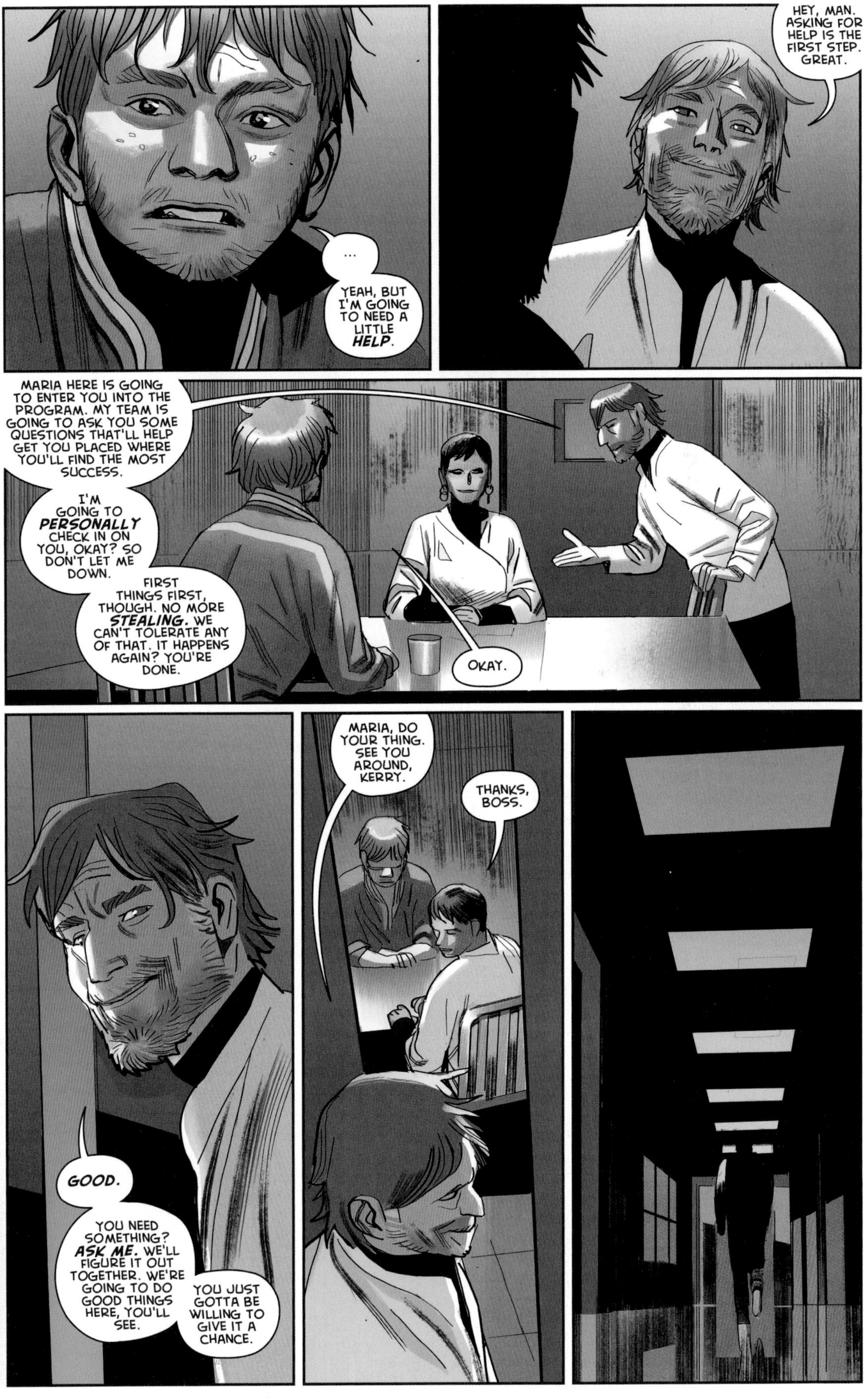

...
YEAH, BUT I'M GOING TO NEED A LITTLE HELP.
HEY, MAN. ASKING FOR HELP IS THE FIRST STEP. GREAT.
MARIA HERE IS GOING TO ENTER YOU INTO THE PROGRAM. MY TEAM IS GOING TO ASK YOU SOME QUESTIONS THAT'LL HELP GET YOU PLACED WHERE YOU'LL FIND THE MOST SUCCESS.
I'M GOING TO PERSONALLY CHECK IN ON YOU, OKAY? SO DON'T LET ME DOWN.
FIRST THINGS FIRST, THOUGH. NO MORE STEALING. WE CAN'T TOLERATE ANY OF THAT. IT HAPPENS AGAIN? YOU'RE DONE.
OKAY.
GOOD.
YOU NEED SOMETHING? ASK ME. WE'LL FIGURE IT OUT TOGETHER. WE'RE GOING TO DO GOOD THINGS HERE, YOU'LL SEE.
YOU JUST GOTTA BE WILLING TO GIVE IT A CHANCE.
MARIA, DO YOUR THING. SEE YOU AROUND, KERRY.
THANKS, BOSS.

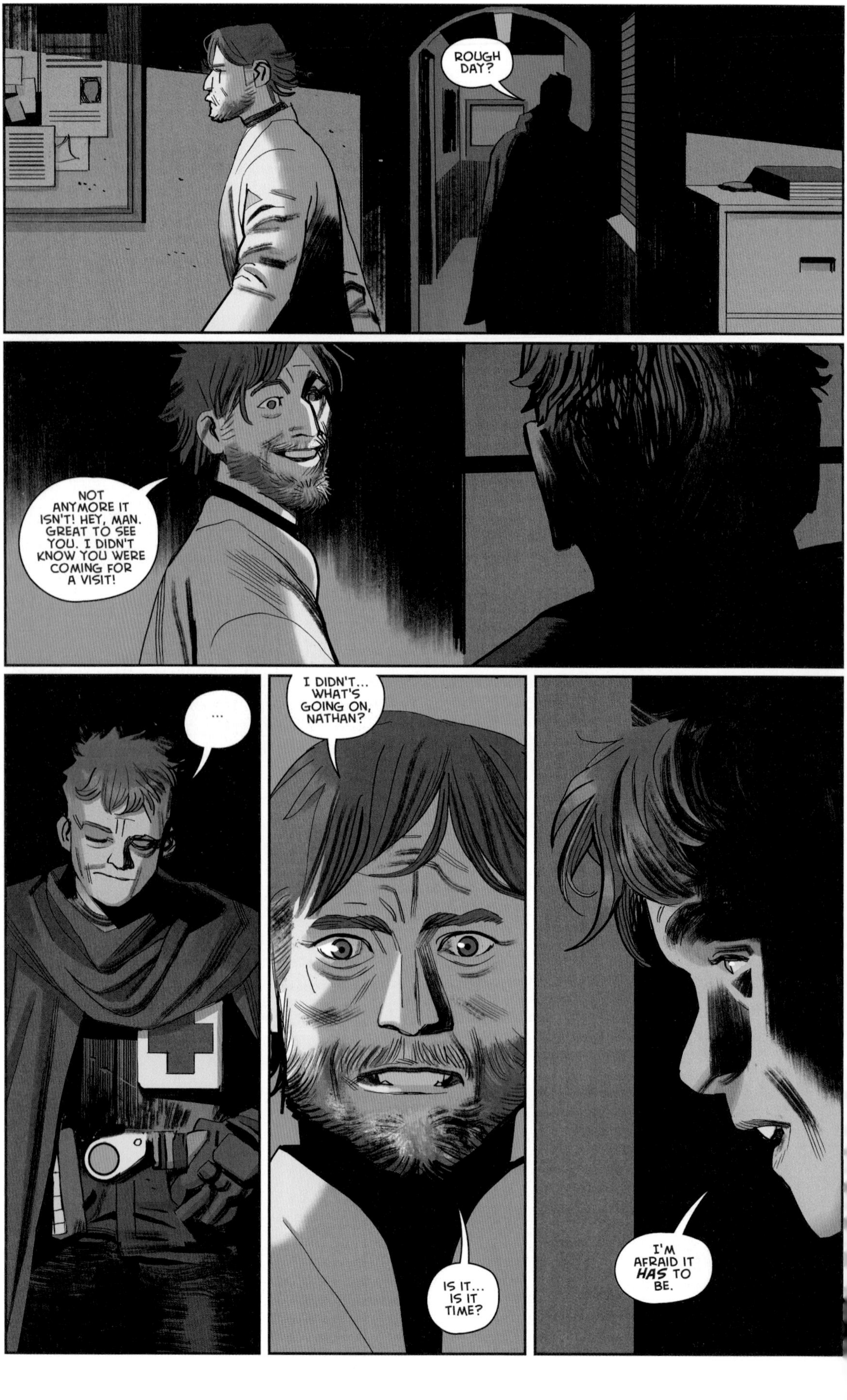
ROUGH DAY?
NOT ANYMORE IT ISN'T! HEY, MAN. GREAT TO SEE YOU. I DIDN'T KNOW YOU WERE COMING FOR A VISIT!
...
I DIDN'T... WHAT'S GOING ON, NATHAN?
IS IT... IS IT TIME?
I'M AFRAID IT *HAS* TO BE.

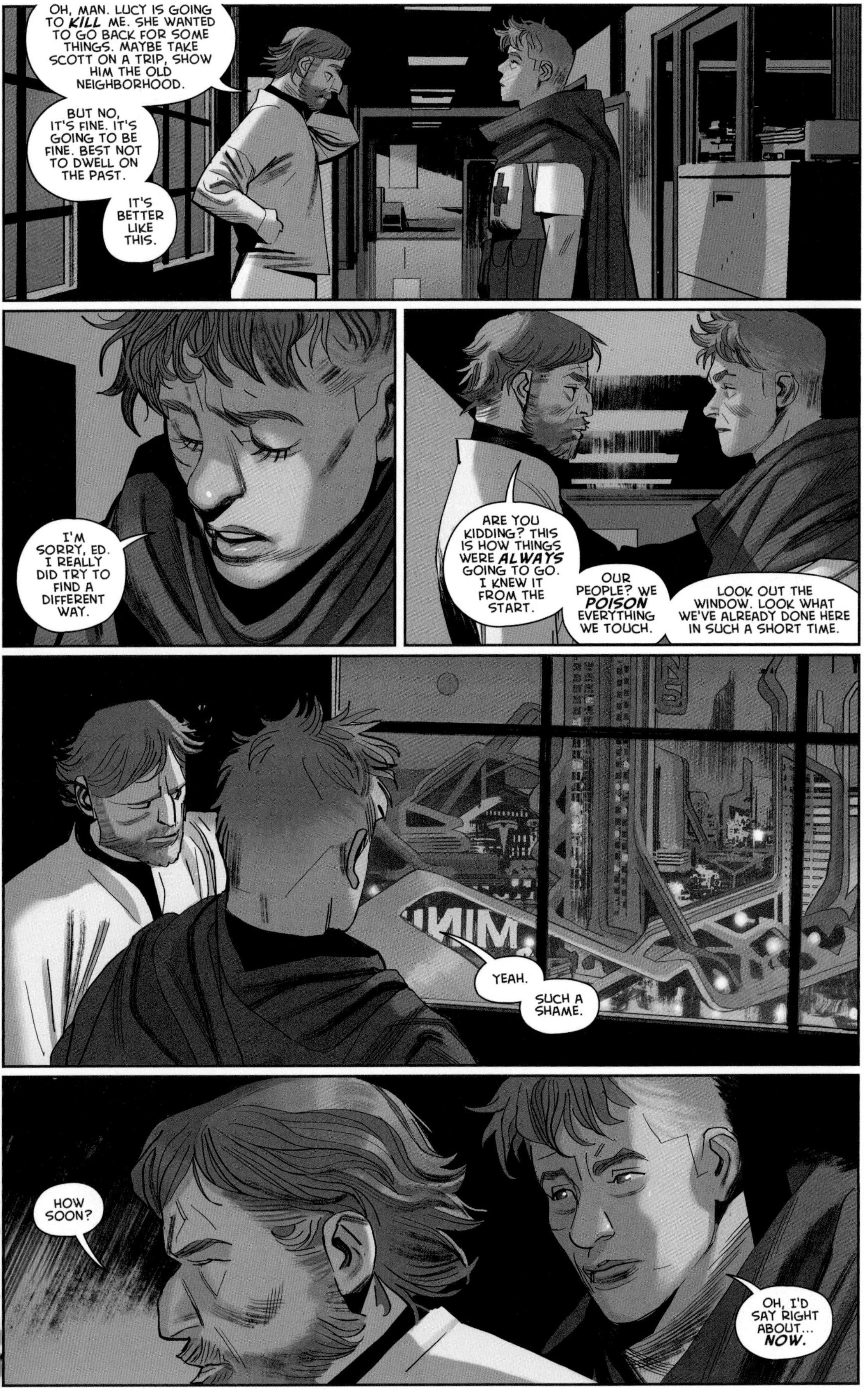
OH, MAN. LUCY IS GOING TO KILL ME. SHE WANTED TO GO BACK FOR SOME THINGS. MAYBE TAKE SCOTT ON A TRIP, SHOW HIM THE OLD NEIGHBORHOOD.
BUT NO, IT'S FINE. IT'S GOING TO BE FINE. BEST NOT TO DWELL ON THE PAST.
IT'S BETTER LIKE THIS.
I'M SORRY, ED. I REALLY DID TRY TO FIND A DIFFERENT WAY.
ARE YOU KIDDING? THIS IS HOW THINGS WERE ALWAYS GOING TO GO. I KNEW IT FROM THE START.
OUR PEOPLE? WE POISON EVERYTHING WE TOUCH.
LOOK OUT THE WINDOW. LOOK WHAT WE'VE ALREADY DONE HERE IN SUCH A SHORT TIME.
YEAH.
SUCH A SHAME.
HOW SOON?
OH, I'D SAY RIGHT ABOUT... NOW.

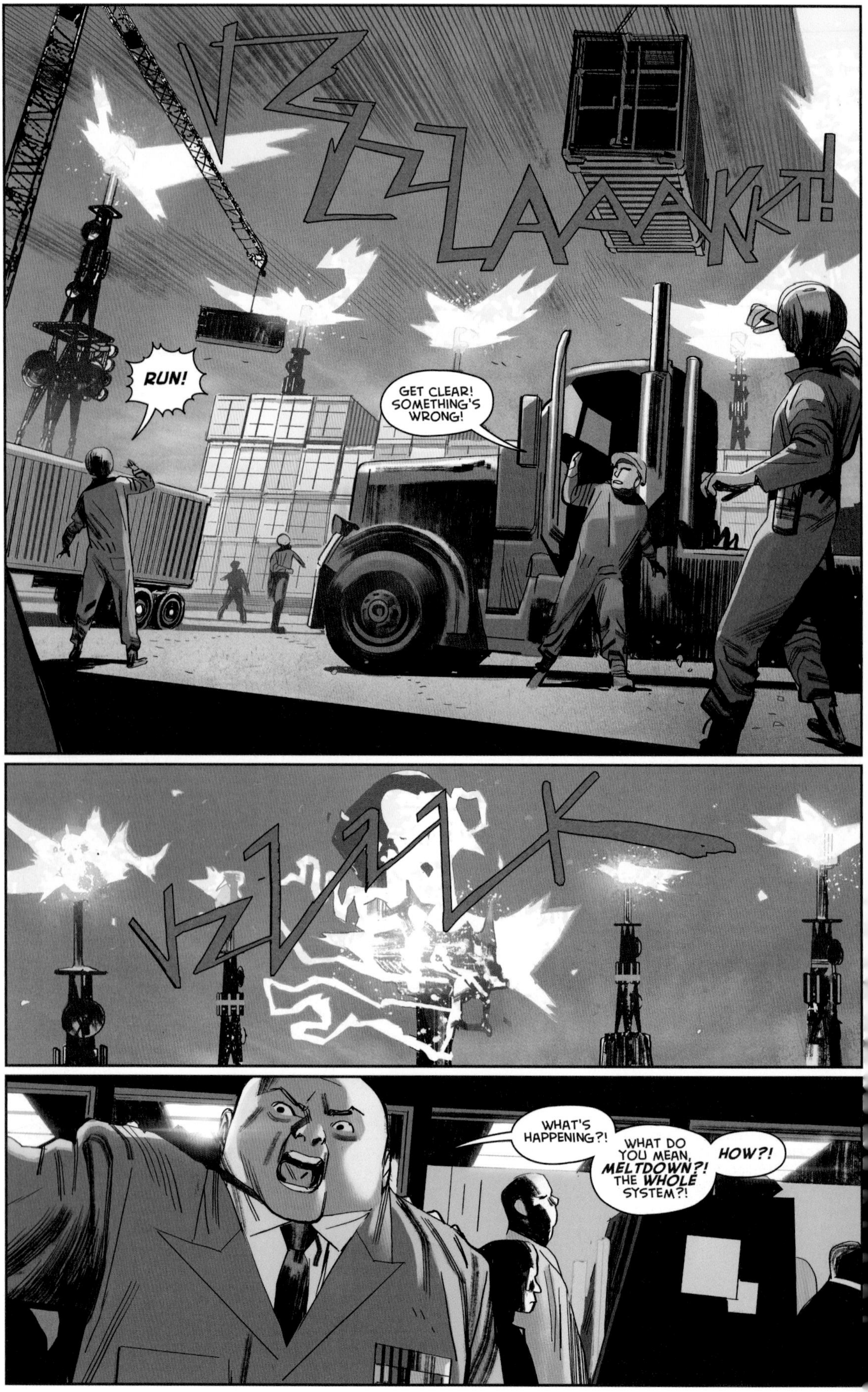
VZZZLAAAAKKT!
RUN!
GET CLEAR! SOMETHING'S WRONG!
VZZZZZK
WHAT'S HAPPENING?!
WHAT DO YOU MEAN, MELTDOWN?! THE WHOLE SYSTEM?!
HOW?!

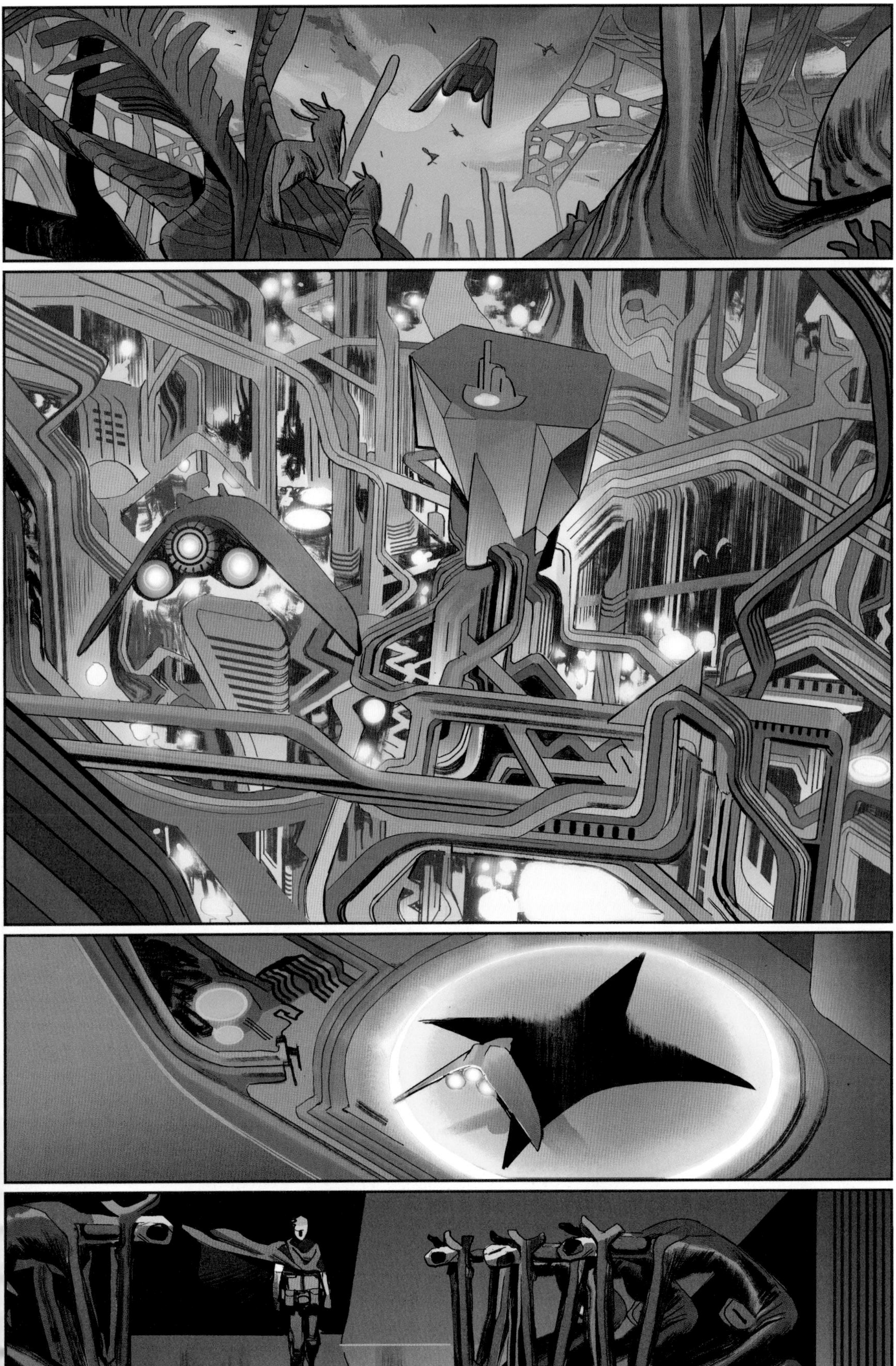

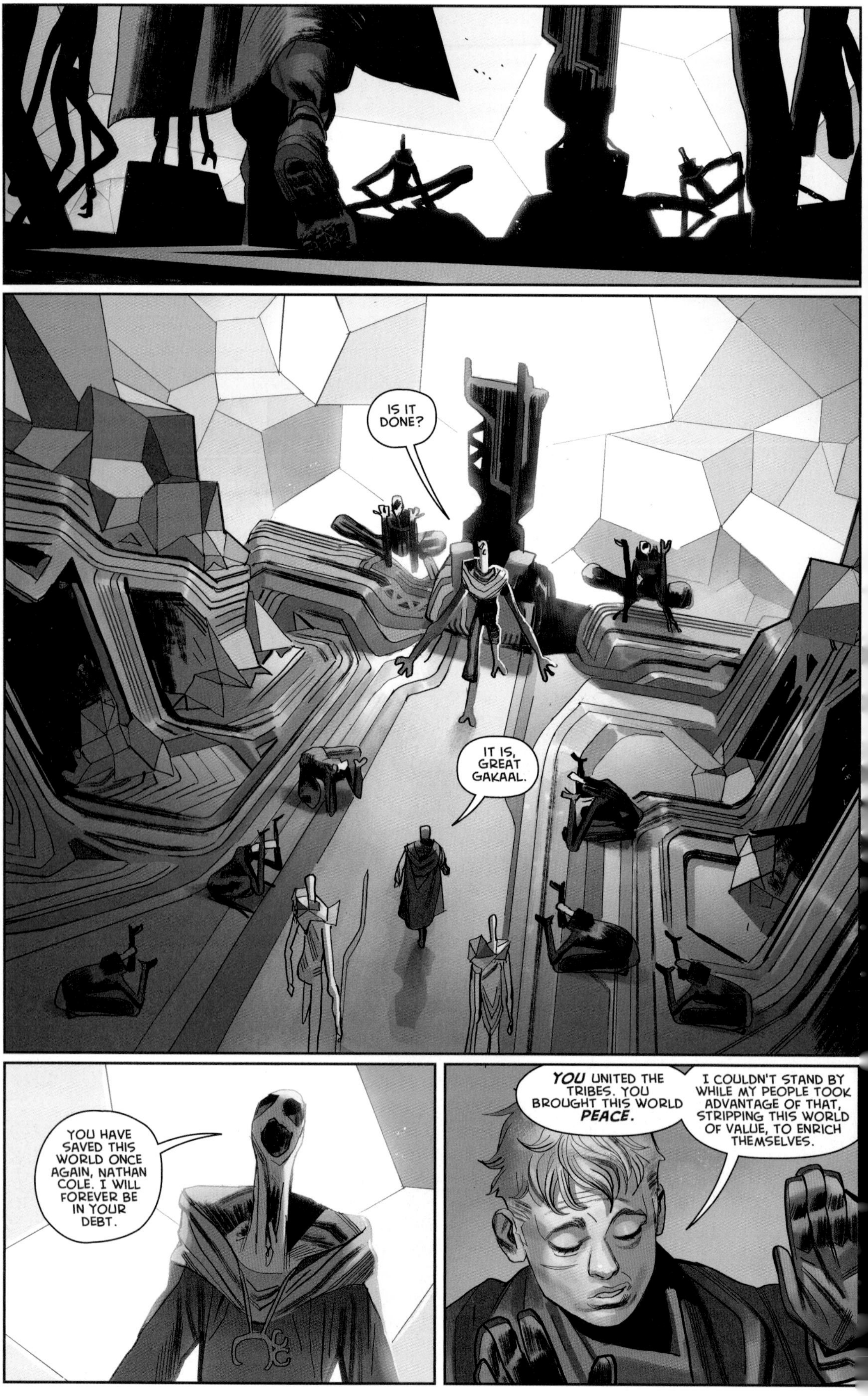

...
IS IT DONE?
IT IS, GREAT GAKAAL.
YOU HAVE SAVED THIS WORLD ONCE AGAIN, NATHAN COLE. I WILL FOREVER BE IN YOUR DEBT.
YOU UNITED THE TRIBES. YOU BROUGHT THIS WORLD *PEACE*.
I COULDN'T STAND BY WHILE MY PEOPLE TOOK ADVANTAGE OF THAT, STRIPPING THIS WORLD OF VALUE, TO ENRICH THEMSELVES.

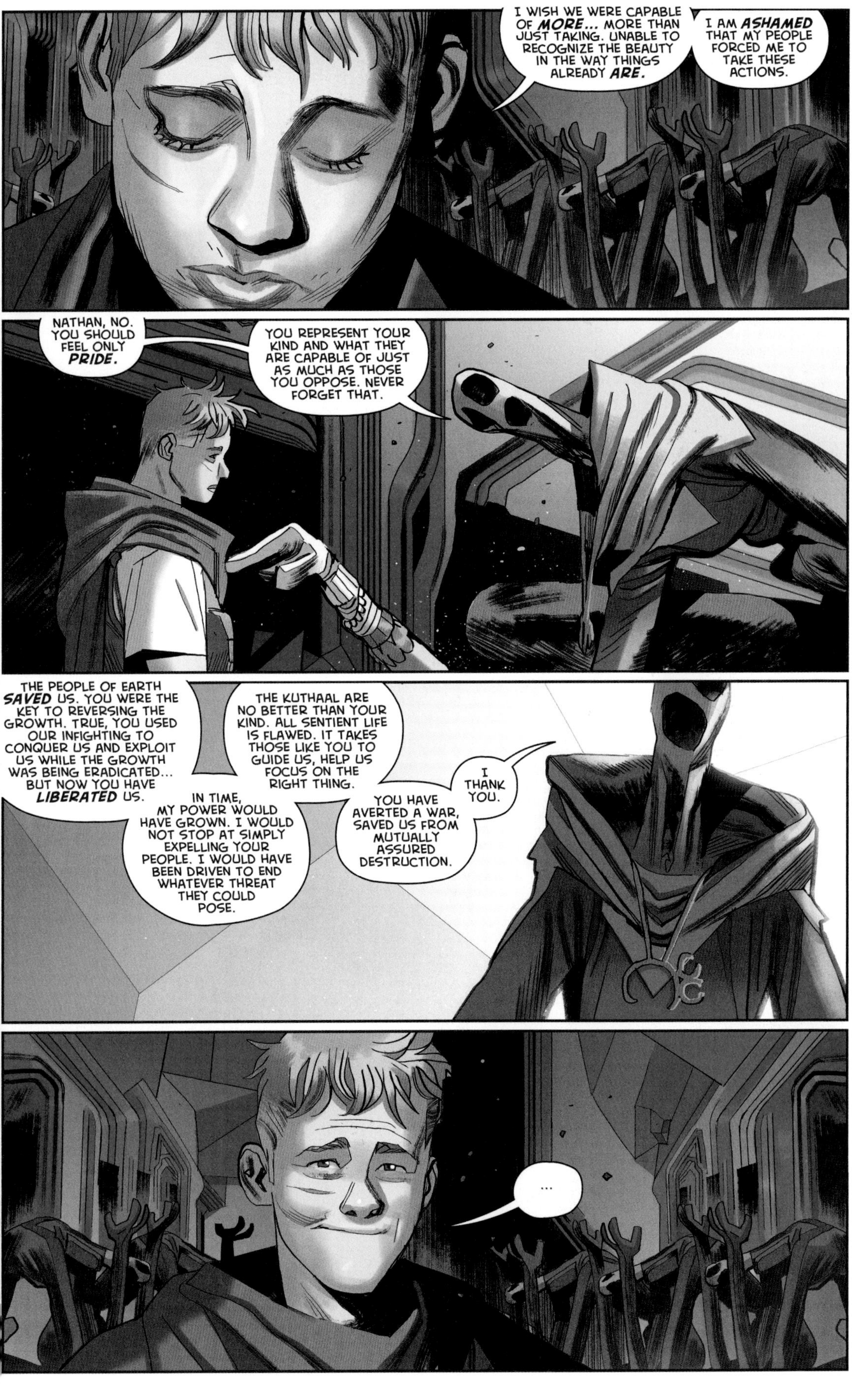

I WISH WE WERE CAPABLE OF MORE... MORE THAN JUST TAKING. UNABLE TO RECOGNIZE THE BEAUTY IN THE WAY THINGS ALREADY ARE.
I AM ASHAMED THAT MY PEOPLE FORCED ME TO TAKE THESE ACTIONS.
NATHAN, NO. YOU SHOULD FEEL ONLY PRIDE.
YOU REPRESENT YOUR KIND AND WHAT THEY ARE CAPABLE OF JUST AS MUCH AS THOSE YOU OPPOSE. NEVER FORGET THAT.
THE PEOPLE OF EARTH SAVED US. YOU WERE THE KEY TO REVERSING THE GROWTH. TRUE, YOU USED OUR INFIGHTING TO CONQUER US AND EXPLOIT US WHILE THE GROWTH WAS BEING ERADICATED... BUT NOW YOU HAVE LIBERATED US.
IN TIME, MY POWER WOULD HAVE GROWN. I WOULD NOT STOP AT SIMPLY EXPELLING YOUR PEOPLE. I WOULD HAVE BEEN DRIVEN TO END WHATEVER THREAT THEY COULD POSE.
THE KUTHAAL ARE NO BETTER THAN YOUR KIND. ALL SENTIENT LIFE IS FLAWED. IT TAKES THOSE LIKE YOU TO GUIDE US, HELP US FOCUS ON THE RIGHT THING.
YOU HAVE AVERTED A WAR, SAVED US FROM MUTUALLY ASSURED DESTRUCTION.
I THANK YOU.
...

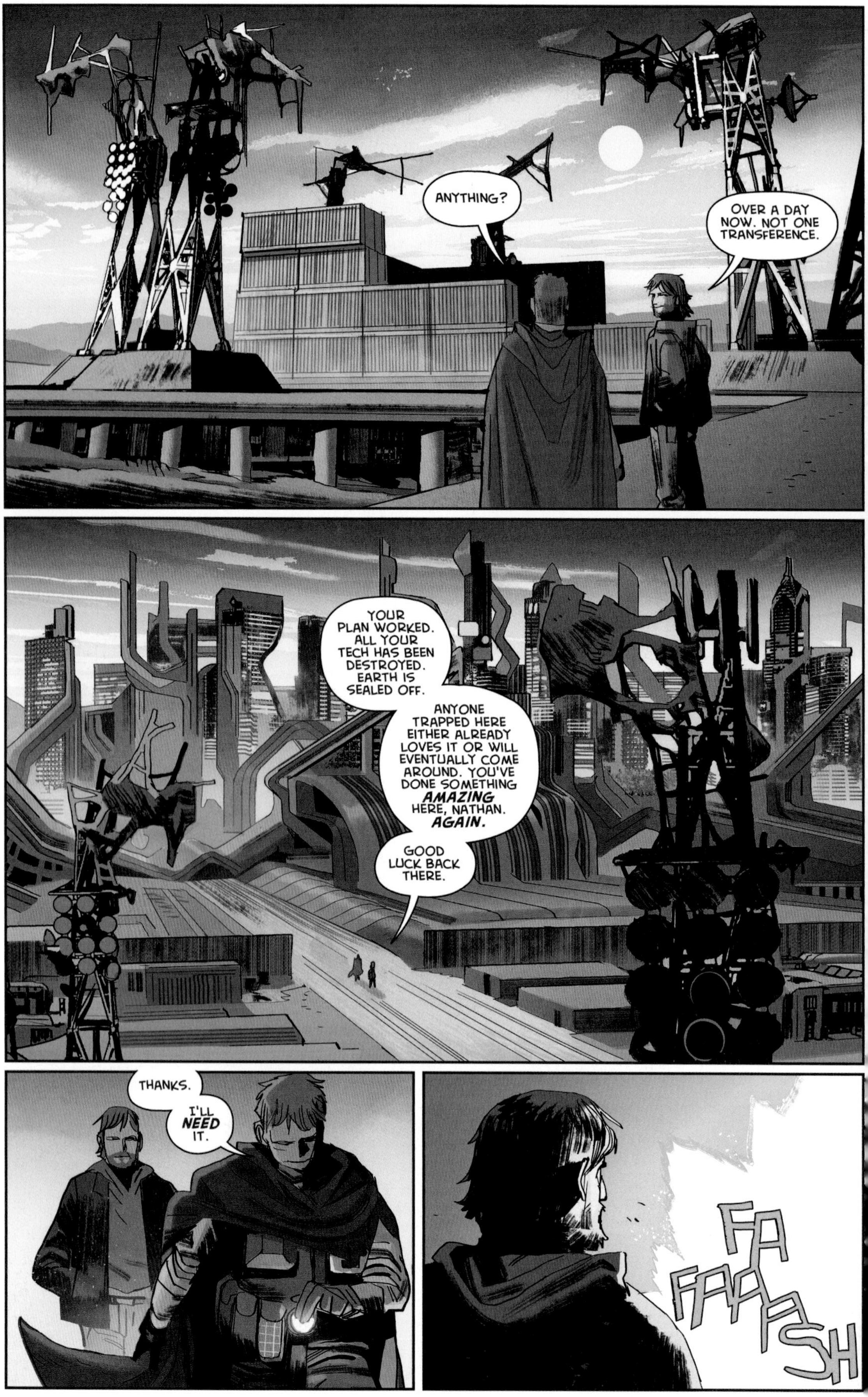

ANYTHING?
OVER A DAY NOW. NOT ONE TRANSFERENCE.
YOUR PLAN WORKED. ALL YOUR TECH HAS BEEN DESTROYED. EARTH IS SEALED OFF.
ANYONE TRAPPED HERE EITHER ALREADY LOVES IT OR WILL EVENTUALLY COME AROUND. YOU'VE DONE SOMETHING AMAZING HERE, NATHAN. AGAIN.
GOOD LUCK BACK THERE.
THANKS.
I'LL NEED IT.
FA FAAAASH

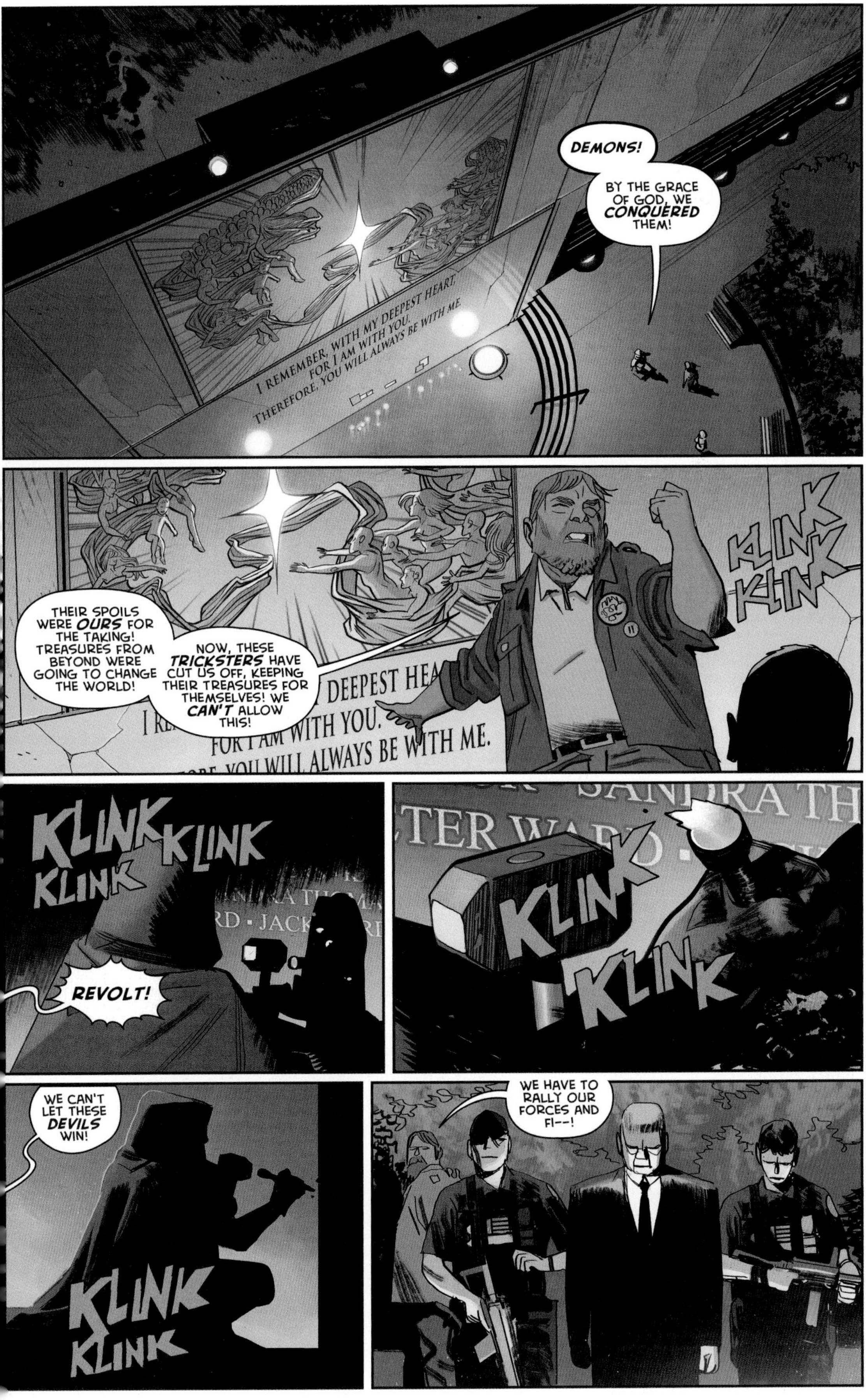
DEMONS!
BY THE GRACE OF GOD, WE CONQUERED THEM!
I REMEMBER, WITH MY DEEPEST HEART, FOR I AM WITH YOU. THEREFORE, YOU WILL ALWAYS BE WITH ME.
THEIR SPOILS WERE OURS FOR THE TAKING! TREASURES FROM BEYOND WERE GOING TO CHANGE THE WORLD!
NOW, THESE TRICKSTERS HAVE CUT US OFF, KEEPING THEIR TREASURES FOR THEMSELVES! WE CAN'T ALLOW THIS!
KLINK KLINK
KLINK KLINK
KLINK
REVOLT!
KLINK
KLINK
WE CAN'T LET THESE DEVILS WIN!
KLINK
KLINK
WE HAVE TO RALLY OUR FORCES AND FI--!

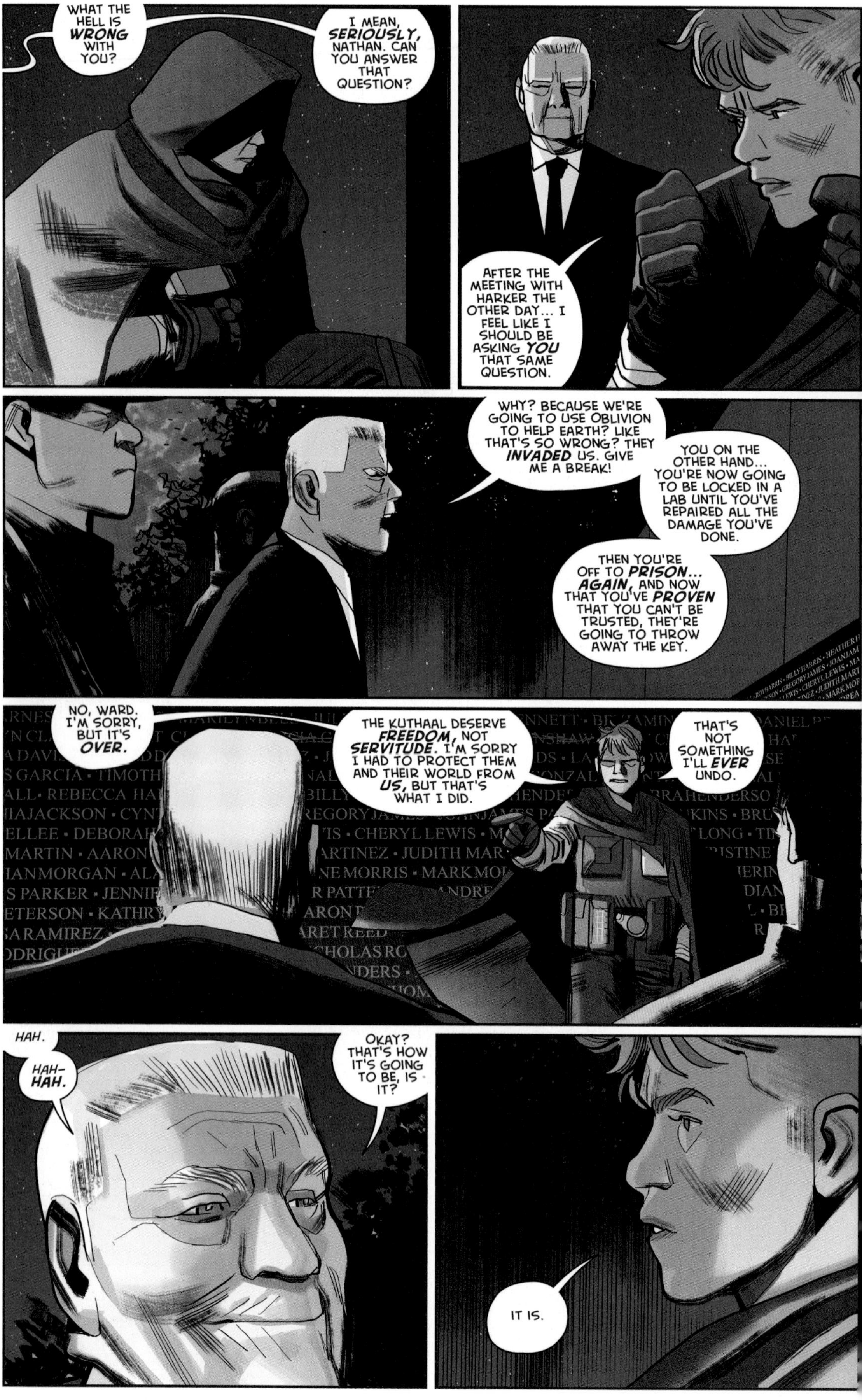

WHAT THE HELL IS WRONG WITH YOU?
I MEAN, SERIOUSLY, NATHAN. CAN YOU ANSWER THAT QUESTION?
AFTER THE MEETING WITH HARKER THE OTHER DAY... I FEEL LIKE I SHOULD BE ASKING YOU THAT SAME QUESTION.
WHY? BECAUSE WE'RE GOING TO USE OBLIVION TO HELP EARTH? LIKE THAT'S SO WRONG? THEY INVADED US. GIVE ME A BREAK!
YOU ON THE OTHER HAND... YOU'RE NOW GOING TO BE LOCKED IN A LAB UNTIL YOU'VE REPAIRED ALL THE DAMAGE YOU'VE DONE.
THEN YOU'RE OFF TO PRISON... AGAIN, AND NOW THAT YOU'VE PROVEN THAT YOU CAN'T BE TRUSTED, THEY'RE GOING TO THROW AWAY THE KEY.
NO, WARD. I'M SORRY, BUT IT'S OVER.
THE KUTHAAL DESERVE FREEDOM, NOT SERVITUDE. I'M SORRY I HAD TO PROTECT THEM AND THEIR WORLD FROM US, BUT THAT'S WHAT I DID.
THAT'S NOT SOMETHING I'LL EVER UNDO.
HAH.
HAH-HAH.
OKAY? THAT'S HOW IT'S GOING TO BE, IS IT?
IT IS.

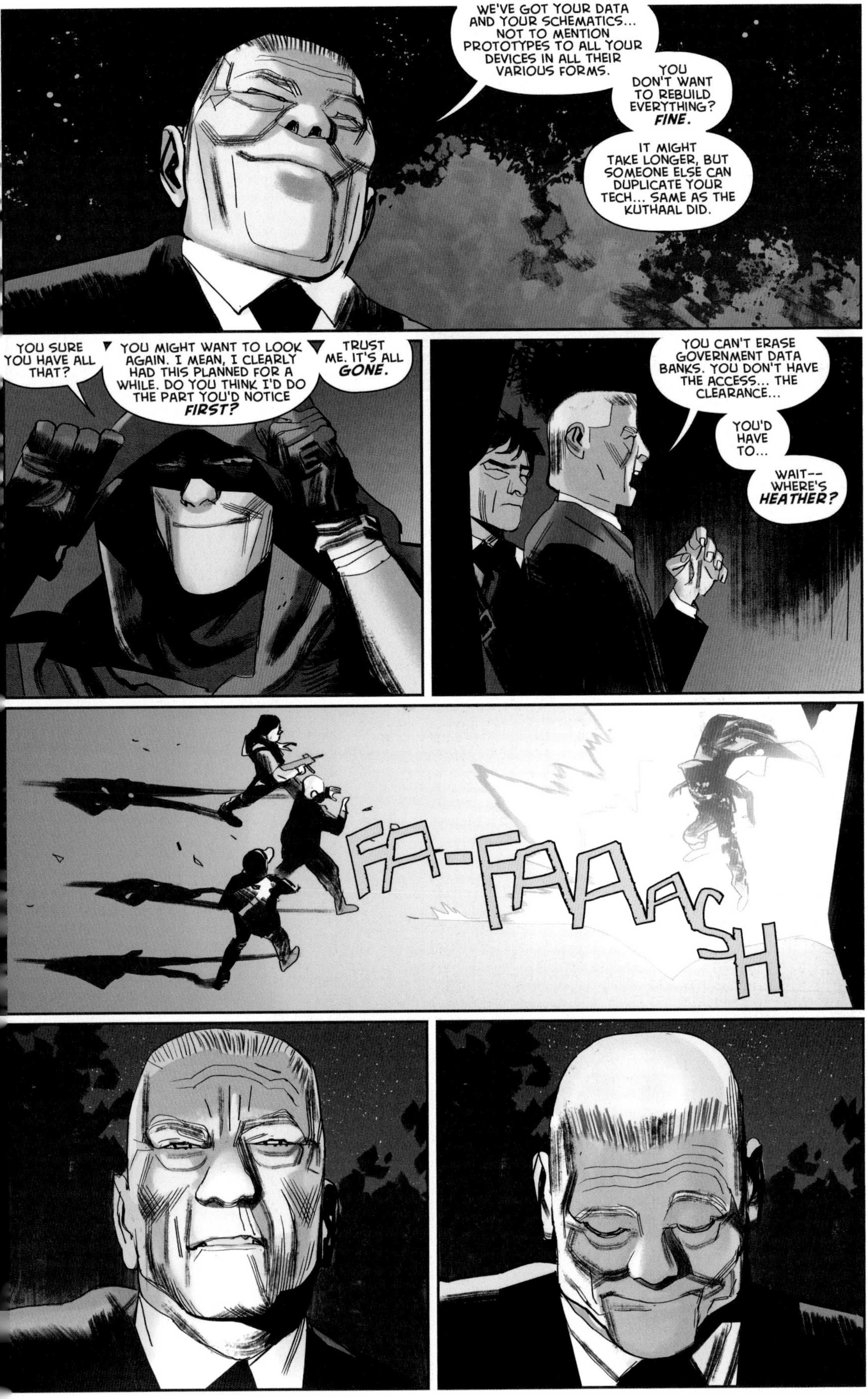
WE'VE GOT YOUR DATA AND YOUR SCHEMATICS... NOT TO MENTION PROTOTYPES TO ALL YOUR DEVICES IN ALL THEIR VARIOUS FORMS.
YOU DON'T WANT TO REBUILD EVERYTHING? FINE.
IT MIGHT TAKE LONGER, BUT SOMEONE ELSE CAN DUPLICATE YOUR TECH... SAME AS THE KUTHAAL DID.
YOU SURE YOU HAVE ALL THAT?
YOU MIGHT WANT TO LOOK AGAIN. I MEAN, I CLEARLY HAD THIS PLANNED FOR A WHILE. DO YOU THINK I'D DO THE PART YOU'D NOTICE FIRST?
TRUST ME. IT'S ALL GONE.
YOU CAN'T ERASE GOVERNMENT DATA BANKS. YOU DON'T HAVE THE ACCESS... THE CLEARANCE...
YOU'D HAVE TO...
WAIT-- WHERE'S HEATHER?
FA-FAAASH

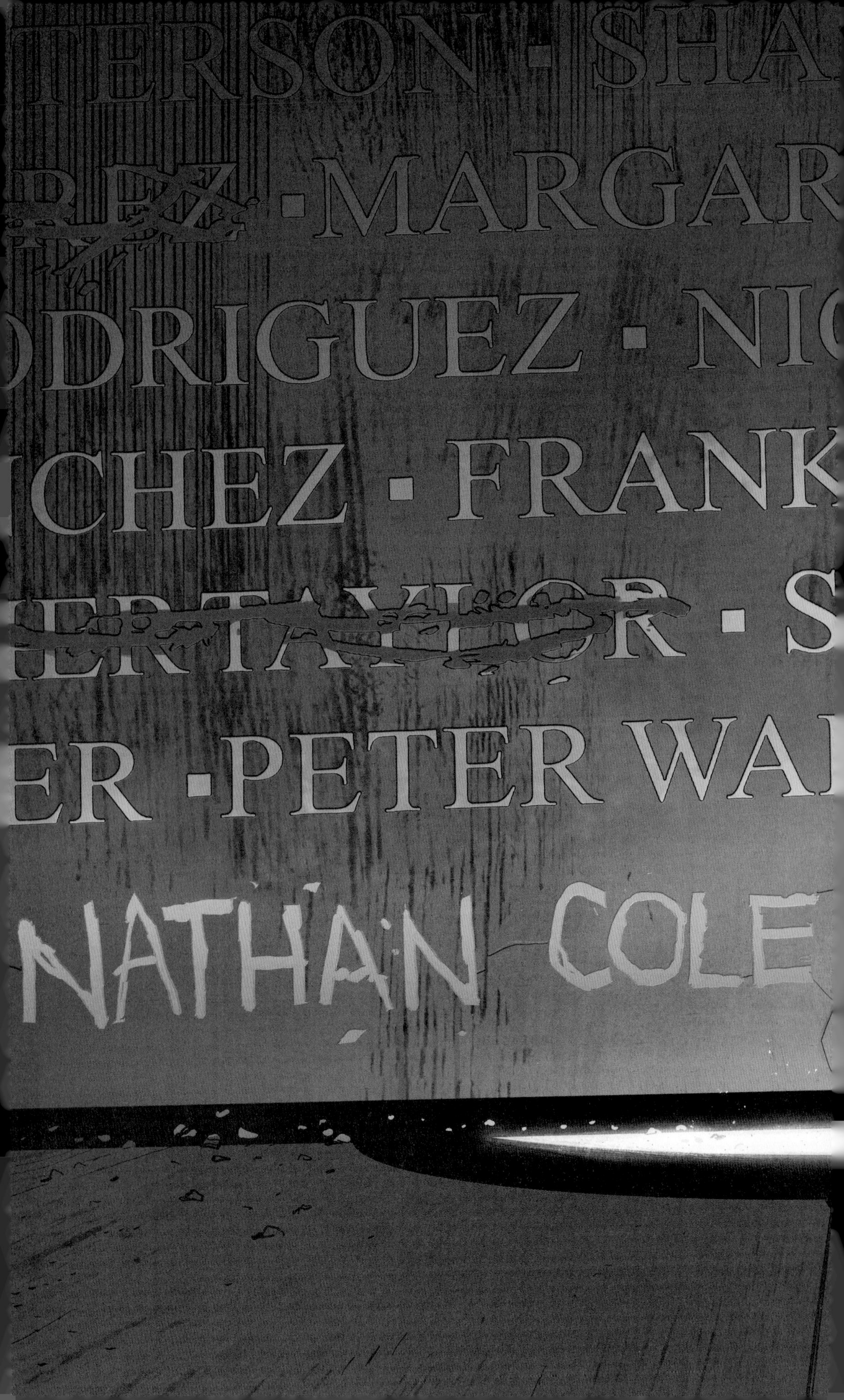

TERSON · SHA

REZ · MARGAR

ODRIGUEZ · NIC

CHEZ · FRANK

ER TAYLOR · S

ER · PETER WAI

NATHAN COLE

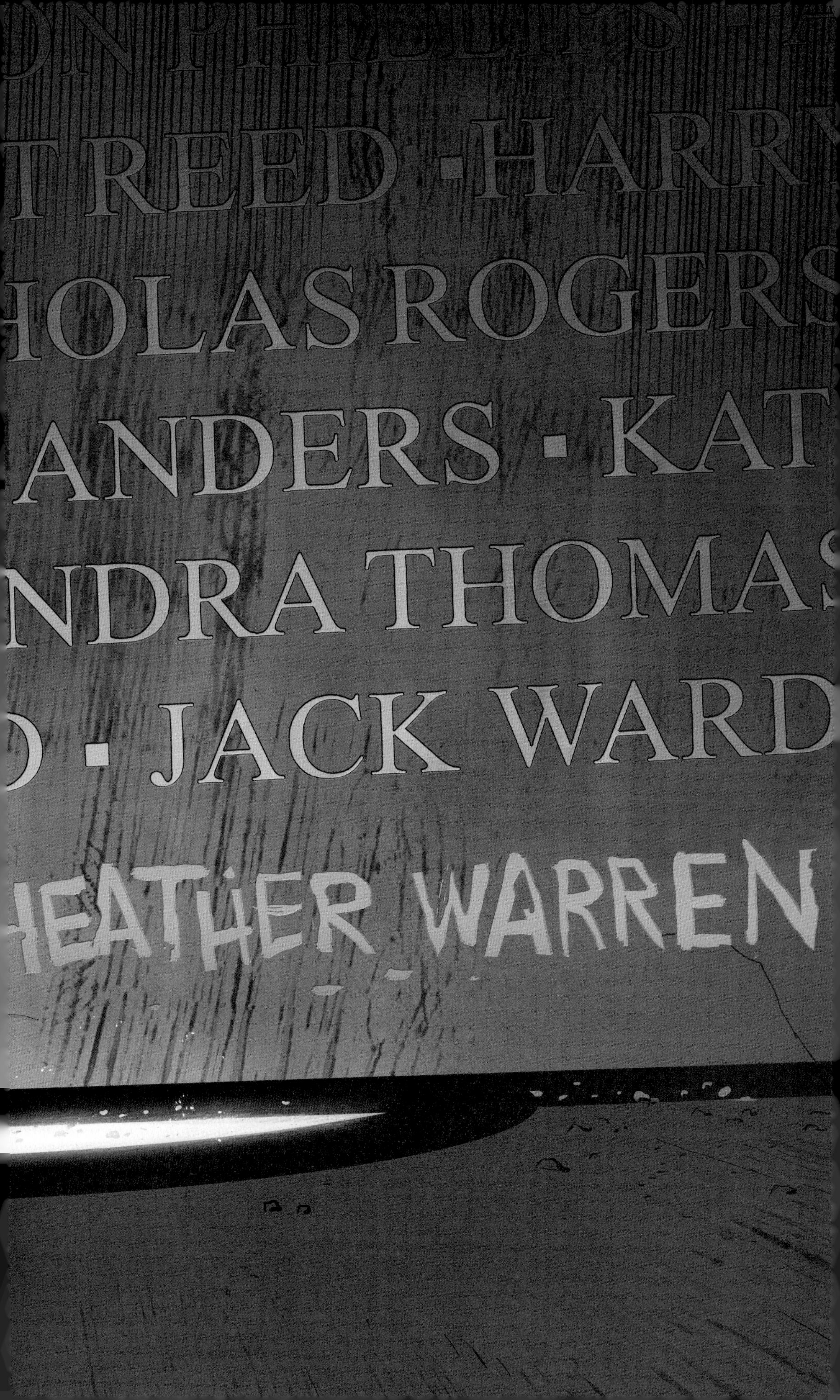
TREED · HARR
HOLAS ROGERS
ANDERS · KAT
NDRA THOMAS
· JACK WARD
HEATHER WARREN

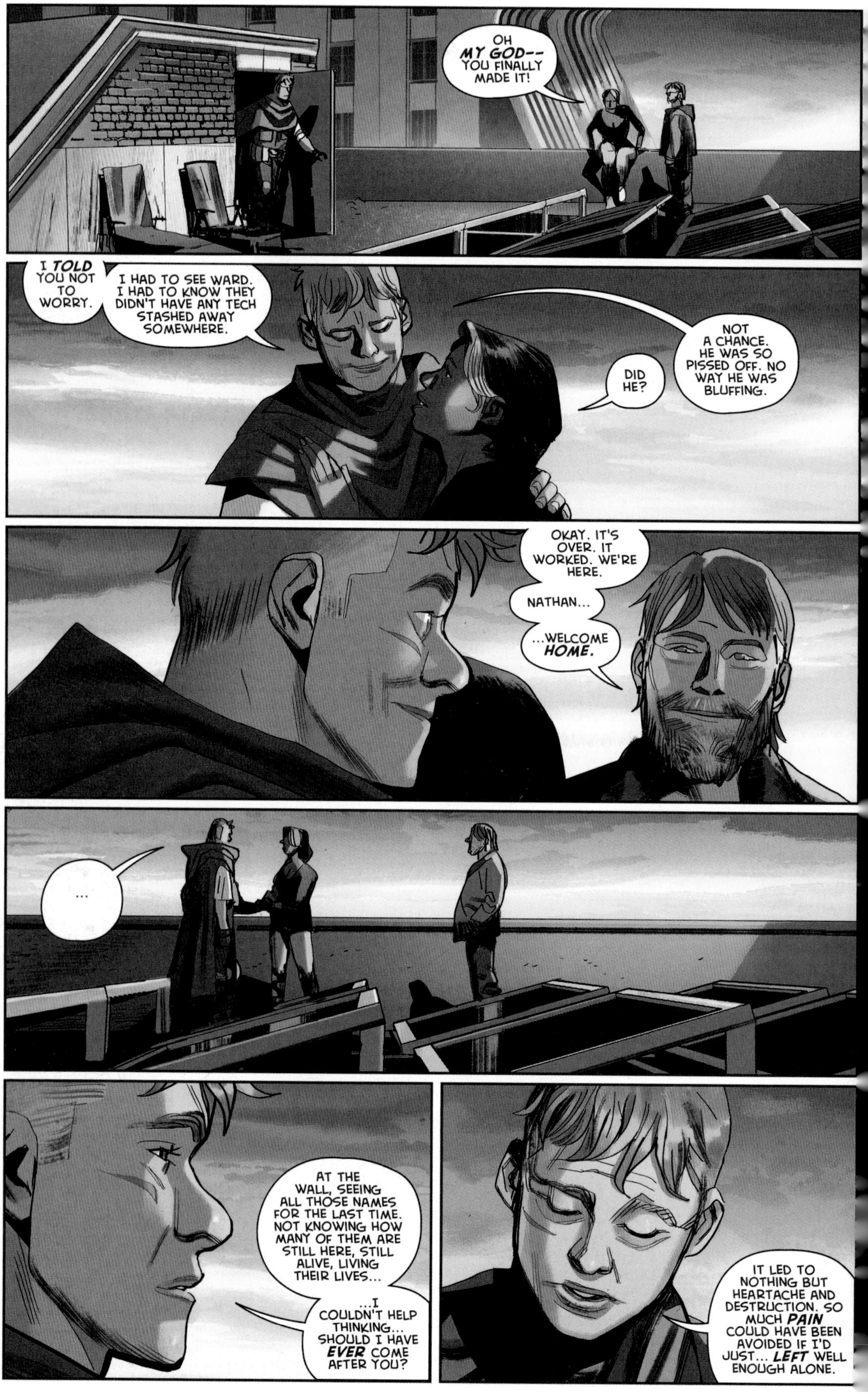

OH MY GOD-- YOU FINALLY MADE IT!
I TOLD YOU NOT TO WORRY.
I HAD TO SEE WARD. I HAD TO KNOW THEY DIDN'T HAVE ANY TECH STASHED AWAY SOMEWHERE.
DID HE?
NOT A CHANCE. HE WAS SO PISSED OFF. NO WAY HE WAS BLUFFING.
OKAY. IT'S OVER. IT WORKED. WE'RE HERE.
NATHAN...
...WELCOME HOME.
...
AT THE WALL, SEEING ALL THOSE NAMES FOR THE LAST TIME. NOT KNOWING HOW MANY OF THEM ARE STILL HERE, STILL ALIVE, LIVING THEIR LIVES...
...I COULDN'T HELP THINKING... SHOULD I HAVE EVER COME AFTER YOU?
IT LED TO NOTHING BUT HEARTACHE AND DESTRUCTION. SO MUCH PAIN COULD HAVE BEEN AVOIDED IF I'D JUST... LEFT WELL ENOUGH ALONE.

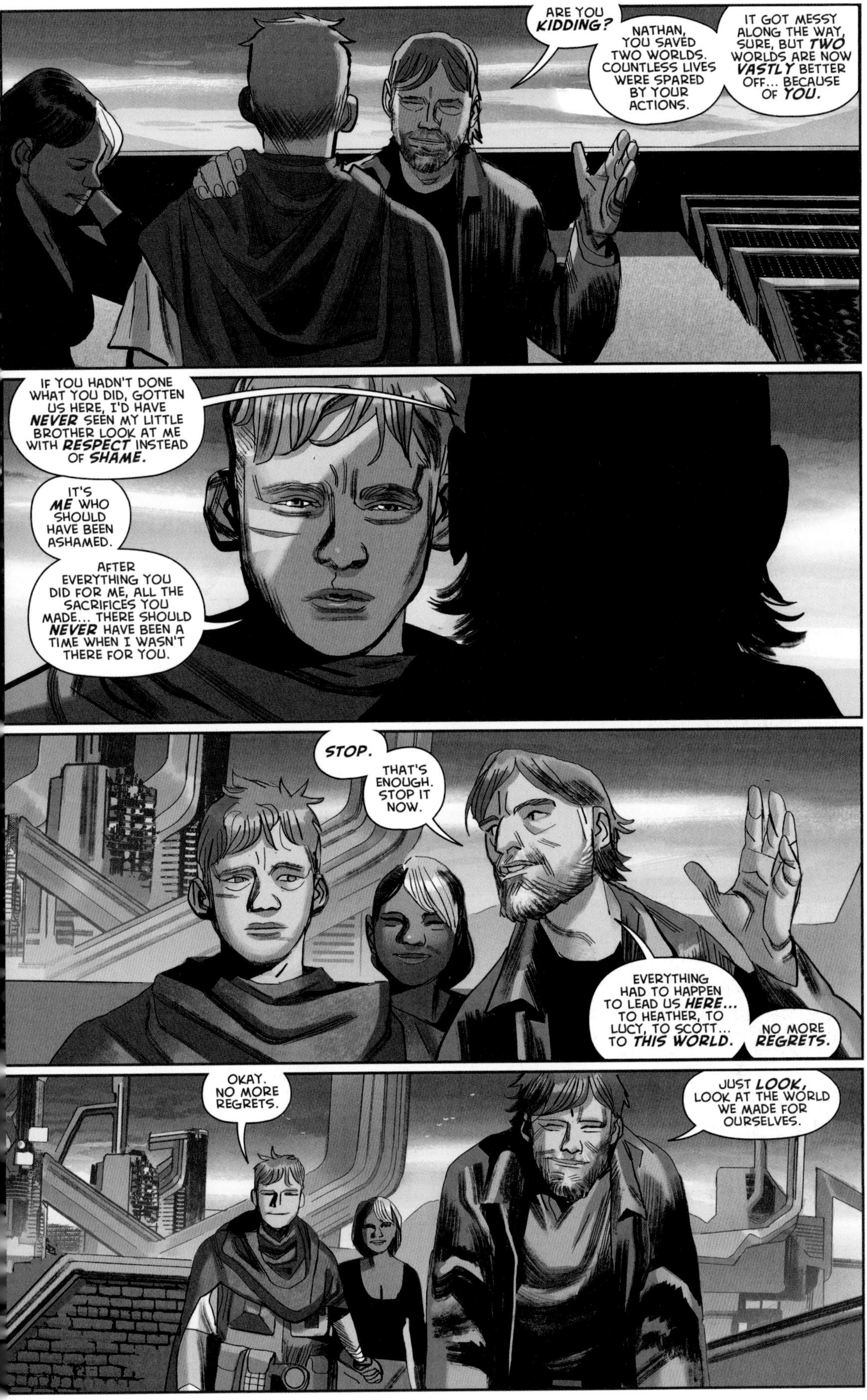

ARE YOU *KIDDING?*
NATHAN, YOU SAVED TWO WORLDS. COUNTLESS LIVES WERE SPARED BY YOUR ACTIONS.
IT GOT MESSY ALONG THE WAY, SURE, BUT *TWO* WORLDS ARE NOW *VASTLY* BETTER OFF... BECAUSE OF *YOU.*
IF YOU HADN'T DONE WHAT YOU DID, GOTTEN US HERE, I'D HAVE *NEVER* SEEN MY LITTLE BROTHER LOOK AT ME WITH *RESPECT* INSTEAD OF *SHAME.*
IT'S *ME* WHO SHOULD HAVE BEEN ASHAMED.
AFTER EVERYTHING YOU DID FOR ME, ALL THE SACRIFICES YOU MADE... THERE SHOULD *NEVER* HAVE BEEN A TIME WHEN I WASN'T THERE FOR YOU.
STOP.
THAT'S ENOUGH. STOP IT NOW.
EVERYTHING HAD TO HAPPEN TO LEAD US *HERE...* TO HEATHER, TO LUCY, TO SCOTT... TO *THIS WORLD.*
NO MORE *REGRETS.*
OKAY. NO MORE REGRETS.
JUST *LOOK,* LOOK AT THE WORLD WE MADE FOR OURSELVES.

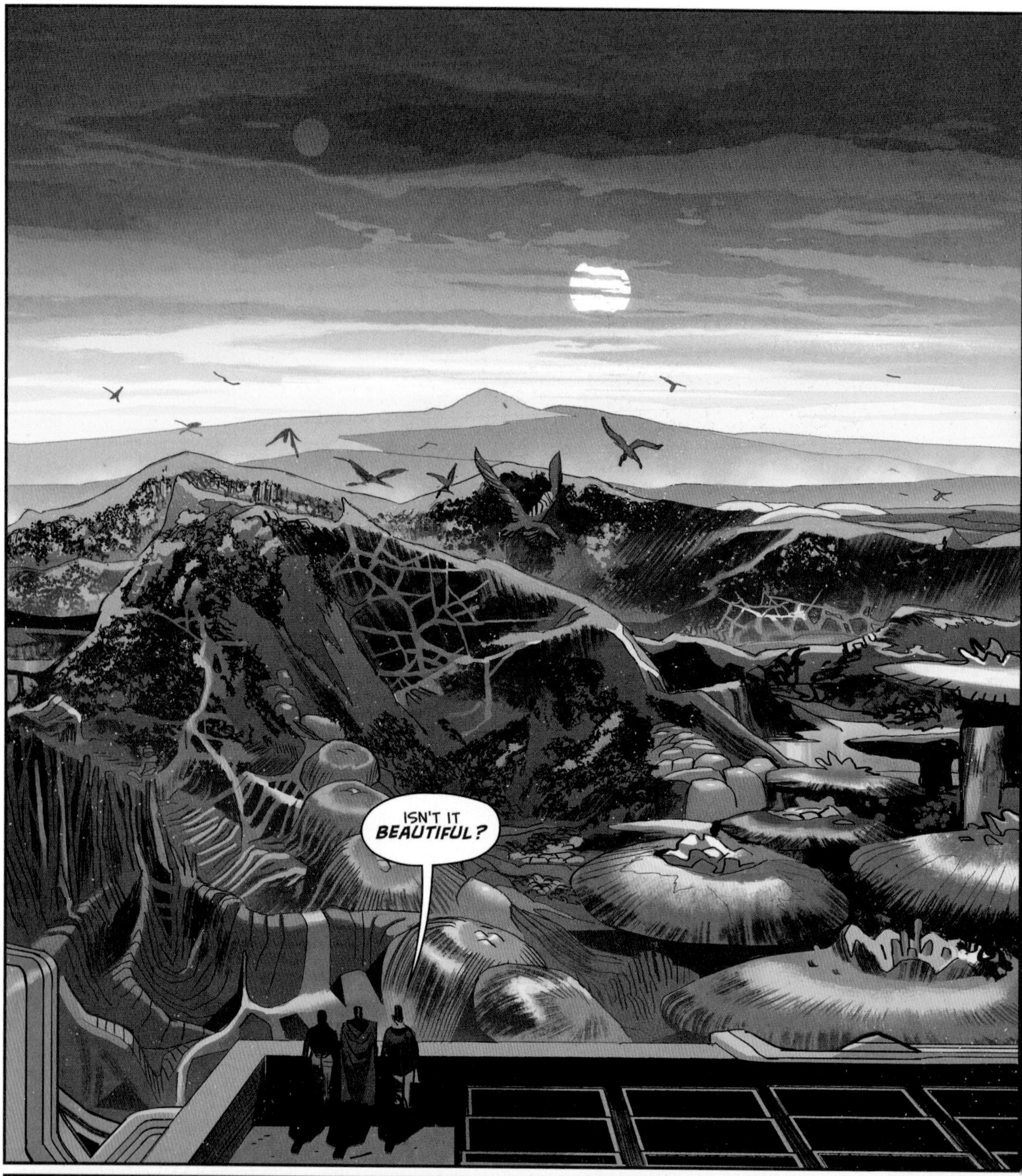
ISN'T IT BEAUTIFUL?

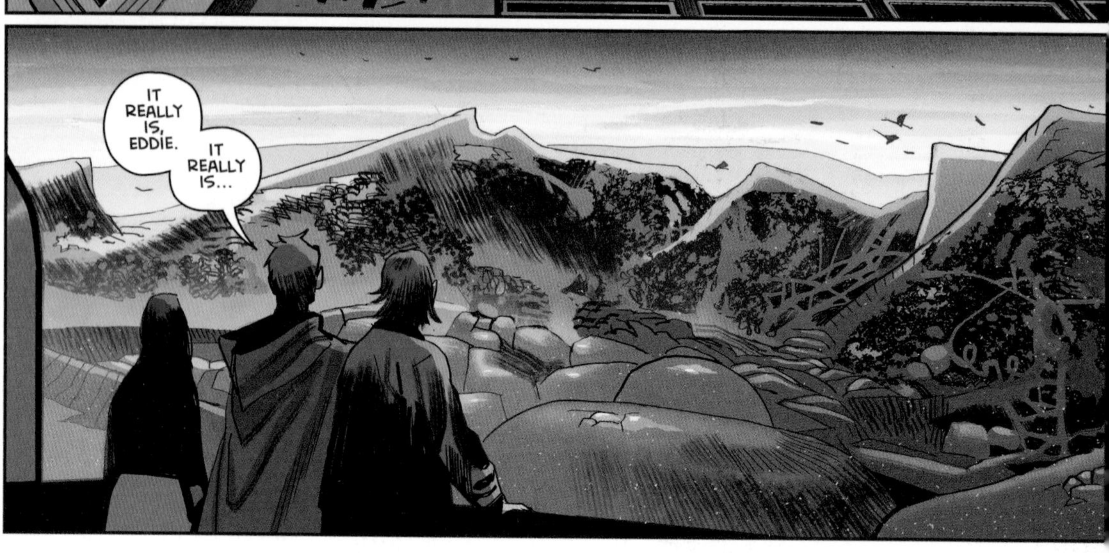
IT REALLY IS, EDDIE.
IT REALLY IS...